COLLECTION

January 2015

February 2015

March 2015

April 2015

May 2015

June 2015

Midnight at the *Oasis*

JANE PORTER
OLIVIA GATES
MEREDITH WEBBER

Published in Great Britain 2015
by Mills & Boon, an imprint of Harlequin (UK) Limited,
Eton House, 18-24 Paradise Road, Richmond, Surrey, TW9 1SR

MIDNIGHT AT THE OASIS © 2015 Harlequin Books S.A.

His Majesty's Mistake © 2012 Jane Porter
To Tempt a Sheikh © 2011 Olivia Gates
Sheikh, Children's Doctor...Husband © 2011 Meredith Webber

ISBN: 978-0-263-25357-3

024-0315

Harlequin (UK) Limited's policy is to use papers that are natural, renewable and recyclable products and made from wood grown in sustainable forests.The logging and manufacturing processes conform to the legalenvironmental regulations of the country of origin.

Printed and bound in Spain
by CPI, Barcelona

His Majesty's Mistake

JANE PORTER

Jane Porter grew up on a diet of romances, reading late at night under the covers so her mother wouldn't see! She wrote her first book at age eight and spent many of her high school and college years living abroad, immersing herself in other cultures and continuing to read voraciously. Now Jane splits her time between rugged Seattle, Washington, and the beautiful beaches of Hawaii, with her sexy surfer and three very active sons. Jane loves to hear from her readers. You can write to her at PO Box 524, Bellevue, WA 98009, USA. Or visit her website at www.janeporter.com.

CHAPTER ONE

ALEJANDRO had to be here.

Had to be.

Because if he wasn't at Mynt Lounge, South Beach's trendiest nightclub, he wasn't in South Beach any longer. She'd checked the other clubs first and she knew Alejandro. He only did cool. He only did chic. It was Mynt Lounge or nothing. And it had to be here because she had to see him.

Ignoring the dozens of young American women queuing outside in stiletto heels and skirts so short they barely covered their assets, Princess Emmeline d'Arcy of Brabant stepped from her cab onto the curb and tucked a long gleaming strand of hair behind her ear. She would make Alejandro listen to reason. She'd make him see her position and surely he'd change his mind once he understood what was at stake.

Her name.

Her reputation.

And even more importantly, the future and security of their child.

Her stomach rose in protest and she willed the nausea to pass. She wouldn't get sick here, not when everything was riding on the next five minutes.

Air bottled in her lungs, shoulders squared, Princess Emmeline d'Arcy of the European commonwealth Brabant headed straight for the entrance, bypassing the line that snaked around the building and down the side street.

Alejandro would honor the promise he'd made her. He'd be a man and keep his word. He had to.

As Emmeline approached the front door, the club bouncer dropped the red velvet rope for her, giving her instant admission into the exclusive club. He didn't know Emmeline personally. He had no idea she was a European royal. But it was clear to everyone present that she was someone important. A VIP. And Mynt Lounge was all about celebrities, models and VIPs. It had, reputedly, the tightest door policy in all of South Beach.

Inside the darkened club, giant stars and metallic balls hung from the ceiling as futuristic go-go girls danced on the bar in nonexistent costumes and white thigh-high boots. A wall of purple lights flashed behind the DJ and other lights shifted, painting the writhing crowd on the dance floor purple, white and gold, leaving corners shadowy.

The princess paused, her long black lashes dropping as she scanned the interior looking for Alejandro, praying he'd be here. Praying he hadn't left South Beach yet for tomorrow's polo tournament in Greenwich. His horses had already gone, but he usually followed later.

A cocktail waitress approached and Emmeline shook her head. She wasn't here to party. She was here to make sure Alejandro did the right thing. He'd made love to her. She'd gotten pregnant. He'd vowed to take care of her. And now he'd better do it.

She wanted a ring, a wedding date and legitimacy for their unborn child.

He owed that much to her.

It had never been her plan to leave Europe, but she'd learned to love Alejandro's Argentina. They could live outside Buenos Aires on his estancia and have babies and raise horses.

It was a different future than the one her family had planned for her. She was to have been Queen of Raguva, married to King Zale Patek, and her family would be upset. For one thing, Alejandro wasn't a member of the aristocracy, and for another, he had a bit of a reputation, but once they were married, surely her mother and father would accept him. Alejandro was wealthy.

He could provide for them. And she believed in her heart that he would provide, once he understood she had nowhere to go, no other options. European princesses didn't become single mothers.

While she'd never wanted to marry King Zale Patek, she did respect him. She couldn't say the same for Alejandro, and she'd slept with him.

Stupid. Stupid to sleep with someone you didn't love, hoping that maybe he did love you, and would want you and protect you…rescue you…as if you were Rapunzel locked high in the ivory tower.

Emmeline shuddered, horrified. But what was done was done and now she had to be smart. Keep it together.

Swallowing convulsively, Emmeline smoothed the peacock-blue satin fabric of her cocktail dress over her hips. She could feel the jut of her hipbones beneath her trembling hands. She'd never been this thin before, but she couldn't keep anything down. She was sick morning, noon and night, but she prayed that once she hit the second trimester the nausea would subside.

From the VIP section in the back she heard a roar of masculine laughter. Alejandro. So he *was* here.

Her stomach fell, a wild tumble, even as her limbs stiffened, body tight, humming with anxiety.

He'd been ignoring her, avoiding her calls, but surely once he saw her, he'd remember how much he'd said he adored her. For five years he'd chased her, pursuing her relentlessly, pledging eternal love. She'd resisted his advances for years, too, but then in a weak moment earlier in the spring, she'd succumbed, giving him her virginity.

It hadn't been the passionate experience she'd hoped for. Alejandro had been impatient, even irritated. She'd been surprised by the emptiness and roughness of the lovemaking but told herself that it'd be better the next time, that as she grew to love him, she'd learn how to relax. She'd learn how to respond. She'd heard that sex was so different when you were emotionally close and she hoped that it was true.

But there hadn't been a next time. And now she was pregnant.

Ridiculous. Horrifying. Especially as she was engaged to another man. It was an arranged marriage, one that had been planned years ago for her when she was still in her teens, and the wedding was scheduled for just ten days from now. Obviously she couldn't marry King Patek pregnant with Alejandro's baby. So Alejandro needed to man up. Do the right thing, and accept his responsibility in this catastrophe.

Shoulders thrown back, head high, Emmeline entered the darkened VIP room, her narrowed gaze scanning the low plush couches filled with lounging guests. She spotted Alejandro right away. He was hard to miss in his billowy white shirt that showed off his dark hair, tan skin and handsome Latin profile to perfection. He wasn't alone. He had a stunning young brunette in a shocking red mini-dress on his lap.

Penelope Luca, Emmeline thought, recognizing the young model who had recently become the new It girl. But Penelope wasn't merely sitting on Alejandro's lap. Alejandro's hand was up underneath the young model's short red skirt, his lips were nuzzling her neck.

For a moment Emmeline couldn't move or breathe. For a moment she stood transfixed by the sight of Alejandro pleasuring Penelope.

And then humiliation screamed through her.

This was the man who'd promised to love her forever? This was the man who wanted her, Emmeline d'Arcy, above all others? This was the man she'd sacrificed her future for?

"Alejandro." Her voice was low, clear and sharp. It cut through the pounding music, hum of voices and shrill laughter. Heads turned toward Emmeline. She was dimly aware that everyone was looking at her but she only had eyes for Alejandro.

He looked up at her from beneath his lashes, his lips still affixed to the girl's neck, his expression mocking.

He didn't care.

Emmeline's legs shook. The room seemed to spin.

He didn't care, she thought again, horror mounting. He didn't care if she saw him with Penelope. He didn't care how Emmeline felt. Because he didn't care for her. He'd never cared, either.

It hit her that it had all been a game for him…to bed a princess. The challenge. The chase. The conquest. She'd merely been a beautiful royal scalp to decorate his belt. And now that he'd possessed her, taken her innocence, he'd discarded her. As if she were nothing. No one.

Fury and pain blinded her. Fury with herself, pain for her child. She'd been stupid, so stupid, and she had no one to blame but herself. But wasn't that her problem? Hadn't that been her Achilles' heel her entire life? Needing love? Craving validation?

Her weakness sickened her, shamed her. Nausea hit her in waves.

"Alejandro," she repeated his name, her voice dropping, breaking, fire licking her limbs, daggers slicing her heart. "I will not be ignored!"

But he did ignore her. He didn't even bother to look at her again.

Her legs shook. Her eyes burned. How dare he mock her this way. She marched closer, temper blazing. "You're a liar and a cheat. A pathetic excuse for a man—"

"Stop." A deep, hard male voice spoke from behind her, interrupting her, even as a hand settled on her shoulder.

She struggled to shake the hand off, not finished with Alejandro yet. "You will take responsibility," she insisted, trembling with rage.

"I said, enough," Sheikh Makin Al-Koury repeated tersely, head dropped, mouth close to Hannah's ear. He was angry, very angry, and he told himself it was because his assistant had gone missing in action, and that he resented having to chase her down like a recalcitrant puppy, but it was more than that.

It was her, Hannah, dressed like…looking like…sex. Sex in high heels.

Impossible. Hannah wasn't sexy. Hannah wasn't hot, but here she was in a cocktail dress so snug that it looked painted on her slim body, the turquoise satin fabric clinging to her small, firm breasts and outlining her high, round ass.

The fact that he noticed her ass blew his mind. He'd never

even looked at her body before, didn't even know she had a body, and yet here she was in a tight shimmering dress with kohl-rimmed eyes, her long dark hair tumbling free over her shoulders.

The thick tousled hair cascading down her back drew his eye again to her ass, and desire flared, his body hardening instantly.

Makin gritted his teeth, disgusted that he was responding to his assistant like an immature schoolboy. For God's sake. She'd worked for him for nearly five years. What was wrong with him?

She tried to jerk away from him, and his palm slid across the warm satin of her bare shoulder. She felt as hot and erotic as she looked, and he hardened all over again, her smooth soft skin heating his.

Stunned that she was being manhandled, Emmeline d'Arcy turned her head sharply to get a look behind her but all she could see was shoulders—endless shoulders—above a very broad chest covered in an elegant charcoal dress shirt.

"Unhand me," she choked, angling her head back to get a better look at him, but she couldn't see his face, not without turning all the way around. Her vision was limited to his chin and jaw. And it wasn't an easy jaw. He was all hard lines—strong, angular jaw, square chin, the fierce set of firm lips. The only hint of softness she could see was the glimpse of dark bronze skin at his throat where his collar was open.

"You're making a fool of yourself," he said harshly, his English lightly accented, his voice strangely familiar.

But why was his voice familiar? Did she know him? More importantly, did he know her? Was he one of her father's men? Had her father, King William, sent someone from his security, or King Patek?

She craned her head to get a better look, but he was so tall, and the club so very dark. "Let me go," she repeated, unwilling to be managed by even her father's men.

"Once we're outside," he answered, applying pressure to her shoulder.

She shuddered at the warmth of his skin against hers.

"I'm not going anywhere. Not until I've spoken with Mr. Ibanez—"

"This is neither the time or place," he said, cutting her short. His hand moved from her shoulder to her wrist, his fingers clamping vise-like around her fragile bones.

He had a tight grip, and she shivered as heat spread through her. "Release me," she demanded, tugging at her wrist. *"Immediately."*

"Not a chance, Hannah," he answered calmly, and yet his tone was so hard and determined that it rumbled through her, penetrating deep to rattle her bones.

Hannah.

He thought she was Hannah.

Her heart faltered. A cold shivery sensation slid down her spine as she put the pieces together. His deep, familiar voice. His extraordinary height. His ridiculous strength.

Sheikh Makin Al-Koury, Hannah's boss. Emmeline stiffened, realizing she was in trouble—she'd spent the past four days impersonating his personal assistant.

And then he was dragging her from the club, through the crowded dance floor and out the front door.

Emmeline's head spun as they stepped outside, away from the blinding lights and gyrating bodies on the bar and dance floor. The heavy nightclub door swung closed behind them, silencing the thumping music.

It was only then that he released her and turning, she looked straight up into Sheikh Al-Koury's face. He wasn't happy. No, make that he was livid.

"Hello," she said, voice cracking.

One of his strong black eyebrows lifted. "Hello?" he repeated incredulously. "Is that all you have to say?"

She licked her lips but her mouth remained too dry and her lips caught on her teeth.

Five days ago it had seemed like a brilliant idea to beg Hannah, the American who looked so much like her, to change places with her for a few hours so Emmeline could escape her security detail at the hotel and confront Alejandro. Hannah had become a blonde and Emmeline a brunette. They'd changed hairstyles, wardrobes and lifestyles. It was to have been for a few hours, but that had been days ago and since then everything had become so very complicated as Hannah was now in Raguva, on the Dalmatian Coast, masquerading as Princess Emmeline, while Emmeline was still here in Florida, pretending to be Hannah.

"Wh-what are you doing here?" she stuttered now, staring up into Sheikh Makin Al-Koury's face, trapped in his light eyes. His eyes were gray, the lightest gray, almost silver, and his expression so fierce her legs went weak.

"Saving you from making a complete ass of yourself," he answered grimly. He had a face that was too hard to be considered classically handsome—square jaw, strong chin, high slash of cheekbones, with a long straight nose. "Have you completely lost your mind?"

Desperation sharpened her voice. "I have to go back in. I must speak with him—"

"He didn't seem interested," Sheikh Al-Koury interrupted as if bored.

Heat rushed through her, heat and shame, because Sheikh Al-Koury was right. Alejandro hadn't been the least bit interested, not with the stunning Penelope on his lap, but that didn't change her goal. It just meant she had to work harder to make Alejandro see reason. "You don't even know who I'm talking about."

"Alejandro Ibanez," he retorted. "Now get into the car—"

"I can't!"

"You must."

"You don't understand." Panic filled her, tears burning her eyes. She could not, would not, be a single mother. She'd be cut off from her family. She'd be out on the streets. And yes, she'd been named an honorary chair for a dozen different charities, but in reality, she had no skills to speak of. If Alejandro didn't help them, how would she and the child survive? "I must speak with him. It's urgent."

"That may be, but there are paparazzi everywhere and your

Mr. Ibanez appeared…unavailable…for a proper discussion. Please get into the car."

It was only then that Emmeline realized that camera flashes were popping right and left. Not because of her—the media thought she was ordinary Hannah Smith—but because Sheikh Al-Koury was one of the world's most powerful men. His country, Kadar, produced more oil than any other country or kingdom in the Middle East. Western powers tripped over themselves to befriend him. And Emmeline's lookalike, Hannah Smith, had been his assistant for years.

"I'll take a cab back to my hotel," she said huskily, nausea washing through her in waves.

Sheikh Al-Koury smiled at her, firm lips quirking as if amused, and yet she knew he couldn't be, not when his silver gaze glittered like frost. "I'm afraid you misunderstood me." He paused, his gaze lingering on her face. "It wasn't a request, Hannah. I'm not negotiating. Get in the car."

For a moment she couldn't breathe, feeling smashed, squashed. He was smiling, though, but that was because he intended to win. Powerful men always did.

Clinging to the last shred of her dignity, she lifted her chin, moved past the paparazzi, and stepped gracefully into the car, her turquoise satin dress swishing across the leather as she slid across the seat to the far side.

Emmeline sucked in a breath of silent protest as Makin settled next to her, far too close. She crossed one leg over the other, trying to make herself smaller. He was too big and physical. He exuded energy, intensity and it made her heart race so fast she felt dizzy.

Emmeline waited until the driver had pulled from the curb to give the name of her hotel. "I'm staying at the Breakers," she said, hands compulsively smoothing the creases marring the satin of her skirt. "You can drop me off there."

Sheikh Al-Koury didn't even glance at her. "I won't be dropping you anywhere. We're heading to the airport. I'll have the hotel pack up your things and send them to the airport to meet our plane."

For a moment she couldn't speak. "Plane?"

"We're going to Kadar."

Her pulse quickened yet again, her hands curling into fists. She wouldn't panic. Not yet. "Kadar?"

His gaze met hers and held. "Yes, Kadar, my country, my home. I'm hosting a huge conference in Kasbah Raha in a few days. Two dozen dignitaries are attending with their spouses. That was your idea. Remember?"

Emmeline pressed the fists down against her thighs. She knew nothing about organizing conferences or hosting international polo tournaments or any of the other dozen things Hannah did as Sheikh Al-Koury's assistant, but she couldn't admit that, not when Hannah was in Raguva pretending to be her. And if Texas-born Hannah could masquerade as a European princess, surely Emmeline could pass herself off as a secretary? How hard could it be?

"Of course," she answered firmly, feigning a confidence she did not feel. "Why wouldn't I?"

Again a strong black eyebrow lifted, his hard, harsh features hawk-like in the darkened limousine. "Because you've called in sick to work four days straight even as you've been spotted living it up all over town."

"I've hardly been living it up. I can't keep anything down, and I've only left my hotel room when absolutely necessary."

"Like tonight?"

"Yes."

"Because you had to see Mr. Ibanez."

Just hearing Alejandro's name sent a shock wave through her, because Alejandro hadn't just rejected her, he'd rejected the baby, too. She exhaled in a rush, devastated. "Yes."

"Why?"

Nausea rushed through her. "That's personal."

CHAPTER TWO

PERSONAL, Makin Al-Koury, His Royal Highness, Prince of Kadar, silently repeated, staring at Hannah from beneath his lashes, stunned that his sensible secretary had fallen for a man who had a woman in every city, as well as a wife and five children back at home.

"So what did he tell you?" Makin said coolly. "That he loved you? That he couldn't live without you? What did he say to get you into bed?"

Her porcelain cheeks turned pink and she pushed the heavy weight of her rich brown hair off her pale shoulder. "That's none of your business."

So Alejandro Ibanez had seduced her.

Makin bit down, his jaws clamped tightly together. He loathed very few people but Ibanez was at the top of the list. Moving in similar polo circles, Makin had witnessed Ibanez in action and the Argentine's tactic for getting women to sleep with him was simple—he seduced them emotionally and then bedded them swiftly. He'd convince a woman that she was special—unique—and that he couldn't imagine living without her. And women fell for it. Hook, line and sinker.

And apparently, Hannah had, too.

He'd known all week that something was wrong with Hannah. His secretary was practical and punctual, organized and calm. She didn't call in sick. She didn't show up late. She didn't make excuses. She was professional. Dedicated. Disciplined. The woman across the seat from him was none of the above.

For the past four days he'd tried to understand what had happened to his efficient secretary.

He'd pursued her as she pursued Alejandro Ibanez, and it wasn't until tonight, when he saw her in the club, that he understood.

She'd fallen in love with Alejandro and the Argentine had callously, carelessly used her before tossing her away, breaking her heart just as he'd broken that of every other woman who came his way.

Makin's chest felt tight and hot, and yet he wasn't a sensitive man, nor was he emotionally close to his employees. He was their boss. They worked for him. He expected them to do their job. End of story.

"Your personal life is impacting your professional life, which is impacting mine," he answered, offering her a small pleasant smile even though he felt far from pleasant on the inside.

Her lips compressed even as her eyes flashed at him. "I'm not allowed to be sick?"

"Not if you aren't truly sick," he said flatly. "In that case, you'd be taking personal days, not sick leave."

Although pale, she sat tall, chin tilted, channeling an elegance, even an arrogance, he'd never seen in her before. "I wasn't well," she said imperiously, her back so tall and straight she appeared almost regal. "I'm still not well. But you can think what you want."

His eyebrow lifted a fraction at her attitude, even as something in him responded to the challenge. Hannah had never spoken to him like this before and he grew warm, overly warm. His trousers suddenly felt too tight, and his gaze dropped to her legs. They were endless. Slim, long, bare, crossed high at her knee—

He stopped himself short. He was not going to go there. This was *Hannah*.

"I don't appreciate the attitude," he ground out. "If you'd like to keep your job, I'd drop it now."

She had the grace to blush. "I'm not giving you attitude. I'm merely defending myself." She paused, considered him from beneath her extravagant black lashes. "Or am I not allowed to do that?"

"There you go again."

"What?"

"Insolent, brash, defiant—"

"I'm confused. Am I an employee or a slave?"

For a moment he was silent, stunned by her audacity. What had happened to his perfect secretary? "Excuse me?" he finally said, his tone so deep and furious that she should have been silenced, but tonight Hannah seemed oblivious to any rebuke.

"Sheikh Al-Koury, certainly I'm allowed to have a voice."

"A voice, yes, provided it's not impudent."

"Impudent?" Her laugh was brittle. "I'm not a disobedient child. I'm twenty-five and—"

"Completely out of line." He leaned toward her, but she didn't shrink back. Instead she lifted her chin, staring boldly into his eyes. He felt another raw rush of emotion, his temper battling with something else…curiosity…desire…none of which, of course, was acceptable.

But there it was. This was a new Hannah and she was turning everything inside-out, including him.

And he didn't like it. Not a bit.

"You disappoint me," he said brusquely. "I expected more from you."

She tensed, pale jaw tightening, emotion flickering over her face, shadowing her eyes.

For a moment she looked fierce and proud and rather bruised.

A fighter without arms.

A warrior taken captive.

Joan of Arc at the stake.

He felt the strangest knotting in his chest. It was an emotion he hadn't felt before, and it was hot, sharp, uncomfortable. He didn't like it. He didn't want to feel it. She worked for him, not the other way around. "I don't know what game you're playing, but it's over. I've chased you from Palm Beach to South Beach but I'm not chasing anymore. Nor am I negotiating. It's my way,

Hannah, or this is where it ends, and you can begin looking for a new job tomorrow."

He saw her chest rise and fall as she took a swift breath, but she didn't speak. Instead she held the air bottled in her lungs as she stared at him, a defiant light burning in her intensely blue eyes.

How could he have ever thought Hannah so calm and controlled? Because there was nothing calm or controlled about her now. No, nothing calm in those mysterious lavender-blue eyes at all. She was all emotion, hot, brilliant emotion that crackled in her and through her as though she were made of electricity itself.

Who was this woman? Did he even know her?

He frowned, his brow furrowing with frustration as his gaze swept over her from head to toe. At work she was always so buttoned-up around him, so perfectly proper, but then, she hadn't dressed for him tonight, she'd dressed for Alejandro, her lover.

The thought of her with Ibanez made his chest tighten again, as something in him cracked, shifted free, escaping from his infamous control to spread through him, hot, hard, possessive. For reasons he didn't fully comprehend, he couldn't stand the idea of Ibanez with her, touching her.

She was too good for Ibanez. She deserved so much better.

His gaze rested on her, and it was impossible to look away. Her satin dress was a perfect foil for her creamy skin and the rich chestnut hair that tumbled down her back. The low square neckline accentuated her long neck and exquisite features. He'd known that Hannah was attractive, but he'd never realized she was beautiful.

Incandescent.

Which didn't make sense. None of this really made sense because Hannah wasn't the sort of woman to glow. She was solidly stable, grounded, focused on work to the exclusion of all else. She rarely wore makeup and knew nothing about fashion, and yet tonight she appeared so delicate and luminous that he was tempted to brush his fingertips across her cheek to see what she wore to make her appear radiant.

The tip of her tongue appeared to wet her soft, full lower lip. His groin hardened as her pink tongue slid across and then touched the bow-shaped upper lip. For a moment he envied the lip and then he suppressed that carnal thought, too, but his body had a mind of its own and blood rushed to his shaft, heating and hardening him, making him throb.

"You're threatening to fire me, Sheikh Al-Koury?" Her incredulous tone provoked him almost as much as that provocative tongue slipping across her lips.

"You should know by now I never threaten, nor do I engage my employees in meaningless conversation. If I'm speaking to you it's because I'm conveying something important, something you need to know." He was hanging on to his temper by a thread. "And you should know that I've reached the end of my patience with you—"

"Not to be rude, Sheikh Al-Koury," she interrupted, before making a soft groaning sound. "But how far away is the airport? I think I'm going to be sick."

For Emmeline, the rest of the short drive to the executive airport passed in a blur of motion and misery. She remembered little but the limo pulling between large gates and then onto empty tarmac next to an impressively long white jet.

She was rushed up the stairs, aided by a flight attendant, and then escorted into a bedroom and through a door to a small bathroom.

The flight attendant flipped on the bathroom lights and then closed the door behind her, leaving Emmeline alone.

Thank God for small mercies.

Perspiration beading her brow, Emmeline crouched before the toilet. Her hands trembled on the pristine white porcelain as she leaned forward, her stomach emptying violently into the toilet bowl.

The acid that burned her throat was nothing compared to the acid eating away in her heart. This was all her fault…she had no one else to blame. She'd been weak and foolish and insecure. She'd reached out to the wrong man in a moment of need, and to make matters worse, she'd approached Hannah, dragging her into this.

Remorse filled her. Remorse and regret. Why wasn't she stronger? Why was she so needy? But then, when hadn't she craved love?

Gritting her teeth, she knew she couldn't blame her parents. They'd done their best. They'd tried. The fault was clearly hers. Apparently even at an early age she'd been clingy, always wanting to be held, needing constant reassurance and affection. Even as a little girl she'd been ashamed that she'd needed so much more than her parents could give.

Good princesses didn't have needs.

Good princesses didn't cause trouble.

Emmeline did both.

Emmeline's stomach churned and heaved all over again, and she lurched over the toilet, sick once more.

Tears stung her eyes. How could anyone call this morning sickness when she was ill morning, noon and night? She flushed the toilet again.

A quiet knocked sounded on the door. "Hannah?"

It was Makin Al-Koury. Emmeline's stomach performed a wild free fall which didn't help her nausea in the slightest. "Yes?"

"May I come in?"

No. But she couldn't say it. She was supposed to work for him. That meant she answered to him. Emmeline's eyes stung. "Yes."

The door softly opened and a shadow fell across the floor.

Blinking back tears, Emmeline glanced up as Makin filled the doorway. Tall and broad-shouldered, his expression was grim. There was no sympathy in his light gray eyes, no gentleness in the set of his jaw or the press of his firm mouth. But then, there'd been no gentleness earlier when he'd yanked her through the nightclub, pulling her onto the street, his hand gripped tightly around her wrist.

Even now, with her knees pressed to the cold tiled floor, she could feel the unyielding grip of his hand on her wrist, the heat of his skin against hers.

He'd been furious as his limousine traveled from the night-club to the airport, and from his expression as he towered above her, he still was.

"Can I get you something?" he asked, his deep voice a raw rasp of sound in the small space.

She shook her head. "No. Thank you."

"You are sick."

She nodded, fighting fresh tears. "Yes."

"Why didn't you tell me?"

Her brow creased, eyebrows knitting. "I did."

His jaw tightened. He looked away, across the small bath, his lips flattening, making him look even more displeased. "Have you seen a doctor?"

"No."

"Why not? You said you can't keep anything down. You should have tests run, or see if the doctor could prescribe something that would help."

"It won't help—"

"Why not?"

She winced at the impatience and roughness in his voice. For a moment his mask slipped and she glimpsed something almost savage in his expression. "Because…"

Her voice faded as she got lost in his light eyes, and it crossed her mind that he might be the world's richest sheikh, but he wasn't entirely modern. Beneath his elegant, tailored suit and polished veneer was a man of the desert.

Because Sheikh Al-Koury wouldn't employ a pregnant, unwed woman, not even if she were American. It was a cultural issue, a matter of honor and respect. Emmeline might not be able to type quickly or place conference calls or create spreadsheets, but she'd spent enough time in the United Arab Emirates and Morocco to be familiar with the concept of *hshuma,* or shame. And an unwed pregnant woman would bring shame on all close to her, including her employer.

"It's just stress," she said. "I'm just…overly upset. But I'll pull myself together. I promise."

He looked at her so long and hard that the fine hair on

Emmeline's nape lifted and her belly flip-flopped with nerves. "Then pull yourself together. I'm counting on you. And if you can't do your job anymore, tell me now so I can find someone who can."

"But I can."

He said nothing for several moments, his gaze resting on her face. "Why Ibanez?" he asked at last. "Why him of all people?"

She hunched her shoulders. "He said he loved me."

His jaw hardened, mouth compressing, expression incredulous. "And you believed him?"

She hesitated. "Yes."

Sheikh Al-Koury choked back a rough growl of protest. "I can't believe you fell for his lines. He says those lines to everyone. But you're not everyone. You're smart. You're educated. You should know better."

"I didn't."

"Couldn't you detect a false note in his flattery? Couldn't you see he's fake? That his lines were too slick, that he's as insincere as they come?"

"No." She drew a swift breath, making a hiccup of sound. "But I wish I had."

Makin battled his temper as he stared down at Hannah where she knelt on the floor, her shoulders sagging, her long chestnut hair a thick tangle down her thin back.

Someone else, someone soft, might be moved by her fragile beauty, but he refused to allow himself to feel anything for her, not now, not after she'd become a temptress. A seductress. A problem.

He didn't allow his personal and professional life to overlap. Sex, desire, lust…they didn't belong in the workplace. Ever.

"I respected you." His deep voice sounded harsh even to his own ears, but he'd never minced words with her before and wasn't about to start now. "And I'm not sure I do anymore."

She flinched, visibly stung, and his gut tightened, an uncomfortable cramp of sensation, and then it was gone, pushed away with the same ferocious intensity he'd applied to the rest of life.

He didn't cater to anyone—male or female. It went against

his belief system. Makin had been his parents' only child and they'd been a very close, tight-knit family. His father, a powerful Bedouin ruler and Kadar's royal prince, was nearly twenty years older than Makin's French mother, Yvette.

When he was growing up, his parents had rarely discussed the past, being too focused on the present, but Makin had pieced enough details together to get a picture of his parents' courtship. They'd met when his mother was just twenty and a film student in Paris. She was beautiful and bright and full of big plans, but within weeks of meeting Tahnoon Al-Koury, she'd accepted his marriage proposal and exchanged her dreams for his, marrying him in a quiet ceremony in Paris before returning to Kadar with her new husband.

Makin had only met his maternal grandparents once, and that was at his father's funeral. His mother refused to speak to them so it'd been left to Makin to introduce himself to his French grandparents. They weren't the terrible people he'd imagined, just ignorant. They couldn't understand that their daughter could love an Arab, much less an Arab confined to a wheelchair.

Makin had grown up with his father in a wheelchair and it was neither terrible nor tragic, at least not until the end. His father was beyond brilliant. Tahnoon was devoted to his family, worshipped his wife and battled to maintain as much independence as he could, despite the degenerative nature of his disease.

Makin was twenty when his father died. But in the years Makin had with him, he never heard his father complain or make excuses, even though Tahnoon lived with tremendous pain and suffered endless indignities. No, his father was a proud, fierce man and he'd taught Makin—not by words, but by example—that life required strength, courage and hard work.

"You don't respect me because I wanted to be loved?" Hannah asked huskily, forcing his attention from the past to the present.

He glanced down, straight into her eyes, and felt that same uncomfortable twinge and steeled himself against the sensation. "I don't respect you wanting to be loved by *him*." He paused, wanting her to understand. "Ibanez is beneath you. He's self-centered and vulgar and the women who chase him are fools."

"That's harsh."

"But true. He's always at the heart of a scandal. He prefers married women or women recently engaged like that ridiculous Princess Emmeline—"

"Ridiculous Princess Emmeline?" she interrupted. "Do you know her?"

"I know of her—"

"So you can't say she's ridiculous—"

"Oh, I can. I know her family well, and I attended her six-teenth birthday in Brabant years ago. She's engaged to King Zale Patek, and I pity him. She's turned him into a joke by chasing after Ibanez all year despite her engagement to Patek. No one respects her. The princess has the morals of an alley cat."

"That's a horrid thing to say."

"I'm honest. Perhaps if others had been more honest with Her Royal Highness, she might have turned out differently." He shrugged dismissively. "But I don't care about her. I care about you and your ability to perform your job with clarity and ef-ficiency. Don't let Ibanez waste another moment of your time. Nor my time, for that matter. Everything about him bores me." His gaze held hers. "Are we clear?"

"Yes," she said huskily.

"Then pull yourself together and take a seat in the main cabin so we can depart."

Using the vanity kit provided in the bathroom, Emmeline washed her face, brushed her teeth and ran a comb through her hair. The thick dark hair still looked strange to her. Emmeline missed her golden-blond color. Missed her wardrobe. Missed her life.

This is how Hannah must have felt when thrust into Emmeline's life.

Lost. Confused. Angry. And Emmeline knew she was the one who'd put Hannah in that position. Changing places with Hannah had been Emmeline's idea. There was no benefit for Hannah. Nothing to be gained by masquerading as a princess. It was Emmeline who'd benefited. She'd been able to slip away from her attendants to seek out Alejandro and tell him about the pregnancy. Only in the end, when she had confronted him, it hadn't mattered. He'd still rejected her.

Emmeline sucked in a slow breath, sickeningly aware that her selfishness and foolishness had impacted so many people. Hannah. King Patek. Sheikh Al-Koury.

What she had to do was fix things. Not just for her, but for everyone.

Once tidy and outwardly calm, she took the seat the flight attendant led her to, a seat not far from Makin's, although he was at work typing away on his laptop.

Emmeline tried to block him from her peripheral vision as the jet taxied down the runway, unnerved by the sheer size and shape of him.

He was tall, solid, muscular. As he typed, his arms flexed and she could see the distinct shape of his thick bicep press against the taut cotton of his shirt. His fine wool trousers silhouetted the hard cut of his quadriceps. Even his hands were strong, his fingers moving easily, confidently, across the laptop keyboard.

She watched his hands for a moment, fascinated by them. His skin was tan and his fingers were long and well-shaped. They reminded her of the hands on Greek statues—beautiful, classic, sculptural. She wondered what his touch would be like, and how his hands would move on a woman's body. Would his touch be light and gentle, or heavy and rough? She wondered how he held a woman, and if he curved her to him or held himself aloof, using her like a piece of equipment.

Emmeline had never wondered about such things before, but her night with Alejandro had changed all that. It changed the way she viewed men and women, made her realize that sex had been romanticized in books and movies and the media.

Sex wasn't warm or fun or intimate. It hadn't been beautiful or something pleasurable.

She'd found it a soulless, empty act. It'd been Alejandro taking her body—no more, no less than that.

Emmeline knew now her expectations had been so silly, so girlish and immature. Why hadn't she realized that Alejandro would pump away at her until he climaxed and roll off to shower and dress and leave?

Her eyes stung, hot, hot and gritty. Even seven weeks later she felt betrayed by her need for love and affection, and how she'd turned to Alejandro to give her that affection.

She'd imagined that sex would fill the hollow emptiness inside of her, but it had only made it worse.

Squeezing her eyes closed, she pulled the soft blanket even higher on her chest as her late grandmother's voice echoed in her head, "Don't cast pearls before swine." But that's what Emmeline had done out of desperation that no one would ever love her.

Emmeline shivered beneath the blanket, horrified all over again by her poor choices.

"Would you like me to turn the heat up?" Makin asked.

She opened her eyes and saw he was watching her. She didn't know how long he'd been watching. "I'm fine," she said unsteadily.

"I can get you another blanket."

"I'm fine," she repeated.

"You're shivering."

Heat crept into her cheeks. He was watching her closely, then. "Just my thoughts."

"Ibanez isn't worth your time. He's a liar, a cheat, a scoundrel. You deserve a prince of a man. Nothing less."

How ironic. Hannah deserved a prince of a man, but she, Emmeline, deserved only scorn.

Emmeline swallowed around the thick lump in her throat, wishing that she could be the smart, capable Hannah he admired instead of the useless spoiled princess he despised.

His disdain for her wounded. It shouldn't. He didn't know her, and she shouldn't let one person's opinion matter, but it did. He'd touched a nerve. A powerful nerve. It was as if he'd somehow seen through her elegant, polished exterior to the real Emmeline, the private Emmeline who felt so unworthy and impossible to love.

She'd always wondered why she felt so insecure, so alone, and then, on her sixteenth birthday, a half hour before her big party, she'd learned that her parents weren't her birth parents after all. She'd been adopted. Her birth mother had been a young unmarried woman from Brabant, but no one knew who her birth father was.

She'd gone to her birthday party absolutely shell-shocked. She didn't know why her adoptive father, King William, had felt compelled to break the news before her party but it had spoiled the night for her. Instead of dancing and celebrating with her guests, she'd found herself wondering about the mother who'd given her up, and if she looked like her, and if her mother ever thought of her.

It had been nine years since that revelation, and yet Emmeline still wondered about her birth parents. Could the fact that she'd been adopted have anything to do with her sense of emptiness and fear of abandonment? Could she have missed that mother who gave birth to her?

"What did you hope to accomplish tonight at the Mynt?" Makin suddenly asked.

She drew the blanket even closer to her chest, trying to capture more warmth. "He said he loved me—"

"Yes, I know," he interrupted impatiently. "You already told me that."

"—and I thought if he saw me tonight, he'd remember how he felt about me," she pressed on as though he hadn't spoken. "I thought he'd remember he'd asked me to marry him."

"He asked you to marry him?" he repeated, incredulous.

Her chin tilted defiantly. Why did he find that so impossible to believe? "Yes."

For a long moment Makin said nothing, absolutely nothing. He just sat there, looking at her as if he felt sorry for her. Just when Emmeline didn't think she could take his pitying silence another moment, he spoke. "Alejandro's already married. Not just married, but a father to five children. The oldest is twelve. The youngest just nine months old."

"Impossible."

"Have I ever lied to you about anything?"

She couldn't answer and, jaw flexing, he looked away, dropping his gaze to the bright screen of his laptop computer.

Blanket pressed to her collarbone, Emmeline's stomach heaved. Alejandro, already married? Father to five? Things just kept getting worse.

CHAPTER THREE

Hours later, Emmeline was woken by the vibration of the jet's landing gear unfolding, wheels in position in preparation for touching down. Half asleep, she glanced out the window but could see nothing below but pale gold...or was it beige? Maybe a little of both. No buildings, no lights, no roads, no sign of life. Just sand.

Emmeline groggily sat taller. Far in the distance she could see a spot of gray color. Or was it green? She didn't know what it was but it couldn't be a city, and there was no sprawling airport, either, and yet here they were making a sharp, steep descent as if they were about to land.

Just moments later, they touched down, the landing so smooth it was but a bump of sound and then the swift application of brakes. They hurtled along the black asphalt runway bordered on both sides by a vast reddish-gold desert. In the distance, in the same direction she'd spotted the gray-green patch, she could see a ragged range of mountains, but even those were copper and gold in the morning light.

She didn't know why, but she'd expected a city. Most of the royal princes she knew in Dubai and the UAE lived in cosmopolitan cities—glamorous centers filled with fashion boutiques and deluxe hotels and five-star restaurants. Sheikhs today were modern and wealthier than the rest of the world, including their European counterparts. They could afford life's every luxury, and they owned jets, yachts, rare cars, polo fields and strings of expensive ponies.

That was the world Emmeline had expected Sheikh Al-Koury to take her to. A sprawling urban city. But instead there was just sand. Sand and more sand. A virtual sea of sand in every direction, all the way to the rough-hewn mountains.

Emmeline had thought she could just put Hannah on a plane and get her here. But she wasn't going to be able to sneak Hannah into the desert and change places with her without anyone knowing. They were in such a deserted spot that all incoming aircraft would immediately be noticed.

"You look disappointed." Makin's deep voice came from across the aisle.

Emmeline's pulse quickened, and his deep husky timbre flooded her with memories—his appearance at the nightclub last night. His harsh opinion of Alejandro. His overwhelming physical presence.

"Why would I be disappointed?" she answered, with a casual arch of her eyebrow.

His silver gaze collided with hers and held. His features were granite-hard, his strong black eyebrows a slash above intense gray eyes. There was a light in his eyes, too, and a curve to his upper lip as if he weren't pleased with what he saw, either.

Her pulse jumped, racing wildly. He was still intense, still overwhelming, and nausea threatened to get the best of her.

"You've never liked the desert and Kasbah Raha," he said softly, his upper lip curling yet again. "You prefer life in Nadir with all the hustle and bustle."

So they truly were in the middle of nowhere. Which meant getting Hannah into Raha undetected would be as nearly impossible as Emmeline getting out.

"That may be so," she answered, hoping he didn't hear the wobble in her voice, "but I love how the morning sun burnishes the sand, turning everything copper and gold."

"How refreshing. You usually dread your time in the desert, saying Raha reminds you too much of your ranch in Texas."

Emmeline valiantly tried to play along. "But I love the ranch. It's where I grew up."

"Maybe. But in Nadir you have friends, your own apartment

in the palace, and numerous social activities, and when you're here, you're very much alone. Or alone with me."

The "alone with him" part sent a tremor of anxiety through her. She couldn't imagine spending another hour alone with him, much less days. She had to get Hannah here. Immediately.

His eyes suddenly gleamed, his full sensual mouth lifting in a mocking smile, and she could have sworn he knew exactly what she was thinking. She blushed, cheeks heating, skin prickling, even as she told herself it was impossible. He wasn't a mind reader. He couldn't possibly know how much he unsettled her.

And yet his gray eyes with those bright silver flecks were so direct, so perceptive she felt a quiver race through her, a quiver of dread and anticipation. He was so different from anyone she knew. So much more…

Makin's long legs stretched carelessly into the aisle and his broad shoulders filled his chair. He was at least six feet two. While Alejandro was handsome, Makin Al-Koury exuded power.

"Fortunately, this time here you'll be too busy assisting and entertaining my guests to feel isolated," he added. "I trust that everything's in place for their arrival?"

"Of course." She smiled to hide the fact that she didn't have a clue. But she'd soon find someone on his staff who would fill her in.

"Good. Because last night I seriously questioned your ability to pull this weekend off. But you slept most of the flight and appear more rested."

"I am," she answered, thinking that it was he who looked utterly fresh despite the fact that they'd been traveling for so long.

"Did you take something to help you sleep?"

"No. Why?"

"You aren't usually able to fall asleep on flights."

She didn't know how to respond to that as she'd learned to sleep on planes at a very young age. She'd grown up traveling. There were always royal functions and goodwill tours and appearances, first with her family and then on her own.

She'd been a shy little girl, and even a timid teenager, but the media never knew that. All they saw was her face and how photogenic she was. By the time she was fifteen, the paparazzi had singled her out, crowning her as the great beauty of her generation. Since then she'd lived in the spotlight, with camera lenses constantly focused on her and journalists' pens poised to praise or critique, and she never knew which until the article was published.

"I think I was too worn out not to sleep," she said, and it was true. All she wanted to do lately was sleep, and apparently that was another side effect of pregnancy. "And you? Did you get any rest?"

"Less than I wanted," he said, lashes dropping over his eyes, concealing his expression. "It was hard to sleep. I was—am— worried about you."

She heard something in his deep voice that made her insides flip-flop.

Genuine emotion. True concern.

He might hate Emmeline but he adored Hannah.

Emmeline felt a sharp stab of envy. What she wouldn't give to be the brilliant, efficient Hannah—a woman worthy of love and respect.

Awash in hot emotion, Emmeline looked away, out the jet's oval window. They'd finally come to a full stop in this vast desert. Uniformed personnel appeared on the tarmac. A fleet of shining black vehicles waited just off to the side of the runway, sunlight glinting off the windows and polished surfaces. Even though it was early, heat shimmered in iridescent waves off the black tarmac and surrounding sand.

This vast hot shimmering desert was Sheikh Al-Koury's world and now that she was here, Emmeline sensed her life would never be the same.

Makin stretched his legs out in the back seat of his custom car, a large, powerful sedan with tinted windows and reinforced panels to make it virtually bulletproof.

There hadn't been an uprising in Kadar in over three hundred years, and it was unlikely there would be in the next three hundred, but trouble could come from outside his country. The fact that he controlled so much oil had put a target on his back years ago. Fortunately, he wasn't a worrier, nor overly preoccupied with his own mortality. Instead he chose to live his life as his father had—without fear.

Makin relaxed a little, glad to be home.

His family had palaces all over Kadar but the rustic tribal kasbah in Raha had always been his favorite. Even the name Kasbah Raha—Palace of Rest—symbolized peace. Peace and calm. And it was. Here in the desert he was able to think clearly and focus without the noise and chaos of modern city life to distract him.

"Let's go over today's schedule," he said to Hannah, as his driver accelerated, leaving the tarmac and the sleek white jet behind. She was sitting to his left, pale but composed. He was glad to see her so calm. It gave him hope that all the personal drama was now behind them. "Which of my guests arrive first? And when?"

He waited for Hannah to reach for her briefcase or her phone but she did nothing. Had nothing. Instead she looked at him, her expression slightly baffled. "I don't…know."

He hesitated, thinking she was joking, not that she normally teased about things like that. But after a beat and a moment of awkward silence, he realized she was serious.

His jaw tightened, lips compressing as he understood that Hannah's personal problems were far from over.

Makin's frown deepened, eyebrows flattening above his eyes. "It's your job to know."

She took a quick breath. "It seems I've lost my calendar."

"But your calendar is backed up on your laptop. Where is your laptop computer?"

Her shoulders lifted and fell. "I don't know."

Makin had to turn away, look at something else other than Hannah. Her helplessness was getting to him. He didn't want to be angry with her, but he found everything about her provoking right now.

He focused on the desert beyond the car's tinted window,

soothed by the familiar landscape. To someone else the desert might look monotonous with miles of red-gold sand in every direction, but he knew this desert like the back of his hand and it centered him now.

"You've lost your computer?" he asked finally, gaze fixed on the undulating dunes in the distance.

"Yes."

"How?"

"I think I must have left it somewhere when I wasn't...well."

"In South Beach?"

"Before that."

He turned his head sharply toward her. Her lavender-blue eyes appeared enormous in her pale face.

"It must have been Palm Beach," she added softly, fingers lacing together. "Just after the polo tournament. I had it for the tournament, but then it was gone."

"Why didn't you tell me sooner?"

"I should have. I'm sorry."

She looked so nervous and desperate that he bit back his criticism and took a deep breath instead. She'd just had her heart broken. She wasn't herself. Surely, he could try to be patient with her. At least for today.

He fought to keep his voice even. "Everything should be backed up on your desktop. When we get to the palace, you can go to your office and print off your calendar and update me later this afternoon."

"Thank you," she whispered.

He drew another breath as he considered her pale, tense face and rigid posture. Her shoulders were set, her spine elongated, her chin tilted. It was strange. Everything about her was strange. Hannah had never sat like this before. So tall and still, as if she'd become someone else. Someone frozen.

Which reminded him of last night on the airplane. His brow furrowed. "You talked in your sleep last night," he said. "Endlessly."

Her eyes met his and her lips parted but she made no sound.

"In French," he continued. "Your accent was impeccable. If I didn't know better, I'd think you were a native speaker."

"You're fluent in French?"

"Of course. My mother was French."

She flushed, her cheeks turning dark pink. "Did I say anything that would embarrass me?"

"Just that you are in terrible trouble." He waited, allowing his words to fall and settle before continuing. "What have you done, Hannah? What are you afraid of?"

A tiny pulse leapt at her throat and the pink in her cheeks faded just as quickly as it had bloomed there. "Nothing."

She answered quickly, too quickly, and they both knew it.

Makin suppressed his annoyance. Who did she think she was fooling? Didn't she realize he knew her? He knew her perhaps better than anyone. They'd worked so closely together over the years that he quite often knew what she would say before she said it. He knew her gestures and expressions and even her hesitation before she gave him her opinion.

But even then, they'd never been friends. Their relationship was strictly professional. He knew her work habits, not her life story. And he had to believe that if she'd gotten herself into trouble, she had the wherewithal to get herself out of it.

She was strong. Smart. Self-sufficient. She'd be fine.

Well, maybe in the long term, he amended. Right now Hannah looked far from fine.

She'd turned white, and he saw her swallow hard, once and again. She looked as if she was battling for control. "Do you need us to pull over?" he asked. "Are you—"

"Yes! Yes, please."

Makin spoke sharply to the driver and moments later they were parked on the side of the narrow road. She stumbled away from the car, her high heels sinking into the soft sand.

He wasn't sure if he should go after her—which is all he'd spent the last week doing—or give her some space to allow her to maintain some dignity.

Space won, and Makin and his driver stood next to the car in the event that their assistance was needed.

Even though it was still relatively early in the day, it was hot in the direct sun, with the morning temperature hovering just under a hundred degrees Fahrenheit. It was a very dry heat, he thought, sliding on his sunglasses, unlike Florida with its sweltering humidity.

Florida was fine, but this was his desert. This was where he belonged. They were just a few kilometers from Kasbah Raha now, and he was impatient to reach the palace.

He spent several months each year at Raha, and they were usually his favorite months.

Every day in Raha he'd wake, exercise, shower, have a light meal and then go to his office to work. He'd break for a late lunch and then work again, often late into the night. He enjoyed everything about his work and stayed at his desk because that's where he wanted to be.

He wasn't all work though. He had a mistress in Nadir whom he saw several times a week when there. Hannah knew about Madeline, of course, but it wasn't something he'd ever discuss with her. Just as Hannah had never discussed her love life with him.

Makin's cell phone suddenly rang, sounding too loud in the quiet desert. Withdrawing the phone from his trouser pocket, he saw it was his chief of security from the palace in Nadir.

Makin answered in Arabic.

As he listened, he went cold, thinking the timing couldn't be worse. Hannah was already struggling. This would devastate her.

Makin asked his chief of security to keep him informed and then hung up. As he pocketed his phone, Hannah appeared, her graceful hands smoothing her creased turquoise cocktail dress. As she walked toward him, she gave him an apologetic smile. "I'm sorry about that."

He didn't smile back. "You're still sick."

"Low blood sugar. Haven't eaten yet today."

Nor had anything to drink, he realized, remembering now that she'd no coffee, tea or juice on the flight, either.

Makin spoke to his driver in Arabic, and the chauffeur immediately went to the back of the gleaming car, opened the trunk, and withdrew two bottles of water. He gave both to the sheikh and Makin unscrewed the cap of one, and handed the open bottle to Hannah.

"It's cold," she said surprised, even as she took a long drink from the plastic bottle.

"I have a small refrigerator built into the trunk. Keeps things cool on long trips."

"That's smart. It's really hot here." She lifted the bottle to her lips, drank again, her hand trembling slightly.

Makin didn't miss the tremble of her hand. Or the purple shadows beneath her eyes. She was exhausted. She needed to eat. Rest. Recover.

She didn't need more bad news.

She didn't need another stress.

He couldn't keep the news from her, nor would he, but he didn't have to tell her now. There was nothing she could do. Nothing any of them could do.

He'd wait until they reached the palace to tell her about the call. Wait until she'd had a chance to shower and change and get something into her stomach because right now she looked on the verge of collapse.

"Shall we?" he asked, gesturing to the car.

CHAPTER FOUR

EMMELINE slowly rolled the cold water bottle between her hands, pretending to study the arid landscape, when in truth she was avoiding Makin's gaze.

She knew he was looking at her. Ever since they'd stopped alongside the road, he seemed quieter, grimmer, if such a thing were possible.

Earlier, by the side of the road, she'd thought she heard his phone ring but she'd only stepped around the car for a minute or two, so if he had talked to someone, it had been a short call.

Her sixth sense told her the call had something to do with her.

Maybe it was paranoia, but she had a cold, sinking sensation in her gut that told her he'd begun to put two and two together and things weren't adding up.

Had he figured out the truth? That she wasn't the real Hannah Smith?

Still worried, Emmeline saw a shimmer of green appear on the horizon. The shimmer of green gradually took shape, becoming trees and orchards as the desert gave way to a fertile oasis.

Fed by an underground stream that came from the mountains, the oasis became a city of red clay walls and narrow roads.

The sheikh's driver turned off the narrow highway onto an even narrower road shaded by tall date palms, the massive green-and-yellow fronds providing protection from the dazzling desert heat.

As the car approached the enormous gates ahead, they swung open, giving entrance into the walled city.

"Home," Makin said with quiet satisfaction as they traveled down yet another long drive bordered by majestic date palms, the heavy fronds like feathered plumes against the clear blue sky.

More gates opened and closed, revealing a sprawling building washed in the palest pink. But as the car continued to travel, Emmeline discovered the palace wasn't just one building, but a series of beautifully shaped buildings connected by trellises, patios, courtyards and gardens. No two were the same. Some had turrets and towers, others were domed, although each had the same smooth clay walls lushly covered in dark purple and white bougainvillea.

The car stopped before the tallest building, three stories tall with intricate gold-plated doors and massive gold, blue and white columns flanking the entrance.

Staff in billowy white pants and white jackets lined the entrance, smiling broadly and bowing low as Sheikh Al-Koury stepped from the car.

Having grown up in a palace, Emmeline was familiar with pomp, protocol and ceremony. Daily she'd witnessed the display of respect all were required to show the royal family, and yet there was something different about the sheikh's staff.

They greeted him with warmth and a genuine sense of pleasure in his return. They cared about him, and she saw from the way he responded to each man, he cared about them.

Makin paused at the ornate entrance, waiting for her, and together they stepped through the tall gold doors, leaving the bright sunlight and dazzling heat behind.

The serene, airy foyer was capped by a high domed ceiling of blue and gold, the cream walls stenciled in sophisticated gold swirls and elegant patterns. Emmeline drew a slow breath, relishing the palace's tranquility and delicious coolness. "Lovely," she said.

The sheikh lifted a brow, and glanced enquiringly at her.

She flushed, remembering she was supposed to be Hannah

and familiar with everything here. "The coolness," she said. "Feels so good after the heat."

He stared down at her a moment, expression peculiar. He seemed to be looking for something in her face, but what, she didn't know.

And then he nodded, a short nod, as if he'd come to a decision. "I'll walk you to your room," he said. "Make sure everything is as it should be."

Emmeline's brow puckered at his tone. Something *had* happened. She was sure of it.

He set off, leaving her to follow, and they crossed the spacious foyer, through one of the many exquisitely carved arches that opened off the entrance, their footsteps echoing on the limestone floor.

He turned down a hallway marked by ornamental columns. Sunlight streamed through high windows. Mosaic murals decorated the ivory walls and large ornate copper lanterns were hung from the high ceiling to provide light in the evening.

They passed through another arch which led outside to a rose-covered arbor. The roses were in full bloom, a soft luscious pink, and the heady scent reminded Emmeline of the formal rose garden at the palace in Brabant. She felt a sudden pang for all that she'd lose once her parents knew she wouldn't—couldn't—marry King Patek, and why. They'd be scandalized. They'd insist she'd get an abortion, something she wouldn't do.

There would be threats.

There would be anger.

Hostility.

Repercussions.

Makin paused before a beautiful door stained a rich mahogany and stepped aside for her to open it.

Hannah's room, she thought, opening the door to a spacious apartment contained in its own building. The high-ceilinged living room spoke of an understated elegance, the colors warmer here than in the rest of the palace. The living-room walls were pale gold and the furniture was gold with touches of red, ivory and blue. She glimpsed a bedroom off the living room with an attached bathroom. There was even a small kitchen where Hannah could prepare coffee and make simple meals.

"The cook made your favorite bread," he said, nodding at a fabric-wrapped loaf on the tiled kitchen counter. "The refrigerator also has your yogurts and milk, and everything else you like. If you won't let Cook send you a tray for lunch, promise me you'll eat something right away."

She nodded. "I promise."

"Good." He hesitated, still standing just inside the doorway, clearly uncomfortable. "I need to tell you something. May we sit?"

She glanced at his face but his expression was shuttered, his silver gaze hard.

Emmeline walked to the low couch upholstered in a delicate silk the color of fresh butter, and moved some of the loose embroidered and jeweled pillows aside so she could sit down. He followed but didn't sit. He stood before her, arms crossed over his chest, his gray linen shirt pulled taut at the shoulders.

He was without a doubt a very handsome man. He radiated power and control, but right now he was scaring her with his fierce expression.

"There's been an accident," he said abruptly. "Last night on the way to the airport, Alejandro lost control of the car and crashed. Penelope died on the scene. Alejandro's in hospital."

It was the last thing Emmeline had expected him to say. She struggled to process what he'd just told her. Her mouth opened and closed without making a sound. She tried again. Failed.

"He was in surgery all night," Makin continued. "There was a lot of internal bleeding. His condition is extremely critical."

Reeling from shock, Emmeline clasped her hands tightly together, too stunned to speak.

Penelope was dead. Alejandro might not survive surgery. And yet both had been so beautiful and alive just hours ago.

Impossible.

Eyes burning, she gazed blindly out the glass doors to the garden beyond. Behind the walled garden the red mountains rose high, reminding her of the red dress Penelope had worn last night. And just like that, the desert was gone and all Emmeline could see was Penelope's vivid red dress against the billowing fabric of Alejandro's white shirt.

Her throat squeezed closed. Hot acid tears filmed her eyes. "Alejandro was…driving?" she asked huskily, finally finding her voice.

"He was at the wheel, yes."

"And Penelope?"

"Was thrown from the car on impact."

Emmeline closed her eyes, able to see it all and hating the movie reel of pictures in her head. Stupid, reckless Alejandro. Her heart ached for Penelope who was so young—just nineteen.

A tear fell, hot and wet on Emmeline's cheek. With a savage motion she brushed it away. She was furious. Furious with Alejandro. Furious that he took lives and wrecked them and threw them all away.

"I'm sorry, Hannah," Makin said, his deep voice rumbling through her. "I know you imagined yourself in love—"

"Please." Her voice broke and she lifted a hand to silence him. "Don't."

He crouched down before her, his powerful thighs all muscle, and caught her chin, forcing her to look at him. His silver-gray eyes glowed like pewter, hot and dark with emotion. "I know this isn't an easy time for you, but you'll survive this. I promise."

Then he surprised her by gently, carefully, sweeping his thumb across the curve of her cheek, catching the tears that fell. It was such a tender gesture from him, so kind and protective, it almost broke her heart.

She hadn't been touched so gently and kindly by anyone in years.

She'd never been touched by a man as if she mattered. "Thank you."

Makin stood. "You'll be all right," he repeated.

She wished she had an ounce of his confidence. "Yes." She wiped her eyes dry. "You're right. I'll shower and change and get to work." She rose, too, took several steps away to put distance between them. "What time shall I meet you?"

"I don't think you should try to do anything this afternoon."

"I know there must be stacks of mail—"

"And hundreds of emails, as well as dozens of phone messages all waiting for your attention, but they can wait a little longer," he said firmly. "I want you to take the rest of the day for yourself. Eat, sleep, read, go for a swim. Do whatever you need to do so that you can get back to work. I need your help, Hannah, but you're absolutely useless to me right now."

She felt her cheeks grow hot. "I'm sorry. I hate being a problem."

He gave her a peculiar look before his broad shoulders shifted. "Rest. Feel better. That would be the biggest help." Then he walked away, leaving her in the living room as if this was where she belonged.

But as the door closed behind him, she knew this wasn't where she belonged. It was where Hannah belonged.

These rooms, the food in the kitchen, the clothes in the closet...they were all Hannah's. Hannah needed her life back.

Emmeline glanced down at herself, feeling grimy and disheveled in her creased cocktail dress, and while she longed for a shower—and food—she had something more important to do first.

She had to reach Hannah. She'd put in calls yesterday but they'd all gone straight to voice mail. Hannah had texted her back, asking when Emmeline planned to arrive. Hannah was expecting Emmeline to show up in Raguva any moment to change places with her before anyone knew the difference. Which obviously wasn't going to happen.

Taking her phone from her small evening purse, Emmeline dialed Hannah's number, praying that she'd actually get through this time instead of reaching Hannah's voice mail again.

The phone rang and rang again before Hannah answered breathlessly. "Hello?"

Emmeline dragged a dark red embroidered pillow against her chest. "Hannah, it's me."

"I know. Are you okay?"

Emmeline squeezed the pillow tighter, her insides starting to churn. "I…I don't know."

"Are you coming here?"

"I…" Emmeline hesitated. "I…don't…know," she repeated, stumbling a bit, feeling dishonest, because she knew the answer. She could never go to Raguva. Not now.

Tense silence stretched over the line and then Hannah asked tightly, "What do you mean, you don't know?"

Emmeline stared at the tall red mountains visible beyond the palace walls. She felt just as jagged as the mountain peaks. She'd flown all night, was seven weeks pregnant, and thousands of miles from Miami where Alejandro lay in critical condition. "I'm in Kadar."

Silence stretched over the line. "Kadar?" Hannah repeated wonderingly. "Why?"

Emmeline's shoulders rose, hunching. "Sheikh Al-Koury thinks I'm you."

Hannah exhaled hard. "Tell him you're not! Tell him the truth."

"I can't." Emmeline felt dangerously close to just losing it. It'd been such a difficult few weeks and she'd been so sure that she could turn things around, make it all right. But instead of things improving, they'd taken a dramatic turn for the worse. "I can't. Not before Sheikh Al-Koury's conference. It'd ruin everything."

"But everything's already ruined," Hannah cried, her voice rising and then breaking. "You have no idea what's happened—"

"I'm sorry, Hannah, I really am. But everything's out of my control."

"*Your* control. *Your* life. It's always about you, isn't it?"

"I didn't mean it that way—"

"But you did mean to send me here in your place and you didn't intend to come right away. You used me. Manipulated me. But how do you think I feel being trapped here, pretending to—" Hannah broke off abruptly.

The line went dead.

Hannah had hung up.

Emmeline stared at the phone, stunned. But what did she expect? She had done an amazing job of messing up Hannah's life.

Makin had met briefly with his staff after leaving Hannah's room and spent fifteen minutes in his office listening to updates from his various department managers before dismissing them all with a wave of his hand.

He couldn't focus on the updates. His thoughts were elsewhere, back with Hannah in her room.

Telling Hannah about Alejandro's accident had been far harder than he'd imagined. He hadn't liked giving her bad news. It didn't feel right. He'd never felt protective of her before, but he did now.

Maybe it was because she wasn't well.

Maybe it was knowing she'd had her heart broken.

Maybe it's because he was suddenly aware of her in a way he hadn't been before.

Aware of her as a woman. Aware that she was very much a woman. A highly desirable woman. And that was a problem.

Mouth compressing, he rose from behind his desk, left his office and set off to meet the Kasbah's director of security, who had promised to give him a tour of the guest wings and go over the security measures in place for the safety of their guests.

The tour was interrupted by a phone call with information that Alejandro was out of surgery and in recovery. He hadn't woken yet, and while the prognosis was still grim, he'd at least survived the nine-hour operation. For Hannah's sake, he was glad.

Call concluded, he and the security director passed through a high, arched doorway and stepped outside. "Which families will be in that building?" he asked, struggling to get his attention back on his life, his work, his conference. He wasn't a man who was easily distracted, but he seemed unable to focus on anything other than Hannah right now.

"The Nuris of Baraka, Your Highness. Sultan Malek Nuri and

his brother Sheikh Kalen Nuri, along with their wives. Sheikh Tair of Ohua."

"And in the building to my right?"

"Our Western dignitaries."

Makin nodded. "Good." He was relieved to see that not only was security prepared, but the Kasbah looked immaculate.

While all of Makin's various homes and palaces were beautiful, Kasbah Raha always took his breath away. The Kasbah itself was hundreds of years old, and lovingly preserved by generations of the Al-Koury family, the colors mirroring the desert—the pink of sunrise, the majestic red mountains, the blue of the sky, and the ivory-and-gold sand.

It was remote. And it was the place he worked best. Which is why he'd never brought Madeline to Raha. Raha was for clarity of thought and personal reflection…not desire or lust. He'd never wanted to associate a carnal pleasure such as sex with Raha, either, but suddenly, with Hannah under his roof, he was thinking about very carnal things instead of focusing on the conference.

Hannah.

Just saying her name made his insides tighten.

And that twinge of tension was enough for him to come to a decision.

This wasn't going to work with her here. He realized they'd only just arrived, but she had to go. The timing was terrible, but there was too much at risk to allow himself to be mired in indecision.

CHAPTER FIVE

STILL flattened from her call to Hannah, Emmeline showered and wrapped herself in her robe that had been unpacked and hung in the closet next to Hannah's wardrobe.

Curious, Emmeline sorted through Hannah's clothes. Hannah's wardrobe wasn't exactly dowdy, but it was practical. Hannah dressed conservatively in keeping with her job.

Stretching out on the bed, Emmeline felt a sudden rush of affection for her lookalike, thinking Hannah was the kind of friend you'd want in your corner. And she'd been in Emmeline's corner, too...

Emmeline didn't remember drifting off to sleep, but hours later the doorbell woke her.

Sitting up, she saw the sun had shifted across the sky and now sat low, hinting at twilight. Pale violet shadows crept across the bedroom and hovered in corners. She headed for the door. One of the palace's kitchen staff stood outside with a gleaming silver trolley.

"Good evening, Miss Smith," the palace staffer greeted her. "His Highness thought you'd want to dine tonight in the privacy of your own room."

A thoughtful gesture on the sheikh's part, she thought, opening the door wider. The man pushed the trolley through the living room out onto the flagstone patio. Emmeline watched as he arranged the tables and chairs closer to the pool and covered the small round table with a cloth from the cart, then dishes, silverware, goblets, candles and a low floral arrangement.

Then with a brief respectful nod to Emmeline, he left, taking the now-empty cart with him. Once he was gone, Emmeline stepped out onto the patio. The table had been set for two. Two plates, two sets of silverware, two water and two wine goblets.

She wasn't dining alone tonight.

And just like that, Emmeline's sense of well-being fled.

The moment Hannah opened the door that evening, Makin knew he'd made a mistake. He should have called her to his office to tell her he was sending her away, summoning her as one would summon an employee, instead of breaking the news over dinner.

He'd thought that talking in private would lessen the blow. But he was wrong. Wrong to speak to her at dinner, in her room.

Worse, she'd dressed for dinner tonight, and she'd never dressed for dinner before.

Why had she put on a frothy cocktail dress? And why those gold high heels that made her legs look silky smooth and endless?

Makin followed her slowly through her gold living room to the garden knowing he was compounding matters, adding insult to injury by staying. One didn't give employees bad news like this. He should go and wait until the morning. Go and wait until he felt calmer, more settled.

But he didn't leave. He couldn't, not when he felt an irresistible pull to stay. Instead of going, he trailed after her through the large sliding glass doors to the garden where a table had been set for two.

Makin's gaze rested on the table and his unease grew.

She'd dressed to match the table setting, her orange chiffon gown a darker, more vibrant shade than the table's rich apricot-and-gold jeweled cloth. Tall tapered candles framed the low floral centerpiece of apricot and cream roses.

Yet another mistake. His chief of staff had misunderstood him.

Makin blamed himself for the confusion. He should have been more clear with his kitchen and waiting staff. He'd requested a quiet meal with Hannah so he could speak frankly with her. He'd asked to have the meal served in her room so he could talk without interruption. It had never crossed his mind that his simple request would get turned into this....

This...

Intimate setting for two.

Makin frowned at the gleaming display of silver, crystal wine goblets and fine bone china.

His frown turned grim as the tall tapered candles flickered and danced, throwing shadows and light across the table, accenting the rich jewel tones of the embroidered cloth. More candles flickered in hammered iron wall sconces. Even the pool and fountain were softly lit as a whisper of a breeze rustled through the tall date palms standing sentry around the perimeter of the garden.

Makin had come to Hannah's apartment hundreds of times over the years, but they'd never dined here before, not alone, not late at night, and certainly never like this.

When they met for dinner, the tone had always been professional, the focus centered on business. She'd attended numerous banquets with him. Had sat across from him at countless perfunctory meals where she took notes and he rattled off instructions. But it had never been this, never the two of them seated across from each other dining by moonlight and candlelight. The lighting changed everything, as did the soft sheen of the embroidered silk tablecloth. The shimmer of fabric, the glow of light created intimacy...sensuality.

She'd never met him in anything but tailored jackets and skirts and demure blouses before, either. And yet she'd dressed tonight. As if this wasn't just a business dinner. As if this was something more...something personal...as if this was a...date.

Just the thought of being alone with Hannah on a date, in a filmy cocktail dress and high strappy gold heels, made him harden.

It was a good thing he'd made the decision this afternoon to send her to a different office to work with different people. A good thing he'd decided to act swiftly. Relationships were tricky, particularly in the work arena, and he'd always been very careful to keep business and personal separate. But now, with Hannah, the line between work and personal life felt blurred. Around Hannah he'd begun to crave…something. And Makin was not a man to crave anything.

"We need to talk," he said roughly, gesturing to the table, deciding he wouldn't wait for dinner to say what he needed to say. He'd just do it right away. Get it over with. He wouldn't be able to relax until he'd broken the news and she'd accepted his decision.

He watched as Hannah sat down gracefully, obediently, at the table and looked up at him, waiting for him to speak. On one hand she was doing everything right—sitting quietly, waiting patiently—and yet everything felt wrong.

Starting with her orange chiffon cocktail dress. And the gold bangle on her wrist. And the fact that she had left her long thick hair loose about her shoulders.

How could he coldly announce he was sending her away, transferring her to another department, when she was looking so good and lovely?

Especially lovely. The *lovely* part frustrated him. He felt tricked. Played.

Hannah didn't wear vivid colors like juicy orange or exotic peacock. She didn't leave her hair loose or smudge her eyes with eyeliner or stain her lips with soft pink color.

He turned his back on her to face the pool. The rectangular blue pool was illuminated tonight with small spotlights aimed at the elegant fountain so that shadows of dancing water played across the back wall. But even the small spotlights hinted at intimacy.

Makin walked around the edge of the pool, ran a troubled hand across his jaw, unable to remember a time when he'd been this uncomfortable. The night was warm but it wasn't the temperature making him miserable. It was the knowledge that this was his last night with Hannah, that tomorrow he'd be sending her away.

He knew it was for the best but still…

Makin rolled his shoulders, trying to release the tension balled in the muscles between his shoulder blades. Even his white shirt felt too snug against his shoulders and his trousers hot against his skin.

"You're making me nervous," she said quietly, her voice soft in the warm night.

He glanced at her, still unable to make sense of this Hannah, or of his ambivalent feelings for her.

For four and a half years they'd worked closely together and as much as he'd valued her and appreciated her skill, he'd never felt the least bit attracted to her. There had never been chemistry. Nor did he want there to be. She was an employee. Intelligent, productive and useful. Three words he used to describe his laptop, too. But you didn't take a computer to bed.

"Why?" he asked equally quietly, seeing the faint tremble of her soft lower lip, and then the pinch of her teeth as they bit down.

The bite of her teeth into that tender pink lip made him hot, blisteringly hot. It was a physical heat, a heat that made him harden and his temper stir.

This was absurd. Ridiculous. Why was he feeling things now? Why was he responding to her now? For God's sake, he was her boss. She was dependent on him. One didn't take advantage of one's position or power in life. Not ever. That lesson had been drummed into him from a very early age.

And yet his hard, heavy erection was very real, as was his drumming pulse.

He was feeling very angry, very annoyed and very impatient. With her, with him, with all of this.

"Something is obviously wrong," she said, sitting tall and still, her slender hands folded in her lap.

His body ached. His erection throbbed. His blood felt like hot, spiced wine, and he was on edge, the night suddenly erotic, electric.

He told himself it was the candlelight and the moon—pale gold and three-quarters full. It was the warm breeze in the palms teasing his senses, making him more restless than usual.

But it wasn't the soft glow of light, or the breeze or the rich, musky scent of roses, but her.

Hannah.

He was absolutely sure he was doing the right thing in sending her to London in the morning. He wouldn't allow doubts to creep in or cloud his thinking. She'd like the London division. She'd be an asset there. By tomorrow afternoon she'd be installed in her new office, meeting her new team, and knowing Hannah, she'd settle in quickly.

But somehow it seemed wrong to break the news to her like this, now, when she looked so beautiful that she took his breath away.

"That's a new dress," he said curtly, his tone almost accusatory.

Bewildered by the sharpness in his voice, her brows pulled together. "No. It's not new. I've had it for a while."

"I've never seen it."

She ran a light hand across her lap, as if smoothing imaginary wrinkles from the silky chiffon. "I haven't ever worn it around you before."

"Why now?"

Her lips pursed and she looked at him strangely. "I can go change if you'd like." She started to rise. "I didn't realize the dress would upset you—"

"It hasn't."

"You're angry."

"I'm not."

"I'll put on something else—"

"Sit." His deep voice rumbled through the garden, sounding too loud as it bounced and echoed off the high garden walls. *It's not her fault,* he told himself. She hadn't done anything wrong. He was the one who'd decided to send her away. She hadn't asked to go. "Please," he added more quietly.

She sank back into her chair, her wide lavender-blue gaze wary.

He closed the distance between them, leaned on the back of his chair and struggled to find the right words. The words that would allow him to put her on the plane to Heathrow tomorrow with the least amount of drama possible. He hated drama. Hated tears.

But closer to her wasn't better. Closer just made him more aware of how very appealing she was.

The pleated orange-chiffon gown left her slim, pale shoulders bare. The dress's neckline was hidden by a wide gold collar. And with her long dark hair loose and her eyes rimmed in a smoky gray, she looked like an exotic princess from a children's storybook. He could almost imagine she was waiting for the brave knight, the noble prince, who could sweep her away, give her that storybook ending.

If he were the sort of royal who believed in that sort of thing.

Which he wasn't. He didn't. He was too practical. Too driven. Too ambitious. He had a purpose in life. A mission. It wasn't enough that he be a great leader for his people. His personal mission was bigger than the borders of Kadar. His mission was to help the world.

It sounded grandiose. Perhaps it even made him sound a bit like a prig. But if his father could accomplish what he had with a brutal degenerative disease, then Makin could accomplish even more.

He had to.

The world was polluting itself to death, choking on chemicals and strangling on debt. The rich were getting richer and the poor, sick and hungry were still suffering and dying at a staggering rate.

For the past five years he'd met privately with powerful, wealthy visionaries from the music industry and high-tech businesses, to pool resources and make an even greater impact around the world. The goal was to get clean water to all people, to help immunize children in all third-world countries, to provide mosquito nets to help protect all vulnerable people from malaria.

Food. Shelter. Education. Safety.

For all children, regardless of religion, race, culture or gender. This was his goal. This was his life's ambition. And this was why he was sending her away.

She'd become a distraction. A liability. And nothing could come between him and his work.

"Sheikh Al-Koury, are you firing me?"

Her uncertain voice broke the silence.

He turned his head, glanced at her, felt a dull ache in his chest.

Damn her. Damn the garden. Damn the moonlight and the orange floaty fabric of her dress that clung to her small, firm breasts and made him want things he couldn't want with her.

"Yes," he said roughly. "No. Not firing. It's a transfer."

"Transfer to where?"

"The London office."

"But I live in Dallas."

"You've always enjoyed London."

"But my home—"

"Will now be London." His gaze met hers. He steeled himself, reminding himself that the only way to pull this off was to be ruthless. Hard. "If you no longer wish to work for me, I understand. But if you do, you'll embrace the challenges of your new position in the marketing and public relations department for the international division."

There. He'd said it. Makin exhaled. For the first time in days he felt relief. He felt in control again.

Silence stretched. The only sound in the garden was the bubble and splash of the fountain and the swish and whisper of palm fronds overhead.

Hannah's smooth jaw shifted, her lips compressed, but still she said nothing, which provoked him. She worked for him, not the other way around. It was her job to accept. Acquiesce. To make this change comfortable and easy for all of them.

"It's a promotion," he said tautly. "Human resources will provide you with temporary housing until you find something you like—"

"I like my job here, with you."

"You're needed elsewhere now."

"Yesterday you needed me here."

"Things change."

Her lips parted ever so slightly as if realizing where this was going, and why.

He hoped she'd gracefully fold, accept his new plan for her. He needed her to concede.

Her gaze turned beseeching. "Alejandro was a mistake. I admit I made a mistake—"

"It has nothing to do with Alejandro—"

"It has everything to do with Alejandro," she cried.

"You're wrong," he countered, torn between wanting to comfort her and crush her because all she needed to do was accept. Give. Agree. Not fight. Not cry. Not make him feel an ounce more emotion tonight.

"I'm not stupid," she said, eyes still shimmering but now flashing with bright hot sparks.

"No, you aren't."

"Then why?" She leaned forward, cheeks flushed, breasts rising and falling with every quick breath. "For four years I have given you everything. For four years I have made your goals mine. For four years I have put your needs before mine. I don't take vacations. I don't use sick days. I don't have a social life. I don't even have a fashionable wardrobe. My life is all about you, and only you."

"All the more reason you need to go to London."

She shot him a withering look, a look that should have cooled his hunger, but it didn't, and he couldn't remember when he'd last felt this way—so raw and physical, so completely carnal.

Before French-born Madeline had been his mistress there had been Jenny, a stunning English woman, and like Madeline, she'd been slim and blonde and very bright. He'd always been attracted to blonde, intelligent women. He took care of his mistresses, too, financially, and physically. When he made love with his mistress, he made sure she was pleasured. He wanted her happy. But he didn't offer love. Nor would he.

It wasn't her fault, he'd told Madeline more than once. It was his. He wasn't sensitive. Wasn't the type to feel certain emotions. Wasn't the type to feel passion.

And yet at the moment Makin literally felt as if he was on fire, his skin hot, nerves sensitive, his body rippling with tension and need. It wasn't rational. And far from civilized. He wanted to grab her, shake her—

He broke off with a shake of his own head. Madness. He'd never wanted to shake a woman before, or drag her from her chair and into his arms. He didn't lose control. Didn't feel strong emotions. So what was happening to him now?

"There will be a bump in your salary, as well as better benefits," he said. "Including another week of vacation."

Her lips curved. "Another week to add to the weeks and months I've never used?"

"Perhaps it's time you started taking those holidays."

"Perhaps it is."

Her tart tone made him see red. Sassy, saucy wench. How dare she speak to him with that attitude? How dare she smirk at him from beneath those long, black lashes as if he was the problem, not she?

What the hell was happening to him? He didn't even know himself at the moment. His shaft ached and throbbed and his hands itched to reach for her, catch her by the wrist and pull her toward him so that he could take her mouth, cover that mocking twist of her lips with his and make her his.

It wasn't a desire but a need. To know her. Feel her. Make her part of him.

His fingers flexed and balled before returning to hard fists. Clearly he wasn't himself.

He wasn't an aggressive man, and he didn't drag women about, and he didn't teach them lessons, but right now he wanted to remind her who he was, and what he was and how he wasn't a man to be trifled with.

He was Sheikh Makin Al-Koury, one of the world's most powerful men. He had a plan and a vision and nothing distracted him from it.

Certainly not his secretary. She was disposable. Dispensable.

Replaceable. And he'd proved it by swiftly organizing the job transfer to London.

"So why this…promotion…now?" she asked, her gaze meeting his and holding, expression challenging.

"I'm ready for a change. And I think you are, too."

Her eyes sparked blue fire. Her eyebrows lifted. "How kind of you to think for me."

"That's not what I meant."

"Good, and I respectfully ask that you don't make decisions for me based on what you think I need. You do not know me. You know nothing about me—"

"That's actually not respectful. And I do know you. I know virtually everything about you."

She laughed. Out loud. Practically in his face.

"If you knew me, Your Highness," she drawled his title, "you'd know who I am." She paused a moment, lashes dropping, concealing the hot bright blue of her eyes. "And who I am not."

Maybe he shouldn't transfer her to London. Maybe he should fire her. Her impudence was galling. He wouldn't have accepted this blatant lack of respect from anyone but her.

"You go too far," he thundered. He hadn't actually raised his voice, but his tone was so hard and fierce that it silenced her immediately.

She fell back into her seat, shoulders tense, lips pressed thinly. For a moment he imagined he saw pain in her eyes and then it was gone, replaced by a stony chill.

"I'm trying to help you," he said quietly.

She looked away, her gaze settling on the bubbling fountain. "You're trying to get rid of me."

"Maybe I am."

And there it was. The truth. Spoken aloud.

He'd said it and he saw by the way she flinched she'd heard it, too.

For a long, endless moment they sat in silence, she staring at the blue ceramic fountain while he stared at her, drinking in her profile, memorizing the delicate, elegant lines of her face.

He'd never appreciated her beauty before, had never seen the high-winged eyebrow, the prominent thrust of her cheekbone, the full, sensual curve of her lips.

His chest grew tight, a spasm of intense sensation. Regret. A whisper of pain. He would miss her.

"Is that it, then?" she asked, turning her head to look at him, dark hair spilling across her shoulder and over the soft ripe chiffon of her orange dress. She was staring deeply into his eyes as if she were trying to see straight through him, into the very heart of him.

He let her look, too, knowing she couldn't see anything, knowing she, like everyone else, only saw what he allowed people to see...

Which was nothing.

Nothing but distance. And hollow space.

Years ago knowing that his father was dying and that his mother didn't want to live without his father, he'd constructed the wall around his emotions, burying his heart behind brick and mortar. No one, not even Madeline, was given access to his emotions. No one was ever allowed that close.

"Is that why we're here having dinner?" she added. "Is that what you came here tonight to say?"

"Yes."

She looked at him for another long, unnerving moment, her eyes a brilliant, startling blue against the paleness of her face. "All right." She shrugged lightly, almost indifferently, and rose to her feet. "Am I excused then?"

"Dinner hasn't even been served."

"I don't think I could stomach a bite now, and it seems a waste of time to sit and make small talk when I could begin getting organized for my flight tomorrow."

CHAPTER SIX

"DINNER hasn't been served," he repeated calmly, leaning back in his chair, stretching out his legs, his broad shoulders square.

Emmeline gazed down at him, thinking that if one didn't know him, one might think he was a gorgeous, easygoing man, the kind of man you'd want to take home to meet the family.

But she did know him. And he was gorgeous but he wasn't easy, or simple or kind.

He was fierce and intimidating and totally overwhelming.

But she was supposed to be Hannah, and Hannah was supposed to like him, even though he'd just transferred her to a new position in London.

"I'm sure the kitchen could send the meal to you in your rooms since I no longer want to eat," she said, masking her anger with her most royal, serene expression.

His dark head tipped, black hair like onyx in the candlelight. "I'm not going to have my staff chasing me all over the palace with a dinner cart," he replied cordially. "I planned to eat here with you. And I will eat here." He paused, and then smiled but the warmth in his eyes was dangerous, as if he were not entirely civilized. "And so will you."

She'd never seen that look in his eye before. Had never thought of him as anything but coldly sophisticated, an elegant Arab sheikh with far too much money and power. But right now he practically hummed with aggression. It was strange—and disorienting.

Emmeline braced herself against the edge of the table with

its opulent settings and gleaming candlelight. Her legs shook beneath her. "You can't force me to eat."

"No, I can't force you. And so I'm asking you. Would you please sit down and join me for dinner? I'm hungry, and I know you've eaten virtually nothing today, and a good meal wouldn't hurt you. You're far too thin these days. You don't eat enough—"

"If I stay and eat, would you at least reconsider your decision to send me to London?"

"No," he answered bluntly. "My decision has been made."

"But you can change it."

"I won't. I stand by my decision. It is the right one."

"Please." Her voice dropped to a husky note and broke. "Please. I don't want to go to London—"

"Hannah."

"I'll do better. I'll work harder." Her voice cracked. "It doesn't seem fair to just throw me away after four years—"

"I am not throwing you away!" He was on his feet and starting toward her but then stopped himself. "And don't beg. You've no reason to beg. It's beneath you, especially when you've done nothing wrong."

"If I haven't done anything wrong, why am I being sent away?"

"Because sometimes change is necessary."

Emmeline's heart felt as if it was breaking. She'd failed Hannah again. She reached up to wipe a tear away before it fell. Her hand was trembling so hard that she missed the tear and had to try again.

"Don't."

"What? I'm not allowed to hurt? To have emotions? I'm supposed to just let you send me away as if I don't care?"

"Yes."

"Why?"

"Because your job is to make my life easier and you're not."

"How terrible."

"But true."

She struggled to catch another tear. "I didn't realize I wasn't allowed to be human—"

"I realize you're disappointed, but this isn't personal, and I'd like you to remain professional. So if you could pull yourself together and have a seat—"

"No."

His nostrils flared. A small muscle popped in his jaw. "No?" he repeated, his voice velvet-soft. "Did I hear you correctly?"

Her lower lip quivered. "Yes."

He moved toward her, a deep hard line between his black eyebrows. "That's insubordination, Miss Smith."

"I won't be bullied."

"I'm not a bully, I'm your boss." He was before her now, and standing so close that she had to tip her head back to see his face. "Or have you forgotten?"

She'd always thought his eyes were a cool silver-gray, but with him just inches away, she could see that his eyes burned and glowed like molten pewter.

"Haven't forgotten," she whispered, her courage starting to fade, as he dwarfed her, not just in height, but in sheer size. His shoulders were immense, his chest broad, his body muscular and strong. But he overpowered her in other ways—made her feel fragile and foolish and terribly emotional.

"Perhaps you'd care to apologize?"

There was a lethal quality to his voice, a leashed tension in his stance. It crossed her mind that she'd pushed him too far, demanded too much. "I'm sorry."

"Sorry for what?" His voice was so rough and deep it sounded like a growl.

She was mesmerized by the tiny gold flecks in his gray eyes. That's why up close his eyes looked warmer. His eyes weren't a cold gray. They had bits of the desert's gold sun and sand in them. "I've botched it all up." Her voice dropped and the air caught in her lungs. "Again."

He was silent, and then he gave his head the slightest of shakes. "I can't do this with you."

She squeezed her eyes closed, nodded her head.

"But I do accept your apology," he added.

Eyes still closed, she nodded again.

"Hannah."

She couldn't look at him, she couldn't, not when she was so overwhelmed by everything.

"Hannah, open your eyes."

"I can't."

"Why not?"

"Because you'll see...you'll see..."

"What?" he demanded, tipping her chin up with a finger.

She opened her eyes, looked up at him, her vision blurred by tears. "Me."

For a long, endless moment he simply stared into her eyes. "And why would that be a bad thing?"

The unexpected tenderness in his voice made her heart seize. "Because you don't like me."

He exhaled hard. "That's where you're wrong."

"Am I?"

"Absolutely." And then his head abruptly dropped, blocking the moon, and his lips covered hers.

It was the last thing she'd expected. The last thing she wanted. She froze, her lips stiff beneath his. For a second she even forgot how to breathe, and the air bottled in her lungs until her head began to spin and little dots danced before her eyes.

His lips traveled slowly across hers, in a light, fleeting kiss that was more comfort than passion. Her back tingled. She shivered and lifted a hand to press against his chest, intending to push him away, and yet her hand seemed to like the feel of his chest, her palm absorbing his warmth, her fingers splaying against the smooth, dense plane of muscle that wrapped his ribs.

Emmeline found herself leaning forward, drawn to his warmth and the heady spice of his cologne and the coolness of his mouth on hers. He nipped lightly at her lower lip, coaxing a response from her and sending a frisson of feeling zipping up her spine. Emmeline shuddered with pleasure, lips parting slightly with a muffled gasp.

Makin's arm wrapped around her waist, drawing her close so that his hard frame pressed against the length of her. He was powerfully built, hard and muscular, and heat radiated from him in waves.

Teasingly his tongue parted the seam of her lips, sending a shock of hot, electric sensation throughout her. She shuddered again, her lips parting beneath his, as her breasts grew heavy, aching, nipples exquisitely sensitive.

She'd never been kissed like this, never felt anything remotely like this. Makin's mouth tasted of spearmint and his spicy cologne filled her nose and his hard jaw was smooth, the skin soft from a recent shave. Her senses swam with the pleasure of it all.

Again he traced the seam of her lips with the tip of his tongue so that she gasped, opening her mouth wider for him. His tongue slid across her soft inner lip even as she felt his hand in the small of her back, a slow, leisurely stroke down over her hips. The lazy caress sent a hot new streak of sensation through her. It felt as if he was spreading fire beneath her skin. She tingled and ached, her womb tightening in need, and she lifted her hands to clasp his face, kissing him back, feeling more urgency.

Makin responded by deepening the kiss, his tongue delving into her mouth to taste her, his lips biting at hers, moving across hers, making every nerve dance to life. She gasped and arched, her hips pressing helplessly against his, making her aware of his thick hot erection. The rub of his erection between her thighs turned her legs to jelly, making her weak.

She'd only been kissed by Alejandro before, and it was that night he'd taken her virginity. His kiss had been hard, and she'd felt no lick of fire in her veins, no deep hot ache between her thighs. She'd felt pressure. A grating and grinding of jaw, lips, tongue and teeth. But there was no grating of anything here. No, Makin was making her melt, dissolving her bones into puddles of thick sweet honey.

Honey of want. Honey of need.

He was driving her wild. He slowly swept his hand back up her bottom to cup the curve of her breast, the palm of his hand so warm against her sensitive skin. She pressed closer wanting a satisfaction she couldn't even name, her fingers tangling, tightening in his shirt.

She heard a hoarse, desperate moan and then realized it was her. She'd whimpered aloud, and if she heard it, he did, too.

Heat rushed through her, a rush of embarrassment and she started to pull away and then his hand found her breast, his fingers catching, kneading the taut nipple and she shuddered and curled back against him, hips, breasts, thighs pressed to him, giving herself over to the hot, intense sensation.

He could have her, she thought, as he sucked the tip of her tongue into his mouth and drew on it, a slow, sensual rhythm that made her pulse throb and her knees press together. She felt hot and wet, her satin thong slick against the softness between her thighs.

He made a rough sound, a sound both primal and male, as he caught the back of her head in his hand, holding her still to kiss her more deeply.

She was drowning in desire, overwhelmed by need. And as he took her mouth, she didn't think she'd ever felt quite so frantic. He could do anything he wanted with her. He could do anything as long as he didn't stop touching her, didn't stop tasting her. She'd never felt so much sensation, never felt such sweet, wild pleasure. He could lift her onto the table and press her against the dishes and cutlery, crushing her into the flowers and she wouldn't protest. He could lift the hem of her dress and slide his fingers beneath the satin edge of her thong and between her thighs where she ached and ached.

He could fill her.

He could.

And then she felt his hand draw the chiffon fabric up over her thigh, and his fingers slide across warm bare skin. She shuddered, and reached up to clasp his nape, and then grab at the ends of his dark, thick hair.

She was empty, so unbearably wet and empty, and she needed him to warm her, needed him to fill her, needed—

"No."

It was just one word, one syllable, and yet he said it loudly, harshly, as he pulled her hands from around his neck and pushed her back, setting her away from him.

"No," he repeated thickly, dark color high in his cheekbones, his breathing still ragged. "I can't do this."

She heard what he was saying but couldn't seem to think of an appropriate response, not when her blood still hummed in her veins and her body felt hot and wet, and there was that terrible ache between her legs.

She'd never known physical desire, had never been truly aroused, and yet all of a sudden she understood why teenagers sat in parked cars and how good girls got themselves into trouble.

They lost control because what they felt was so good.

They forgot the dangers because pleasure could be so addictive.

"That shouldn't have happened," he added. "I apologize. It won't happen again."

"It's okay—"

"No. No, it's not. It's wrong. I have a mistress. I don't want this from you."

And then he left her without a second glance.

Stunned, she slid into the nearest chair, her hands falling numbly to her sides.

She felt shattered.

Even now she could feel the dizzying heat of the kiss, and the scorching warmth of Makin's hard body against hers. She could still smell the tantalizing hint of his fragrance lingering in the air—or was it on her skin? It was a scent of sandalwood and spice, a smell that reminded her of this desert of his—warm, exotic, golden.

But then his words returned to her, *No. I don't want this from you,* and she cringed with shame, and the gorgeous pleasure faded away.

His words hurt.

Exhaling slowly, trying to stop the rush of pain, she got to her feet, took a step, and then another, until she was walking around the pool. For several minutes she just made herself move. It was easier when she was moving not to feel so much. Not to hurt so much. Easier to work through his bruising disdain.

And then finally, when she'd walked herself to a place of quiet and calm, she was able to tell herself that the sheikh had overreacted.

It was a kiss, just a kiss, nothing more. He might be upset but there had been no great impropriety. They hadn't undressed, they weren't lying down, hadn't touched intimately.

And yet...

She stopped, ran a hand along her neck and down to the valley between her breasts. It had been a hot, explosive kiss. A kiss that had seared her, burned her, made her understand what she wanted from a man.

Hunger. Fire. Passion. All the things she'd been taught to believe were bad, wicked...and yet when she was in his arms, it hadn't felt wicked. It had felt sweet.

She'd felt good. Beautiful and strong and lovely. Emmeline rarely felt lovely. The world heralded her as her generation's great beauty but she didn't feel beautiful. She'd never felt like anything special until just now....

Biting her lip, she turned away, confused. Conflicted.

How could something that felt so good be wrong?

When she'd been in Makin's arms she hadn't felt any shame, any guilt, nothing but pleasure. And she refused to feel shame now. She wouldn't let the kiss become ugly, wouldn't let the dizzying pleasure turn to disgust.

Swallowing hard, she smoothed the silky chiffon hem of her dress over the heated skin of her upper thigh. Just the whisper of fabric against her sensitive skin made her insides turn over and her breasts tighten as she was flooded with another scalding rush of desire.

This is how good girls go bad, she thought ruefully, slipping one gold high-heeled sandal off, and then the other. This is how eligible ladies ruined their chances. Not on men like Alejandro, men who kissed too hard with their jaws and tongues, but men like Makin who could make a woman feel wonderful and beautiful inside and out.

And even though Makin Al-Koury had hurt her after with his harsh rejection, the kiss itself had been amazing.

The kiss had made her feel amazing. As though she'd actually mattered.

Smiling wistfully, she picked up the shoes by the thin gold straps and rose. Leaning across the table, Emmeline blew out the candles, one by one, and then, shoes in hand, headed into Hannah's apartment.

She was sliding the glass doors closed when the doorbell chimed. Had Makin returned?

"Good evening, Miss Smith," the uniformed kitchen staff greeted her as she opened the door. "Sheikh Al-Koury is taking his dinner in his own room, but said you'd want something to eat."

Emmeline's smile slipped.

That was the moment she remembered that the kiss, so good and melting and bittersweet, hadn't been meant for her. Makin thought he'd kissed Hannah Smith.

The kiss—the one he'd regretted—had been for Hannah. But if he regretted kissing Hannah, his perfect secretary, how would he react if he knew he'd kissed Emmeline d'Arcy, the princess he despised?

Emmeline choked back a strangled laugh. Her eyes stung and burned. She swallowed once and again. And then she did what she'd been taught to do her entire life—she arranged her features into a formal but polite smile—and graciously thanked the kind kitchen staff for bringing her dinner.

That kiss, he thought, *that kiss...*

It was two-thirty in the morning and Makin was still up, his thoughts unusually chaotic, and he climbed from bed, giving up the illusion of trying to sleep.

He was angry he'd kissed her, angry with himself, angry with his loss of control.

He never lost control.

And that kiss...

It threatened to change everything. It had made him feel things he didn't feel. Hadn't thought he could feel. Holding her, tasting her had been intoxicating. He'd felt like someone else. Someone different.

He'd felt.

And suddenly he didn't want to send her away, on to London and a new position, but he wanted to keep her here, for him, with him. Not as his assistant but as his woman.

But he had a woman. He had Madeline. And until tonight he'd been happy with her as his mistress.

Had been, he silently repeated, brow furrowing, his expression darkening as he paced the length of his bedroom once and again.

Why was he so tempted by Hannah? Was Madeline not enough for him anymore?

Skin hot, emotions hotter, Makin opened the tall glass doors and walked out onto his balcony. Moonlight turned the garden below silver and white. A fountain splashed and he leaned against the elegant iron railing, aware that his attraction to Hannah was stronger than anything he'd ever felt for Madeline or Jenny or any woman in years.

But then, he'd always deliberately chosen beautiful women who were cool and calm…composed. His mistresses accommodated him, never challenging him or disturbing his focus.

Everything about Hannah disturbed his focus.

He shouldn't like it, shouldn't allow it. He'd never wanted fire or intensity with his women before. He was too practical. He wanted convenience, companionship and satisfaction. And he had all that with Madeline. When in Nadir he saw her two, maybe three times, a week. If she chafed at their limited time together, she never said so. She greeted him with smiles and easy warmth, and there was never pressure to be anything but present. It was enough. Enough for her, enough for him.

He liked their routine in Nadir. He'd join her around nine or ten in the evening. They'd have dinner, a little conversation, sex, and then he'd return home. He never stayed the night. He never wanted to. And it was the kind of relationship that worked for him.

What kind of mistress would Hannah be? He pictured installing her in a beautiful house overlooking the royal gardens in Nadir, pictured working all day then going to her at night. Pictured her opening the door, wearing something orange and filmy, or perhaps a sleek black satin evening gown with a thigh-high slit up the front. Makin hardened.

He wouldn't want dinner. Or talk. He'd want her. Immediately. He'd want to take her there in the hall, slip his hands beneath the fabric and find her soft sensitive skin and make her shudder and whimper against him.

And then he'd want her again in the bedroom, beneath him on the bed, pale thighs parted, her breasts rising and falling as he rose up over her, plunging slowly, deeply into her, filling her, making her cry out his name.

Body aching, shaft throbbing, Makin turned, leaned against the railing and gazed into his bedroom glowing with yellow light, wishing Hannah were in his bed now. He wanted her now. Needed her, needed release.

His hand slipped down his belly, reaching into his loose pajama pants to grip his heavy erection. He palmed himself once, twice, his grip firm as he pictured her blue eyes, the curve of her lips, the firmness of her breasts and the ripeness of her hips and ass.

He would take her from behind, and then flip her over, and take her again, this time drawing her down onto his shaft so that he could watch her face as he made her come.

He wanted to make her come. He wanted to make her come over and over…

Madness.

This was exactly why he had to send her away. He didn't want to feel this much for a woman, didn't want to become emotionally involved. He had a job to do, a plan for his future, a plan that didn't include sex in hallways and restless nights and hot, erotic thoughts.

He liked cool women, cool, calm, sophisticated women. Women who didn't provoke or challenge or arouse him to the point he couldn't think or sleep.

As she had tonight.

He'd been with Madeline for three years and yet he'd never once lost sleep thinking of her. But tonight he felt absolutely obsessed with Hannah.

Thank God she'd be gone in the morning.

The sun poured through his office window, casting a glare on the computer screen, making his eyes burn.

Makin felt like hell.

It had been a rough night. A long night. He'd ended up going to bed just hours ago, and then sleeping badly, and now he was back at his desk at seven drinking cup after cup of coffee, hoping to wake up, gain some clarity and, with any luck, shake his sense of guilt and shame.

He'd treated Hannah badly last night and he was still angry with himself for losing control, for allowing lust and desire to cloud his thinking. He shouldn't have kissed her, shouldn't have reached for her, but that wasn't her fault. It was his.

He'd apologize to her later, just before he put her in the limousine on the way to the airstrip. And then he'd move forward. He wouldn't look back.

It was good. Everything was good. Hannah would be off after breakfast, his guests would arrive midafternoon, and he had sorted out his priorities.

Ringing for a fresh pot of coffee, Makin woke up his computer and checked the headlines of the various international papers for world news. He usually devoted an hour to reading his preferred papers every morning, and was reading the online version of *The New York Times* when he came across a link with the heading Argentine Polo Star in Fatal Crash.

Alejandro's accident had finally hit the newswire.

Curious to see if there was an update on Alejandro's condition, Makin clicked on the link and pulled up the article. He skimmed the piece but the article didn't cover anything new.

Makin looked at the three photos accompanying the story next. The first was one of Ibanez on his horse on the field, one posing with his team at the recent Palm Beach tournament, and

one in which Alejandro was snapped talking with the Princess
Emmeline of Brabant.

He ignored the first two photos, intrigued by the last. It was
a recent photo, he saw, taken a week ago in Palm Beach at the
polo tournament he'd hosted and Hannah had organized.

It wasn't the most flattering photo of either Ibanez or the princess, and Makin suspected they probably weren't even aware
they were being photographed. Alejandro looked angry and the
princess was in tears. It didn't require a lot of imagination to
figure out what the fight was about. Perhaps the princess had
discovered that there were other women? Women like Penelope.
Women like Hannah.

Thinking about Hannah, Makin clicked on the photo, enlarg-
ing it. He felt a flicker of unease as he studied the princess.

She looked far too familiar, as if he knew her, but how
could that be? He'd only been in the same room with Princess
Emmeline once and yet looking at this picture, he felt as if he
knew her…intimately.

Impossible.

He studied the photo intently, drawn by Emmeline's eyes and
her expression.

He knew that expression. He knew those eyes.

His uneasiness increased.

He copied and pasted the photo onto his desktop and enlarged
the picture once more, studying it carefully, analyzing the princess's slender frame, the tilt to her head, the twist of her lips.

She was clearly desperately unhappy. And while that wasn't
his problem—the princess was most definitely not his problem—
he recognized that face. It was the face he'd seen all night in his
troubled dreams.

Hannah's.

A thought came, unbidden, and it made him even more uncomfortable than before.

Holding his breath, Makin opened the photo folder on his
computer, pulled up the photo taken in Tokyo last year at a business dinner. It was a photo of Hannah accepting a ceremonial
kimono. The shot had been taken at an angle, just like the photo

of the princess talking to Ibanez. Hannah's hair had been pulled back in a low ponytail, much like the princess's chignon at the polo match.

He enlarged Hannah's photo and dragged it next to the shot of the princess.

The resemblance was uncanny. Their profiles were so similar. The chin, nose, brow. Even the eye color. Change the hair color, and they could be the same. Maybe identical. And to think they'd come so close to meeting each other in Palm Beach. They'd both been there at the polo field...they'd both attended Sunday...

Could they...could Hannah be...

No. No. It was too incredible, too impossible. People didn't switch places...that was a ludicrous idea, something that only happened in Hollywood movies.

And yet, when he glanced from the photo of Emmeline to the one of Hannah and back again, comparing the faces, the profiles, the lavender-blue eyes, he thought, *It could be done.*

Change the hair, swap the clothes, mask the accents and Hannah and the princess could easily pass for each other. Makin was rarely truly shocked by anything but he was blown away now. Dumbfounded, he crossed his arms over his chest and stared through narrowed eyes at the computer screen.

Why hadn't he seen it before? Why hadn't he picked up on the differences...the changes? Hannah's sudden extreme thinness. Her fragile beauty. The emotion in her eyes.

Hannah, the Hannah with him here in Raha right now, wasn't Hannah at all. She was Princess Emmeline d'Arcy, the twenty-five-year-old royal from Brabant engaged to King Zale Patek of Raguva.

Which meant he hadn't kissed Hannah, but Princess Emmeline.

It hadn't been Hannah who had captured his imagination and turned him on, it was Emmeline.

It was Emmeline he'd wanted. Emmeline who had created a night of hot, erotic thoughts.

Unbelievable.

He drummed his fingers on the desk.

Unthinkable.

He didn't know what game she was playing, but he'd soon find out.

Unforgivable.

He slapped his hand down hard on the desk and got to his feet. Time he paid a call on the princess.

CHAPTER SEVEN

EMMELINE answered the knock on her door, hoping against hope it was breakfast as she'd rung for eggs and toast a half hour ago, but it wasn't anyone from the kitchen on her doorstep. It was Makin Al-Koury, looking elegant and polished, if a tad forbidding in his black trousers and black shirt.

He must have just showered and shaved because his dark hair still gleamed, the skin on his bronze jaw was taut and smooth and she caught a whiff of his spicy sandalwood cologne. "You're up early," she said, her pulse racing, her stomach a knot of nerves.

"We're usually working by seven-thirty," he answered. "You've been taking it easy and sleeping in."

There was something rather chilling about his smile this morning and her heart faltered and plummeted, making a dramatic swan dive right to her feet.

Locking her knees, she forced herself to look up and meet his gaze head-on. His eyes were light and glacier-cool, like mist rising off ice.

Last night the kiss had felt so good, but now, in the clear light of day, she knew it had been a dreadful mistake. Sheikh Makin Al-Koury was too big, too powerful, and far from civilized. He might have millions and billions of euros, and expensive toys and homes scattered across the globe, but that didn't make him easy, or comfortable or approachable.

"No wonder you're sending me away. I've become unforgivably lazy," she answered lightly, forcing a smile as she placed an unsteady hand over the narrow waistband of her ivory lace skirt, hoping he'd be fooled by her bravado.

"No one can be perfect all the time." He smiled at her. "How are you this morning?"

"Good."

"And you slept well?"

He was still smiling but she felt far from easy. "Yes, thank you."

"Excellent." He paused, gazed down at her, his expression inscrutable. "In that case, I trust you feel well enough to take some dictation?"

"Dictation?" She hoped he didn't hear the slight stutter in her voice.

"I need a letter written, a letter that must go out today. I'm hoping to put it on the flight with you."

"Of course." Emmeline fought panic and reminded herself that she could do this. She could play the game a little longer... pretend a little longer... "Would you like me come to your office?"

"That's not necessary." He put a hand on the door and pushed it all the way open. "I'm already here."

Emmeline stepped aside to let him in. "I just need some paper and a pen."

"You'll find both in your desk in the bedroom," he said helpfully. "In case you've forgotten."

She darted a quick look into his face, trying to understand where he was going with this, because he was most definitely going somewhere and she didn't like it. "Thank you."

Heart hammering, stomach churning, she headed to the bedroom to retrieve the pad of paper and a pen from the desk, and then hesitated at the mirror hanging over the painted chest of drawers. She looked elegant this morning in her ivory silk blouse and matching lace skirt. She'd pulled her dark hair back and added a rope of pearls, and Emmeline could only pray that her polished exterior would hide her anxiety. She didn't know anything about taking dictation. She'd never dictated a letter, either, but she'd never let the sheikh know that.

Back in the living room, Emmeline sat down on the edge of the pale gold silk couch, pen poised. "I'm ready."

He glanced at her pen hovering above paper and then into her eyes. He smiled, again, all hard white teeth. "I'm not sure how to start the letter," he said. "Perhaps you can help me? It's for an acquaintance, King Zale Patek of Raguva. I'm not sure about the salutation. Would I say 'Dear Your Royal Highness'? Or just 'Your Highness'? What do you think?"

Emmeline's cheeks grew hot. She fought to keep her voice even. "I think either would work."

"Good enough." The sheikh sat down on the couch next to her, far too close to her. And then he turned so that he fully faced her. "How about we start with 'Your Royal Highness'?"

She swallowed, nodded and scribbled the words onto the top of the page before looking up at him.

"Something has come to my attention that cannot be ignored. It is an urgent personal matter, and I wouldn't bring it to you if it weren't important." He paused, looked over her shoulder to see what she'd written. "Good. You've almost got it all. And it's very nice handwriting, but I'd appreciate it if you took short-hand. It's hard to get my thoughts out when you're writing so slowly."

She nodded, staring blindly at the notepad, so hot and cold that she barely registered a word he said.

She couldn't do this. Heavens, how could she when she couldn't even breathe? Couldn't seem to get any air into her lungs at all. Was she having a panic attack? It had happened once before, on the night of her sixteenth birthday after her father had broken the news about her adoption.

She'd nearly collapsed that night as her throat had seized.

Her throat felt squeezed closed now. Her head spun. And it was all because Sheikh Al-Koury was sprawling on the couch next to her, taking up all the space, as he dictated a letter to her fiancé, King Patek.

A letter about an urgent personal matter.

Emmeline's head swam.

What could Makin Al-Koury possibly have to say to King

Patek that was urgent or personal? If they were close friends, the sheikh wouldn't have her dictate a letter. He'd send Zale a text, or an email or pick up the phone and call. No, a formal letter was reserved for acquaintances. And bearing bad news.

"You missed a line," Sheik Al-Koury said, leaning close to point to the page. "The last thing I just said, about me discovering some disturbing information concerning his fiancée, Princess Emmeline d'Arcy. Write it down, please."

He waited while she slowly wrote each word.

"Your handwriting is getting smaller," he said. "Good thing I'll have you type it before sending. Now to continue. Where were we? Right, about his duplicitous fiancée, Princess—"

"I have that part," she interrupted huskily.

"Not duplicitous."

"You didn't say it the first time."

"I said it now. Put it in. It's important. He needs to know."

Her pen hovered over the page. She couldn't make it move. She couldn't do this anymore.

"Hannah," he said sharply. "Finish the letter."

She shook her head, bit her lip. "I can't."

"You must. It's vital I get this letter off. King Patek is a good person—a man of great integrity—and one of the few royals I truly like. He needs to be told, at the very least warned, that his fiancée can't be trusted. That she's unscrupulous and amoral and she'll bring nothing but shame—"

"If you'll excuse me," she choked, rising from the couch, eyes burning, stomach heaving. "I don't feel so well."

Emmeline raced to the bathroom, closed the door and sat down on the cold marble floor next to the deep tub. She felt so sick she wished she'd throw up.

Instead she heard Sheikh Al-Koury's words swirl and echo around in her head. *Duplicitous. Unscrupulous. Amoral.*

They would be her mother's words, too. There would be no one to take her side or speak up for her in defense. Her family would judge her and punish her just as they always had. Just as they always did.

The bathroom door softly opened and a shadow fell across the white marble floor. Jaw set defiantly, she glanced up at Makin as he filled the doorway, a silent challenge in her blue eyes.

Makin gazed down at the princess where she sat on the floor, a slender arm wrapped around her knees.

Considering her precarious situation, he would have thought she'd be timid or tearful, or pleading for forgiveness, but she was none of those things. Instead of meeting his gaze meekly, she stared him in the eye, her chin lifted rebelliously, her full lips stubbornly compressed.

One of his eyebrows lifted slightly. Was this how she intended to play it? As if he was the villain and she the victim?

How fascinating.

She was a far better actress than he'd given her credit for. Last night she'd moved him with her touching vulnerability. He, who felt so little real emotion, had felt so much for her. He'd wanted to strap on a sword and rush to her defense. He'd wanted to be a hero, wanted to provide her with the protection she so desperately seemed to need.

But it had all been an act. She wasn't Hannah, nor was she fragile, but a conniving, manipulative princess who cared for no one but herself.

The edge of his mouth curled. She hadn't changed. She was still the imperious, spoiled princess he'd met nine years ago at her sixteenth-birthday ball. He'd never forget that her father had thrown her a huge party, inviting everyone who was anyone, and she'd spent it throwing a tantrum, crying her way through the evening.

Embarrassed for her father and disgusted by her histrionics, Makin had left the ball early, vowing to avoid her in the future. And he had. Until now.

His narrowed gray eyes searched hers, thinking that in the past nine years little had changed. She still epitomized everything he despised in modern culture. The sense of entitlement. The fixation on celebrity. The worship of money. Skating through life on one's looks.

And yes, Emmeline was stunning—he wouldn't pretend that he hadn't wanted her last night—but now that he knew who he was dealing with, and *what* he was dealing with, his desire was gone. She left him cold.

Makin leaned against the white marble vanity, hands braced against the cool, smooth stone surface. He was furious and he needed answers, and he would have them now.

"You don't have the flu," he said shortly, his deep voice hard, the sharp tone echoing off all the polished stone.

She opened her mouth to protest and then thought better of it. "No."

"And you weren't sick yesterday because you had low blood sugar."

Her chin inched higher. "No."

Didn't she realize the game was up? Didn't she understand that he'd figured it out? That he knew who she was and that he was livid? That he was hanging on to his control by a thread?

Makin didn't speak, battling for that control, battling to maintain the upper hand on his temper when all he could see was red. "How far along are you?" he asked, when he could trust himself to speak.

Her eyes, those stunning lavender eyes, opened wide. They were Hannah's eyes, the same lavender-blue of periwinkles or rain-drenched violets, which made him suddenly hate her more. "The truth," he bit out.

She just stared at him, expression mutinous, lips firm. There was nothing weak or helpless about her now. Even sitting on the floor she looked regal and proud and ready to fight him tooth and nail.

How dare she? How dare she play the entitled princess here? Now? She should be begging for mercy, pleading for leniency.

"I'm waiting," he gritted impatiently, fully cognizant that if she were a man he wouldn't be using words right now, but his fists. Just who did she think she was, waltzing into his life as if she belonged here? He flashed to last night in the garden and how he'd reached for her, and kissed her, wanting her more than he'd ever wanted any woman. And it galled him—infuriated him—that she'd succeeded in making a fool of him in his own home.

"Seven weeks," she said at last, eyes darkening, the lavender-blue luminous against the pallor of her face. "Give or take a day."

Give or take a day, Makin silently repeated. God, he detested her. Detested everything about her, and everything she represented. "I take it Alejandro Ibanez is the father."

She nodded.

"And that's why you were at Mynt making a scene."

Her cheeks suddenly flushed, turning a delicate pink. "I didn't make a scene. He was making a scene—" She broke off, bit savagely into her lower lip and looked away, expression tortured.

For a moment, just a moment, Makin almost felt sorry for her. Almost, but not quite. "And my second question, Your Royal Highness, and an even more important question is, what have you done with my secretary, Hannah Smith?"

Emmeline's head jerked back around, her gaze wary as it met his. "What do you mean?"

For a moment he saw only red again, blazing-hot red, but then his vision cleared. "I'm not in the mood for games, princess."

"I...I don't know what you mean."

He was angry, so very, very angry, that he could have easily dragged her up from the floor and taught her a lesson. "You *know* what I mean."

"But I *am* Hannah."

Makin gritted his teeth so hard his jaw ached and his temple throbbed. "Don't insult my intelligence, Your Highness. You'll just make me angrier—"

"But I am—"

"—Emmeline d'Arcy, Princess of Brabant," he finished for her, his tone sharp and withering. "You've been masquerading as my secretary, Hannah Smith, for the past three days—maybe longer. That's the part you'll want to explain, starting right now."

"Sheikh Al-Koury—"

"How about we drop the titles? Cut out all the pretense of formality and suggestion of respect? You don't respect me, and I certainly don't respect you. So I'll call you Emmeline, and you can call me Makin, and, with any luck, I'll finally get the truth."

She slowly rose to her feet, smoothed her ivory skirt with

the overlay of fine Belgian lace, which accentuated the rounded shape of her hips and the high, firm buttocks. Blood coursed through his veins. He suddenly felt hot and hard and even angrier.

How could he still want her? It boggled his mind that he could find her attractive now, after all of this....

"How did you find out?" she asked quietly.

"By chance." He looked down at her and his lips curled faintly, self-mockingly, even as his body ached with the need to take her, possess her. It wouldn't be gentle though. "I was reading *The New York Times* online, and came across a link to an article about Alejandro's accident. One of the photos accompanying the story was a shot of you and Alejandro talking at the polo tournament I hosted in Palm Beach."

"The only photo I took was with the Argentine team—"

"This wasn't a posed photo. It was candid. You were behind the stables and neither of you were happy. You looked as if maybe you were having a fight." He saw the light dawn in her eyes and realized he'd been right. They had been quarreling, and probably about the pregnancy. Of course Ibanez wouldn't want the child. He'd probably insisted she get an abortion, and for a moment Makin felt a flicker of pity for the princess but then squashed it. Emmeline d'Arcy deserved whatever she had coming. He wouldn't spare her a moment's concern.

"You were crying," he added flatly, harshly, refusing to let her get under his skin again, reminding himself that she was shallow and selfish and without one redeeming virtue. "That's when I knew." He paused, studied her pale face. "I knew that expression." *And I knew those eyes,* he silently added.

Now that he knew who was who, he could see how different Emmeline's eyes were from Hannah's. They might be the same shade, that astonishing lavender-blue, but the expression wasn't at all similar. Hannah's gaze was calm and steady, while Emmeline's was stormy and shadowed with emotion. If one didn't know better, one might think that Emmeline had grown up in a tough neighborhood, fighting for every scrap of kindness, instead of having lived an easy life in which luxury had been handed to her on a silver platter.

His chest grew tight. He told himself it was anger. But it wasn't just anger, it was betrayal.

He'd started to care for her, just a little. Just enough for him to feel used today. Played.

And no one played Makin.

"So what have you done with Hannah?" he asked, his tone icy with disdain. "I want her back. Immediately."

For a moment the princess didn't speak and then she took a deep breath, squared her shoulders. "She's in Raguva." She hesitated. "Pretending to be me."

"What?" Makin rarely raised his voice but it thundered through the marble bathroom.

She stood tall, appearing nonchalant, but then she ruined the effect by chewing nervously on her bottom lip. "I needed to speak with Alejandro about my pregnancy, but he wouldn't take my calls, not after that talk we had at the polo field following the tournament. I was desperate. I had to see him. I needed his help. So I begged Hannah to switch places with me for a day so I could go to him in person."

"And you couldn't go to him as yourself?"

"He was avoiding me, and even if he would see me, my staff and security detail wouldn't let me go. They'd been given orders by my parents to keep me away from him, and they were determined to follow those orders."

"Your parents were right not to trust you."

She shrugged, walked past him, leaving the bathroom. "Probably."

"Probably?" he demanded, following her. "Is that all you have to say?"

Her shoulders rolled, shrugging. "What do you want from me? An apology? Fine. I apologize."

Makin stood inside the bedroom doorway, astounded by her lack of concern. She was suddenly the epitome of calm and cool. How was such a thing possible? "When exactly did you switch places with my assistant?"

"Last Sunday. The twenty-second." She moved across the bedroom to enter the walk-in closet. She pulled an armful of clothes out and carried them to the bed.

She was packing.

She must assume that she was going somewhere.

"That was a week ago," he answered, leaning against the door frame, arms folded over his chest. Why pack now? Where did she think she was going? To London? On his plane? At his expense? How fascinating.

Emmeline nodded, emerging from the closet with a half dozen pairs of delicate high heels.

His brow lowered as he watched her place the shoes in tidy pairs on the bed next to her other garments. "And just how long were you planning on leaving my secretary in Raguva, Your *Highness?*"

Emmeline glanced up from the shoes, wincing at his sarcasm. He'd finally gotten to her. "I...I don't know," she confessed, sitting down on the edge of the bed next to her clothes and shoes. "I haven't figured that part out."

His gaze raked her up and down, expression merciless. "Unbelievable." His chest felt blisteringly hot while the rest of him remained cold.

She didn't answer. She didn't even try.

He took a step toward her, and then another, hands clenched at his sides. "Who do you think you are? How could you put my assistant in this position? Do you know what you've cost her?"

And still she said nothing.

"Her job." He was so angry, so very angry and yet Emmeline appeared remote, detached, as if she were above the fray. "She's gone. Fired. I've no need of her services anymore—not here with me, or in London, or back in Dallas, either. She's gone, finished, so be sure to give yourself a good pat on your back."

Emmeline's body jerked, shoulders twisting. "But you've made it clear that there was no one like Hannah—"

"There wasn't. But you changed that when you asked her to shift her loyalty from me to you—"

"She didn't. She hasn't!" Emmeline leaned urgently forward.

"She is still very loyal to you. Completely loyal. She loves working for you."

Finally, he thought. Finally some reaction. Some emotion. But it was too little, too late, for all of them. He shrugged indifferently. "Good. She's yours. She can now work for you."

"Please don't do that. Please. Hannah loves her job."

"Maybe she should have thought of that before she headed off to Raguva, pretending to be you." He started for the bedroom door, but paused to turn to look at the princess who still sat frozen on the edge of the bed. "And I'm not sure why you're packing. I don't know where you think you're going, or how you're getting there. Because you're in my desert, my world, princess, and you're stuck here with me."

And then he was gone, leaving the apartment with his emotions running high, temper hot, feeling even angrier and more punitive than he had an hour before.

There would be consequences. And she would not like them.

CHAPTER EIGHT

EMMELINE'S legs shook as the door closed behind Makin. She'd been shaking ever since he'd confronted her in the bathroom with the truth. Shaking with fear.

But now he was gone and she was glad. Glad he'd left her alone. Glad the truth was finally out. She'd hated lying to him. Hated pretending to be his perfect Hannah. And now she didn't have to lie anymore.

It was better now that he knew the truth. Even if it meant he'd never speak to her again. Better this way. Better to be honest about everything.

And he could say what he wanted about her. He could ridicule her and despise her, but she wouldn't give him the ability to hurt her anymore. Emmeline left the cool serenity of the white, apricot and gold bedroom for the garden.

She paced the private courtyard with the intensely sweet perfume of antique roses scenting the air as the hot yellow sun beat down, heating her skin. For many this palace would be a kind of paradise. But Emmeline had grown up in palaces surrounded by high stone walls and uniformed soldiers who changed position every four hours. She'd never been the tourist on the outside, admiring the pageantry and elegance. She'd been the captive royal inside the palace walls, locked in for her own protection.

And now, Kasbah Raha was just one more beautiful gilded cage.

One more luxurious but secure building to hold her, confine her, trap her.

And Makin was one more powerful man who thought he could intimidate her. Belittle her. Control her.

But she was done being manipulated and controlled. It was time she grew up. Wised up. Opened her eyes and used her brain. She had a good brain, too, and at twenty-five it was time she owned her life and made decisions for her future.

A future with a baby. *Her* baby. And how she loved her baby already. Her baby was the most important thing now.

"You look like a tiger in the zoo."

Emmeline jumped at the sound of Makin's deep voice and turned to see him inside the doorway, in the cool shadows of the air-conditioned living room. "So much for privacy," she said, folding her arms across her chest.

He shrugged. "You didn't answer the door."

"So you just let yourself in?"

"If I'm concerned about the safety of one of my guests."

"And so now you're concerned about me?"

He shrugged again. "I'm responsible for all the guests in my home."

The edge of her mouth curled up. "Did you forget something? Or have you thought of another way to humiliate me?"

"I don't have to, Your Highness. You do a great job of humiliating yourself." He gestured toward a bench in the dappled shade. "But I do have news. Sit."

She bristled inwardly at his sarcasm but refused to let him see how much he affected her. There was no reason for him to affect her. She told herself she didn't care for him. Certainly didn't need him. They were equals. And adversaries. "I'd rather stand."

"You're seven weeks pregnant. I'd rather you sit."

It was clear from the curt tone that he expected her to obey, but he forgot that he had no power over her. "You might, but I'd ask you to remember that I'm not Hannah—"

"Trust me, I do," he cut her off with a sigh. "So sit. There is something I must tell you, and it's not easy."

Emmeline's stomach fell and her knees went weak. Alarm shot through her. "Alejandro?" she whispered.

"Yes."

She put a hand to her belly, sixth sense telling her that Makin's news wasn't good.

Crossing to the marble bench in the dappled shade, Emmeline sat down, feeling the tug of the lace skirt around her hips and how her ivory silk blouse clung to her damp, warm skin.

"I'm sorry," he said simply.

Emmeline's heart sank into the pit of her stomach. "What happened?"

"He went into cardiac arrest a couple of hours ago. And even though they had the best doctors and nurses in all of Miami, they couldn't get his heart beating again."

It took her a second to process everything. "He's gone."

"Yes."

She closed her eyes, besieged by wildly different emotions. Shock, grief, regret. But the grief and sorrow weren't for herself, or Alejandro. They were for Alejandro's five children. Their lives would now be changed forever.

"Are you feeling faint?" Makin asked.

She shook her head, opened her eyes. "No."

"This must be quite a blow."

"Yes."

"I am sorry."

She pushed a loose tendril of hair back from her face. "You didn't like him."

"He was a father."

She nodded. "I feel for his children," she answered, realizing now that her child would never have the chance to know his or her father. "I wonder if they know yet. I wonder if his wife knows."

"Isn't that a bit hypocritical?"

"What?"

"To pretend you care about his family…?"

"Why shouldn't I?"

"You chase Ibanez, sleep with him—"

"I didn't know he was married until you told me, and I didn't chase him. He chased me."

"So that makes it okay to sleep with a married man?"

"No! Heavens, no! I'm horrified, disgusted. I made a terrible mistake."

"And your engagement? Did you not know about that, either?"

She swallowed around the thick lump filling her throat. No wonder Makin enjoyed ridiculing her. She sounded pathetic. Stupid beyond belief. "I did."

"That's a relief, because I'd hate to think that everyone but you knew."

She winced. Blood rushed to her cheeks again. "He pursued me, not the other way around. Some days he'd call or text over and over, and this went on for years."

"So you're saying it *is* okay to cheat?"

"*No.* But I wasn't married to Zale yet, and I was still hoping to marry for love, not money. My parents knew I didn't want an arranged marriage. I wanted a love match, and I thought since Alejandro loved me, we would have that."

"If you didn't want to marry Zale, why didn't you say no? Why enter the arrangement in the first place?"

Makin Al-Koury was a powerful man, and he understood a great deal about politics and economics. But he didn't know everything. He didn't know what it was like to be a woman. Much less a beautiful, sheltered young woman with no vocation, few practical skills and a numbing lack of real world experience. Emmeline's only purpose and power lay in her marriage ability. "Because I didn't have a choice."

"You were forced into the arrangement?"

She shrugged, worn out from trying to make him understand. He'd been raised by different parents, who had a different plan for him than hers had had for her. "There are different kinds of pressure. It's not always about physical force. Women can be intimidated emotionally, psychologically—" She broke off, shook her head. "But that's neither here nor there. The fact is, I have known since I was a little girl that my parents would choose my husband for me. They made sure that from a young age I knew my duty."

"Apparently they didn't. Because everyone but King Patek knows you've been hooking up with Ibanez over the years."

Emmeline flushed. "That's not true. We *never* hooked up."

"So you're not pregnant?"

"*Yes*. Yes, I did sleep with him. But it was only one time, and he was my...first." Her voice wobbled. "I was a virgin until then."

Makin snorted with derision.

Emmeline's flush deepened, heat spreading through her body until she tingled all over. "Believe what you want. I don't have to answer to you, or impress you, or try to make you like me. You and I will never see eye to eye—" She broke off abruptly and turned away, horrified to discover that she was about to cry.

Thank God he didn't say anything right away, or laugh. Thank God there was just the bubble and splash of the fountain. But the silence stretched too long. Emmeline glanced at Makin and saw his expression.

Hard. Unforgiving.

She swallowed around the lump in her throat and lifted her chin, refusing to be cowed by his judgment, knowing that others would look at her the exact same way. Including her parents. It would hurt. But it wouldn't kill her. Over time she'd learn to weather the disapproval without letting it get to her. She'd learn she could stand on her own two feet just fine.

"I know you don't think much of me," she said. "But I will be a good mother. I will do what's right for my child, starting with seeing a doctor as soon as I get back to Europe."

"Then let's stop wasting time and get you on a plane for Brabant—"

"I'm not going to Brabant. I'm going to London."

"Not back to Brabant?"

"No. Never."

"But that is your home, your country—"

"Not anymore."

"You can't change your birthright, Your Highness. You are descended from one of the oldest royal families in all of Europe. Your bloodline ties you to the very country."

"I will find a new country to call home. Lots of royals do it."

"Yes, in countries where monarchy has been replaced by democracy or socialism, but Brabant is still a constitutional monarchy and as far as I know, you are the rightful heir to the throne. Why would you give that up?"

"Because I'm not the rightful heir," she said huskily, walking away from him to approach the pool. "I'm not a true heir at all—"

"That's ridiculous."

She shrugged. "But true. And that's why I won't be going home, and why I won't be asking for forgiveness or mercy. I don't have to tell my parents anything. I'm twenty-five, of majority, and have access to the trust set up for me by my late grandfather. If I am careful, it's more than enough for me to live on."

"And your child?" he asked. "If you walk away from them, he or she may never be accepted by your family."

"I am sure he—or she—won't be," she said after a moment.

"Certainly not, if you plan on running away...hiding in the English countryside?"

"I wouldn't be hiding. I'd be living quietly, raising my child with, I hope, some privacy and dignity—"

"You hope?" His mouth tightened. "Is that your bright plan? To hope to have some privacy and dignity?" He made a rough, low sound of disgust. "Good luck, Your Highness. You're going to need it." With another low, derisive snort, he turned around and walked away.

She drew a quick breath, feeling as if he'd slapped her. "I might be running away but you're great at walking away," she called after him, hands curling into fists, her voice vibrating with emotion.

"What?"

"You can do it because you have power," she said as he turned to face her. "Most of us can't. We have to stand there and take it. But you don't have to. You're a man, and one of the world's richest. Everybody needs you. Everybody wants your approval or your protection. It must feel good."

He started back toward her. "How dare you speak to me in

that tone of voice? You are a guest in my home. You are completely dependent on me—"

"I didn't ask to be."

"No, you didn't ask. You forced yourself on me by impersonating my assistant."

"Then let me go."

"I would love you to go."

She visibly flinched, stung. And yet, why did she care what he thought? Why did he have the power to hurt her? Swallowing hard, she walked around the pool and toward the house. "Great. That makes two of us. If you'll have a driver take me to the airstrip, I'll fly out immediately."

"With what plane?"

She stopped short. "The one you were going to send Hannah on."

"Oh, my plane. But that was for Hannah. You can send for your own."

"I don't have my own plane."

"I guess you'll need to ask your parents."

She clamped her jaw tight. "That's exactly what I meant when I said you love your power. You want the world to think you're this good, caring person. You put on conferences and host events and fund research, but you do it to prove you are superior."

"Someone should teach your some manners."

"It won't be you. You have none."

"Perhaps I should drop you off along the desert highway… see if any of my good Bedouin tribe members happen along and let you hitchhike a ride home. Or they may not. You might end up as desert road kill."

"What a gentleman."

"No. Wouldn't claim that one at all. But then, why do I need to be a gentleman? You're no lady."

"Having fun now, are you?"

A hot light flickered in his silver eyes. "No. Not at all. So help me understand what it is you want from me. Do you want pity? Sympathy? Poor Emmeline, poor little princess, she's been so mistreated—"

"Go to hell," she gritted, walking past him into the living room. He was so appallingly chauvinistic. So arrogant and self-righteous that she couldn't even believe this was the same man she'd kissed last night. And last night had been lovely. For a moment last night she'd felt something beautiful and good but all the goodness was gone, leaving her shaken and disillusioned.

"Where are you going?" Sheikh Al-Koury demanded, his sharp voice followed her into the living room.

"To finish packing. Your Bedouin tribesmen sound delightful compared to you."

CHAPTER NINE

WHEN Makin Al-Koury decided to act, he acted swiftly. And this time he'd acted so swiftly Emmeline's head still spun.

She couldn't quite believe she was seated on his jet as it taxied down the runway preparing for takeoff only thirty minutes after she'd told him his Bedouin tribesmen sounded delightful.

In retrospect, it probably wasn't the smartest thing to say. But then, Emmeline had struggled with containing her emotions ever since she was a child. One day she would learn control. One day she'd bite her tongue.

But until then, she'd suffer the consequences as she was suffering now.

Because she wasn't just flying to Brabant. She was being accompanied home by Sheikh Makin Al-Koury who had decided that she couldn't be trusted to make it home to see her parents. No, he'd decided to escort her all the way to the d'Arcy palace and leave her in her parents' care.

What a prince.

The jet was picking up speed, racing down the narrow black runway they'd landed on just twenty-four hours before.

It was déjà vu. Everything was as it had been—they were buckled into the very same seats they'd sat in on the way to Raha. She felt the same emotions, too. Anxiety. Dread. Fear of the unknown.

Emmeline felt Makin look at her as she choked on a gasp when the jet lifted off the ground in a dramatically steep ascent.

"Nervous flyer?" he asked.

"No." She forced herself to take a deep breath. She wasn't a nervous flyer, but she certainly hadn't expected to spend the rest of the day in Makin's company. It had been a tough morning and now it would be a very long day. "Just a little queasy from takeoff."

He hesitated, before asking gruffly, "Do you need anything?"

Her head snapped up in shock, lips parting slightly at his audacity. Did she *need* anything? Was he serious?

He was hauling her—by force—across the Middle East to Europe, to return her—against her will—to the royal palace in Brabant, and he wondered if she needed anything?

This. This was exactly what she didn't get. This is exactly what she didn't understand about him.

If he was so angry with her—and he was—then why did he care about how she felt? Why ask her about her comfort, or pretend to care about her well-being?

"Aren't your first guests arriving this afternoon?" she answered, suppressing her confusion, realizing she'd never understand him.

"Yes."

"You won't be there."

"I am fully aware of that."

"I thought this conference was so important to you."

"It is."

"Then shouldn't you be home, welcoming everyone, instead of flying twenty-nine hundred miles to haul me before my parents?"

"I thought it prudent to get you out of Raha before my guests arrived."

She saw his expression and understood. "You thought I'd be disruptive."

She saw that she'd hit the nail squarely on the head.

He didn't trust her. He thought she was a loose cannon, causing trouble wherever she went.

A weight settled in her chest, making it hard to breathe. He was no different than her parents. He looked at her and saw what he wanted to see instead of who she really was.

Chest tight, Emmeline glanced away, out the window at the sea of gold sand below. *Let Makin think what he wants,* she told herself. *It doesn't matter...he doesn't matter...*

And yet in a small part of her heart, she could admit that maybe he did.

It had happened when he'd kissed her.

In Makin's arms she'd felt not just safe, but...desirable. Beautiful. And she never felt beautiful as a woman. She never felt like a real woman...and she hadn't, not until Makin kissed her, bringing someone to life inside of her.

The kiss had been the most amazing thing she'd ever felt. And she'd wanted more.

"I'm not dangerous," she said hoarsely, unable to hold the words in, or hide the hurt.

"You didn't say dangerous, you said disruptive."

"I wouldn't have embarrassed you."

"I couldn't have taken the chance."

"What about your guests? You're not even going to be there now to greet them as they arrive."

"My friend Sultan Nuri of Baraka has promised to do the honors."

Emmeline knew Malek Nuri, had seen him and his wife, the European princess Nicolette Ducasse, at a number of social events over the years. They were a gorgeous couple and so very happy together. "Does he know why you're not there? Does he know that you feel compelled personally to hand me over to the executioner?"

"You are so dramatic."

"So I've been told."

"As well as emotional."

Blood surged to her cheeks. "And you are so critical."

He studied her from beneath lowered lashes. "I hit a nerve, didn't I?"

"I've been criticized for being emotional my entire life."

Makin had been angry when they'd boarded the plane but now, seated across the aisle from Emmeline, he found it impossible to remain upset with her. He didn't know if it was because

she bore such a strong resemblance to Hannah, or if it was because Emmeline was an enigma, but he was intrigued by her
and wanted to know more about her. "Who criticizes you?"

"My parents, particularly my mother."

"What's her complaint?"

"She has many." Emmeline wrinkled her nose. "But the chief
one seems to be my excessive emotion."

"Excessive…how?"

She ticked her mother's complaints off on her fingers. "I'm
sensitive. I talk fast. I get nervous. I cry at the drop of a hat."

His lips twitched. "Do you cry at the drop of a hat?"

"Depends on the hat."

He grinned, amused, liking this Emmeline. She was unpre-
tentious. Funny. Direct. "Have you and your mother always had
a strained relationship?"

"Since birth."

"Why?"

"I wish I knew."

She suddenly sounded very serious and his brow furrowed.
She'd changed into jeans and a white peasant blouse before the
flight, and right now with her hair loose and no makeup, she
looked young and fresh. Appealing. Like the kind of girl you'd
want to take home to meet your parents, and he suddenly wondered what his parents would have thought of Emmeline d'Arcy.
They'd known of her, of course, but due to his father's health,
they'd never met her.

"I was emotional as a boy," he said abruptly. "Sensitive. I'll
never forget my mother pulling me aside when I was around
eight or nine and telling me I was a big boy now and too old to
cry."

"Do you remember why you cried?"

"My father had fallen out of his wheelchair. I was scared."

"But that would be frightening."

"I would see worse things."

"Sounds like you had to grow up at quite a young age."

He shrugged. "My mother needed me. It was important I be
strong for her, and my father."

Emmeline's expression was troubled and Makin realized the conversation had become too personal. He swiftly changed the subject to lighten the mood. "I've never seen you in jeans before."

Emmeline glanced down, crossed her legs, running a hand over her thigh as she did so. "They're Hannah's. And Hannah's top. I found them buried in the back of her closet." She suddenly looked at him. "I'm going to return them to her. I promise. I'll have them dry-cleaned and—"

"That's between you and Hannah. I imagine she's had to wear your clothes in Raguva. I can't picture her playing princess in her wardrobe of brown, beige and gray."

Emmeline smiled crookedly. "She doesn't really have a couture wardrobe."

"No. She's too practical for that."

Emmeline ran a hand over the worn denim again. "I've never owned a pair of jeans like these. They aren't the designer ones. They're real. Broken in, so soft."

"Hannah was raised on her father's ranch in Texas, just outside of San Antonio. Has she told you some of her stories about her life on the ranch?"

Emmeline shook her head.

"I think she found it lonely on the ranch. Her father raised her. She didn't have a mother. She grew up riding and roping and helping with roundups."

"Such a different life than mine."

"I can't see you on a ranch."

"Neither can I, but I do ride. Not Western-style, of course. I used to compete."

"Dressage?"

She grinned. "No, jumping. I was quite good." She must have seen the disbelief in his eyes because she laughed and added, "I really was. Even made the Brabant Olympic Equestrian team at twenty."

"You participated in the Olympics?"

"Well, I made it there, but ended up getting thrown in my first event. It was a nasty fall, and for almost twenty-four hours

I had no feeling below my chest. Thank goodness full sensation eventually returned, but that was the end of my riding. I'm not allowed to compete again."

"I had no idea."

"I can't imagine you reading tabloid magazines, so it's unlikely you'd know I was mad about jumping. It's not exactly mainstream news."

"Your accident would have made headlines."

"It was mentioned that I was thrown, but there was a massive earthquake the next day, and the focus turned to real news."

"How many years ago was that?"

"Five." She glanced down at her middle and pressed a hand to the peasant blouse, flattening the cotton fabric over her still-flat stomach. "That's how I met Alejandro. He was at the course when I was thrown and he came to the hospital to check on me. The nurses wouldn't let him in. Alejandro being Alejandro—" She broke off, swallowed. "—he told them he was my fiancé, and they let him in."

Makin thought he'd known Princess Emmeline all of these years. He thought he'd known everything important about her—beautiful, fashionable, chic, as well as soft, pampered and lazy. He'd imagined that her only ambition was being seen and photographed. Instead she'd spent years training in a highly competitive, dangerous sport. She'd been thrown from a horse. She was far stronger than he'd ever imagined.

"That's how the rumors and talk started," she added. "About Alejandro and me. But we weren't involved. There was nothing between us, not until March."

"But over the years you were seen with him, time and again."

"Because he would search me out. Never the other way around. I was never interested in him. He wasn't my type. I know you don't believe me, but I worked very hard to rebuff him. Only, I think that backfired. The more I pushed him away, the more determined he was to win."

Looking at her stunning features—the high cheekbones, the angled jaw, the full mouth—he could believe it. She was beyond beautiful. She had a rare, luminous quality, as though there was a light inside of her making her shimmer and glow. "Men like the chase," he said.

"So I've learned." She tried to smile but it didn't reach her eyes. "He didn't love me. He didn't even want me. He just wanted to…oh, what's that English expression? Score. He just wanted to score." She met his gaze, smiled mockingly. "And he did. Now he's gone. I'm pregnant. And nothing will ever be the same, will it?"

He felt such a sharp tug of emotion that it almost took his breath away. She'd been through a difficult time and things weren't going to be getting any easier. He suddenly knew she needed a friend, someone in her corner. Someone who would be there for her. "You're right. It won't be."

"I'm scared."

He felt another inexplicable tug on his emotions. Gone was the glossy, glamorous princess who had sailed through life untouched by the problems of ordinary mortals. She looked young and real and heartbreakingly vulnerable. "You could end the pregnancy. No one would be the wiser."

"*I* would."

"It'd be the best thing for you."

"But not for the baby!" she flashed hotly, color suffusing her cheeks. "And I know you don't like Alejandro—"

"This has nothing to do with him," he interrupted sternly. "And I'm not a proponent of abortion. But I think you have to be very practical right now, think hard on your choices. You are Princess Emmeline d'Arcy and the world holds you to a different standard."

"Perhaps. But I could no more abort the pregnancy than amputate an arm or leg. I love this baby, and I want this baby and am prepared to make the necessary sacrifices to ensure that he or she has the best possible life."

Makin regarded her steadily, torn between admiration and concern, aware that the road ahead of her would not be easy. But life wasn't about making the easy decision, it was about making the right decision, and if keeping the baby was the right thing for her, then he supported her one hundred percent. Life was fragile and precious and full of unknowns.

Makin was all too familiar with the fragility of life. He'd known since he was a teenager that he'd never be able to have children due to the gene he'd inherited from his father. And so at twenty, six months after his father's death, Makin had elected to have a vasectomy to ensure that he couldn't carelessly or accidentally impregnate his partner. He simply could not take the risk of passing on such a fatal, painful disease to his children. It had been bad enough watching his father suffer. He couldn't imagine his own children suffering the same fate.

"Then you need to be strong," he said to Emmeline at length. "You need to hold tightly to your convictions and do not let anyone sway you from what you believe is right and true."

They traveled in silence for nearly forty minutes and then the captain announced that they would be starting their descent momentarily.

Emmeline looked out the window and then at Makin. "We're still flying over desert."

"We're stopping in Nadir to refuel. We'll only be on the ground fifteen or twenty minutes." He paused, studied her brown hair, aware that it wasn't her true color. "Do you have a personal hair stylist?"

"Yes. She's in Raguva with Hannah."

"Which means she could be anywhere." He saw Emmeline's expression and clarified, "Hannah's no longer in Raguva. She left the palace early this morning and should be on her way back to Dallas now."

"So King Patek knows?"

"He discovered the truth last night."

"My parents must know then, too."

"I did send word we were on the way and had to stop and refuel. They aren't expecting us until midafternoon."

"It's going to be pretty ugly when we get to Brabant," she said slowly.

"You have to face your family sooner or later."

"Then later seems preferable."

"Right now, maybe. But it's always better to confront problems head-on. I act as soon as I can. It saves heartache down the road."

"That's why we're on the plane now. Better to get me home quickly than delay and risk more trouble."

"Exactly," he agreed, and then realized how it must sound to her. He tried to soften the blow. "My father taught me not to sweep things under the carpet or play ostrich by burying your head in the sand. People will think you're ashamed or have something to hide."

"But I do feel shame. I'm not proud to be a single, unwed mother. I've made so many appearances trying to educate young girls, wanting them to be smart and careful, and yet I've failed to do the very thing I preach."

"As you said, you made a mistake."

"A terribly stupid one."

Makin's insides tightened, his chest knotting with sensation, and he realized now it wasn't Hannah he'd wanted to send away yesterday. It was this person, this woman. Emmeline. Not because he disliked her, or because she'd failed him in some way, but because she was making him care. Not about grand or important things like politics and economics, but about something very small and personal. Her.

He did care for her. He was glad he was accompanying her home, if only to lend his moral support. "What's done is done," he said. "You can't go back. All you can do is go forward."

"Yes."

"But I don't think you should go home like this." He indicated her hair. "Not as a brunette. Since your stylist isn't available, I know someone who could help. She can meet us at the airport and board the plane when we refuel."

Emmeline touched her hair. "You're sure she'll come?"

"She's on my payroll."

"She's your stylist then?"

"No. She's Madeline's."

"Madeline?"

"My...mistress."

Emmeline frowned. "That's right. You mentioned her last night." She hesitated. "Does Madeline mind that her stylist will help with my hair?"

"I don't know." He shrugged, suddenly uncomfortable and impatient. He wished he hadn't mentioned Madeline. There was no need to bring her up, and he certainly had no desire to discuss her with the princess. "Risa is an expert at doing hair on this jet and she'll have you back to your natural color by the time we arrive in Brabant."

Just a little over an hour later, they were back in the air after refueling in Nadir.

Risa, the hairstylist, had brought everything she might need in a large trunk. She had various boxes of color, foil squares, cotton strips, shampoo and conditioner, as well as a hair dryer, curling tongs, styling creams and finishing sprays.

On board, Risa immediately mixed color and applied it to Emmeline's hair, taking little strips here and there and wrapping them in foil.

Now Emmeline sat on the bed flipping through one of the magazines Risa had brought with her while she waited for the color to finish processing, but her mind kept wandering from the magazine to Makin. Why did he have a mistress? What was the point of a mistress? Why not a girlfriend…or a wife?

A knock sounded on the door. It was Makin. He opened the door a crack. "Are you decent?"

"I'm dressed. But not sure how decent I look," she answered, setting the magazine aside.

He opened the door wider. "You look like an alien," he said, taking in the pieces of foil and purple cream.

Emmeline smiled wryly. "You're not supposed to see this part."

"Where's Risa?"

"In the galley kitchen rinsing the bowls and brushes." Emmeline closed the magazine and slid her legs off the bed. "Risa's good, by the way. She knows what she's doing."

"She worked in Paris for ten years for a top salon before Madeline hired her away."

"Risa told me Madeline's blonde." Emmeline didn't know why she said it.

"She is," he agreed.

Emmeline waited for him to elaborate but he didn't. "Have you always had a mistress?"

Makin blinked. "What kind of question is that?"

"I'm curious. And you've asked me very personal things. I don't know why I'm not allowed to know anything about you."

"I never said you weren't."

"Good. So, why a mistress instead of a girlfriend? What's the point of having a mistress?"

He hesitated a moment than shrugged. "Convenience."

Her brows knit together. "For you?"

"Yes."

"And what's in it for her?"

"Comfort. Security."

"Financial security, you mean?"

"Yes."

"Because it doesn't sound as if there is emotional security."

"I wouldn't say that—"

"Because you have all the control. It's a relationship on your terms. You see her when you want, and she must be available whenever you call. Which, by the way, is horrible."

"Madeline's not unhappy."

"How do you know she's not unhappy?"

"Because she's never said she was."

"Maybe she's afraid to complain—"

"Madeline's not afraid of me."

"But she can't feel all that secure. She's not in a relationship with you—"

"Time to change the subject."

"Do you love her?"

"That's none of your business."

"Do you plan on marrying her?"

"Again, none of your business."

"But she's been your mistress for three years."

"Risa told you that, didn't she?"

"Don't blame her. I ask too many questions."

"I can believe that," he said dryly.

Emmeline flushed. "It's just that I would hate to be someone's mistress. I would hate to spend my life waiting for someone to call me or come see me."

"Madeline has friends in Nadir, and a busy social life attending parties and fashion shows."

"I'd rather be poor and have someone to love me, than to have lots of money and no love."

"You can say that because you wear couture and get invitations to the most exclusive parties—"

"But clothes and parties aren't real. Clothes and parties are frills...window dressing. I'd rather someone like me—want me—for me, than for what I have in a bank account."

Makin suddenly smiled and shook his head. "You're like a little dog with a bone. You're not going to drop it, are you?"

She looked at him for a long moment before smiling reluctantly. "I'm sorry. I guess I did get a little carried away."

"I admire your strong convictions."

Her smile stretched wider. "You know, you're not all bad, Sheikh Al-Koury. There are some good things about you."

"Just hours ago you were saying I was a power monger."

She blushed, not sure if she should laugh or cry. "Haven't forgotten. And I haven't forgotten that we're not friends. And that we don't like each other."

His lips curved faintly. "You're incorrigible. I don't think anyone could control you."

"Many have tried."

For a moment he just looked at her, his hard features set, his gray eyes narrowed. "You can't move to England. You'd be miserable."

"No."

"You would. You'd be living in a fishbowl. You couldn't go anywhere without a half dozen paparazzi following you."

"Not in the country."

"Most definitely. You are Princess Emmeline d'Arcy. Once the media discovers you are pregnant and single, you will never be left alone. The tabloids will haunt you. Photographers will shadow you. The paparazzi aren't going to disappear just because you want to live quietly."

"Well, I can't stay in Brabant, locked behind the palace gate, under my parents' thumb. It's not healthy."

"Don't you have a home of your own in Brabant?"

"My grandparents left me an estate in the north. It's quite pretty, a small castle with gorgeous grounds—orchards, a rose garden and even a small wood with a lake for fishing—but my parents have said that it'd cost too much for me to actually live there. Staffing it, running it, security. And so it's mine, but unlivable."

"I thought you said you had some money of your own now? That you'd come into your majority?"

"I do, but it's not enough to fund the running of a château, and my parents won't help cover the difference, nor will they ask the taxpayers to help. And I do agree with that. Our people don't need me being a burden. That's why I thought that I would just go somewhere else, like England, and find a small place that I could afford."

"I think your citizens would be hurt if you left them. They love you."

She thought of the large crowds that turned out every time she made an appearance, all ages, waving flags and carrying flowers, of all the little children who lifted their faces for a kiss. "And I love them. They have always been so very good to me. So loyal. But now I am pregnant, and it will bring them shame, which doesn't seem right. I was to have been their perfect princess, a replacement for my aunt Jacqueline who was a most beloved princess. She's been gone longer than she was alive, and yet they still mourn her."

"She was stunning."

"She was so young, too, when she died. Just twenty."

"But now you create a new life," he said firmly. "A new royal baby for your citizens to love and adore."

Emmeline throat ached with emotion. "But I'm not royal—"

"What?"

She nodded. "And Alejandro is a commoner so the baby won't be given a title, or be in line for the throne. That's how it works in Brabant." Her voice broke. "That's why I had to marry King Patek. I had to marry a royal, a blue blood. And obviously I can't marry Zale now—can't marry any royal—and so I'm no longer in line for succession. Which means, my child won't be, either."

"I don't understand. How can you not be royal? You are King William and Queen Claire's daughter—"

"*Adopted* daughter." Emmeline's eyes met his. She hesitated, struggling to find the right words when none of them felt good. "They adopted me when I was six days old. Apparently I'm a bastard, which even today brings Claire, my adoptive mother, endless shame."

He looked dumbstruck. "Do you know anything about your birth parents?"

"Only that my birth mother was a Brabant commoner. Young, pregnant and unwed."

"And your father?"

"No one knows anything about him."

"You can't find out?"

Emmeline shook her head. "It wasn't an open adoption. My birth mother had no idea who would be adopting me, and my parents are very private. I had no idea I was adopted until I was sixteen." She paused, tugged on the cuff of the blouse with unsteady fingers. "My father broke the news to me just before my birthday party."

Makin's eyes narrowed fractionally. "The actual day of your birthday?"

She shrugged. "I know it sounds childish, but it crushed me. I'd had no idea, and then suddenly my father was telling me I was illegitimate—a bastard—born of sin." Her lips twisted wryly. "There I was, in my beautiful party dress and brand-new high heels, my first real set of heels, feeling so grown-up and excited. Then Father called me aside and took it all away. I don't think he meant to hurt me as much as he did. But to call me a bastard? To tell his only daughter that she was a product of sin?"

Her smile slipped for a moment, revealing raw, naked pain. "I fell apart. I think I cried the rest of the night. Silly, I know."

"It would have been shocking for anyone."

"Maybe." She was silent a moment. "So you see, I understand the stigma and shame of being illegitimate. I know what it's like to be judged and rejected. Who knows who my birth parents were, or why they had to give me up for adoption? But they did, and they must have imagined it was the best thing for me. And maybe it was. But I do know this—I want my child—he or she is not a mistake. And I will do everything in my power to ensure that he or she has the best life possible."

CHAPTER TEN

EMMELINE sat on the edge of the bed while Risa blew-dry her hair with a big round brush, aware that once she was home, it would be absolute hell. Her mother would lose her temper, probably scream at her that she was stupid. Her father would look morose and deeply disappointed and let her mother do all the talking. It was how they handled problems. It was how they handled problems like her. Not that she'd ever done anything to be considered a problem before, but it was how they'd always viewed her.

Sometimes Emmeline thought she should do something outrageous to give them cause for complaint, as the worst thing she'd ever done—until now—was skinny-dipping while visiting her cousins in Spain. She'd been twelve and it had seemed so daring to swim naked at night in the palace pool. Thirteen-year-old Delfina had suggested it and ten-year-old Isabel had endorsed the idea so Emmeline, nervous and giggling, joined them. And it had been fun, up until the time the palace security reported them to their parents.

Aunt Astrid had given them a scolding but Emmeline's mother had been furious. She'd demanded to know whose idea it was, and when Delfina didn't speak up, Emmeline took the blame to protect her cousins.

Emmeline had expected that her mother would spank her and that would be the end of it. Instead her mother spanked her and sent her home to Brabant.

The spanking had been bad, but being sent away from her cousins in disgrace, so much worse.

In the fourteen years since then, not a lot had changed. Her parents were still distant, her mother rigid. Emmeline could only imagine their reaction to the news that she was pregnant. She was too old to be spanked or sent away, so what would they do this time? Lock her in a tower and throw away the key?

"Almost done," Risa said, turning off the blow-dryer.

Which meant they were almost there, Emmeline thought, hands knotting into fists.

While Risa was styling Emmeline's hair in the rear cabin, Makin sat in his seat in the main cabin replaying the last several conversations he'd had with Emmeline in his head.

She wasn't who he'd thought she was. She wasn't shallow, either. Just sheltered and naive.

How could you hate someone for being sheltered? Inexperienced?

He couldn't.

He understood now that she'd panicked back in March. She'd turned to Alejandro out of desperation, wanting someone to love her, knowing her prospective bridegroom didn't. She'd made a gross error of judgment, but she wasn't a terrible person. He couldn't condone her actions, but he couldn't dislike her anymore. Not when he understood how painful it had been for her to be married off to the highest bidder, as if she were an object instead of a smart, sensitive and shy young woman with hopes and dreams of her own.

Makin suddenly wished he hadn't been so quick to put Emmeline on the plane for Brabant. But it was too late to turn around. All he could do now was offer her his support and let her know she wasn't alone.

An hour later they were in the back of a limousine sailing toward the palace. Just before landing Emmeline changed into a black pencil skirt and a chic black satin blouse, which she accessorized with a long strand of ivory pearls. Her hair, now a gleaming golden blond, was drawn into an elegant chignon at the back of her head. She wore pearls at her ears.

She was nervous, beyond nervous, but she squashed every visible sign of fear, flattening all emotion, refusing to let herself think or feel. Things were what they were. What would happen would happen. She would survive.

"Not that it matters, but I'm not a fan of arranged marriages," Makin said abruptly, breaking the silence. "They're popular in my culture, but it's not for me."

She looked at him, surprised that he had shared something personal. "Your parents didn't try to arrange anything for you?"

He shook his head. "They were a love match. They wanted the same for me."

"Are they still alive?"

"No. They died quite a few years ago. My father first—I was twenty—and my mother the year after." He hesitated. "We expected my father's death. He had been ill for a long time. But my mother...she was still young. Just forty-one. It was quite a shock. I wasn't at all prepared to lose her."

"An accident?" she murmured.

"Heart attack..." His voice drifted off and he frowned, his strong brow creasing. "Personally, I think it was grief. She didn't want to be without my father."

Emmeline looked at Makin and the emotion darkening his eyes. Until he'd kissed her last night, she'd imagined him to be cool...cold...and quite detached. Now she was beginning to understand that with him, still waters ran deep. His cool exterior hid a passionate nature. "They were happy together?"

"Very. They had an extraordinary relationship, and they were devoted to each other, from the day they met until the very end. I was lucky to have parents who loved each other so much, and to be part of that circle of love. It made me who I am."

"So why haven't you married?" she asked, noting that he, too, had showered and dressed just before they landed. He now wore a gray shirt and black trousers, and the crisp starched shirt was open at the collar and exposed the hollow of his throat. His skin was the burnished gold of his desert, perfectly setting off his black hair and striking silver eyes.

And it was a good question, she thought, waiting for him to answer. He was gorgeous. Brilliant. Ridiculously wealthy. He would be the catch of the century.

His broad shoulders shifted. "I haven't met the right one."

"And what would she be like?"

"I don't know. I haven't met her yet. But I'll let you know the moment I do."

Makin saw her lips curve and her eyes dance as she laughed at him. He wouldn't have thought he'd like her laughing at him and yet he found himself amused by her amusement. She didn't laugh often, but now she came alive, mouth lifted, dimples flashing, light dancing in her eyes. She was joyous...mischievous... happier and younger than he'd ever seen her and it crossed his mind that he would do almost anything to see her smile like this again.

He glanced from her eyes to her appealing lips, and suddenly Makin wanted to touch her, kiss her, part those soft, full lips and taste her again as he had last night in the garden.

He'd thought it was the candlelight and moonlight and dark purple sky bewitching him, but now he knew better. He knew it was her. She was the magic. But he had Madeline, and Emmeline was pregnant. They each had their own path, a path they had been destined to travel.

"I have a plan," he said firmly, hating that his body had hardened and he felt hot and restless next to her. He couldn't let her affect him this way. He did have a plan—he had a vision—he'd vowed to do something significant with his life and he would.

If his father could be as successful as he had been with a disease so brutal and debilitating, a disease that destroyed his spine and his limbs, eventually robbing him of movement and speech, trapping his brilliant mind in a wasteland of a body, then Makin should be able to move mountains.

But he couldn't move mountains if he got distracted. One day he'd have time for more. But not now.

Not now, he repeated, his gaze moving to the pearls around her neck. He'd never been a fan of pearls. They reminded him too much of old ladies and uptight college girls in cashmere twinsets, but Emmeline made pearls look glamorous. No, make that sexy. The long strand around her neck hung between her breasts almost to her waist. They slid across the black satin of her blouse as she moved, outlining one soft swell of breast and then the other. He found it almost impossible to look away from the luminescent pearls.

He stifled a groan as he felt yet another hot surge of desire, his attraction to her now complicated by his desire to protect her. He didn't know when he'd begun to develop feelings for her, but he did care about her, and there was nothing simple about their relationship anymore.

"Not far now," Emmeline said quietly, the laughter gone from her voice.

The car was speeding from the freeway to a quiet city street, and she was focused on the old buildings passing by, but her expression was serene, her blue eyes clear and untroubled.

If one didn't know better you'd think she was heading to a fashion show and luncheon instead of an excruciating encounter with her parents.

If one didn't know, he silently repeated, realizing he'd never known her. Realizing he'd always looked at the externals— the impossibly beautiful young woman, her effortless style, her placid expression—and had imagined that she sailed through life unmarked, untouched, unconcerned with the human fray.

He'd been wrong.

Emmeline suddenly turned her head and looked at him. For a moment she just looked into his eyes, cool and composed, and then her lips slowly curved up. "Is there something on my face?" she asked, arching a winged eyebrow, looking every inch a princess. "Or perhaps something green in my teeth?"

He nearly smiled at the something green in her teeth. She was funny. All these years he'd thought he'd known her, but he hadn't. He'd known of her, and then he'd projected onto her, but he'd gotten her wrong.

She wasn't stiff and dramatic and petulant. She *was* emotional, but she was also smart, warm, with a mischievous streak running through her.

"I have a feeling you were a handful as a little girl," he said.

She wrinkled her nose. "I must have been. Until I was thirteen I thought my name was Emmeline-get-in-here-you're-in-trouble-d'Arcy."

Makin laughed softly, even as his chest suddenly ached. She *was* funny. And sweet. And really lovely. Heartbreakingly lovely and he didn't know why he'd never seen it before.

Was it because she was so pretty? Was it because she looked like a princess that he had assumed the worst?

"I'm glad I had the chance to spend the past few days with you," he said. "When you get past the body guards and ladies-in-waiting and multitude of assistants, you're quite likable."

She choked on a laugh. "Careful. Don't be too nice. I might think we were friends."

It crossed his mind that she could probably use a friend. He was beginning to understand there wasn't anyone in her life to protect her. It was wrong. "So tell me, how will it go once we reach your home?"

The warmth faded from her eyes. "It won't be pleasant. There will be hard things said, particularly from my mother."

"She has a temper?"

"She does. She can be…hurtful."

"Just remember, sticks and stones might break your bones…"

"…but words will never hurt me…" She finished the children's rhyme, and her voice trailed off. She smiled a little less steadily. "It'll be fine."

That smile nearly pushed him over the edge.

He understood then that it wasn't going to be fine. It wouldn't be fine at all.

He looked away again, out the window at the elegant gray eighteenth-century buildings lining the square. It was raining, just a light drizzle, but the gray clouds made the afternoon feel dark and gloomy. The only color on the streets were the rows of trees leading to the adjacent park, lushly green with new spring growth.

"It seems bad now," he said, aware that he was in danger of becoming too involved, caring too much. He needed to step back. Put some distance between him and Emmeline. He was merely bringing her home, returning her safely to her family.

"But this will pass. In fact this time tomorrow you could have a whole new set of problems."

"Oh, I hope not," she answered with a cool, hollow laugh as the palace gates loomed before them. "I think I have enough on my plate. Don't you?"

Entering the palace salon where her parents waited was like walking into a minefield, Emmeline thought several minutes later. She hadn't even walked all the way through the salon doors before her mother exploded in anger.

"What were you thinking? Were you even thinking?" Queen Claire d'Arcy was on her feet in an instant, her voice a sharp ricochet of sound. "Or was your intention to humiliate us?"

"Absolutely not," Emmeline answered firmly, forcing herself to keep putting one foot in front of the other, closing the gap between them. In a dim part of her brain she knew that Makin was behind her but he was the least of her worries now. "I would never want to humiliate you—"

"But you did! Zale Patek didn't give us a specific reason why he felt it necessary to break off the engagement, only that he was concerned about a lack of compatibility. *Compatibility*," the queen repeated bitterly. "What does that even mean?"

"He was merely being polite. The fault is mine."

"Why am I not surprised?"

Emmeline ignored the jab. "I'm sorry to have disappointed you—"

"When haven't you?"

"—and will try to make amends."

"Good. At least we agree on something. You are to return to Raguva immediately and beg His Highness for forgiveness. Do whatever it is you must do, but do not return without his ring on your finger—"

"I can't."

"Emmeline, it's not an option. It's your duty to marry him. Your duty to provide heirs for him—"

"I can't, Mother. I'm already pregnant."

The grand salon, coolly elegant in white and gold, went

strangely silent. For a moment there was no sound, no motion, and then her mother sank into her chair by her father's side.

Finally her mother's head tipped. "What did you just say, Emmeline?"

Emmeline glanced at her father, who, so far, hadn't said a word. True to form he sat silent and grim, letting her mother do all the talking. "I...I'm..." She drew a deep breath. "...nearly eight weeks pregnant."

"Please tell me I heard you wrong." Her mother's voice dropped to a whisper.

"I wish I could." Emmeline's voice sounded faint to her own ears.

"And of course it's not Zale Patek's."

"No."

"Slut."

Emmeline heard Makin hiss a breath, but she didn't even flinch. She'd expected this. Had known it wouldn't be pleasant. And it wasn't.

"How dare you?" Claire choked on the words. "You ungrateful girl! How dare you throw every good thing we have done for you back in our faces?"

Emmeline felt rather than heard Makin move to her side. "I'm sorry," she said quietly.

"That's it? That's all you have to say for yourself? You ruin your chances, you ruin us, and you're *sorry?*"

Emmeline lifted her chin, determined to stay calm, determined to remain strong. Tears would serve no purpose, just make her look weak and emotional. Instead she'd accept the consequences, no matter how painful. It'd been her decision to sleep with Alejandro. Now she had to deal with the repercussions. "Yes. And while this is the last thing I wanted to happen, it has, and I'm going to take responsibility."

"And may I ask who the father is? Or is that secret knowledge?"

Emmeline's lips parted but Makin spoke first.

"I am," he said clearly, his deep voice firm.

Emmeline turned to face him, jaw dropping in shock, but he

didn't even look at her. He was staring straight at her mother, a snarl twisting his lips. "I am," he repeated fiercely, "and I would like a little bit of respect, please."

Emmeline's legs turned to jelly, even as her head spun. She reached for Makin. "What are you doing?" she choked, as his fingers curled around hers.

"Making this right," he growled.

She shook her head frantically. "It won't…it won't, trust me."

"No. It's time you trusted me." And then with a small, hard smile in her parents' direction, he walked Emmeline out and closed the doors behind him.

In the hall Emmeline's legs threatened to give out. "Do you have any idea what you just did?" she said, holding his arm tightly.

"Yes." He frowned at her. "You're feeling faint, aren't you?"

"A little."

He swore beneath his breath and swung her into his arms. "I should not have brought you back!"

"But you did. Now, put me down. I'll be fine in a moment."

He ignored her, exiting the hall for the grand foyer with the blue-painted dome, and began to climb the stairs two at a time.

"Makin, please. I can walk."

"Not going to have you faint and risk having you, or the baby, hurt," he answered, continuing up the marble steps with single-minded focus. "Isn't your room up here somewhere?"

"On the second floor, yes. But I won't faint—"

"Good." He shifted her weight in his arms as he reached the top stair. "Right or left?"

She peeked over his shoulder, saw the familiar hall with ivory-painted woodwork, gleaming chandeliers overhead and the pale gold-and-ivory carpet runner underfoot. "Right. But I can walk—"

"Fantastic. Which room?"

"That one," she said, nodding at a closed door. "And you didn't need to claim the baby. I was going to tell them the truth."

"The truth?" he repeated, leaning down to turn the knob and

push the door open, giving her a whiff of his subtle spicy cologne, the scent that always made her insides curl.

"Yes," she answered breathlessly, growing warm and warmer. "It's what you told me to do."

"Until I saw your mother in action and thought she was the devil."

"Makin."

"I did. I still do." He crossed the bedroom floor with the same long strides that had eaten up the stairs and hall. "No wonder Alejandro seemed like an attractive option. Your mother is terrifying!"

"She didn't terrify you."

His arms tightened around her. "No. But she did make me angry."

Emmeline inhaled sharply as he held her even closer to his chest. His body was muscular and hard. His spicy fragrance teased her senses and she could feel his heart thudding beneath her ear. Alejandro had been cold in bed. She didn't think Makin would be cold. She didn't think he'd be detached or indifferent, either.

The thought of Makin in bed with her, naked next to her, was both thrilling and terrifying. He was beyond gorgeous, but too big...too strong...too overwhelming in every way.

She was glad when he placed her on the bed and she scooted to the middle to try to clear her head.

He gazed down at her, his arms crossing over his chest, emphasizing the width of his rib cage. "You're an adult, Emmeline. You don't owe them your soul."

"My mother thinks I do."

"I noticed." He shook his head in disgust. "That's why I spoke up. She wanted a name, so I gave her one."

"But that's just going to make things worse, Makin. She's going to expect you to provide for the baby—"

"I will."

"No, you won't. It's my baby and I'm responsible. Not you."

His strong jaw firmed in protest, and she didn't think he'd ever looked quite so powerful and primitive and male.

"And so what do you want me to do, Emmeline? Just leave you here with them? Allow your parents to ride roughshod over you?"

"I can manage them."

"Just like you did in the salon?"

Heat rushed to her cheeks and she jerked her chin up. "It wasn't that bad."

"Have you lost your mind? That was horrendous. A blood-bath. If it had been your father speaking I probably would have punched him."

"Makin!"

"I'm serious."

"I appreciate your support, I do, but telling them you're the baby's father isn't the way. We have to go tell them the truth before it's too late." Her voice broke and a tendril of pale hair slipped from her chignon to tumble against her cheek. "And please understand that while I appreciate you speaking up for me, it's time I stood on my own two feet—"

"So what do you want me to do?" he interrupted. "Stand by and do nothing? Allow your mother to attack you? Destroy you?"

Her heart suddenly ached. Hot tears filled her eyes. "Sticks and stones, Makin, remember?"

He held her gaze for an endless span of time. "But the rhyme has it wrong. Words can hurt. They were crushing you."

For a second she couldn't breathe: her chest on fire, her heart in pain. "She doesn't really mean it," she whispered. "It sounds worse than it is. Mother just has a temper."

"She crossed the line, Emmeline. She said too much."

"She did. But she'll calm down and feel bad later. She eventually always apologizes.'"

"That doesn't make it right."

Her shoulders twisted. "I know. But this is how it's always been and I'm not going to change her now."

"So what do you want me to do?"

"Go back to Kadar. Focus on your conference. It's an important conference for you."

"But you're important, too."

Her lips twisted wryly. "Not as important as all those dignitaries gathered at Kasbah Raha."

His light eyes searched hers. "I won't let them hurt you anymore, Emmeline."

"They won't. The worst is over."

His jaw flexed, a muscle popping, tightening near his ear. "You're sure of that?"

She suppressed all thought but freeing him. This wasn't his mess, or his mistake, and she couldn't let her life take over his. "Yes." She held out her hand to him. "And I hope we can part as friends."

His hand slowly enveloped hers, his gaze holding hers captive. "Friends," he repeated slowly.

She nodded, forcing a smile to her lips to hide her sudden rush of emotion. She would miss him. She'd grown to like him. Probably far more than she should. "Can we stay in touch? Maybe we could drop each other a line now and then?"

"That sounds like a plan."

CHAPTER ELEVEN

AFTER Makin left, Emmeline stayed in her room and even took dinner there, unable to face anyone.

She wished Makin had stayed.

Not because she needed him to fight her fights, but because he was good company. Interesting company. And he made her feel interesting, too.

She liked that he listened to her when she talked, liked how his eyes rested on her mouth, his brow furrowed intently. No one had ever talked to her as much as Makin had. No one had ever cared so much, either.

She fell asleep missing him, and woke up thinking of him and was grateful when her father sent for her during her morning coffee, if only to get her mind off Makin.

Emmeline's hands shook as she finished buttoning her navy silk blouse. She'd paired it with a long skirt the same color and added a wide, dark chocolate crocodile belt at her waist that matched her high heels. It was a mature, elegant, subdued look, perfect for the morning after yesterday's histrionics.

She slipped a necklace of Murano glass beads around her neck, the beads a swirl of gold, bronze and blue, and wondered if her mother would be waiting in the library or if this was to be just a father-daughter talk. One of those unbearably tense conversations her father had with her, where he talked and talked, and she listened and listened?

Regardless, she had to go. Dressed, with her hair drawn back into a smooth ponytail, and just mascara on her lashes, she left her room for the library, each step making her stomach churn.

Makin must be back in Kadar now, surrounded by his beloved desert and his important work. She felt an ache in her chest, near her heart.

Emmeline knocked firmly on the library door and waited for King William to permit her to enter. When he did, she found him seated at his enormous desk searching for an item in the center drawer.

"I had no idea," he said, frowning into his open drawer as she crossed the room to stand before his desk. "I wish you had spoken up."

She folded her hands in front of her, her own brow furrowing; she wasn't at all sure what he was referring to but she knew better than to interrupt.

"It would have helped if you'd explained, might have made the scene in the salon less uncomfortable." He looked up at her now, blue gaze reproving. "It was damn uncomfortable. Especially with Al-Koury there."

She sucked in a breath, hating the butterflies she got every time Makin's name was mentioned. "Yes, Father."

"But at the same time, I understand why you didn't say anything. I understand that Al-Koury wanted to speak to me first, and I appreciate the courtesy. I'm glad he's a gentleman and wanted to ask for your hand properly—"

"What?"

"Although to be quite honest," he continued, "Al-Koury should have come on his own, asked for your hand, before traveling with you. It is irregular, what with you being engaged to Zale Patek. A bit presumptuous. Put me in the hot seat, especially with your mother. But you're both human. Things happen."

"Father," she said sharply.

But he wasn't listening to her. He never did. His shoulders rolled as he just kept talking. "But it's not quite so easy for your mother. She's struggling to take it all in as she's very traditional and hasn't adapted to the way young people do things today. In her mind, you don't get pregnant and then married. You marry and then have the baby."

Emmeline blinked at him. Her father was speaking French but it could have been Mandarin or Egyptian. Because what he was saying didn't make sense at all.

King William lifted a hand. "But I promised Al-Koury we wouldn't criticize you, and we won't. I also promised that we'd focus on the positives, and so let me congratulate you. Al-Koury will be a good husband. And you know I like Patek, I do. But Sheikh Al-Koury…he's big money. Serious money. One hundred billion, two hundred billion, maybe more—"

"Father!"

"You're right. I shouldn't mention his wealth. But it is important, and he and I are to sit down later and discuss the pre-nup. You had quite a contract with Zale Patek. I'll negotiate just as hard for you with Al-Koury."

"Father."

"Yes, Emmeline?"

"I don't understand."

"Don't worry about the pre-nup. That's between him and me. And the lawyers, of course. His are flying in as we speak." He paused, looked at her for a moment and then smiled. "Your mother wouldn't approve of me saying this, but she's not here. I'm proud of you, Em. To snare one of the world's richest men. That says something. He's not an easy man to please and it's obvious he dotes on you. Congratulations, my dear. You did very well."

"When did you speak with him?" she asked, her voice strangled.

"Last night. After you'd gone to rest. He came to see me."

"He said he was going home," she whispered.

"Maybe to his room. We gave him the Ducalle Suite. I personally thought we could have done better but your mother isn't entirely happy about a sheikh for a son-in-law, but she'll come round. She always does."

"He's still here?"

"Of course."

She swallowed hard. "Father, there's been a mistake."

He closed the drawer hard. The entire desk rattled. "How so?"

"We're not…we're not…engaged."

"Well, you weren't. Not until Makin asked for your hand, and I've given him permission to marry you. I'm sure he'll give you the ring today—"

"Father, he doesn't love me. He barely likes me."

His eyes rolled. "Certainly liked you enough to get you pregnant."

"But Father—"

She was drowned out by the shrill ring of the telephone on his desk. It was a large antique phone and took up an entire corner of the table.

"I've said all I intended to say," he said, raising his voice to be heard over the ring. "The sheikh will be asking for your hand this morning. He'll put a ring on your finger and your mother should be calm soon. Now I must take this call—"

"He's not the father. It's not his child."

"Emmeline, I can't hear you over the phone. Please, go. I'll see you tonight at seven. We're meeting for drinks and then a celebratory dinner. See you then."

In the hallway, Emmeline put her hands on her hips and took a deep breath and then another, trying to process everything her father had said.

Makin hadn't gone home? He'd stayed and spoken with her father? He'd asked for her hand in marriage?

What was the sheikh thinking?

Wishing she'd had more than coffee and a roll for breakfast, Emmeline set off for the Ducalle Suite but Makin didn't answer the door. She knocked a second time, harder.

A maid popped her head out of a room from across the hall. "Sheikh Al-Koury is downstairs, Your Highness. He's having coffee on the terrace."

Emmeline grimly thanked her and headed for the large terrace where she found Makin at a table outside enjoying breakfast in the morning sun.

"What have you done?" she demanded, voice shaking as she marched toward him. She'd missed him this morning and had wanted to see him, but not on these terms.

"Sorted things out," he answered calmly, stirring a half tea-spoon of sugar into his coffee. "Made things right."

"No! You didn't make things right, Makin. You made things worse."

"How so?"

"My father is in the library rubbing his hands gleefully, an-ticipating getting his hands on some of your money, which won't ever happen as we're not getting married."

"I told him we are."

"Apparently you did. But you didn't ask me—"

"I didn't, no, not yet. But you need to be protected, and by marrying me, you will be protected—"

"How arrogant."

"But true."

"But I won't marry you. I don't want to marry you."

"Why not?"

Her eyebrows arched. "You need reasons?"

"Yes."

She shook her head, incredulous. "You're arrogant, control-ling, and you keep mistresses."

"I've already ended my relationship with Madeline."

"You're mad!"

"Don't be shortsighted. This is the best thing for the baby, and in your heart you know it."

"It might be the best thing for the baby, but it's not the best thing for me."

"Why not?"

"I didn't want this kind of marriage. If I'd wanted an arranged marriage I would have married Zale. But I didn't. And I don't need you and my father making bargains in his library."

"You are being dramatic."

"Maybe I am," she choked, pulling out a chair across from him and sitting down heavily. "But you know we're not suitable.

You know we're not compatible and you only asked for my hand because my mother was screaming."

"She does have a loud voice."

"See?" Emmeline was near tears. "You asked my father for my hand because you hate excessive emotion, and weren't comfortable with the shouting and crying, and so, to keep from feeling powerless, you took control the only way you knew how."

He sipped his coffee and returned the cup to the saucer. "Is that how it was?"

"Yes."

"Interesting, but not true. It *was* a scene in the salon yesterday, and your mother showed a side of her personality that I've never seen before, and hope to never see again, but Emmeline, you're mistaken if you thought I felt powerless. I knew exactly what I was doing."

For a moment she couldn't think of a single thing to say. *"What?"*

"I knew what I was doing when I left your bedroom. I fully intended to speak for you."

"But you did it out of pity," she whispered, suddenly chilled. "You did it because you couldn't bear not to do anything."

He looked at her long and hard, his dense black lashes concealing his expression. "You still have it wrong. I didn't do it because I couldn't bear not to do anything. I did it because I could do something. And I wanted to do something."

"But how does it help?"

"Because it changes everything. It gives your baby a name and a family. By marrying me, your child will have legitimacy, security and respect. He or she will want for nothing."

"Except your love."

"You can't say that. You don't know that."

"But I *do*. I was a baby adopted by well-meaning people, and they gave me every material thing they could, but it was never enough. I never felt wanted. I never felt loved. And I won't do that to my child. Not ever!"

Emmeline didn't wait for him to respond. She turned and practically ran, dashing down the terrace steps to the stretch of emerald lawn. She hurried across the lawn, her high heels sinking into the grass with every step, her emotions wildly chaotic.

When she turned and disappeared around a tall yew hedge, the grass gave way to gravel and the path led to the rose garden and Emmeline let out a hiccup of sound.

She hated him, hated him, hated him!

How could he do this to her? She'd trusted him. Trusted him to protect her.

Emmeline blinked back tears and walked in circles around the rose garden, but her quick steps failed to soothe her. Her emotions ran even hotter.

She felt betrayed by Makin. Worse, she knew he was right.

Marrying him would change everything.

Marrying him guaranteed her child a life of unknown luxury and protection. There would be private jets and private schools and round-the-clock security. The baby would be envied, admired, doted on by all simply because he or she was Sheikh Al-Koury's child.

Amazing what money and power could do.

And she'd be a fool to walk away from that kind of power and security just because she wanted more. Because she needed love.

Emmeline swallowed hard, torn between the knowledge that Makin could provide a good life for her child and the desire to be free and independent, aware that freedom and independence would come with a price.

People would talk. People could be cruel. People could make her baby's life a living hell.

Emmeline paused, her gaze skimming the rosebushes. It was too early and cool yet for the roses to be in bloom and they still looked sharp and thorny, still shorn from the pruning they'd had several months before. She felt like the rosebushes—bare, prickly, unlovable.

"I'm not King William." Makin's deep voice came from behind her, at the entrance to the rose garden, and he sounded furious. "Nor am I Queen Claire. I am Makin Tahnoon Al-Koury, and I am here because I choose to be here. I didn't have to fly to Brabant with you. I could have put you on the plane and sent you off. But I didn't. I wanted to travel to the palace with you. I wanted to be there when you announced you were pregnant—"

"You wanted to see me humiliated?"

"No. I wanted to make sure you were all right. And when I listened to your mother tear you apart yesterday, I realized you needed me. You needed someone to stand up to her and tell her to back off. You needed someone to believe in you. Someone to protect you. And I can. And I will."

"But why? You might be altruistic when it comes to third-world nations, but you've no patience with spoiled, cosseted, self-indulgent royals like me."

"Obviously, I didn't know you. I thought I did, but I was wrong. But now that I do know you, there's so much to like—"

"Like, not love. You don't love me. You don't. And you can't pretend you do."

His silver-gray gaze raked over her, from the top of her pale golden head to the tips of her dark heels. "I don't have to love you to want you." He paused to allow his words to register, his expression intense. "And I do."

She stared at him, her heart starting to race. "You mean… my body."

"I mean you."

"But you don't want *me*."

His lips curved, his expression dark and dangerous. "Oh, but I do," he said, closing the distance between them and drawing her toward him.

She stiffened as she came into contact with the hard heat of his body, and she flashed to the kiss in the garden in Raha. The kiss had been lovely and yet overwhelming—hot, intense, beautiful, but it had made her want and need. She couldn't let herself go there again. Couldn't risk letting her heart hope again. "No," she choked, trying to twist free.

His head dipped, his mouth slanting across hers, silencing her protest.

It wasn't a light kiss or a tentative kiss. Makin kissed her hard, his lips parting hers with ruthless intent. She shuddered as his tongue plundered her mouth, taking and tasting her as if she already belonged to him.

But she didn't. She belonged to no one and she struggled to free herself, but he was too strong. She couldn't escape. Panic flooded her. She wouldn't be bought and sold. Wouldn't be handed over from one man to another. She wouldn't go through life spineless and powerless.

Furious, she bit Makin in the lower lip.

He cursed and lifted his head, arms loosening around her. His eyes glowed like molten silver. "What was that for?"

She punched him in the arm. "You don't own me!"

"Of course I don't. You're a woman, not a piece of property."

"Then why make a deal with my father before you come to me?"

"Because I was trying to help you—"

"You're just like him. Just like all of them. You don't respect me. You don't respect women—"

"Absolutely not true," he snapped, cutting her short. "I admired my mother immensely. She handled complex, difficult situations with dignity and grace, and I respect her more than anyone else I've ever met."

"What did she do that made her so admirable?"

"What didn't she do? She was a modern European woman married to a sheikh in the Middle East. She had to cope with my father's illness. She modeled strength and courage for me. And most of all, she was loving. She loved my father." He hesitated, shrugged. "She loved me."

"And that makes her remarkable."

"Yes."

He said it with such conviction and authority that she immediately believed it. And the fight suddenly left her.

Emmeline exhaled in a hard whoosh of air. "But you work so hard to accomplish things…"

"I do. But that's because there isn't a lot I need for me. I'm financially solvent. I'm blessed with good health. I've always felt loved and wanted. And so I can afford to focus on others, which allows me to give back."

"And so there's nothing you want? Nothing you need?"

"I didn't say that. Because I do want something. I want you."

His deep voice sent a thrill through her. *I want you.* There was such authority and purpose in his voice. Such firm conviction that she felt another ripple of shock and pleasure.

Alejandro had said he'd wanted her, but he'd always been the charming playboy, handsome but flirty and playful. Makin Al-Koury was far from flirty and playful. Makin was fierce and powerful and supremely focused. When he said he wanted her, she felt it in her bones.

"But why me?"

He was silent a long moment, his features hard, lashes lowered over his intense gaze. "You have no idea of your worth, do you?"

"I'm an expensive headache, Sheikh Al-Koury. A constant problem requiring attention." She smiled and yet her eyes burned.

"Everyone needs attention. And princesses—particularly beautiful princesses—are notoriously expensive."

She laughed, and his gaze dropped to her mouth as if he found it absolutely fascinating.

"I did some research on your riding career last night after you'd gone to bed," he added.

"Did you?"

He nodded. "Even watched several videos of you competing. You were extraordinary, Emmeline. Does your family have any idea of how gifted you are?"

She shifted uncomfortably. "I'm not that gifted. When I finally made the Olympic team I fell—"

"Listen to yourself. You *made* the Olympic team." His voice dropped, deepened. "You *made* the Olympic team. And I repeated that for your benefit because your family seems to have done nothing but break you down when they should have built you up and given you confidence and support and unconditional love."

Emmeline had to look away, absolutely overwhelmed by the fierceness in Makin's voice. She knew him well enough to know he meant every word he was saying. He truly believed she deserved support and love…unconditional love…and it staggered her. Made her ache for all the things she'd never known and made her hope for all the things she still wanted.

Love. Security.

Happiness.

After a moment when she was sure she had her emotions firmly in control she looked up into Makin's face, studied his lip. "Did I hurt you?"

He licked the inside of his lip. "Just a little blood. Nothing serious."

"I drew blood?"

"You have a mean bite."

She knew he was teasing her but she felt bad. "I'm sorry."

"I'm fine. And I'm glad you got mad. I'm glad you have some fight in you. Life isn't easy and one can't just lie down and die when things get hard."

"Is that what you would teach the baby?"

"Absolutely."

"Even if she's a girl?"

"Especially if she's a girl. Life's difficult and you're going to be confronted by adversity, and you're going to get knocked down. But that's just part of life and so you get up and shake yourself off and keep going."

"I thought only weak people got knocked down."

"Everybody gets knocked down. The secret is the getting up again. That's why I value mental toughness—resilience. You don't want difficulties to break you. You want them to make you stronger."

She was silent as she processed this. "Marrying you is definitely the right thing for the baby, but it's not easy for me. I have a lot of pride. I don't like being dependent on others. I don't want others to come in and fix my mistakes, or sort out my problems for me. That's my job. I'm not helpless or stupid—"

"Good. Because I'd never marry a woman who was."

Emmeline looked at him a long moment, her pride warring with common sense. Marrying him would be the best thing for the baby. It would give her child a home, a name, legitimacy. And yet it wasn't that simple. Emmeline had hopes and dreams… there were things she'd wanted for herself. Like marrying the man she loved.

"It would be so easy to just give in, Makin, and let you be Prince Charming and allow you to sweep me off my feet and right all the wrongs…but that's not what I want from a man. Not anymore."

"What do you want?"

"To be the prince. To wear a sword and ride off on the white stallion and slay my own dragons." She laughed at the picture she'd painted, but it was true. She was tired of being helpless and broken. Tired of needing fixing. "There is a strong person inside of me. I just have to find her. Free her."

"I think you're on your way," he answered, taking her hand and slipping his fingers through hers.

Makin's hand was warm, strong, and she glanced down at their entwined fingers, at the gold of his skin against the pale ivory of hers. It felt good to hold his hand. She felt good with him at her side. Maybe one day she could be a woman like Hannah or his mother. Maybe one day he could respect her…maybe even love her. "Did you really end things with Madeline?"

"Yes."

"Why?"

"Because when I marry you tomorrow I am forsaking all others."

"You mean that?"

"Of course."

"So…our marriage…will be real?"

"Absolutely."

"Oh."

"You look shocked."

"Not shocked. Just nervous."

He led her to the bench near the sundial, and sat down, and drew her onto his lap. Emmeline blushed as she felt the warmth of him through his trousers, and the corded muscles of his thighs against her backside, and shifted uneasily. "Why nervous?" he asked, running a hand over her ponytail.

She liked the feel of his hand on her hair. It felt good. Warm. Soothing. As well as a little sexy. "I...don't have a lot of experience."

"You said Alejandro was your first."

"Yes. And it wasn't good. I didn't like it."

He shifted her around to look into her face. "The first time isn't usually the best."

"I don't think I'd enjoy it after thirty times with him. It just wasn't...good."

"Did you like kissing him?"

She shook her head. "It didn't feel like anything."

"Did you like kissing me?"

Heat surged to her cheeks. She looked away. "It was all right," she admitted grudgingly.

"Just all right?"

She glanced back at him. His lips were twitching. He was trying not to laugh. "Are you fishing for compliments?"

"No."

"Sounds like it."

"No, I'm quite confident in that department—"

"Maybe a little too confident."

"You think so?"

"Quite possibly."

"Let's test that theory, shall we?" he asked, dipping his head, his mouth slanting across hers.

As Makin's head dropped, he breathed in her fragrance—fresh, light, sweet—and he hardened instantly. But he kissed her slowly this morning, taking his time, aware that he had all the time in the world because she would be his. She'd be his wife. His lover. The mother of his child. Call it fate or karma, but she was meant to be his, and now he kissed her as if it was the first time and he was just discovering the shape of her lips, and the softness of her mouth.

He felt Emmeline tremble against him, leaning toward him, and he held her closer, but even then, he refused to rush.

Maybe one day she could be a knight or brave prince, but she wasn't there yet. She didn't believe in herself yet. Didn't even know who she was yet.

Right now Princess Emmeline reminded him of Sleeping Beauty. She needed to be woken with a kiss, a proper kiss, a kiss that would let her know she was beautiful and desirable and safe.

He'd never hurt her. He'd always protect her. She needed to know that first. And then she needed to know how much he wanted her.

Because he did.

He slid the tip of his tongue along her upper lip, finding nerves in the delicate skin, and felt her nipples harden against his chest. His tongue flicked the other lip and he heard the hitch in her breath.

She was growing warm and pliant against him, her body molding to his, and it took all his self-control not to unbutton her blouse or pull up her skirt to get at her bare skin. He wanted to feel the seductive softness of her skin, and explore her tempting curves. He ached to have her naked and wet and open, but he'd make sure she was ready. Not just physically, but emotionally.

Emmeline's first time had hurt her. Her second time needed to be perfect.

Reluctantly he lifted his head. He gazed down into her eyes. They were darker now, deep purple, and cloudy with passion. "Marry me, Emmeline."

"And what do you get out of this, Makin?"

His lips brushed hers, sending an electric shiver dancing up and down her spine. "You."

CHAPTER TWELVE

THEY were supposed to be having a pre-dinner cocktail with her parents that evening in the elegant wood-paneled chamber her father favored, but her mother hadn't yet appeared.

Emmeline was sitting on the narrow loveseat with Makin at her side but she couldn't get comfortable, not when his thigh pressed to hers.

He was warm and making her warmer. And she couldn't relax. Her thoughts were absolutely chaotic and running wild at the moment.

But then, they had been all day, ever since she'd woken up and discovered that Makin had asked her father for her hand.

Which made no sense. At all.

Why would Makin do that? He said he wanted her. But that made no sense, either.

It really didn't.

Emmeline shot Makin a mistrustful glance from beneath her lashes. He was big, powerful, wealthy, gorgeous…he could have anyone…and he said he wanted her?

No. Impossible. Her father had to be paying him something. But Makin was one of the richest men in the world. He didn't need money…

"If your father wasn't here, I'd kiss that look off your face," Makin growled at her, his voice pitched so low only she could hear him.

Emmeline cradled her glass of ice water closer to her stomach and hissed, "Stop acting like a caveman. I'm not something you can just tackle and drag next to the fire."

"No? I quite like the idea."

She cast him another reproving glance. He didn't quell in the slightest, but then, Makin was tall, strong, thickly muscled. "You're unbearable. Now please scoot over. You're crowding me." Which was true. They were smashed together on this tiny settee as if they really were a newly engaged couple. *A couple in love.*

He was a horrible man.

A horribly confident and terribly appealing man.

She wondered yet again what he'd be like in bed.

Emmeline's insides suddenly flipped, her breath catching in her throat, her breasts exquisitely sensitive.

"It's called cozy, Emmie."

"Well, I don't like it." Because sitting this close to him, she couldn't see, hear, feel or think of anything but him. And the way he kissed. And how his hands felt on her. And how she felt when he was holding her...

She liked it when he held her. Liked his mouth on hers, and her body against his and she'd never felt this way about anyone before. She'd never wanted anyone before and she wanted Makin. But she wanted more than just lips and hands and skin. She wanted all of him.

Which was so confusing...

"I didn't pick this room, or the couch," he retorted.

True. This was the room reserved for close friends and family, and despite the high ceiling and tall windows framed in rich dark green velvet curtains, the chamber was filled with petite antique pieces that had been passed down for generations. Pieces that had been made hundreds of years ago for people who were definitely smaller than they were today.

"I wonder what's keeping your mother," her father said with a frown. "Perhaps I should go check on her?"

"I can go, if you'd like?" Emmeline offered, seeing an opportunity to escape.

"No need for you to race around in your condition," William

answered, setting his drink on an end table. "You stay and relax. I'll enquire after your mother."

Makin glanced down at her as the door closed behind her father, a lazy smile playing at his lips. "Nice try."

She stood up, walked away from him. "This is all so…fake."

"How so?"

"Our engagement—"

"No, that's real. I asked for your hand in marriage, and we are getting married tomorrow." He paused. "By the way, you look incredible." His voice deepened with appreciation, his gaze slowly drifting over her bared shoulder to the pink-and-plum shirred fabric shaping her breasts and outlining her flat tummy, before falling to a long train of pale pink at her feet. "I don't think I've ever seen you look better."

She glanced down at the asymmetrical neckline of her dress and then lower, to where the plum color gave way to the pink over her hips. It was a very slim, very body-conscious evening gown and in another month or two she'd start to show and she wouldn't be able to wear it. "It's the dress," she said, touching the bodice covered in crystals. "Couture does that for a woman."

"It's the other way around, Emmeline. You make the dress." He held his hand out to her. "I have something for you."

She shivered as she glanced at him where he sat on the small antique couch. He was huge and the couch was tiny and she could still remember the way it had felt to sit so close, the heat of his hip warming her, the corded muscle of his thigh pressing against hers. "You make me so nervous, Makin."

"Why?"

"I don't know. But every time I look at you, I get butterflies."

"Then I'll come to you." He left the couch, walked toward her and, removing a ring box, he snapped it open.

Emmeline blinked at the enormous diamond ring cradled by the darkest blue velvet.

"Give me your hand," he said.

Her fingers curled into a fist. She couldn't take her eyes off the ring. The diamond was huge. Four carats? Five? "Is that what I think it is?" she whispered, mouth drying.

"Yes."

"I can't wear that."

"Why not?"

"It's ridiculous, Makin. Far too extravagant. Something small and sentimental would have been nice—"

"It's my mother's wedding ring."

"Oh." She exhaled in a whoosh, and looked up at him apologetically. "I'm sorry. I didn't mean it that way—"

"You jump to conclusions too quickly."

Her heart was racing now. She felt almost sick. "I know. Another fault of mine," she murmured, putting her left hand in his. She was shaking as he slid the ring onto her finger. The stone was an immense princess-cut diamond, and smaller diamonds crusted the narrow band.

The ring was stunning. It glinted and sparkled as it caught the light.

Tahnoon Al-Koury had given this ring to Yvette, Makin's mother. Makin now gave it to her. Her heart suddenly ached. "It's really lovely," she said huskily.

"And so are you."

Her head lifted. Tears shimmered in her eyes. "I'm not. Not really."

"How can you say that, Emmeline?"

"Because I'm not."

"Have you looked in a mirror?"

"Yes."

"And what do you see?"

"Faults, flaws—" She broke off, bit hard into her bottom lip. "Makin, I'm not the woman in the magazines. I'm not that beautiful, glossy princess."

"Thank God."

Her head jerked up. Her eyes met his.

"I don't want a wife who is beautiful but fake, Emmeline. I want someone real. And you, Emmeline, are real."

He was prevented from saying more by the arrival of her parents. Her mother led them to dinner in the Crimson Dining Room. The table, of course, was impossibly elegant, with the royal china being used on top of heavy silver chargers. Crystal glittered beneath the antique chandeliers and dinner was subdued, conversation stilted, for the first half hour of the meal. But the wine was flowing freely, and as the second course was removed, Queen Claire became livelier.

Emmeline glanced nervously at her mother, aware that alcohol always made Emmeline's father quieter and her mother more chatty. Claire was becoming extremely chatty—practically verbose.

Makin was still on his first glass of wine and Emmeline wondered what he was thinking.

Makin caught her glance and smiled at her, which made her stomach do a funny nosedive.

He was really too good-looking. Feeling jittery and shy, she glanced down at her left hand resting in her lap to study the enormous engagement ring. It was the whitest stone she'd ever seen, and the exquisite cut continued to catch the light, glinting bits of blue, white and silver fire.

She glanced at him again and discovered he was looking at her, his silver-gray gaze intense.

Tomorrow night at this time they'd be married. Husband and wife. And from what he'd said earlier, he intended to be a real husband to her....

"Don't say I didn't warn you," Claire repeated, gesturing for one of the footmen to fill her wineglass again. "She's always been a problem. From the time she was an infant. There has never been a baby that cried so much."

Emmeline felt Makin's gaze on her again, but this time she looked pointedly away, a small, tight smile on her face. She wasn't a problem. She didn't know why her mother always seemed to think she was. It's not as if Claire had ever taken time to know her. They were rarely alone together. Her parents had busy, important lives and Emmeline had been raised by hired help—nannies and tutors—before being sent to a very small private girls' boarding school in France not long after she turned fourteen.

The boarding school had a reputation for being strict, but

Emmeline had been happy there. There was order to the day and the rules were logical and consequences appropriate to the crime. Emmeline didn't mind that fraternizing with boys was absolutely forbidden.

School was the place she could escape her mother's unsmiling gaze and the tension that permeated the d'Arcy family palace.

"You can't really blame her, Claire, she was quite small at birth," her father interjected, rousing himself from his usual silence. He glanced at Makin, brow furrowing, bushy gray eyebrows pulling together. "She was not even four pounds when we got her. I think the nanny tried five different formulas before we found one she could tolerate."

"See? Emmeline has always been impossible to please," Claire added thickly. "Even as an infant, she had a temper. She'd cry for hours. Refused to be comforted."

"Babies cry," William said.

Emmeline glanced at her father, surprised that he was defending her. He rarely took on her mother, but perhaps the wine tonight had given him liquid courage.

William's expression softened as he gazed at her. "You look lovely tonight, Emmie."

She was touched by the compliment. Her lips curved in a smile. "Thank you. It's the dress—"

"It's not the dress," William interrupted. "It's you. You've grown up and you are…you look…just like her."

"Who, Father?"

"William!" Claire rebuked.

But William lifted a hand as if telling his wife to be quiet. "Your…mother."

"I'm her mother," Claire corrected stiffly.

"Birth mother," William amended.

Goose bumps covered Emmeline's arms and the fine hair at her nape stood on end. Stunned, she glanced at Claire and then back to her father. "Did you know my birth mother?"

"Yes," her father answered after the faintest hesitation. "And we think, in light of tomorrow's ceremony, you should know who she was, too."

Emmeline's pulse raced. Her hands shook in her lap. "Who was she? What was she like? Did you ever meet her?" The questions tumbled from her as fast as she could say them.

"Of course we met her," Queen Claire answered brusquely. "We wouldn't adopt just any baby. We couldn't raise just any child. We adopted you because you were…different."

"Different?" Emmeline repeated wonderingly.

Claire took a sip of wine. "Special," she added coolly. "You weren't just any baby. You were royal."

A moment ago Emmeline's heart had raced. Now her blood seemed to freeze in her veins. *"Royal?"*

"Your mother was Princess Jacqueline," her father said, getting to his feet. "My sister."

Emmeline shook her head. "No…I don't…no…"

"It's true," Claire said flatly, slurring a little as she stared into her now-empty wineglass with some consternation. "William's baby sister. You were, what? Ten years older than her?"

He stood next to the table, fingertips pressed to the cloth. "Twelve." He sounded grave. "She wasn't planned. My parents had given up on having another. She was quite a surprise." His voice suddenly quavered. "My parents adored her. I did, too. No one imagined that by sending her away…no one could have dreamed…it was a mistake, a terrible, terrible mistake."

Emmeline's head spun. "I don't understand. My aunt Jacqueline died at twenty from a rare heart condition—"

"That was a fabricated story her parents told the public to cover the sordid facts of Jacqueline's death," Claire said with great relish. "Your mother died giving birth to you. Now you know the truth."

For a moment all was silent and then Emmeline spoke. "All these years you've known, but you hid the truth from me. Why?"

"It didn't seem relevant," Claire answered.

Emmeline exhaled in a rush. "Perhaps not to you, but it's everything to me."

Claire banged her hand on the table. "And why is it so important?"

"Because."

"That's it?"

"Yes." Emmeline rose, stood for a moment with her fingertips pressed to the table. "It's how I feel. And I have a right to feel what I feel. I have a right to be who I want to be. I think I'm going to have coffee and dessert later. If you'll excuse me."

She turned now to Makin and offered him a devastating smile. "Would you care to join me, darling?"

Makin would never forget that moment. He would have clapped if it had been appropriate. It wasn't.

But this…this was why he wanted her. This was why she was his.

She was brilliant. Stunning. Majestic.

He'd listened to the revelation regarding her birth mother in silence, disgusted that William and Claire had kept the truth from her and even more disgusted that tonight's dinner was when they'd chosen to share the news.

But they had. And Emmeline had handled it with grace, strength, dignity.

He loved her for it.

She was every inch the royal d'Arcy princess. Daughter of Europe's beloved Princess Jacqueline d'Arcy.

Jacqueline would have been proud.

He rose to his feet, buttoned his black dinner jacket. "Yes," he said simply, firmly, and offered her his arm.

Emmeline's legs felt like jelly as they exited to the hall and she was grateful for Makin's arm. Grateful for his support.

Her legs continued to feel like jelly as she climbed the stairs to her room and she held his arm tightly, thinking she couldn't have gotten through this without him.

He gave her confidence. He made her feel safe. Strong. Good.

As if she truly mattered.

And somehow, with him, she almost believed she did.

Emmeline swallowed hard as they approached her room. "Never a dull moment around here, is there?"

"No," he agreed, opening the door for her and then following her inside.

She wandered around the room for a moment, too agitated to sit.

She wasn't the daughter of a Brabant commoner. Her mother had been Princess Jacqueline, Europe's most beautiful royal, and she'd died in childbirth. She'd died giving life to her.

It was terrible. Tragic. But at least Emmeline now knew the truth.

"So now you know," Makin said quietly, arms folded across his chest. "It was a horrible way to find out, but at least you know. There are no more secrets. No more skeletons in the closet. It's all out in the open."

Emmeline turned, looked at him. "If she hadn't had me, she'd be alive."

"If her parents hadn't sent her away to give birth in secret, she would have lived."

"You think so?"

"Yes."

She nodded, and rubbed her arms. "And here I am, twenty-five years later, single and pregnant, too."

"Yes. But things happen, mistakes happen, and we learn from them. We grow from them. And I look forward to starting a family with you. I think it's going to be quite interesting."

Her lips curved in a tremulous smile. "It certainly will be a change."

"And an adventure." He smiled back at her. "You're good for me, you know. You're shaking things up. Making me feel alive."

"And you give me confidence. I'm already stronger because of you."

"You were always strong. You just didn't know it."

"I wish it were true."

"It's true." He closed the distance between them, and took her hands in his, kissing one palm and then the other, and finally her mouth.

He was just deepening the kiss when her bedroom door opened and a muffled cough came from the hall.

Makin lifted his head and, blushing, Emmeline faced her father who was standing in the hall holding an enormous garment bag. "It wasn't all the way shut," William said gruffly. "I can come back later."

"No," Emmeline said, cheeks still hot. "Come in, please."

William hesitated. "I don't know if this will fit, but it was Jacqueline's. She wore this gown for her debutante ball. Mother saved it, and I thought perhaps you might want to wear it for the wedding…." His voice drifted off. He swallowed uncomfortably. "You might already have something—"

"I'd love to wear it," Emmeline interrupted him, taking the garment bag from him. It was surprisingly heavy. Must have a huge skirt. "But you didn't have to bring it here yourself. You could have sent it with one of the maids in the morning."

"I know. Claire said the same thing, but I wanted to see you. To make sure you were okay."

"Come in," she repeated, carrying the garment bag to the bed.

"I shall go," Makin said, "and let you two talk." He dropped another kiss on Emmeline's lips before walking out, closing the door quietly behind him.

William stood in the middle of the room, hands in his pockets. "My timing is terrible."

"I'm glad you're here. There are so many things I'd like to know."

"I imagine there are." He hesitated. "I know it sounds cruel, what my parents did, sending Jacqueline away to give birth. But they were old-fashioned, and they'd been raised in a time where unplanned pregnancies were hushed. Covered up. They thought they were doing the right thing. They truly believed they were protecting Jacqueline. They had no idea it would turn out the way it did."

"I don't remember my grandparents as cruel," she said, sitting down on the bed next to the garment bag.

"They weren't," he agreed. "And losing Jacqueline destroyed them. She was their baby. They never recovered from her death.

After the funeral, Father moved to the dowager's château on the edge of the city, and Mother remained here to be close to you."

"Did Grandmother spend time with me?" Emmeline asked.

"She did. In the beginning. She was with you almost every day. Claire had to fight her for you. They had terrible rows—" He broke off, laughed as he sat down heavily, but the laugh sounded like pain. "I'm so sorry. Emmeline, we got it all wrong. We just tried to protect Jacquie, and then you, and it didn't work. The truth is so much better. Remember that."

She nodded, thinking that this was the time to tell him. He'd opened the door for her, created trust. Now all she had to do was tell the truth and confess that Makin wasn't her baby's father, that Alejandro Ibanez was, tell him that with Alejandro gone, Makin had offered for her out of some misguided sense of duty.

She knew her father would free her of the engagement. He couldn't possibly insist on her marrying Makin once he knew the truth.

But before she could find the right words to break the news, William reached for her hand and he carried it to his cheek. "You don't know how happy I am for you." He squeezed her fingers, overcome by gratitude. "It means so much to me that you have what your mother never had. The opportunity to marry the man you love, to have a normal life…or as normal as you can as a princess."

Emmeline's throat sealed closed as she watched the emotions—pain, relief, hope—pass one by one over his lined face. He'd had a far harder life than she'd ever imagined. "It's difficult to have a normal life when you're a royal, isn't it?" she said to him.

"It is. Especially when you're as beautiful as you are." He kissed her forehead. "I'm glad you have Makin. He's not the sort to indulge in make-believe. You can rest assured he's marrying you for all the right reasons. Now get some sleep, my dear. Good night."

CHAPTER THIRTEEN

MAKIN watched Emmeline walk down the palace chapel on her father's arm. King William wore his black royal uniform, a military dress coat from when he'd served in the Brabant Air Force as a twenty-year-old. His posture was as erect and proud as if he were still a military man.

But it was Emmeline who held Makin's attention, Emmeline who took his breath away in her mother's white debutante gown with a tiara on top of her golden head.

More ivory than ice-white, the strapless, heart-shaped bodice hugged her breasts and rib cage before nipping in dramatically at Emmeline's small waist. The very full silk skirt was covered in a pleated swirling pattern made to look like overblown roses, with the beaded ivory silk flowers growing larger as they moved toward the hem. The skirt's pleated silk caught the light and created shadows. Makin didn't think she could have picked a more beautiful gown to be married in.

For Emmeline, the brief wedding ceremony passed in a blur of sound and motion. There was the sound of the organ playing something too loud and bright. She and her father walked down the chapel aisle, the pews empty except for her mother in the front and the bishop waiting at the altar with Makin.

She felt her father kiss her and then give her hand to Makin. She heard the bishop's voice, and then heard Makin saying words, repeating the vows. She repeated the same vows. The bishop spoke again and then there was the exchange of rings. Makin lifted her veil and kissed her on the lips.

And it was done.

They were married.

There was an even briefer gathering after, consisting of wedding cake and champagne. Emmeline had a sip of champagne and a couple of bites of cake but couldn't eat or drink more than that.

She caught a glimpse of her reflection in the Gold Drawing Room mirror, seeing the swish of her full silk skirt from the back and the small, corseted waist. The dress hadn't needed to be altered a bit. It fitted Emmeline perfectly, which meant she and her mother had been the same size. Small. Slender. Elegant.

Emmeline suddenly wanted out of the dress, away from Brabant. This was the old life. She was ready for the next.

"Have you had enough cake and champagne?" she asked Makin.

His gaze held hers a moment, the silver depths warm. "Yes."

"I have, too. I'm going to go change."

"I'll call my flight crew, let them know we'll soon be on the way."

Upstairs, Emmeline had nearly finished changing into traveling clothes—a trim designer suit in taupe and pink. She'd just slid her heels on and was putting in the first of her pearl earrings when her bedroom door opened and closed.

Emmeline turned around to find her mother standing awkwardly by the door. "I came to offer my help, but you've already changed," Claire said crisply.

"Yes," Emmeline agreed, attaching the other earring. "Everything's packed. Just need to switch out my purse and I'm ready to go."

"Have you rung for someone to take your bags?"

"The maid did."

"Do you need…any money, or anything…before you go?"

Emmeline's lips curved but the rest of her face felt hard. "No. Makin's loaded. He'll take care of everything."

"Emmeline!"

Emmeline's eyes burned, and she swallowed with effort, her

throat aching with suppressed emotion. "What do you expect me to say, Mother? Two days ago you made it perfectly clear how you felt about me. That I was an embarrassment, a problem, nothing short of a failure—"

"I never called you a failure!"

"But an embarrassment and a problem."

The queen took a slow breath. "You haven't been an easy child."

"But I'm not a child, Mother. I'm twenty-five…a woman who is going to have a child, and I can promise you this, I will never tell my child that he or she is a problem or an embarrassment. What a horrible thing for a mother to say to her daughter."

"I was caught off guard."

"Apparently you're always caught off guard."

Silence descended in the room, twilight casting long shadows across the bedroom floor, turning the rose-patterned carpet into shades of lavender and gray.

Claire cleared her throat, and again. "Perhaps I haven't been the best mother," she said after a moment. "But I tried. I did. I realize now it wasn't enough. You were always so emotional, so needy—"

"Not again." Emmeline closed her eyes at the familiar refrain.

"Hear me out. I don't express things well, Emmeline. I'm not good with words like you are. I'm not comfortable sharing my feelings. I never have been. But that doesn't mean I don't… love…you."

"Hard word for you to say, isn't it?"

"Yes."

"I've never heard you say *love* before." Emmeline locked her knees, lifted her chin. Today she would not fall apart. She would not leave in pieces. "You've never once told me you loved me."

"Because it wasn't necessary. I was your mother. You were my daughter—"

"And children like tenderness. They like affection. I craved it, Mother. Morning, noon and night."

"I know. You have such strong emotions, you feel everything so intensely. Just like your mother." Her voice quavered.

"Everybody loved your mother. Her death devastated your grandparents. It broke William's heart, too, because he was Jacqueline's big brother. He adored her. That's why he wanted you."

"And you didn't."

"No, Emmie, I did. I wanted you and I tried my best with you, but you were inconsolable as an infant. You cried for the first six months of your life, day and night. Your grandmother was always reaching for you, wanting to comfort you, and I'd tell her no, that you were my daughter and I wanted to hold you. And I did. I used to walk with you in the nursery, back and forth, for hours. William would come up at two in the morning and he'd see me with you, and he'd tell me to come to bed. But I wouldn't. I was so determined to be a good mother. I was so determined to find a way to make you love me." She broke off, tears filling her eyes. "You never did."

"But I have always loved you. As a child I wanted nothing more than your approval. But you couldn't give me that."

"You were just so like her."

"Like Jacqueline."

Claire nodded.

"And you resented me for that," Emmeline concluded.

"I think I did."

"Why?"

"Because I wanted you to be like me."

Seated in the limousine next to Makin, Emmeline stared out the window, overwhelmed. So much had happened in just a handful of days. Alejandro's death. The revelation that Princess Jacqueline was the birth mother she'd never known. Her marriage to Makin. And then the scene with Claire in her bedroom. It was a lot to take in.

"Are you all right?" Makin asked, his voice a deep rumble in the darkness of the car.

"Yes," she answered faintly, her face averted, her gaze fixed on a point far away. Her heart felt battered. Bruised.

"Did something happen when you went upstairs after the ceremony?"

"How do you know?"

"I can see the change in you. I hear it in your voice."

It amazed her that he could already read her so well. "My mother came to see me."

"What did she have to say?"

Emmeline felt a hot rush of emotion and she closed her eyes so he wouldn't see. "She wanted me to know that despite appearances, she loved me. And I told her that I'd always loved her."

He was silent a moment. "But it wasn't exactly warm and satisfying?"

"No." She laughed, a quick, sharp laugh even as she blinked back tears. "But then, nothing with my mother ever is."

On board the plane, Emmeline curled into her chair and gave in to sleep.

While she slept, Makin called his close friend, Sultan Malek Nuri, to see how the Raha conference was going. Malek relayed that everything was going well, but, of course, everyone wished Makin was there.

"When do you return?" Malek asked. "I'd thought it was today, but maybe it's later tonight?"

"No. I'm actually en route to Marquette."

"Your Caribbean island?"

"Yes." Makin hesitated, wondering how to share his news, as Malek's wife Nicolette and her sisters were quite friendly, as well as distantly related, to Emmeline. Malek and Nicolette were also aware that Makin had never been a fan of Emmeline's. "I just got married," he said, believing the best way through something was directly.

"You…what?"

"I married Emmeline d'Arcy."

Malek Nuri was successful because he knew when to speak and when to hold his peace. But he did neither now. He laughed, a great rich laugh of pure amusement. "Makin, my friend, I thought you were just seeing her safely home."

"I was."

"What happened?"

"I couldn't let her go."

Emmeline didn't wake until they were in their final approach and close to landing.

"Where are we?" Emmeline asked, looking out the window. She'd expected a sea of sand, but instead it was blue underneath. Water.

"The Caribbean. We'll be landing on my island Marquette in the next few minutes, but look out the window, we're about to be treated to an incredible sunset now."

He was right. The sun was low in the sky, a great red ball of fire moments away from dropping into the ocean. The horizon was already turning orange and purple and Emmeline felt a thrill of pleasure. "It's gorgeous," she said.

"Dramatic, isn't it?"

She smiled, amused by his word choice. "So sometimes dramatic is good?"

His gaze met hers and held. "Yes. Sometimes dramatic is perfect."

On the ground a driver in a white open Jeep met them at the airstrip and drove them across the estate to a sprawling plantation house. The two-hundred-and-fifty-year-old house had been built in the colonial style, with a steep thatched roof, high ceilings and thick stone walls to keep the interior cool.

On entering the house, Emmeline discovered she could see the ocean from virtually every room, with the last lingering rays of light turning the sea into a parfait of purple, lavender and red.

The house itself was furnished in the dark woods of the colonial style, with a mix of Spanish, French and English antiques, furniture brought over from Europe during the sixteenth and seventeenth centuries. The fabrics, though, were all soft and light—white linens, red, green and blue cheerful tropical cotton prints.

It was a happy house, she thought, following Makin on the

tour that ended in the spacious master bedroom with windows everywhere.

By the time they finished the tour, her luggage had already been brought in and a maid had unpacked her clothes into the large mahogany dresser and closet.

Makin left her so she could bathe and change for dinner. With the door closed, Emmeline did a little twirl, her nerves almost getting the best of her.

So this was it. No more solo rooms. They were married. They'd share the master bedroom from now on.

She battled her panic by walking slowly around the bedroom, trying to get comfortable even as her gaze avoided the bed. It looked as though it was custom made, with a massive king-size frame, and it was draped with sheer white linens. She knew that it was in this bed that Makin would want to consummate the marriage tonight—

She broke off, shook her head, unable to finish the thought.

Take it one step at a time, she told herself. *Bathe, dress, meet Makin for dinner, and then worry about the rest later.*

It was a good plan, she thought thirty minutes later, but it wasn't going to work.

She couldn't do this. Couldn't meet him for dinner and then go to bed with him as if it was the normal thing to do. She barely knew him. Had kissed him a few times, but that wasn't a relationship.

She was still panicking when the maid knocked on the door and asked if Her Highness needed assistance. The maid, like the rest of the staff, spoke French.

"Yes," Emmeline answered. "Can you please let Sheikh Al-Koury know I'm not feeling well and won't be able to join him?"

"You won't be joining him for dinner, Your Highness?"

"That's correct. Please tell him I don't feel well and I'm going to bed."

CHAPTER FOURTEEN

HE didn't even knock. He just barged through the bedroom and into the bath where she was still chin-deep in now-tepid water.

"What's wrong?" he demanded, his gaze sweeping from the top of her head, where her blond hair was piled high in a knot, to the tips of her toes peeping from the water at the foot of the tub. "What's happened? Do you need to see a doctor?"

"No."

"You're not well?"

"No."

"Are you cramping? Are you queasy?"

"No!" She swallowed guiltily and slid a little deeper into the hot water. "I'm just…tired."

"Tired?"

"Yes. And I think I should just go to bed…you know…right now instead of after dinner."

"So you're not sick?"

"No. Not sick."

He swore beneath his breath and pushed a hand through his black hair, ruffling it on end. "So you're perfectly fine?"

"Other than feeling tired, yes."

He straightened, jaw tightening as his hands fisted at his side. "Do you have any idea how scared I was for you? I thought you were in pain. I thought you were miscarrying—"

"I'm not. And nothing's wrong. Okay? I was just…" She shook her head, looked away before glancing back at him. "Avoiding you."

"That's what this is all about?"

"Yes. I was nervous about consummating the marriage so I decided to stay in the bath and hide. Feel better?"

"No."

Now she felt foolish, embarrassed and angry with herself. Why did she think she could be the hero in a story if she wasn't even brave enough to face her husband? "I'm a coward, Makin. You know that. I'm shriveling to nothing in this cold bath because I'm hiding from you. Does that make you feel better?"

"No. But this will." And he leaned over the tub and scooped Emmeline from the bath, carried her soaking wet into the bedroom where he dropped her on the bed.

Before she could scramble backward, Makin moved over her, catching her wrists in his hands, pressing them down onto the bed, and straddled her hips with his thighs. "Stop hiding," he gritted through clenched teeth. "Stop running away and start living."

"Get off!" she choked, furious.

"I will when I feel like it," he answered, his gaze slowly sweeping over her wet puckered breasts. "Because isn't that what you do? You leave me outside, sitting by myself, waiting for my bride to join me when my bride in reality has no intention of joining me."

"I wanted to."

"If you wanted to, you would have come. Instead you send a maid to tell me you're going to bed."

"I was afraid!" she cried, trying desperately hard to twist free.

"Of what?"

"Of you. Of this." She was panting from exertion and frustration.

"And what's so scary about this?"

"All of it. Being naked. Being touched. Being known."

"Get over it. Because I'm going to touch you and know you and make you feel good if it's the last thing I do."

The heat in his eyes made her heart lurch. Emmeline drew a

panicked breath which only emphasized the rise and fall of her bare, gleaming breasts. "Even if I say I don't want to?"

"You knew when we got married it would be a real marriage, and it's going to be." His gaze wandered slowly down her body, from the thrust of her collarbone to the peaked swell of her breasts, down her ribs to her small waist and rounded hips. "You have the most beautiful body, Emmeline. I can't wait to touch you and taste you, everywhere."

"I can," she huffed.

He had the gall to laugh as he lowered his head to kiss her collarbone. His mouth brushed across the length of the fragile bone and goose bumps covered her skin, making her nipples pebble tighter. "At least your nerve endings there work," he murmured, his mouth working its way down her collarbone to the upper slope of her breast.

Heat washed through her as his lips closed around one peaked breast, his mouth wet and warm against the cool hard nipple. She shuddered as he sucked, tension coiling deep inside her, making her aware there were things she didn't know, had never felt.

He moved to the other breast, laved the other nipple with attention even as his hands stroked her flat stomach and the curve of her hips.

He knew exactly how to make her feel. And she was feeling so much.

He was sucking harder on the nipple, and Emmeline pressed against him for relief, but it was impossible to find when his mouth was driving her wild. The pressure, tight and rhythmic, made her aware of how empty she felt, how much she needed him.

And she did need him. She needed him to touch her, kiss her, lick her, fill her. She'd let him do anything if he'd satisfy the aching emptiness within her. She'd never felt so tight and so hollow at the same time. Her body throbbed with the worst of the need between her legs.

His hand trailed down her flat belly, caressing her abdomen, skimming her belly button before stroking lightly across one jutting hipbone. She hissed a breath as his palm circled over the hipbone, sending sparks of sensation shooting through her. Her inner muscles squeezed, gripping nothing and yet she'd never felt so hot or wet before. She could feel the dampness of her own body, the hint of moisture at her thighs.

His fingers brushed over the hipbone again and then down her outer thigh and back up. Again and again he traced her thigh as his mouth followed the path his hand had just taken, tongue on her belly, circling her belly button and then outlining the curve of hipbone.

"Open your legs," he said, kissing the hollow where her thigh joined her pelvis. It was such a light kiss and yet she shuddered.

"Can't," she gritted and shuddered yet again as he kissed her through the golden curls at the juncture of her thighs. His warm breath made her go hot and then cold and little spots danced and exploded against her mind's eye.

"Why not?" he asked, sliding one finger down the front of her, through the curls and between her lips to touch her.

Emmeline gasped, eyes opening wide, and tried to scoot away. "I'll lose control."

"That's what you're supposed to do."

"No. Not good. Not good at all."

She heard him smother a laugh. "Why not?" he asked, stroking her again, his finger sliding up, then down once more, sliding deeper this time, over the tight bud to her slick inner folds.

"I'll feel too much," she gasped, thinking she was already feeling way, way too much. "And fall apart and that's never, ever good."

"But if you don't fall apart, you don't experience pleasure. And pleasure is a good thing."

He was still stroking her, and she was finding it harder and harder to focus on anything but the delicious sensations he was creating with his touch. But the pleasure wasn't just sexual, her entire body felt sensitive, intense and alive.

This time she didn't resist as he parted her legs and shifted his body to settle between her thighs.

She knew where he was, but it was still a shock when his mouth covered her sex, his lips and tongue touching, tasting her.

"Makin," she choked.

His tongue and fingers together caressed her, and the sensation seemed to grow, building, teetering between pleasure and pain.

Her hips rose as the tension coiled in her belly, tight and hard and far from soothing. His tongue stroked her, his fingers teased her, one filling her, sliding in and out and matching the flick of his tongue.

"Dammit," she choked, her body so hot, her skin growing damp. She wanted something else, wanted release but didn't know how to get it, find it, not when the pressure kept building until she felt mad with it.

"Can't, can't, can't," she repeated wildly, and just then he sucked on her sex, drawing tight on her until she arched and screamed, everything within her shattering, her body convulsing against his mouth, around his finger.

For long moments she struggled to catch her breath as her body jumped and jerked, exquisitely sensitive from head to toe. She'd never felt anything like that in her entire life. "That's an orgasm," she said, dazed.

She felt Makin smile as he kissed the inside of her trembling thigh. "Yes. That's an orgasm."

She drew a rough breath. "I can see why that could be addictive."

"See? You do need me," he said and the husky tone of his voice sent another wave of sharp pleasure racing through her.

"Maybe," she said sleepily.

"Just maybe?" he repeated, sitting up to look down at her.

With a jolt she realized he was still dressed. The sense of pleasure dimmed, overshadowed by a feeling of impropriety. Good girls didn't lose control…good girls didn't enjoy sex… good girls—

"Don't do it," he said curtly, interrupting the punitive voice within her, the one constantly taking her to task.

"Do what?" she asked.

"Ruin this by overthinking things."

"According to you, not thinking got me into trouble in the first place."

"Yes. But I'm not trouble. I'm your husband, and what we do together is a good thing, and you felt good until you started letting fear take over." He was unbuttoning his shirt, and then peeling it back from his powerful shoulders. His chest was all bronze muscle, his stomach so hard it looked as if it'd been carved from stone. "I don't subscribe to fear."

Her eyes grew round as his feet hit the ground and he stood next to the bed, unbuckling his belt and unzipping his pants, stripping his remaining clothes off one by one.

Alejandro had been naked with her that one night in March, but she hadn't really looked at him. Everything that night had been a haze of panic and fear, but Emmeline found it impossible not to look at Makin.

He was all male, incredibly male, from the wide shoulders to the tapered waist to the corded muscles of his thighs, and that didn't even include his very big, very erect member.

Her gaze locked on the length of his erection and it was a little too impressive. But then, everything about him was big.

Intimidating.

"That," she said, gulping, "will not fit in me."

His lips curved but his eyes burned with heat. "It will. Your body is an amazing thing."

"It's too big."

"You're very wet."

She cringed, shoulders rising to her ears. "It hurt with…him."

"You were a virgin, and it didn't sound as if he was gentle."

"And you will be?"

He stretched out on the bed next to her, his weight resting on his elbow. "Have I ever hurt you?"

His eyes were holding hers, his gaze intensely warm.

"No," she whispered.

"Nor would I. Ever."

Emmeline couldn't breathe, overwhelmed by emotion. He was so strong and sure of himself and she wanted to be that strong for him. "Promise?"

"Yes."

He lowered his head, covering her mouth with his. The kiss was extraordinarily slow, almost languid, as he took his time exploring the shape of her lips, the softness inside her mouth, knowing just how to turn her on again and make her feel.

Pretty soon her breath was catching in her throat, and her toes were curling with pleasure and her still-warm body grew hot.

He kissed her until she was reaching for him, her arm linking around his neck, needing to draw him even closer to her.

She loved it when he shifted and moved over her, welcoming his warmth and the weight of him. He was so big and hard and it felt right against her softness. She practically purred as his chest crushed her breasts, the hard planes of muscle rubbing across her tight nipples.

She was the one who parted her thighs, allowing him to sink between her hips, and then twisted her hips to slide the tip of his erection from her belly to between her legs. She exhaled hard when his shaft's large silken tip pressed against her wetness, the tip brushing across nerves that still felt sensitive from before.

It would be so easy to come again, she thought, as Makin kissed her deeply. His tongue probed her mouth, sliding across her lips and tongue even as his shaft slid across her slick opening.

She whimpered as he rubbed the tip up and down her once more. "Anything hurt?" he asked, looking into her eyes.

His eyes were so cool and yet hot, silver flecked with glowing gold. He was hard and fierce and focused and determined, everything she wasn't.

Her chest suddenly felt unbearably tight, and the backs of her eyes stung. If she weren't so afraid she could love him. If she weren't so afraid of being left, rejected, broken, she could give herself to him.

But she was afraid. "No," she whispered, heart aching.

"I want you," he said.

Her arm tightened around his neck, her heart twisting, contorting, emotions on fire. "Take me."

Makin did, slowly filling her, groaning a little at the tightness of her hot sheath. She was almost too tight, and he feared hurting her. He paused, focused on her mouth and kissing her, and making her feel good. He could feel her grow hotter, wetter, and she was adjusting to his size. He pushed in deeper, still hanging on to his control. This time she wiggled beneath him, taking more of him. Makin groaned deep in his throat.

Once he was buried all the way in her, he rocked his hips, moving forward just enough to press against her.

She gasped and he knew that hitch in her voice. Makin pushed her long tumble of hair back from her neck, kissed her neck and slowly withdrew before plunging back in.

She gasped again. Blood surged within him, making his skin tingle and his erection grow even harder.

He kissed her neck and the pink tips of her breasts as he slowly thrust in and out of her tight, hot body. He could hear her breathe and see the color storm her cheeks and the deep flush suffuse her breasts.

Makin used her breathing to tell him where she was and what she needed. It was easy to delay his pleasure. He'd learned control years ago but she was something new and gorgeous, and he wanted to make her feel good again, wanted to see her come this time, and when she began to breathe in little pants he knew she was close to shattering.

His fingers moved between their bodies as he increased the tempo, his hips driving harder and deeper into her body, only to withdraw and drive deep again. He touched her, lightly circling the small delicate nub with the pad of his finger. He felt her grow still beneath him, tensing, and he knew she was right there, ready. He touched her again even as he thrust deep and she screamed.

This time he didn't let up. He kept thrusting in and out and she writhed beneath him, her inner muscles clenching him, squeezing him, wrenching his control away so that he couldn't hold back any longer. Makin felt as if he exploded, his body violently releasing into hers, and then shuddering with aftershocks.

It was the most intense orgasm he could remember. His entire body throbbed. But it wasn't just physical. His chest ached, too.

Makin kissed her, savoring the softness of her mouth and the way her lips parted beneath his. She tasted warm and sweet. She tasted like his.

Sensation ripped through him, centered in his chest. For a moment he couldn't catch his breath. It was a pain unlike any he'd felt in years…a pain he'd only experienced twice before. When his father died. And then his mother. It was pain created by love.

Makin lifted his head, gazed down into Emmeline's blue eyes and he finally understood why he'd claimed her. Why he'd insisted on marrying her and taking her away from her parents.

He loved her.

He needed her.

He wanted her.

Why hadn't he seen it before? Why hadn't he understood what he was feeling?

"Makin?" she whispered.

He stroked her hair, realizing now his desire to protect her. To make her his. It was because she *was* his. She'd been made for him and he was here, born, created, for her. "Everything's good," he said, and he meant it. Everything was truly good.

Emmeline lay in the huge four-poster bed with the cool cotton sheet pulled to her chest, listening to Makin breathe.

He'd been asleep for an hour now, but she couldn't relax, couldn't sleep.

She liked him too much. Far too much. And that scared her.

She'd married him to provide legitimacy for her baby, and yet here she was, falling for him. And falling for him was wrong. It was dangerous.

She wanted to be brave and fearless. Wanted to wield a sword and fight dragons, but the only dragons in her life were the dragons and demons inside of her. And those were still too big for her to vanquish.

Twenty-five years of fear and insecurity didn't disappear in a week. Twenty-five years of needing acceptance didn't end after a night of sex.

The bad thing about fear was that it created more fear. And she was afraid now.

Afraid of opening herself up and being crushed. Afraid to feel and love only to discover more pain.

She couldn't do more pain. Not yet.

And so the only way to protect her heart was to guard it, and yet around Makin she had so little control. Around him she felt emotional and terrifyingly vulnerable.

Was this love? Could love be so full of fear?

She turned onto her side to look at him. The wooden shutters were partially open and moonlight fell across the bed in strips. A finger of light illuminated Makin's mouth. It was a firm, generous mouth that knew how to kiss her senseless, make her weak in the knees.

Gently she reached out to touch his cheek, a light touch, the briefest caress, as she didn't want to wake him. He needed his sleep.

He was a good man.

Better than she deserved.

CHAPTER FIFTEEN

EVEN though she'd been awake half the night, Emmeline woke at six and quietly slipped from bed to go dress in the spacious walk-in closet. She changed into a long cotton skirt and a knit top and then grabbed her sandals and headed outside for an early walk.

Skirting the island villa's immense and gorgeous gardens, she descended the different terraces to walk the length of the cove, on the beach of soft, powdery, pale sand.

Her head ached from lack of sleep. Her heart felt even worse.

Makin heard her leave the bed and watched as she tiptoed from their room with sandals in her hand. He knew she hadn't slept well, knew she'd been waiting impatiently for dawn so she could escape.

After she left, he rose and showered and headed toward the kitchen for coffee.

Cook was already in there, baking. She greeted Makin effusively and poured him a cup of steaming-hot coffee while asking where he and the queen would like to have breakfast. The edge of his mouth lifted as he imagined Emmeline's reaction to being called his queen. "Outside," he said, still smiling faintly, "on the upper terrace. Her Highness is out for a walk, so I'll wait to eat until she's returned."

He carried his coffee outside and leaned against the balustrade. He was still savoring his drink when Emmeline appeared on the lower terrace, cheeks pink, golden hair tousled. She looked young and fresh in her ruffled coral cotton skirt and white knit top, unbelievably appealing.

"You went to the beach?" he asked as she climbed the stone stairs to join him on the upper terrace.

"Yes. Looking for shells."

"Did you find any?"

She turned her hand over and showed him the three delicate shells in her palm. "These."

"Pretty," he said, admiring them before glancing up at her. "But do be careful. The old staircase at the lower terrace worries me. It should have been replaced years ago."

"I'll be careful."

"Did you sleep well?" he asked.

"I did. And you?"

So she wouldn't tell him the truth. She didn't trust him. Was determined to hide. "I was worried about you."

She looked down at the shells in her hand. "Why?"

"Because I care about you."

"Then don't worry. I'm great." She smiled then, a quick tight smile that didn't reach her eyes. "Have you eaten yet? I'm starving!"

After breakfast they spent the day snorkeling, sunbathing and swimming, both in the ocean and the big pool, and then mid-afternoon, after a long, leisurely lunch, Makin excused himself to take care of some business while Emmeline took a much-needed nap.

She woke up slowly, stretching lazily, her gaze fixed on the bright blue sky and turquoise water outside the bedroom window.

She'd slept well, and must have dreamed something lovely because she felt good, better than she had in days.

She liked Marquette. Could get used to coming here. And she'd enjoyed spending the day with Makin today. Earlier, as they swam and snorkeled and splashed in the pool, she'd laughed easily and felt happy. The real kind of happiness. But that kind of happiness scared her. It made you vulnerable, made you hurt when it ended.

Leaving bed, Emmeline disappeared into their ensuite bath to shower and wash her hair, taking time to blow it dry. With her towel wrapped around her toga-style, she headed back to the bedroom to figure out what she'd wear for that evening.

Makin was stretched out on the bed now, hands behind his head, a hot, hungry light in his eyes. "I almost joined you in the shower."

She blushed and tugged her towel tighter. "I shower alone," she said primly.

"Not for long."

Cheeks rosy, she disappeared into the closet.

"Cook has re-created our wedding dinner for us," Makin called to her.

"That's nice of her," she answered, emerging with a long ivory satin gown pieced together by long ropes of pearls. The dress had such a daringly low back and delicate beaded straps that Emmeline immediately thought of a harem girl. "What is this?" she asked, giving the hanger a shake.

"One of the dresses I ordered for you."

"When?"

"Yesterday when we were flying from Brabant. You were asleep and I was bored so I did a little online shopping."

She turned the dress toward her, inspecting the delicate label which she knew had been hand-sewn into the dress as the last step. "It's couture. This isn't something you buy online."

"I emailed the designer and requested a couple of dresses for the honeymoon."

"And how did you get it here so fast?"

"Had a plane go get it."

"Just like that?"

He shrugged. "I thought you'd look good in it."

"That's a ridiculous amount of money."

"I have a ridiculous amount of money."

She shook her head, lips pursing as she struggled not to smile. "You're shameless."

"I know. But you like my confidence." He left the bed and approached her, his gaze slowly examining her, starting at the top of her head and working his way down, possession darkening his eyes. "Maybe we should skip dinner tonight again," he said, drawing her into his arms, dipping his head to nuzzle her neck.

Her lips parted in a silent gasp as his mouth found nerves behind her ear, then along the column of her neck before kissing the hollow at her throat. "But Cook has re-created our wedding dinner," she protested hoarsely.

He found her lips, kissed her slowly, thoroughly, until she was clinging to him, her hands fisted in his shirt.

He lifted his head, gazed down into her eyes, and Emmeline blinked up at him, dazed. "Maybe we don't need dinner," she said breathlessly.

He smiled but there was a dangerous light in his eyes. "I don't, but you do. You're not eating enough, and you're eating for two." He gently but firmly set her back. "So I'll go shower and dress in the other room, but I will have you tonight, Emmeline. So do what you have to now, because later you'll be mine."

Pulse unsteady, Emmeline rang for a maid as she needed help fastening the tiny hooks of the seductive gown.

Finally dressed, Emmeline brushed her hair again, leaving it loose, and then did her makeup, focusing on her pale pink lips and dark smoky eyes. Finished, she rose from the dressing table, stepped back and glanced at herself in the mirror. As she turned, the long ropes of pearls swayed, brushing against her bare back, and the thin satin fabric strained to contain her breasts, while it kissed her belly and slid over her thighs. It was such a daring gown. It hinted at passion and seduction and very hot sex.

Sex. That's what they had together, wasn't it?

Hot sex, good sex, and she'd have to learn to be happy with that. Not to want more.

House staff bowed to Emmeline as she walked through the villa and directed her to the garden. In the garden more staff pointed her to the terrace below, the middle terrace, where a white silk tent had been erected on the lawn overlooking the sea, with torches at each of the tent's four corners, the long bamboo poles buried deep in the ground. Emmeline's pulse matched the torches tonight, her heart jumping and twisting like the gold flames.

As she climbed down the upper staircase to the middle terrace, she spotted Makin inside the tent, his back to her, his face toward the sea. He was wearing a white linen shirt and oatmeal linen slacks and she didn't think he'd ever looked quite so regal.

"Do you ever wear traditional robes?" she asked him as she crossed the lawn and entered the tent where a table had been set for two. The tablecloth, a stunning watery blue silk, was the same clear blue of the ocean. A vase of white orchids and plumeria was in the center of the table while low white votive candles were nestled among the crystal and sterling silver.

"I do for business in Kadar. Sometimes at home. Why? Would you like me to wear the *thawb* and *keffiyeh* my countrymen do?"

"I don't know," she answered. "Maybe. Might help me to remember you really are Sheikh Al-Koury."

"Instead of…?" he prompted curiously.

"You." She swallowed hard, butterflies flitting wildly inside her tummy.

"And what am I?"

"Gorgeous."

He looked unaccountably pleased. "Am I?"

"You know you are!" she exclaimed, turning away, embarrassed to have even said that much.

Her gaze fell on the sitting area created in front of the table. A low couch was upholstered in the same matching blue silk as the tablecloth, with throw pillows in white. More white candles glowed in glass hurricanes on the ground. Emmeline could smell something tantalizing in the air and didn't know if it was his fragrance or the plumeria or a combination of the two.

"This is so beautiful and romantic," Emmeline said, suddenly overwhelmed by the need to be in Makin's arms, close to his chest. In his arms she felt good. Safe. In his arms she could almost believe he loved her…could almost believe that sex would be enough.…

"My staff is very happy for us," he answered, filling a slender flute with icy-cold sparkling water for her, and then another for him.

"Just because I can't drink, doesn't mean you can't."

He shrugged, powerful shoulders rolling. "I don't need to drink to be with you. In fact, I prefer not to drink."

"Why?"

"I enjoy you too much."

She blushed, and took a seat on the low couch, her body suddenly sensitive and tingling everywhere.

She could feel Makin's gaze rest on her and it just made her heart race faster. He still overwhelmed her, but now it was in a sexy, wicked sort of way. She'd never felt beautiful with anyone but Makin before, had never felt so important before. In his eyes, she mattered.

Her heart turned over and hot emotion washed through her and suddenly Emmeline wasn't sure she could live without him.

She needed him. Wanted him. And yet love wasn't a sure thing.

Emmeline went hot and cold and her fingers tightened on the stem of the flute.

"Are you all right?" he asked, concern deepening his voice.

She nodded. "Yes." She forced herself to smile, the warm breeze caressing her, making her think of his hands on her skin. "Just a little overwhelmed...but in a good way."

"I hope so. I like having you here for me. It feels right. Makes the island feel like home."

Her heart ached all over again. She blinked back tears. "I love being here, too."

"You enjoyed today?"

"Very much."

"What did you enjoy most?"

She thought for a moment. "Swimming...snorkeling. The coral reef was amazing. So many beautiful fish."

"My mother loved it here, too. She believed it was very healing."

"Marquette was her island then?"

"My father bought it for her as a wedding gift. Growing up we spent many holidays here, but I haven't been to Marquette in years."

"Why not?"

"I'm not a boy anymore. I have work. Am usually too busy for pleasure trips."

She frowned a little at his intense work ethic. He was so driven, so ambitious. "Even men need to relax."

"My mother used to say the same thing to my father."

"And did he listen to her?"

"Most of the time."

"Good. So you have to listen to me, too."

Makin smiled at her, amused.

He'd told Malek Nuri that he'd married Emmeline because he couldn't let her go—which was true—but now looking at her in her daring pearl-and-satin gown, he knew it was more that that. He'd married her because she was made for him, destined for him, fated.

In Kadar her tears had moved him, but her laughter was twice as powerful. When she smiled at him he felt invincible. For her, he thought he could do anything.

And he would.

The evening passed slowly for Makin though. He didn't want to spend two hours at a table eating and talking, not when he found Emmeline and her satin-and-pearl gown so damn distracting. All evening the ropes of pearls and slinky satin fabric had teased, hugging her curves and revealing her smooth, flawless skin.

He was delighted when she passed on an after-dinner coffee. Back in their bedroom he shut the door, locking it and turned to discover Emmeline lifting her hair off her neck and presenting her back to him. "I'm going to need your help getting me out of this dress," she said.

Makin groaned under his breath. She looked like Aphrodite in that position, head slightly forward, hair piled in golden waves, arms up, her long slim back gorgeously exposed. And she was his.

Would always be his.

He hardened instantly, desire surging through him, making him feel even hotter and hungrier as his gaze swept over her, taking in the gleaming hair, the creamy nape, her bare back covered by just those long delicate strands. During dinner he'd been fascinated by the way the pearls draped across her skin, attached from the beaded shoulder straps of her gown to the dip in her spine where the ivory satin fabric just barely covered her bottom. Now he just wanted his hands on her bottom. Wanted to feel the softness of her skin on his.

And even though he was impatient to have her, he held himself in check, knowing she was still learning about sex and love. So he unhooked her gown carefully until the dress spilled to her feet in a tumble of silk and pearls.

The gown had been too bare for a bra. She stood now in just her high strappy heels and that tiny scrap of satin she called a thong.

Stifling another growl, he drew her backward and held her against him, his hands on her hips, her round pert butt pressed against his straining shaft.

God, he wanted to bury himself in her. Spread her thighs, drag her down on him and have her ride him.

But not yet.

His head dipped, he kissed the side of her neck, felt her shiver in response. He slid one hand from her hip up over the indentation of her waist, to her ribs to cup a bare breast. Her nipple was tight and hard against his palm and he rubbed it, teasing it, imagining it in his mouth, against the wet heat of his tongue.

She wiggled against him, her breast in his hand, the firm globes of her butt rubbing up and down along his erection and his control nearly snapped.

"Want you," he said thickly.

She turned in his arms, a tiny smile curving her lips, a bright glow in her eyes. For a moment he thought she looked happy, truly happy, and his heart turned over.

Makin caught her face in his hands, kissed her deeply, before stripping off his clothes. Naked, he sat down on the edge of the bed and pulled her onto his lap, lowering her slowly onto his hard shaft until she was settled firmly on his thighs, his erection embedded deeply inside of her.

With his hands on her hips he guided her, helping to set the rhythm he knew she liked. She was wet and slick and as he lifted her up and down on him, he felt her breathing quicken, heard her small quick gasps of pleasure. It was the sexiest sound and made him surge harder and deeper into her hot, wet body.

She came first and then he, and, spent, he dragged her backward on the bed to lie in his arms.

For long minutes they were quiet.

"Do you always do the right thing?" Emmeline asked, breaking the silence.

"I try," he answered, his voice deep, husky in the dark.

"Do you ever worry that doing the right thing might not always be the right thing?"

"No."

She turned restlessly in his arms, the sheets sticking to her damp skin, resenting him just a little for his confidence. How nice it must be never to doubt oneself! "But doing the right thing might not always be right," she persisted. "Doing the right thing might actually be the worst thing you can do."

"How so?" he asked, lazily, lifting her hair in his hand, letting it slide through his fingers.

Makin's ease with her made her almost crazy. He seemed so content, so calm and self-assured. It wasn't fair. She never felt calm and content. She almost always felt as if she were one step away from disaster.

"My uncle adopted me out of duty," she said, drawing a deep breath, "just as you have married me out of duty. I worry that you and my uncle have both made the same mistake. Your decisions weren't based on love, but doing the right thing, and I worry that later you might come to resent me the way Claire resented me. I think she wanted to be my mother but then felt burdened by the responsibility."

"I'm not William or Claire, so I can't answer for them, but I can answer for me. You will never be a burden. I chose to make you my wife. There was no gun to my head, no external pressure. It was a decision I freely made and, Emmeline, I'm a man of my word. I've made a commitment to you and the baby and you are now my family. Both of you."

"But someday you'll want children of your own," she said, "and I'm afraid you'll love them more—"

"No."

"You will." She rose up on her elbow to look down at him. "It's natural."

His hand wrapped around a fistful of hair and he gave it a gentle tug. "Emmeline, I won't ever have biological children. I can't."

"Why not?"

"My father's disease is genetic." After the slightest pause he continued, "I didn't get the disease itself, but I carry the genes. I can't take the risk of having children and giving them my father's disease. The disease ravished my father. The end was brutal. He suffered terribly."

"But you talked about starting a family…"

"And I will. There are so many children in this world that need parents, love, a stable home. I've always planned on adopting."

"Were you ever going to tell me?"

"I'm telling you now."

"Yes, but what if I married you hoping to have children with you?"

"But you didn't."

"What if I want more children?"

"I hope you do. As an only child, I always wanted brothers and sisters. I'd love to adopt down the road, give our little one siblings."

"And we would adopt those?"

"Yes."

"And you would love all of them, regardless of their parentage?"

"Yes."

"How can you be so sure?"

"Because they'd be ours, yours and my children."

She lay back down next to him, facing him, scooting as close to him as she could, wanting to absorb his warmth and strength. She wished she could tell him how much she loved his strength and his confidence. She wished she could let him know that he inspired her…made her want to be bolder, more courageous.

"You really will love my baby?" she whispered, face tipped up to his.

"Yes," he answered, smoothing her hair back from her face. "I will be a good father. I had a great father. He taught me what love is."

Emmeline's eyes felt heavy but she wouldn't let herself fall asleep. She wanted to look at Makin.

She didn't know how he'd done it, but she'd fallen for him, fallen hard and fast.

She loved him. But she didn't trust love. In fact, loving him made everything worse.

Because now he had the power to hurt her. Now he could break her heart.

And maybe he did want her, but Emmeline knew that sexual desire waned, and she feared that when the newness of their coupling wore off, he'd lose interest.

He'd go. If not physically, then emotionally. And that would drive her mad. She'd feel like desperate Emmeline again, the girl who couldn't ever get enough love. And Emmeline hated being needy. She'd hated that she wanted so much more than her parents could give. And the truth was, she already wanted more from Makin. Sex wasn't enough. She couldn't just be his woman in bed when he needed release. She wanted his heart.

Fighting tears, Emmeline leaned forward and gently touched her lips to his.

If only she were different.

If only she were someone stronger. Calmer, tougher, someone less brittle. Someone like Hannah. Maybe then she could trust. Maybe then she could believe there was something good about her, something someone could love.

But she wasn't Hannah. Regretfully, she wasn't anything like Hannah.

* * *

Emmeline's morning walk felt like a death march. She walked in circles on the beach, arms wrapped around her waist as she faced the truth.

She couldn't do this anymore. Couldn't remain in this paradise and swim and play and make love to Makin as if this was really a honeymoon.

This was no honeymoon. It was hell. She was living in hell and it was her fault.

She'd fallen in love with Makin. She wasn't supposed to fall in love. She was supposed to have been smart, strong, safe.

Instead, she loved him and needed him, and the depth of her emotions terrified her. They were too much.

If only she hadn't fallen in love with him then maybe she could have played the game…floated through a marriage of convenience with dignity and grace. But there was nothing dignified about what she was feeling.

She felt consumed by fear, consumed by need and pain. There was no way Makin could ever love someone like her…someone so fearful and broken…someone so damaged.

He'd soon discover just how much she needed him and it would overwhelm him. Her needs overwhelmed everyone.

Better to leave now while she could. There was no way she was strong enough for a prolonged goodbye. Better to do it quickly and cleanly, one hard cut today, a total break, and then move on.

Emmeline exhaled in a quick rush, knowing she was kidding herself. It wouldn't be a clean break. It'd be brutal, but she'd have to be brutal with Makin to make him leave.

She inhaled sharply, her heart hurting, burning, as she pictured him walking away.

He'd be okay, she told herself, shoving a hand across her mouth to stifle a cry. He'd be fine. He was tough. Strong. He'd survive without her. She was the one who might not make it without him.

Makin was standing on the upper terrace, staring out over the sea, when she returned from her morning walk.

He didn't look at her as she climbed the steps and Emmeline

knew immediately something was wrong. He leaned against the wall, his gaze fixed on the ocean, the morning breeze ruffling his dark hair.

"Nice walk?" he asked casually.

"Yes."

"You're okay?" he persisted.

She tugged a wild tendril away from her eyes. "Yes. Why?"

"I thought I heard you crying while you were walking below."

A lump rose to her throat. She had been crying, but she didn't want him to know. "No."

"I could have sworn it was you."

The lump grew bigger. Emmeline's mouth quivered and she bit ruthlessly into her bottom lip. "It was the wind."

He finally looked at her. His gaze shuttered, expression cool. "I can still hear it in your voice."

She forced a smile, closed the distance between them and kissed his shoulder. He was so tall, so powerful, and completely addictive. "You're imagining things," she said lightly, knowing that soon she'd tell him it was over. Sometime in the next hour or two everything would change forever. "I'm going to go shower and dress. Have you had breakfast already?"

"No."

"Give me fifteen minutes and I'll be right back."

Emmeline headed for their bedroom aware that Makin watched her every step until she disappeared inside the house. He knew something was wrong. He'd press her for the truth this next time, and she would tell him.

It happened just the way she'd expected. They were still at breakfast, lingering over coffee, talking about what they wanted to do that day when Makin abruptly told her he knew she was upset, that he'd been awakened last night by the sound of her crying.

"Don't tell me nothing is wrong," he said flatly. "Obviously something is. What?"

He didn't skirt problems but ran directly at them, head-first. Emmeline felt a rush of intense love and admiration. He really was good, strong. He needed someone at his side who was as good and strong.

She was neither.

Nor would she ever be.

"I changed my mind," she said quietly, toying with the handle on her cup. "I changed my mind," she repeated, louder, more firmly. "I can't do this after all."

"Do what?" he asked, almost too gently.

She steeled herself against regrets, wouldn't tolerate second thoughts. "Do...this...be here with you like this, as if I'm really your wife."

"You *are* my wife."

She forced herself to meet his eyes, hold his gaze. "I'm not, not truly."

His shoulders squared. He seemed to grow even taller. "You said the vows. You have my ring on your finger."

Emmeline glanced down at the enormous stone weighting her finger. Her heart turned over. His mother's ring. Suddenly frantic to be free of all this emotion, fear and pain, she tugged the ring off her finger and held it out to him. "Take it, then. I won't wear it again."

"No."

"I can't do this. I thought I could. But I was wrong. It won't work. I'm not the right woman for you, I'm not a woman who can love you the way you want—"

"You don't know what I want."

"I do. You want a woman like your mother, you want a good woman, a loving woman, a woman who will make your life magical and special, who will love you no matter what...but I don't know how to love like that."

He studied her for an endless moment, his expression grave, gray eyes empty. "I don't believe you. I think you're just scared—"

"I don't love you, Makin." It killed her to say it. It was a lie, an absolute lie, but she knew she had to be brutal, knew she had to hurt him, and she did. She saw his expression change, his features harden because she knew then with absolute certainty that she did love him. But he couldn't know or he'd never let her go. She battled for composure. "I will never love you."

Again he looked at her, no emotion in his mouth or eyes. "Why not?"

If she was going to cut the ties that bind, if she was going to set him free—set them both free—she couldn't just go through the motions. She had to make the cut sharp and deep.

Brutal, she told herself, *be brutal and finish this.*

Her lips curved and she forced a mocking note into her voice. "Do you really need to ask?"

"Yes."

She shrugged carelessly even as her heart burned. "You'll never be Alejandro."

He didn't even blink. He made no sound. He just looked at her, intensely, searchingly, and she kept her smile fixed, her lips curving cruelly. "I loved him," she added. "You know I loved him—"

"You told me you never did."

Another indifferent shrug. "I know what I said, but it was a lie. An act. I was playing you the entire time."

Finally, a flicker of emotion in his silver eyes. "Why, Emmeline?"

The husky note in his voice was almost her undoing. She struggled to breathe when her throat was squeezing closed. She couldn't do this, couldn't be so hurtful and hateful. But if she didn't hurt him badly, he'd forgive her. He was that kind of man. So she had to be hideous. Terrible. Beyond redemption. She had to make sure he let her go.

Forever.

"Because sometimes we play games to get what we want."

"And what did you want?"

"A name for my baby. A story to give the press."

"And I'm that story?"

She nodded. "Even when we divorce, I will tell everyone you fathered my child. When the baby is born, I will give him or her your name. I can be a divorcée and have a good life. I just couldn't as an unwed pregnant princess."

"I could demand a paternity test, make the results public."

"You wouldn't."

"I would."

"You married me to do the right thing. You are a man who believes he can make a difference, and you do."

"But now you're done with me."

Her chest constricted, her heart was on fire. "Yes."

"You used me."

"Yes." She extended her hand, the ring balanced on her palm. "Take it. Give it to your next wife. Let's hope you make a better choice than you did with me."

Makin pushed away from the table without a word. Emmeline waited, feeling as if life as she knew it had come to an end.

There would never be another Makin Al-Koury. There would never be a man with his grace or strength or courage.

She sat for another fifteen minutes hoping against hope that he'd come back, grab her, shake her, kiss her, tell her she was a fool. Because she was a fool. A frightened fool.

But he didn't return.

Instead she heard the distant roar of an engine. Emmeline froze, cold all over. It was Makin's plane.

Makin was leaving her.

Emmeline rose, stood in place, her heart thudding heavily, hollowly in her ears.

What had she done? What had she done to him? To them?

She raced from the terrace to the upper garden, and the distant roar of the jet's engines grew stronger. Panic flooded her. What was the matter with her? What was she thinking? When would she stop being so afraid?

She had to stop him, had to catch him, had to let him know she was wrong. Emmeline dashed down the stone stairs of the terraces. The plane would be taking off any minute. There was no way to reach the runway in time but maybe she could catch the pilot's attention, maybe Makin would see her on the beach.

Emmeline tore down the narrow wooden stairs, taking the white painted steps two at a time, running across the sand to the water.

The engines grew louder. She spun around, waving her arms overhead as the white jet appeared directly over her. It rose swiftly into the sky. She ran deeper into the water, waving madly. Surely Makin would see. Or the pilot. *Someone.*

But the jet kept banking right, ascending steeply, soaring over the ocean, letting Marquette fall behind.

Emmeline's arms fell to her sides. For several minutes she just stood there as waves crashed and broke against her legs.

He'd gone. He'd gone just as she feared he would.

Because she'd chased him away.

CHAPTER SIXTEEN

EMMELINE stayed on the beach for an hour, and then another, unable to leave the cove. Her legs wouldn't hold her. She couldn't stop crying. She'd never hated herself so much in her entire life, and that was saying a lot because Emmeline was an expert in self-loathing.

But enough was enough.

When would she grow up? Become that strong prince with the sword who was slaying dragons instead of the princess in the tower?

When would she be someone she could admire? When would she stop acting out of fear?

She'd hurt Makin because she was afraid he'd hurt her. She'd gathered her love for him and turned it into a weapon, slashing out at Makin as if he was the dragon.

He was no dragon. He was a prince. A hero.

The man she adored with all her heart. Even though it was a broken and battered heart.

But hearts mended and love could heal and she could become stronger. She could become brave. She just had to tell Makin the truth.

That she loved him…more than she'd loved anyone…and she would work on changing if he would just be patient. If he'd just give her the chance.

And somehow, in her heart, she knew he would. Because he was that kind of man.

She wiped away tears with the back of her arm. She should

go back to the house. She'd been on the beach for hours but she needed to gather her composure. Even though Makin was gone, she couldn't be seen with a swollen, red face—princesses didn't cry in public—and so she lingered for another half hour on the beach, watching a storm move across the horizon, ominous clouds gathering in the sky.

The first raindrops fell as the wind blew in a gust that lashed at the palm trees. Emmeline cast a glance at the now-dark sky. The clouds were black. The wind began to howl. Brushing the sand off the back of her skirt, she quickly headed for the stairs.

The wind buffeted Emmeline as she climbed the old staircase, and for a moment she paused, feeling the stairs sway and creak. She shuddered a little as they swayed again. Suddenly there was a loud pop and crack and Emmeline grabbed the staircase rail as she felt the wooden stairs begin to collapse.

The baby, she thought in panic, as the wooden structure folded in on itself like a row of dominoes and she scrambled backward, leaping into the soft wet sand just as the entire staircase came crashing down.

Emmeline sat up and put a hand to her middle. She hadn't fallen hard. It hadn't been a very high jump. She hadn't even had the wind knocked out of her. The baby couldn't have been hurt.

But it was a wake-up call, she thought, stepping away from the wooden debris. She needed to be more careful.

Getting to her feet, she shouted for help. The wind was so loud she was sure it devoured her voice. She shouted again anyway. And again. No one came.

The rain slashed down and the wind tore at her hair and Emmeline sat on the wet beach with her arms wrapped tightly around her knees as she struggled to think of a way to get off the private beach.

She couldn't think of anything that might be safe. She'd have to ride the storm out.

Time slowed, blurred. Minutes became hours. Darkness was now rapidly descending, and the wind still howled, but Emmeline thought she heard an engine.

Had Makin returned? Had he heard she was missing and flown back to find her?

But no one could fly in this weather, and the intense winds would make it impossible to land safely on the small island airstrip.

Emmeline fought panic. The wind kept screaming, the tide kept rising, and the waves were breaking just feet away from her now. If the tide got much higher, she'd be swimming soon.

She suddenly stilled. Was someone shouting her name?

Could it be? Or was it more wishful thinking?

A light glowed overhead. Someone *was* up there. She rose unsteadily shouted for help.

The yellow light shifted. "Emmeline?"

Makin.

Her heart stopped. "Down here! Makin, I'm here!"

He moved the lantern, crouching on the edge of the terrace above her, at the place the staircase used to be. She couldn't see his face, the lantern too low, shining down on her, but she found his size and shape so very reassuring.

"What are you doing out here?" he shouted.

"I was trying to find you—"

"Have you lost your mind? It's a bloody hurricane!"

"It wasn't when you left."

"Stay right there. Don't move."

He reappeared in minutes, anchoring a long rope in one of the metal rings which had supported the stairs.

Emmeline squinted against the darkness, trying to see through the rain, as Makin took the rope, wrapped it around his waist and rappelled down the crumbly face of the cliff. He was like a pirate in one of those old movies, leaping from the rigging of one tall ship onto the rigging of another.

With the lantern flickering she could see that the rain had soaked his shirt, flattening the fabric, outlining his back and the corded muscles in his arms.

He continued his descent until he could reach her. "Give me your hand," he said, bracing his feet against the rock.

"Makin, you can't—"

"Don't! Don't ever tell me what I can and can't do. I know what I can do. Now give me your hand."

Biting her lip she put her hand into his. His fingers immediately closed around hers. "Hold tight," he commanded, as he slowly pulled her into the circle of his arms, his body sheltering hers as he adjusted his grip on the rope.

"Turn and face me," he said, his voice in her ear. "Wrap your legs around my waist—"

"Makin—"

"Not interested, Emmeline. Do as you're told. Slide up and wrap your legs around my waist. Lock your feet by your ankles. And hang on tight. Got it?"

She nodded against his chest and, heart pounding, she felt him begin the arduous climb back up the cliff.

The rain was pouring down and she could feel his heart thud against hers as he lifted them, hand over hand, up the rocky face.

Makin was breathing hard as they reached the top. With one foot on the top of the cliff, and the other still planted on the rocky face, he pushed Emmeline onto the flat terrace before pulling himself up and over to join her.

Emmeline stared at him wide-eyed as he dragged a hand through his hair and shoved it off his face. "You are in so much trouble," he gritted through clenched teeth. "You have no idea how angry I am. You could have been hurt. You could have hurt the baby—"

"I was trying to stop you."

"I was coming back."

"I didn't know." She was shivering now, chilled by her wet clothes as well as his furious expression. "And I'd said all those terrible things, Makin, said hateful things, and you were right to go—"

"I would never leave you."

"But you took off—"

"I had something to do."

"I didn't think you were coming back."

"You have so much to learn, but I'm not doing this now. Go to the house. Shower, dress, have a snack and then meet me in the living room in half an hour. You do not want to be late. Understand?"

Emmeline showered, dressed, sipped some hot sweet tea and nibbled on some buttered toast and was in the living room in twenty minutes, not thirty. Makin wasn't there. But someone else was.

A tall, lean man with graying blond hair and darkly tanned skin turned around when he heard the click of her heels. He was wearing jeans and cowboy boots and a Western-style belt with an enormous oval silver buckle.

"Oh, excuse me," Emmeline said, drawing up short. "I didn't realize we had a guest."

The man was as tall as Makin and just as broad through the shoulders. He had piercing blue eyes and a firm mouth above a hard, uncompromising chin. "My God," he muttered. "Jacqueline."

Goose bumps covered Emmeline's arm. "What did you just say?"

"Unbelievable," he said, taking a step toward her, his expression incredulous. "You look just like her."

He was an American, with a Texas drawl. A real cowboy? "Who?" she whispered.

"Your mother."

For a moment she couldn't breathe. "You knew her?"

"Yes."

"You know who I am?" she asked faintly.

"My other daughter."

Emmeline's legs buckled. She reached for a chair and sat down. "*Other* daughter?"

He nodded, brow furrowed, blue eyes darkening with emotion. "Hannah's twin."

"Hannah?" she choked.

"Hannah Smith. Your sister."

Hannah was her sister? Her twin? Impossible. Impossible. "How...what...?" Emmeline shook her head, unable to get the words out.

"Princess Jacqueline had twins." It was Makin who spoke.

He'd quietly entered the living room a few moments earlier and moved to Emmeline's side. "Two baby girls, and you were separated at birth. One baby went to Texas, and the other to your family in Brabant."

Emmeline leaned forward, covered her mouth as she stared across the room to the American. "I can't believe this..."

"I finally put it all together yesterday," Makin said, his hand on her back. "I called Jack to confirm my suspicions. Once I told him what I knew, he got on the first flight he could for St. Thomas, and I brought him here."

Emmeline couldn't look away from the blond, weathered Texan with his boots and jeans. "You're really my...father?"

Jack Smith nodded. "I had no idea there were two of you," he said gruffly. "I can't believe I didn't get to raise both of you. I should have."

Her eyes burned and she drew a quick breath. "What was she like? My mom?"

"Like you." Jack's voice deepened, roughened. "Smart. Kind. Funny. And the most beautiful thing I'd ever seen in my life."

Emmeline dashed away tears. "You loved her?"

"More than I can say."

The three of them had dinner and they talked nonstop, Emmeline asking questions and Jack answering them with Makin just listening.

Now and then during dinner Emmeline would have to brush away tears and she'd look at Makin and discover him watching her and the expression on his face...the look in his eyes...it nearly broke her heart.

He didn't just want her body. He didn't just want sex. He wanted her.

He cared for her.

He might even love her.

Blinking back tears she turned her attention to her father who was telling her how he'd met her mother. Jacqueline had been on a goodwill tour of North America and Jack, a Texas Ranger, had been assigned to her security detail while visiting Texas.

"We fell in love somewhere between Austin and San Antonio.

We made love just once. It was hurried and risky, but I loved her. I was crazy about her and had imagined appearing before her parents in Brabant and asking for her hand. But after she returned home, I never heard from Jacqueline again. I had no idea she was pregnant until one day a woman shows up on my ranch with an infant, tells me that Jacqueline has died and this is our daughter."

"And this woman never told you there had been another baby?" Emmeline asked, leaning forward.

He shook his head. "No. Not a word, and I can assure you, that if I had known about you, Emmeline, I would have come for you. And no one, not even the King and Queen of Brabant, could have kept me from you."

Emmeline glanced at Makin and then back to her father. "Does Hannah know about me? That I'm really her sister?"

Makin nodded. "She does now."

"I want to see her."

"She's on the way," Jack said. "She should be here in the morning."

Later, after everyone had gone to bed and the house was dark and quiet, Emmeline turned to face Makin. "You really do love me," she whispered. "I wasn't sure before. I thought it was just sex you wanted, or maybe a woman like Hannah—"

"Oh, no, I definitely don't want Hannah." He put a finger to her lips when she opened her mouth to protest. "She is brilliant and your twin sister, but I don't feel even a spark of attraction for her. Now you...I can't keep my hands off you."

Emmeline closed her eyes, lips parting as he kissed the side of her neck, her collarbone and lower, on her breast. "You'd better stop, Makin. I won't be able to talk pretty soon."

"Good. We've talked enough for tonight."

"But there are things I have to say—"

"You don't."

"I do. I need you to forgive me for saying hurtful things and pushing you away—"

"I already have." He tucked a long strand of hair behind her ear. "I love you."

"You should hate me for hurting you, for saying unkind things."

The edge of his mouth lifted. "I can't hate you. I could never hate you. You were scared. I know that."

"It's that easy? No grudges? No simmering anger? No lingering resentment?"

He laughed softly, pulling her onto his chest, and kissed her again. "No."

"Why not?"

"Because you're my wife—"

"Even if it's by default?"

He laughed again and kissed her slowly. "Not by default. This is fate, my darling. You were made for me."

"Even with all my flaws and faults?"

"You're not flawed. You're just you, and real, and perfect for me."

"I love you, Makin."

"I know."

"You do?"

He nodded, kissed her gently, and then again, this time deepening the kiss so that his tongue teased hers, tasting her. "Yes."

"How?"

"Because you can't contain your feelings—"

"I knew it!"

He laughed softly and kissed her again. "And that's a good thing, Emmeline. I need your warmth and your energy and your passion for life. I've spent these past fourteen years pouring myself into my work but I'm ready to have more...I want and need more. I want and need you."

"Why? Why me?"

"I have no idea, but no one has mattered to me here," he said, pausing to touch his chest, just over his heart, "until I entered Mynt and saw you there in that tight little turquoise dress. And I came alive. For you."

"You really, truly do love me!"

"I really, truly do. And we're good together. We're meant to be together."

"How can you be so sure? We've only been together a week."

"My father knew my mother just days before he married her. They had twenty wonderful years together."

She exhaled carefully, her heart so full it ached. "I would love to have twenty wonderful years with you."

"Not me. I want at least forty."

She had to blink back the hot rush of tears. "That does sound better."

"At least forty," he repeated. "We can watch our children grow, marry and have children. How does that sound?"

"Like the very best happily-ever-after ending I've ever heard!"

EPILOGUE

Seven months later

It was a bright winter morning in Nadir, at the city's best hospital in the wing reserved for the Al-Koury royal family. It had been a long night for those in the labor and delivery room, though, and Emmeline had been grateful for her husband's and sister's support.

Nineteen hours of contractions had left Emmeline exhausted and the pain was just getting worse.

Gripping Hannah's hand tightly, Emmeline cried out as the latest contraction gripped her belly. The contractions were right on top of each other now with no rest time anymore. "Hurts," she choked, perspiration beading her brow, body trembling uncontrollably.

"You're almost there," the nurse said soothingly.

Emmeline shook her head. "Really hurts."

Makin glared at the nurse. "Give her something for the pain, now!"

"Too late," the nurse answered crisply, stepping around the sheikh and checking the monitor that tracked Emmeline's and the baby's heart rates. Both were doing just fine.

"What do you mean, too late?"

The nurse stepped around Makin again. "The baby is crowning. He or she is here."

But Makin was beside himself. "And where the hell is the doctor?"

"On his way. But your little one is impatient to see the world and has decided not to wait." The nurse gave Emmeline a calm, encouraging smile. "Your Highness, on the next contraction you are going to take a deep breath and push—"

"Without giving her something for the pain?" Makin demanded.

"No, Makin, she can't," Hannah snapped at him from the opposite side of the bed, exasperated by his bellowing and the only one in any condition to tell him to pull himself together. "You insisted on being in here," she added tartly, pointing to the door, "but you're not helping Emmeline when you roar like that. So help her, or go."

Makin's jaw hardened as he swallowed, but his expression softened the moment he glanced down at Emmeline. "I'm sorry," he apologized, smoothing her hair back from her damp face. "I hate seeing you in pain."

"I'm okay."

"Not okay," he corrected, leaning over to kiss her. "You're amazing."

"All right, Your Highness," the nurse said, watching the contractions build on another machine. "It's time to meet your little one. Take a deep breath and push. Give me everything you can."

With Hannah squeezing one hand, and Makin holding the other, Emmeline focused all her energy on bringing her baby safely into the world.

"That's it," the nurse exclaimed. "You did it. Your daughter is here."

And then the baby cried, a loud piercing cry.

"Oh, Emmie, she's gorgeous!" Hannah exclaimed, leaning over to kiss her sister's cheek. "Congratulations!"

A girl, a daughter, Emmeline silently repeated as she glanced from the nurse who held the squalling infant, to her husband, Makin, who only had eyes for the newborn.

"May I hold her?" he asked the nurse gruffly.

"Do you want to wait until I clean her up?"

"No. I've been waiting forever to meet my daughter."

Emmeline's eyes filled with tears as the nurse handed the slippery, shrieking baby to Makin. He held her close to his chest, his big arms cradling her securely, as if that's what his arms were made to do. "Jacqueline Yvette," he said softly, and the baby stopped kicking and crying.

"What do you think of the name?" he asked Emmeline, carrying the tiny infant around the foot of the bed and over to meet her mother for the first time.

Emmeline gazed down at her naked baby daughter nestled in Makin's powerful arms. She was a red-faced little thing with a thatch of dark hair and a big strong kick. "It's perfect," she said huskily.

Makin leaned over to kiss her. "Just like her mother."

Blinking back tears, Queen Hannah Jacqueline Patek quietly slipped out of the room to go tell her husband that the next generation of beautiful royal princesses had just been born.

* * * * *

To Tempt a Sheikh

OLIVIA GATES

Olivia Gates has always pursued creative passions —singing and many handicrafts. She still does, but only one of her passions grew gratifying enough, consuming enough, to become an ongoing career—writing.

She is most fulfilled when she is creating worlds and conflicts for her characters, then exploring and untangling them bit by bit, sharing her protagonists' every heart-wrenching heartache and hope, their every heart-pounding doubt and trial, until she leads them to an indisputably earned and gloriously satisfying happy ending. When she's not writing, she is a doctor, a wife to her own alpha male and a mother to one brilliant girl and one demanding Angora cat. Visit Olivia at www.oliviagates.com.

To my mother.
No words can describe how relieved
I am that the worst is over.
Here's to many, many more books with
us together.

One

Harres Aal Shalaan tightened his shroud, narrowing the opening across his eyes to a slit. He didn't need more than that to monitor his target.

The midnight wind buffeted him, pelted him with sand as he stilled once more, flattened himself at the uppermost edge of the dune. His cloth-smothered breathing still rivaled the wind's hubbub across the endlessness of the desert in his ears.

He absently reached for his sand car much as he would have his prized horse. The vehicle wasn't there. He'd left it behind over two miles away. Any closer and the engine noise would have transmitted across this sound-hurling landscape. Ideally, he would have dragged it to this vantage point, but that would have slowed him down at least twenty minutes. Twenty minutes he couldn't afford.

He wouldn't let the stationary status of the scene he'd been watching for the past five minutes fool him. Everything could change at any moment. Then it would be too late for him to intervene.

For now, all remained the same. The two sentries guarding the only entrance were huddled around a makeshift container where a fire struggled for survival against the merciless desert wind. Three more guard duos surrounded the weather-eaten, sand-brick cabin. From inside the shabby construction, gaslight flickered through the seams of shoddy wooden shutters.

He had to give it to the Aal Ossaibis. The Aal Shalaan's rival clan had constructed a watertight plan, and at the spur of the moment, too. This cabin was in the middle of nowhere. Literally. The nearest inhabited areas were over five hundred miles away in any direction. It was an ideal place to hold a hostage.

The hostage Harres was here to free.

He only found this place because he'd deduced the identity of one of those who hired the people inside the cabin. Since he'd uncovered the plot early enough, he'd managed to tag all the players in transit. He'd followed their phone signals before coverage vanished two hundred miles away. He'd since employed all the technology at his fingertips, and found this place only through some advanced satellite triangulation.

Anyone with less specific knowledge and less-than-limitless access and power at his disposal would have been stymied. Even with all of his resources, he never would have found it if not for his timely deductions.

And time was running out. From what he'd learned of the enemy's plans he had less than twenty minutes to complete the extraction. It was then that the masterminds of this kidnapping would arrive to interrogate the hostage and they'd be bringing their army of guards along.

Under any other circumstances, he wouldn't have considered this the ticking bomb he did now. He would have been here with his own major strike force. The very appearance of his finest Black Ops men would have forced anyone with any survival instincts to throw down his arms in surrender.

But as Zohayd's Minister of Interior and head of Central Intelligence and Homeland Security, he no longer knew whom to trust. His team tonight consisted of three men from his highest-ranking teams whom he would trust with his life. They didn't just work under him—they were family, prince soldiers who, like him, would give their lives for their kingdom. Though in other circumstances he trusted many of his men the same way, he couldn't afford the luxury of belief right now. There was too much at stake, and mixed loyalties could tip the whole region into chaos. He had to treat everyone else as suspect.

How could he not when the royal palace itself had already been breached? He wouldn't put infiltrating his ministry and operations, the forces responsible for keeping Zohayd secure, beyond the royal house's enemies.

He closed his eyes. He could still hardly believe it.

A conspiracy to overthrow his father as king and the Aal Shalaans as the ruling house of Zohayd had been brewing right under their noses for months now. The priceless Pride of Zohayd jewels, believed universally throughout the tribes to give the royal house the right to rule, had been stolen and replaced with fakes just in time for Exhibition Day, when they were to be paraded in public for all to see. No doubt the thief planned to publicly expose the jewels as fakes and begin the chaos that would see the Aal Shalaans removed from power.

For the past weeks, Harres had been casting his net throughout the region using information his brother Shaheen and his new wife, Johara, had secured. Early that morning,

Harres had gotten a lead that might take him straight to the conspiracy's mastermind.

A man claiming to be an American reporter was said to be in possession of all the vital details of the conspiracy.

Within twenty minutes, Harres had arrived at the man's rented condo. But their enemies had already made their move. The man had been gone. Abducted.

Harres hadn't missed a beat since, had followed the trail of the abductors to this desolate place. He had no doubt what the orders of the ruthless patriarch of the Aal Ossaibis were. Extract the info from the man, then let the desert claim him and his secrets.

That alone was reason enough for Harres to be out here. No one would be unjustly hurt on Zohaydan soil on his watch. Not even if it was someone whose agenda was to bring the Aal Shalaans down. Not even if it was this T. J. Burke.

T. J. Burke. The man was an enigma. In his databases Harres possessed up-to-the-moment information on every reporter in the world. He kept tight tabs on each since they wielded the most dangerous weapon of all, the media and its inexorable effect on global movements and the manufacturing of worldwide public opinion.

But T. J. Burke had slipped under his radar. Since Harres had learned of the reporter's existence, the unprecedented had happened. He'd failed to learn anything about the man. It was as if T. J. Burke had come into existence the moment he'd arrived in the region one week ago.

He'd found one reference to the only T. J. Burke who'd ever been in the region, an American IT specialist who'd worked for a multinational corporation in Azmahar. But that man had gone back to the States just over a year ago. A few months later, he'd been tried for the crimes of fraud and embezzlement, perpetrated while he'd been in

Harres's region. He was now serving a five-year sentence in a maximum-security penitentiary and was still securely in his cell as of a couple hours ago.

The current T. J. Burke had probably latched on to the name, or else he'd come up with a random persona for his fictional character and it coincided with an actual person's identity.

Which drove Harres to one conclusion. The man must be a spy. An uncanny one at that, hiding his origins from Harres's networks, and his movements and affiliations, too.

But he would save T. J. Burke even if he were the devil. Once he had him safe, he would extract the info he had. If it was what he hoped, what he feared, he would see what impossible price this man had intended to demand for the invaluable info and double it. Then he'd do everything in his considerable power to ensure he'd never resell it.

The sentries were nodding off in front of the fire now. He signaled to Munsoor, his second-in-command. Munsoor relayed his order counterclockwise to Yazeed at the cabin's south side, who then relayed it to Mohab at its west.

Twice they simultaneously fired their tranq darts, each felling their designated sentries.

Harres erupted to his feet. In seconds he was jumping over the guards' crumpled bodies and landing soundlessly on the stone steps leading to the cabin's door. The others were converging on him.

He exchanged a terse nod with his men, seeing only their intense gazes in the eerie combination of steady-as-time starlight and erratic firelight. They'd deal with any surprises. He'd go straight for their target.

He pushed on the door. It swung open with a creak that gutted the silence.

His gaze swept around the dim interior. Burke wasn't there. There was another room. He had to be there.

He bounded to its skewed door, slowly pushed it open.

A slim, trim-bearded man in a sand-colored quilted jacket rounded on him.

A heartbeat stretched as their eyes clashed.

Even in the faint light, Harres did a double take at the impact of the man's gaze, which seemed to be spewing electric azure. Then there was the rest of him. He seemed to glow in the gloom, both with an incandescent tan and a shock of gleaming gold hair spiking around his face.

Next heartbeat, Harres tore his gaze away, assessed the situation. This was a bathroom. Burke hadn't been using it. He'd been attempting an escape. He'd already pried the six-foot-high window open even with his hands tied in front of him. Harres had no doubt his captors wouldn't have made the mistake of tying them like that. Which meant the man had enough flexibility to get his hands where he could use them. A minute more and he *would* have escaped.

It was clear he didn't know there was nowhere to escape to. He must have been either knocked out cold or blindfolded on the way. But from what he'd seen in Burke's eyes, Harres bet he would have tried to escape regardless. This man was one who'd rather be shot in the back escaping than in the face while he pleaded for his life. He was beyond canny. He was resourceful, fearless.

And he'd be dead if Harres didn't get him out of here.

Harres had no doubt his captors would rather kill the man and lose the info his mind contained than let it fall into Aal Shalaan hands.

Observations segued into action. He lunged, grabbed the man's arm. Next second, he could swear a rocket launched through his teeth and exploded behind his eye sockets. It took him seconds to realize what had happened.

The man had hit him.

Still half-blind, Harres ducked, employing his other senses to dodge the barrage of blows the man rained on him. Harres charged him again, detained him in a crushing bear hug. He had no time for a more intimate introduction to those fists that packed such an unexpected wallop.

The man writhed in his hold with the ferocity of a tornado, almost breaking it.

"Quit struggling, you fool," Harres hissed. "I'm here to save you."

Seemed the man couldn't decipher Harres's words through the shroud covering his mouth. Or he didn't believe him. The man simultaneously delivered a bone-cracking kick to his left shin and kneed him. Harres barely avoided that last crippling impact, marveling at Burke's agility and speed even as he squeezed the man harder. The much smaller, wiry man would give him a run for his money if he had the use of both hands and more space.

Harres wrenched the cloth from his mouth, plastered the man against the uneven stone wall, a forearm against his throat applying enough pressure to make him stop fighting, pushing his face up to his so they again made eye contact.

A buzz zapped through him again as those glowing eyes slammed into his, as the body he imprisoned seethed against his with a mixture of defiance and panic.

Harres shook away the disorientation, firmed his pressure. "Don't make me knock you out and carry you like a sack of dirty laundry. I don't have time for your paranoia. Now, do as I tell you, if you want to get out of here alive."

He didn't wait for the man's consent. But in the second before he wrenched away, he thought he saw the fearful hostility in Burke's eyes soften. He filed away the observation for later dissection as he began dragging Burke back where he'd come from.

A fire exchange ripped the night, aborted his momentum.

Reinforcements must have arrived. His heart stampeded with the need to charge to his men's aid. But he couldn't. They'd all signed on knowing that only securing their target mattered. Anything—and anyone else—was expendable.

Feeling his blood boiling and curdling at once, he turned to the man. They'd have to use the escape route he'd already secured.

The man was ahead of him, already turning there. Harres snatched a dagger from the weapon belt around his thigh, slashed Burke's tethers, put it away, then bent to give him a boost so he could climb out of the window. And the man did another uncanny thing. He leaped up from a standstill, like a cat, clutched the six-foot-high ledge for the moment it took him to gain leverage and impetus to catapult himself through the opening. He cleared it in one fluid move. In a second, Harres heard the distinctive sound of someone hitting the ground on the other side of the wall in a rolling landing.

Was this guy an acrobat? Or was he a Black Ops agent, too?

Whatever he was, he was far more than even Harres had bargained for. He just hoped the tenacious sod didn't take off, forcing him to pursue Burke once he got out of here. It would take him more than the three seconds flat the man had taken to clear that tiny hatch with his size.

In about ten seconds, Harres flipped himself backward through the opening, the only way he'd been able to get enough leverage to squeeze himself through. As he let his mass drag him down, meeting the ground with extended arms, he had an upside-down view of the man's waiting silhouette. So

Burke was intelligent enough to know where his best chances lay.

He landed on flat palms, tucked and flipped over to his feet, standing up and starting to run toward the man in one continuous motion. "Follow me."

Without a word, the man did.

They ran across the sand dunes guided only by Harres's phosphorescent compass and a canopy of cold starlight. He couldn't use a flashlight to find his trail back to his sand car. There was no telling if any of their adversaries had slipped his men's net. A flashlight in this darkness would be like a beacon for the enemy to follow and all this would have been for nothing.

He ran with his charge in his wake, telling himself the others were safe. He wouldn't know for certain until they reached their own helicopter several miles away and entered coverage zones where he could communicate with them.

For now, he could think only of getting T. J. Burke to safety.

Ten minutes later, he felt secure enough to turn his senses back to the man. Burke was keeping up with him. The rhythm of his feet said he was running faster than Harres to make up for the difference in the length of their legs. So not only an agile and ready fighter, but in great shape, too. Good news. He hadn't been looking forward to hauling the guy to the sand car if he collapsed. But it was clear there was no danger of that. Burke was pacing himself superbly. No gasping, just even, deep inhalations and long, full exhalations.

And again something…inexplicable slithered down Harres's body as those sounds seemed to permeate the night, even with his own ears being boxed by the wind. The sensation originated from somewhere behind his breastbone and traveled downward, settling low, then lower.

He gritted his teeth against the disturbance as they reached his sand car. He jumped inside the open-framed, dune-buggy-style four-wheel vehicle. "Get in behind me."

Without missing a beat, Burke slid behind him on the seat, spread his legs on either side of Harres's hips, plastered his front to his back and curled himself around him as if they'd been doing this every day.

A shudder spread through Harres as he revved the motor. In seconds, he was hurtling the sand car over the dunes, driving with even more violence than the urgency of the situation dictated.

He drove in charged silence, catapulting the car over dune edges, crashing it in depressions, spraying sand in their wake and pushing the engine to its limit. With every violent jolt, the man's arms tightened around his midriff, his legs grabbing him more securely, his cheek pressing deeper into his back until Harres felt they'd been fused together.

His breath shortened by the moment as the heat of the man's body seeped through every point of contact, pooled in his loins.

Adrenaline. That was what it was. Discomfort. At having someone pressed so close, even in these circumstances.

Yes. What else could it possibly be?

In minutes, the crouching silhouette of his Mi-17 transport helicopter came into view. It was the best sight Harres had ever seen. He'd not only managed to reach their way out, but now he could get the man off of him.

He screeched the sand car into a huge arc, almost toppling it before bringing it to a quaking stop by the pilot's door.

He wrenched Burke's hands from his waist and leveraged himself out of the car in one motion. The man jumped out behind him, again with the stealth and economy of a cat, then waited for directions.

He took in details now that his vision was at its darkness-adapted best. With his windswept golden hair and those iridescent eyes, Burke looked like some moon elf, ethereal, his beauty untouched by the ordeal—

His *beauty?*

"Jump into the passenger seat and buckle yourself up." He heard his bark, knew all his aggression was directed at his insane thoughts and reactions. "I'll stuff the car in the cargo bay—"

The crack of thunder registered first.

Second, comprehension. A gun's discharge.

The shock in the man's eyes followed.

Last, the sting.

He'd been hit.

Somewhere on his left side, level with his heart. He had to assume not in it. He didn't feel any weakening. Yet.

Someone had slipped his men's net, had managed to sneak up on them. This could be the last mistake he ever made.

He exploded into action, charged the man to stop him from taking cover. They had no time for that.

He shouldn't have worried. Burke was no cowering fool. He was bolting to the helicopter even as more and more gunshots rang around them. He now knew the shot that had connected had been random. That was no sniper out there. That still didn't mean whoever it was couldn't hit a huge target like the chopper.

In seconds they were in their seats and Harres had the monster of a machine roaring off the ground, levitating into the sky.

He pressed the helicopter for all the altitude and velocity it was capable of. In less than a minute he knew they were too far for anyone pursuing them on foot or ATV to even spot anymore.

Only then did he let himself investigate his body for the

damage it had sustained. It had no idea yet. All it reported back was a burning path traversing his left side back to front just below his armpit. Flesh wound, he preferred to assume. Maybe with some bone damage. Nothing major. If no artery had been hit.

But the idea of losing blood too fast and spiraling into shock gave way to more pressing bad news. The chopper was losing fuel. The pursuer had hit the tank.

He eyed the gauge. With the rate of loss, the fuel wouldn't take them back to the capital. Nor anywhere near the inhabited areas where he could make contact with his people.

He had to make a detour. Head for the nearest oasis. At fifty miles away it was still four hundred and fifty miles closer than any other inhabited area. The inhabitants hadn't joined the modern world in any way, but once he and Burke were safely there, he would send envoys on horseback to his people. The trek would probably be delayed by a sandstorm that was expected to cut off the area from the world soon, a week or two during which his brothers and cousins—the only ones who knew of his mission—would probably think him dead. When weighed against his actual survival, and that of his charge, that was a tiny price to pay.

His new plan *would* be effective. Land in the oasis, take care of any injuries and contact his people. Mission accomplished.

Next minute, he almost kicked himself.

Of all times to count his missions….

The leaking fuel wasn't their only problem. In fact it was their slighter one. The damage to the navigation system had taken this long to reveal itself. The chopper was losing altitude fast. And there was nothing he could do to right its course.

He had to land now. Here. Or crash.

He turned to Burke urgently. "Are you buckled in?"

The man nodded frantically, his eyes widening with realization. Harres had no time to reassure him.

For the next few minutes he tried every trick he'd learned from his stint as a test pilot to land the helicopter and not have it be the last thing he did in his life.

As it was, they ended up crash-landing.

After the violent chain reaction of bone-powdering, steel-tearing impacts came to an end, he let out a shuddering breath acknowledging that they had survived being pulverized.

He leaned back in his seat, watching the interior of the cockpit fade in and out of focus. Had he lost too much blood or were the cockpit's lights fluctuating? He had no doubt the chopper itself was a goner.

He'd deal with his own concerns later. After he saw to his passenger.

He unbuckled his belt, flicked the cockpit lights on to maximum, turned to Burke. The man had his head turned against his seat, his eyes wide with an amalgam of panic and relief. Their gazes meshed.

And there was no mistaking what happened then.

Harres hardened. Fully.

He shuddered. What *was* this? What was going on? Was his body going haywire from the stress?

Enough of this idiocy. Check him for injuries.

He reached for him. The man flinched at his touch, as if Harres had electrified him. He knew how he felt. The same charge had forked through him. This had crossed from idiotic to insane.

He forced in an inhalation, determined to erase those anomalous reactions, drew Burke by the shoulders into the overhead light. The man struggled.

"Stop squirming. I need to check you for injuries."

"I'm fine."

The husky voice skewered through him even though he could barely hear it with the din of the still-moving rotors.

And a conviction slammed into him.

He would have thought he was beginning to hallucinate from blood loss. But he'd been feeling these inexplicable things long before he'd been hit. So he was through listening to his mind, and what it thought it knew, and heeding his body. It had been yelling at him from the first moment, just as his every instinct had been. He always listened to them.

Right now they were telling him that, even in these nightmarish conditions, they *wanted* T. J. Burke.

And knowing himself, that could only mean one thing.

He stabbed his fingers into the unruly gold silk on top of T. J. Burke's head, his body hardening more at the escaping gasp that flayed his cheek.

He traced the dewy lips with his thumb, as if to catch the sound and the chagrined shock at what he sensed was an equally uncontrollable response.

He smiled his satisfaction. "So, tell me, why are you pretending to be T. J. Burke, bearded investigative reporter, when a modern-day bejeweled Mata Hari would suit you far better?"

Two

T. J. Burke wrenched away from the cloaked, force-of-nature-in-man-form's hold, panted, voice gruff and low, a tremor of panic traversing it. "Did you hit your head in the crash?"

The man bore down again without seeming to move, making the spacious cockpit of the high-end military helicopter shrink. The smile in those golden eyes that seemed to snare the dimmest rays and emit them magnified, took on a dangerous edge. The danger was more spine-shivering for being unthreatening, more…distressing, with the response it elicited.

Then the colossus drawled in that deeper-than-the-desert-night baritone. "The only hit to the head I got tonight was courtesy of those neatly trimmed, capable hands of yours."

"Since I hit you with the intention of taking your head

off, I probably dislocated something in there. Your good sense, seemingly. Maybe your whole brain."

The man pressed closer, the freshness of his breath and the potency of his virility flooding every one of T.J.'s senses. "Oh, both my sense and my brain are welded in place. It would take maybe…" his eyes traveled up and down T.J.'s body like slow, scorching hands "…ten of you to loosen even my consciousness."

"It took only one of me to do so earlier," T.J. scoffed, not sure the supply of air in the cockpit would last much longer. "I almost took you down. With both hands literally tied, too."

"You can sure take me down, just not by hitting me. Your effect on me has nothing to do with your physical strength and is certainly not proportionate to your size."

"Is that all you got? Cheap shots at my size?"

"I'd never take any kind of shot at you." Again the man's eyes seemed to emit a force field that gathered T.J. into its embrace. "And then, I think your size is perfection itself."

Drenched in goose bumps and feeling the heart that had barely slowed down start to hammer again, T.J. smirked. "Sure you're not concussed? Or is this the way you usually talk to other men?"

The insult seemed to burn to ash in the rising temperature of the man's smile. "It's not even the way I talk to women. But it's the only way I'll talk to *you*. Among other things. Every other possible thing."

T.J. pressed against the passenger door. "So you somehow got it into your head that I'm a woman? And now you're all over me? Just minutes after barely surviving a devastating crash and landing God knows where in this forsaken, sand-infested land? And you can't hear how ridiculous you sound?"

"What's ridiculous is that you thought a fuzzy beard and

an atrocious haircut would disguise the femininity blasting off you. It got me by the…throat, from the first moment. So why don't you drop the act and tell me who you really are?"

"I *am* T. J. Burke!"

Painstakingly chiseled lips spread to reveal teeth so white they were almost phosphorescent in the dimness. "My bearded beauty, only one of us has testosterone coursing in his bloodstream right now. Don't make me offer you… tangible proof."

T.J. glowered at him, tried not to show any weakness, to meet him on the same level of audacity. "Is it the…tangible proof proving that you're attracted to small blond men?"

A chuckle rumbled deep in that huge predator's gut, zigzagged all through T.J.'s system like deadly voltage. "First thing you have to learn about me so we can move on is that I am insult-proof. I wouldn't even sock you if you *were* a man. But my body knew you weren't from the moment I laid eyes on you in that filthy hole, against all evidence and intel. So will you admit it on your own, or will you make me…establish proof myself?"

T.J. shrank back farther against the door as the man's right hand rose. "Lay a hand on me, buster, and have it chomped off."

"With the way I'm reacting to you, there's nothing I want more than your teeth on every part of me. But if anything proves your femininity, it's that so-called threat. A man would have told me he'd break my hand or tear it off, or something suitably macho."

"So you have men regularly threatening to do that? And women chomping away at any part of you they can reach?"

The man narrowed his eyes, concentrating the intensity of his amusement. "You're an expert at diversion, aren't you? Give it up, already. I'm on to you. So on to you that not even a bullet is dulling my response."

"A *bullet?*" T.J felt both eyes almost pop out with shock. "You're hit?"

The man nodded. "So will you take pity on an injured man and bestow your name on me? Make it your real one this time. And let me see how you look without that rug on your face."

"Oh, shut *up*. Are you really injured or are you playing me?"

The man suddenly sat up from his seemingly indolent pose, tugged T.J.'s right hand. T.J. ended up pressed against him, chest to chest, face in his neck, arm around his massive torso. The sensation of touching a live wire came first. Then that of sickening viscosity scorched everything away.

Before T.J. could jerk back in alarm, the man meshed his right hand in T.J.'s hair, pulling gently until their gazes once again melded. "See? I'm bleeding. For you. I might die. Can you be so cruel as to let me die without knowing who you are?"

T.J. wrenched away from him, one hand drenched in the thick heat and slickness of his blood. "Oh, just shut *up*."

Those lethal lips twitched. "I will if you start talking."

"You don't need me to talk, you need me to take care of this wound."

"*I'll* take care of it. You talk."

"Don't be stupid. Your intercostal arteries might be severed, and those bleed like gushing faucets. You might think you're stable, but there's no telling how bad your injury is, what kind of blood loss you've suffered. Your blood pressure could plunge without warning. And if it does, there's no bringing it back up!"

"Spoken like an expert. Been shot before?"

"I've treated people who were. People who weren't too stupid to jump at my offer to help them."

"Is that any way to talk to the man who took a bullet for you? And will you peel that thing off your face, already?"

"I can't believe this! You might slip into shock at any moment and you're still trying to prove this lame theory of yours?"

He just smiled, imperturbable, immovable.

"Okay," T.J. gritted. "I'll talk. After I take care of you."

"I'll let you take care of me. After you talk."

"Come *on*. Where is this chopper's emergency kit?"

"I'll tell you after you tell me what I want to hear."

"Not the truth, huh? 'Cause I already told you that."

The man backed away when T.J. lunged at him, hands reaching out to expose his wound. "Uh-uh-uh. No touching until you admit you're a woman. I only let women touch me."

T.J. glared into eyes that had a dozen devils dancing in them. "You're really out of touch with the reality—the *gravity*—of your situation, aren't you? But what do you care if I admit it or not? You *know* it, after all. And then, I'm not going to merely *touch* you, I'm going to bathe in your blood."

The appreciation in the man's eyes expanded, enveloped T.J. whole. "I knew you were a bloodthirsty wench when you almost sliced me in half with the power of your glare alone. Then you tried to powder my teeth *and* transform me from a baritone to an alto."

T.J. felt a smile advancing, dispelling the frown that by now felt etched on, and had to admit…

That man was lethal. In every sense of the word.

But though he was teasing, his irreversible deterioration

might actually come to pass. There was no telling how serious his injury was without a thorough exam. "And to think you seemed intelligent. Guess appearances can be deceiving."

The man's lips twisted. "You can talk."

"Oh, but I thought my appearance didn't deceive you for a moment, that my 'femininity' kicked you like a mule."

The man sighed, nodding in mock helplessness. "*Aih.* But if I do succumb, remember, it's your doing, in every way."

"Give me a break." T.J. exhaled forcibly then scratched at the beard.

Then she snatched it away.

She yelped as a blowtorch seemed to blast her nerve endings, forcing her to leave the beard dangling over her lips. She rubbed at the burning sensation, gave her tormentor a baleful glance. "Happy now, you pigheaded, mulish ox?"

"A one-man farm, eh? No one has ever flattered me as you do." She glared at him as he oh-so-carefully removed the rest of the beard, making the adhesive separate from her skin with a kneading sensation instead of a stinging one.

Then he pulled back, massaged her jaw and cheeks in an insistent to and fro, soothing her skin with the backs of those long, roughened, steel-hard fingers. She moaned as a far more devastating brand of fire swept her flesh from every point of contact.

He groaned himself. "*Ya Ullah, ma ajmalek.* How absolutely beautiful you are. I thought I'd seen all kinds of beauty, but I've never laid eyes on anything like you. It's like you're made of light and gold and energy and gemstones."

Heat rose through her at his every word. When she'd first seen him, she'd been freezing with dread and the desert's chill. But when she'd turned to him in that filthy bathroom, his very presence had sent animation surging into her every cell. The crash had drained her, but the heat of his solicitude, his awareness and appreciation, the stoking of his challenge, had been melting away the ice that seemed to have become a constituent of her bones.

She still couldn't believe he'd seen through her disguise. No one had during the week she'd been in Zohayd. Her captors hadn't, and she'd spent a whole day in their grasp. But he'd sensed her femininity in moments, with his senses almost blinded by the night's dimness, the urgency and her disguise. He'd also had no tactile evidence, with the buffer of clothes—especially her jacket and the corset flattening her...assets.

Yet he'd known. And just as he'd felt her vibes, she'd been immersed in his. She'd felt every hot granite inch of his formidable body, smelled him over the overpowering stench of her prison, over the dispersion of the desert and the deluge of post-accident mayhem. She'd heard each inflection of his voice through the din of her inner cacophony and the madness of their escape and crash.

And instead of reacting to his maleness as she had to her captors'—with dread, revulsion, aggression and desperation—she was finding it bolstering, soothing and, if she could believe her body's reactions in these insane circumstances, arousing.

She hadn't found a male this arousing in...ever.

And to find this man so might mean it was *she* who'd hit her head. Or something. There must be something wrong, if all she wanted right now was to snuggle into him and hold on tight.

As if responding to her need, mirroring it, he leaned in, pressed his face lightly into her neck, breathed her in and groaned again with intense enjoyment. "Even with male cologne and all the traces of your ordeal, you smell heavenly. And you still haven't told me your name, *ya jameelati*."

She pulled back from his hypnosis, from the idiocy of her untimely weakness. She had to patch up this obdurate hulk. "And you still think if you ask me enough times I'll give you a different answer."

His eyes stilled on her. Then he nodded, as if coming to a decision. "So your name is T.J. What do the *T* and *J* stand for?"

She blinked. "You believe me?"

"Yes. My instincts about you have been right-on so far. They're saying you're telling the truth now. They even insist you probably haven't developed the ability to lie."

"You make me sound like an incontinent blabbermouth. I gave my kidnappers nothing."

"Withholding the truth is not lying. It can span the spectrum of motives, from fear to nobility. Doing it under threat of harm or worse is courageous. But in almost all situations, telling an untruth is cowardly. And I had no doubt of your courage from the first moment. So, with that established…your name?"

T.J. drew in a shaky inhalation then blurted it out. "Talia Jasmine. Satisfied? Now where is that damned emergency kit?"

She heard his intake of breath, felt it sweeping inside her own chest like an internal caress. But it was the wonder that flared in those preternatural eyes that started her shivering again. With everything but cold.

Without a word, he reached overheard, opened a compartment and produced a huge emergency bag.

She pounced on it. Relief swamped her as she made a lightning-fast inventory of the contents. Everything she could possibly need.

She took out a saline bag, hooked it in an overhead protrusion, dragged his right arm over her lap and pushed the needle into his vein, then secured it with adhesive tape and turned the drip to maximum for quickest fluid replacement.

He tugged at her chin, pressed something to her lips. A bottle of water. She suddenly realized she was beyond parched. She downed the bottle in one go. He watched her as if he wanted to gulp her down himself, to decipher and assimilate her.

She licked her lips, cleared her throat. "Okay, I need you to expose the wound and hold this flashlight over it for me. Better do it in the back of this monster so you can lie down."

He smiled in that seriousness-melting way of his. "I can give you two out of three of your demands. I can with pleasure take off my clothes. And I can shed light on the mess I made when all of my senses were so focused on you that I missed the pursuer who could have killed me with one haphazard shot. I shudder to think where that would have left you."

"As if I'm in such a great situation now," she mumbled under her breath as she snapped on gloves.

"We're both in one piece, with me only slightly punctured, which in a hostage-extraction op is about the best possible situation. But I have to inform you I had to sacrifice the back end of the chopper to preserve the cockpit while crash-landing. I doubt there's any space back there for even one of *your* species to stretch out."

She looked up from preparing her surgical tray. "My species? Women you mean? Last I heard we were a gender."

"Felines." His smile widened as he reached for the swathe over his head to start the process of exposing himself...his *wound* for her. "I know of nothing else capable of exiting a six-foot-high window with as much economy of movement and grace."

"They're called gymnasts. I was one till I hit eighteen. Seems my abilities reactivated under duress."

He finished unfurling the yards of material from his head in movements she could only describe as…erotic. This was a man used to barricading himself in mere cloth before plunging into the desert, pitting his wiles and will against its cruelty and capriciousness.

Suddenly all thoughts evaporated. The last coil fell off, and a mane of gleaming mahogany cascaded in layers of satin luxury to his shoulders.

She swallowed. "You should talk."

"Oh?" One formidable wing of an eyebrow quirked as he shrugged off the outer layer of his night-colored desert raider/ninja/Black Ops hybrid outfit. He seemed to grow bigger in only a skintight, high-collared, long-sleeved top.

She gave him an encompassing gesture. "You should be on stage playing the Lion King yourself. With minimal or no makeup."

And he gifted her with another of those amused rumbles that proved his great feline origins.

Then he tried to yank off his top and groaned, his face twisting in obvious pain. "Seems raising my left arm won't be one of my favorite activities for a while."

"Do you have a change of clothes on board?"

"Yes. And other supplies that I'll access once we're done with this."

"Okay, then." She swept scissors off the tray and proceeded to cut off his top.

He hissed as the coolness of the blade slid against his hot skin, groaned as she reached the parts that had stuck to his wound, then growled as her gloved hands glided over his flesh, separating the adhesions and palpating the edges of his wound.

There should only be pain. But to ears that were hyperaware of his merest inflection, the pleasure was unmistakable, too.

Tremors invaded her hands, traveling all the way from her core. And this from gloved and accidental contact while exploring his wound. What would touching him with no barriers do to her if she were exploring his power and beauty for pleasure instead?

Work, idiot. Stop fantasizing about this hunk of impossible virility and just patch him up. You're probably in ten different types of shock and hallucinating most of this anyway. Moron.

Continuing her raucous inner abuse, she worked in silence.

Suddenly a realization dawned on her. All the time she'd been filling hypodermic needles with local anesthetic, analgesic/anti-inflammatory and broad-spectrum antibiotic, he'd been handing her vials, receiving filled syringes and placing them in the correct sequence on the tray like the best of her long-term assistants. He continued to help her with total efficiency and obvious knowledge of what went where and would be used when as she prepared forceps, scalpels, sutures, cautery, bandages, wipes and antiseptics.

He hadn't been bragging when he'd said he'd take care of his wound. This was a man versed in more than hostage-retrieval ops. He was no stranger to field emergency procedures.

Just who and what was he?

She opened her mouth to ask and one of those fingers she'd bet could bend steel feathered down her cheek again. The gentleness of his touch almost pulverized her precarious control. Tears churned at the back of her eyes. She swallowed them along with any questions.

He asked them of her. "You weren't exaggerating when you said you'd treated bullet wounds before. Just who are you, my heaven's dew?"

Her hands stilled from checking her supplies before she started the procedure.

No one had ever realized the meaning of her name.

"Your parents are to be applauded for choosing such a name to befit your wonder and delicacy."

She shot him an affronted look. "I'm not delicate!"

His smile filled with teasing indulgence. "Oh, but you are, incredibly so."

She narrowed her eyes at him. "How's your jaw?"

Something hot and delighted rumbled deep in his chest, revved in her bones like a bass line made of urges instead of sound. "My jaw will always remember its meeting with your fist. But sheathe your claws. Delicacy doesn't equate with fragility when describing you, but with refinement mixed with delectability wrapped around a core of resourcefulness. That's what you are. An exterior of pure gold, a filling of sheer delight and a center of polished steel."

Her lips twitched. "You sure you didn't hit your head? Or are you always so ready and free with spontaneous poetry?"

"I'm the very opposite. Women call me a miser with words. I never say what I don't mean. What I don't feel. It's no wonder I was chosen for law enforcement and not diplomacy."

"So among the hordes of women who've stampeded through your life, I'm the only one who, in the aftermath of a rescue mission out of a *Mission Impossible* movie, has moved you so much you've found your inner poet."

"You've summed it up perfectly."

He suddenly turned around and lay back, placing his head and shoulders on her lap.

He grinned up at her as she froze, stared down at him. "This is the only place I'm lying down around here."

She gulped, looked into his upside-down eyes and repressed the urge to smooth her hands over his face, to thread her fingers through that incredible mane fanned over her lap, and most insane of all, to bend down and kiss his forehead before she started poking him with needles and slicing him with scalpels.

Before she succumbed to any of those ridiculous urges, he transferred the tray she'd prepared to the floor, then turned to his side to present her with an optimum view of his injury.

She almost choked when he looked up from his sideways position and purred, "And that's the best way to hand you instruments as you work."

She gave a jerky nod and a throat-clearing cough, hoping to expel any mind-fogging stupidity.

Then proceeded to examine his wound.

Harres looked up at this enigma in a woman's form whom he'd saved. And who was in turn saving him.

He held the flashlight at an optimal angle for her. And while she injected his side with local anesthetic, he examined her.

She was beyond beautiful. Unique. Magical. He hadn't told her the half of it when she'd charged him with being poetic.

She finally made that throat-clearing noise he'd come to realize meant she was fighting for composure. And he bet it had nothing to do with the medical part of their situation.

"Okay. The bullet made a clear track through your muscles. It hit the tip of your scapula, grazing three ribs.

No tendons or nerves are severed. There is muscle damage at the bullet's entry point, then as it came out the front it tore a four-inch wound in your skin. But the bleeding is the worst of it, since a few arteries have recoiled out of reach. I'll have to widen the wound and deepen it, to fish them out and cauterize them, and for future drainage. I'll place deep sutures to repair the most traumatized tissues, but will leave the wound open to drain for later closure, once the swelling goes down, so no infection is trapped within."

As she spoke, she continued to implement her plan with flawless execution. He continued to assist her.

Every minute brought more unprecedented sensations. It wasn't just physical reactions to feeling her firm, warm thighs beneath his head, or breathing her hot, intoxicating scent with every breath. He'd never experienced this synergy, not even when working with his brothers or his men. He'd never let another person take charge of anything while he was around, let alone his own physical well-being. He'd never lusted after a woman anywhere near this intensely, let alone while simultaneously respecting the hell out of her capabilities, relying on her efficiency and wanting to pamper her with all he had and protect her with his life.

Was this real, or was everything being amplified by the circumstances combined with a dose of blood loss, survival elation and gratitude?

But when he added in his mounting physical response and mental appreciation, he was back to square one.

This *was* as real as anything got. And from the way she kept stroking him with her eyes after she finished each step and with her hands after each cut as if to apologize for the necessity of hurting him to heal him, from the way her hands and lips trembled at his merest indication of discomfort, he knew.

It was just as real for her.

It didn't matter who they were, or how and when they'd met. What they'd done since, the seeming lifetime of life-changing events and feelings they'd experienced together, meant they could leap over most stages of development and acknowledgment of attraction.

She finished the procedure and he sat up, helped her wrap his torso in bandages. As she began to draw back, he couldn't bear it. His right hand wove into her hair, kept her close, brought her closer. And she lurched away.

He stilled, his heart jolting with the same force.

After a long moment, he removed his hand, whispered, "Are you afraid of me?"

"No." Relief deflated him at her vehement denial. Then she grinned sheepishly at him, boosting her beauty to dizzying heights. "Which might be the stupidest thing I've ever thought or felt, considering I'm in the middle of nowhere with a hulk of a man in a hostile land where I know no one. But there you go. I'm not afraid of you. Not for a second. I'm…the very opposite."

Warmth flooded him at her admission. He'd been right. She felt the same way.

Another unknown urge took him over, the desire to tease her, even as he wanted to devour her. "Now that's a little white lie. You were so afraid of me for at least a few seconds that you almost gave me a permanent disability."

"That was before I saw your face, heard your voice. Before that, you were this…huge chunk of night that had come to claim me."

"You were right about the coming to claim you part." He reached out to her again, slid a hand around her waist, drew her to him. "So are you going to tell me where you learned to perform field surgery like that?"

"In medical school, where else?"

"You mean you *are* a doctor?"

"Last I heard that's what came off said school's production line."

"So everything I thought you were was false, from your gender to your profession. Is there no end to your surprises?"

A grin trembled on her dimpled but now colorless lips. "Now why would there be?"

The urge to capture her lips, nibble color and warmth back into them surged inside him, almost brimmed over into action.

"No reason at all, *ya shafeyati*."

"What does this mean?"

"My healer."

"So how do you say 'my rescuer' in Arabic?"

"Monqethi."

She repeated the word after him, that voice that even when she'd tried to deepen and roughen it had coursed through him like an intravenous aphrodisiac now becoming a vocal caress that soothed his insides, infused his every cell.

Then she heightened her exquisite torture. "And 'my hero'?"

His vocal cords locked against the tide of temptation. He whispered, *"Buttuli,"* listened to her hypnotic melody begin to repeat it, before his control snapped.

He swooped down and took the rest of her tremulous homage inside him, along with that breath that had been tormenting him with its arousing fragrance. She gave him more, in one gasp after another, opened for him.

He wanted to drown in her, drown her in him, give her a glimpse of the need and ferocity she ignited in him. His lips claimed hers as if he'd brand her, his tongue thrusting deep, breaching her, draining her of moans and sweetness.

She took it all, seeming unable to meet his passion yet overwhelming him with her surrender.

"Talia…*nadda jannati*…my heaven's dew…"

"Not fair," she moaned into his lips. "I don't know your name…let alone what it means."

He drew in her plump lower lip, suckled it until she cried out and took his tongue deeper.

"Harres…Harres Aal Shalaan." He started to translate, had said only "Guardian—" when she gasped then pushed him away.

He stared down at her, all his being rioting, needing her back against him, her lips crushed beneath his, her heat enveloping his suddenly chilled body.

She gaped up at him.

Then she finally rasped, "You're an Aal Shalaan?"

Harres nodded, already acutely sorry that he'd told her.

Now it would end, the spontaneity of the attraction that had exploded to life between them. Now that he'd told her who he was, nothing could ever be the same. There hadn't been a woman of the thousands he'd met in his life, the hundreds who'd pursued him, no matter how attracted to him they were, who'd seen him as anything but an amalgam of status, power and money. He was never just a man to them. He'd cease to be just a man to her now.

He exhaled, his gaze leaving her kiss-swollen lips in regret as he waited for artificiality to settle into her guileless eyes, for calculation to take hold of her open-book reactions. He'd often chafed at the trappings of his status and position and wealth. He now positively cursed them.

Then she again did the last thing he could have expected.

Her gaping became a glare of such revulsion and hostility,

he might as well have turned into a slimy creature before her eyes.

Then she spat, "You're one of that pack of highborn, lowlife criminals?"

Three

Harres stared at this woman who'd just called him and his family a pack of criminals. And he did the only thing he could.

He threw his head back and belted out a guffaw.

Now that the local anesthetic was wearing off, his wound protested the uninhibited movement, stabbed him with a burning lance of pain. It wasn't any hotter than the glare of abhorrence Talia still scorched him with. Seemed his mirth only poured fuel on her sudden antipathy.

But he couldn't help it. There was no way he could control his relief, his thrill, that instead of fawning over him, she looked ready to sock him again.

Then she did. On his good arm, hard enough to sober him a bit, save him from tearing loose her meticulous suturing efforts with laughter.

"Don't you laugh at me, you aggravating jackass!"

As if in response to her anger, the wind exploded with sudden fury around the helicopter, rocking the wreckage.

She didn't seem to notice as she braced herself, her incandescent eyes riddling him with azure-hot holes.

And he just loved it.

He raised a placating hand, tried to pretend a measure of sobriety. It was far harder than anything he'd done tonight. Right along with not reaching out and dragging her back against him. The woman sabotaged his propriety sense and either caressed, aroused or tickled all others.

"I wouldn't dare. And then, this is delight, not ridicule." His left hand rubbed the sting of her blow, as if to trap the feel of her flesh against his, even in anger. His lips were still burning with the memory of capturing hers, his tongue from tangling with hers, tasting her intoxication and swallowing her whimpers of pleasure. All of him still tingled from having her, ton of clothes and all, pressed against him. He wanted to get this confrontation out of the way so he could have her there again. "And it's your doing again, you and your endless surprises."

She balled her fists, her bee-stung lips pressing into an ominous line. "How about I give those a fitting end? By fracturing your nose."

Her aggression made the pleasure bubbling inside him spill again into a chuckle as he gave his aching jaw a reminiscent rub. "To go with my jaw?" He turned his face, presented her with a three-quarters view of said nose. "Or do you think it could do with a new one?" He shook his head at her chagrined hiss. "Whoa, that alone could have done the job. It's a good thing I didn't tell you my name when you had your scalpels deep in my flesh."

Her eyes became slits of enraged challenge. "But now I know it, and I'll have those scalpels there again while debriding the wound before closing it. Over many stages.

Or it will fester. And don't tell me you can take care of it yourself, 'cause we both know you can't. Most of the wound track is where you can't reach it. And next time, maybe my nerve block won't be as…effective."

He gasped in mock shock. "You not only flaunt your power over me, you'd abuse that power, disregard your oath to do no harm? You would torment me while I'm under your scalpel? You'd gloat at my helplessness and need, and take pleasure in my pain?" He let excitement at her implied threat spread his lips. "I can't wait."

Her eyes swept him with now blue-cold disdain. "So you have an extreme form of masochism among your perversions, huh? Figures."

"Not to me, it doesn't. At least, it didn't. But I *am* discovering I'd welcome anything from you."

She snorted. He shook his head as he huffed another chuckle. He couldn't believe it himself, how fully he meant that.

Sighing, admitting that for the first time in his life, he was experiencing something beyond his control, he reached for what had survived of his bloody clothes. And though she aimed more detestation at him, he felt her unwilling coveting spread over every inch of his cold flesh, heating it from the inside out. He shuddered at the caress of her eyes over every bulge and stretch of his muscles as he carefully pulled his clothes back on.

His satisfaction rose. Her reactions to him had not only alternated between delightful and brutal honesty, they were as overpowering as his. Her mind might be telling her to slash him open, but everything else was clamoring for his nearness, delighting in his every detail. And of course that was making her madder. At him.

He'd finished dressing before it occurred to him to try the heater. It was still working.

He turned his gaze back to her with a smile, and she slammed him with a disapproving scowl.

"*Now* you turn on the heater. Were you trying to see how long you can last before you succumb to hypothermia? Or were you hoping I'd offer you the best remedy for it?"

"Flesh-on-flesh warming." He almost shivered with imagining the mind-melting sensuality of such an act with her. "And now you've cornered me. I must admit either that I was such a remiss male that I didn't think of it, or such an inefficient field officer that I didn't remember the onboard heater. Will I get leniency points if I cite my reason for failing to think of it to be preoccupation with your golden self?"

"Nah. I have another explanation. You didn't think of it because you're cold-blooded like all *your* species. Snakes."

A laugh overpowered him and sent another bolt of pain through him. "Ah, I've never been so inventively insulted before. I can't get enough of whatever spills from your mouth."

Her smile was one of condescension and disgust. "I'm such a refreshing acid bath after all the slimy, simpering sweetness you usually marinate in, huh, you jaded jerk?"

He put a protective hand to his side as he laughed again and groaned in pain simultaneously. "What you are is literally sidesplitting. It is positively intoxicating what an irreverent, fearless wildcat you are, *ya nadda jannati*."

"Don't you dare call me that again!" she growled.

"Talia…"

She slammed her fist on her thigh in chagrin. "And don't call me that, either. I'm T.J.—no, *Dr.* Burke to you. No—I'm nothing to you. So don't call me anything at all!" He began to say her name again but she bulldozed over his insistence. "And now I take back everything *I* called you.

You're not *monqethi* or *buttuli*. You're just one of those self-serving, criminal dictators. Or wait—since you were sent to retrieve me, you're probably one of their lower ranks, maybe even disposable. Not that it makes you any better than the higher-ups."

Everything inside him stilled.

Then he slowly asked, "You don't know who I am?"

"You're an Aal Shalaan," she spat the name. "That's all I need to know."

Would knowing exactly who he was change her attitude? For the better? By now, he was hoping it would. Her antagonism, now that it seemed there to stay, was fast losing its exciting edge.

Then he inhaled. "I'm not just an Aal Shalaan. I'm Harres."

"Yeah, I heard you the first time. But just Harres, huh? Like you're Elvis or something!"

"Around here? I'd say I'm more Captain Kirk. And you really have no idea, eh?"

Her eyes narrowed on him. "So you're some big shot?"

He huffed, the last traces of elation snuffed. "The third-biggest shot around, yes."

He saw that lightning-fast mind of hers reach the conclusion. She still stared at him, as if expecting him to say something else to negate his declaration and her deduction.

He quirked a prodding eyebrow at her. He wanted to reach the new status quo his identity always triggered and be done with it.

She shook her golden head dazedly, her lips opening and closing on many aborted outbursts, before she finally managed to voice one.

"You're *that* Harres Aal Shalaan?"

"You mean there are others? And here I thought I was the one and only."

"And here I thought the dumb-blonde stereotype had been long erased. Clearly not in Zohayd, if you think I'll believe *that*."

"Actually I think you're superiorly intelligent and extensively informed. In general. In this specific case, I think you're suffering from severe and very damaging misinformation."

"Fine. One of the hallmarks of superior intelligence is an open mind. So here's my mind, wide as the desert and ready for amending info. What is the king's second son and Zohayd's worshipped minister of interior doing on a hostage-retrieval mission?"

"You see? Brilliant. You cut to the core of logic in any situation like an arrow. And as the question is the only one to be asked, the answer is as singular. I couldn't entrust anyone else with retrieving you. I had to be here myself. And I thank the circumstances that necessitated my presence."

She cracked a bitter laugh. "Sure, because it turned out to be me, and I'm unique, magical, and our meeting under these circumstances is an unprecedented and unrepeatable act of munificent fate, and all that over-the-top drivel."

His hands itched with the need to capture that proud, obstinate head, subdue her resentment, resurrect her hunger.

But he knew that would backfire. He was finally realizing the gravity of the situation. The depth of her prejudice. He had no idea what had formed such an iceberg within her, but if he wasn't careful, all his efforts to win her trust would be wrecked against it.

He let the last trace of the smile go. This needed to be serious, heartfelt. That would be easy. He didn't have to act either sentiment. "A few minutes ago, before learning my identity turned you from an ally into an enemy, you would have agreed with all that you now consider devious nonsense."

Her eyes lashed him with more vexation. He realized that her belief that she'd been taken in was exaggerating her anger. "Sure I would have. I was being worked by a master manipulator. But then, after I escaped being interrogated to death by a gang of desert hooligans, anyone would have seemed a knight in camouflage to my fried mind and senses. But you're not being very clever. Telling me who you are was the worst mistake you could have made. You would have served your goal far better if you'd let me believe you were small fry, one of the hundreds of 'princes' with the odd drop of Aal Shalaan blood. Exposing yourself as the premium pure brew only makes you more accountable for the crimes your family perpetrated. It makes you the enemy I'm here to bring down."

Talia watched her words sink into Harres Aal Shalaan.

She'd managed to wipe away that indulgent smile that had seemed permanent on his face a couple of minutes ago. Now she'd gone a dozen steps further, causing his expression to be engulfed in a tide of grimness.

She almost bit her tongue, but she might get poisoned by the venom flowing from it.

But she couldn't stop. Disappointment urged her to pour it out before it ate through her. Her hero, her savior, the man who'd risked his life to rescue her, was an Aal Shalaan. And not just any Aal Shalaan. One of the four big guns. And the one who had as much jurisdiction and even more law-enforcement power than the king himself. Which meant only one thing.

He had more to lose than any other member of his family.

He had *everything* to lose.

And she was using her considerable provocation powers to declare herself in a position to affect those incalculable losses. While she was stranded in the desert with him, with no way of rejoining humanity except through him.

Any bets she ever would now?

She held her breath for his reaction. So rage and indignation and—damn him—*him* were loosening every last one of her discretion screws. But not to the point where she'd lost track of the possible, and expected, consequences.

He lowered his gaze, relinquishing hers for the first time. She watched the long sweep of his downcast lashes as they stilled, her heart ramming her ribcage. Next time he raised those eyes he'd take off the mask of geniality and tolerance. They'd be cold and ruthless. And he'd no longer be her persuader but her interrogator, not her rescuer but her warden.

Then he raised his eyes and almost had her keeling over in his lap.

Those golden orbs were emitting a steady energy, a calming power that seeped through hers, into her brain, flooding her whole body.

The son of a…king was trying to hypnotize her!

And he was almost succeeding. Even now.

So. She'd gravely underestimated him. She'd thought, with the novelty of her resistance depleted, his facade of endless patience and indulgence would crack, exposing his true face. That of an all-powerful prince used to having people cower before him. But it seemed he was also an infallible character-reader, realized that intimidation would get him nowhere with her. So he wasn't playing that card just yet. Not before he gave all the others in his formidable arsenal a full demo.

So Prince Harres Aal Shalaan wasn't who he was just

because he'd been delivered into the royal family, hadn't qualified for his position in the family business because he'd grown up playing desert raiders. He evidently had staying power, was in command of himself at all times. He had long-term insight and layered intelligence, remained on top of any situation. And he had uncanny people skills and truckloads of charisma, made willing followers of everyone he crossed paths with.

He had of her, too. But no more.

The bucket of drool stopped here.

Then he spoke in that polyphonic voice of his, which made her feel as if it was coming from all around her, from inside her, and she almost revised her certainty. Almost.

"I don't know what you've been hearing about the Aal Shalaans, or from whom, but you've been misled. We're neither despots nor criminals."

"Sure. And I'm supposed to take your word for it."

"Yes, until I'm in a position to prove it. I would at least demand you grant us the benefit of the doubt."

"Oh, if I had any, I'd grant it. But I don't, so I won't."

"Won't you at least make your accusations and give me a chance to come up with a defense?"

"I'm sure you can come up with anything you wish. You'd fabricate enough evidence to confuse issues with reasonable doubt. But this isn't a court of law, and I'm not a judge. I'm just someone who knows the truth. And I'm here collecting evidence to prove it."

"To prove what?"

"That you're not all above reproach as you paint yourselves to be."

He gave a shrug with his right shoulder. It was eloquent with concession and dismissal. The man spoke, expressed, with every last inch of his body. "Who in any place of power doesn't have someone with a beef against them?

Ruling a country isn't all plain sailing. Laws and rulings are contested, whether economic, military or judicial, by others with opposing views or interests. In my own peacekeeping and business capacities, I'm sure my decisions and actions always leave someone disgruntled. That doesn't mean I'm evil. I've certainly done nothing criminal in my life."

"Oh, you're too clever to do something overt. But you, Mr. Peacekeeping Entrepreneur, manipulate the law, and people. Like you did me. Like you're still trying to. But I'm on to you. I'm on to your whole family. That you call yourselves a royal family doesn't make you any less criminal. Many so-called rulers were deposed then brought to justice for crimes against their people. As you one day, and soon I hope, will be."

Okay. She'd done it. She'd ensured her place at the top of his blacklist.

And again, the tenacious man refused to get it over with and validate her fear, release his mask.

His face remained the very sight of sincerity, his voice the very sound of earnestness. "You can believe what you wish, Talia. But I will also say what I wish, my version of the truth. I would have come to save you, no matter who you were. And whomever I saved would have been safe with me. Whatever your agenda is, you are safer with me than with your own family. You scoff now, but when you weren't applying your prejudice to me, you, too, believed it was an act of fate for us to share this, to feel this powerfully about each other, to see the other for what we truly are without the help or hindrance of identities and history. I now urge you to look beyond what you think you know, to what you *do* know. Of me. You're a doctor, and you're used to seeing people stripped to their basic nature during emergencies. You've seen me as I really am through the best tests of all—the litmus of mortal danger, and your own valiant efforts at exercising your potent provocation."

She gaped at him for a long moment.

Then she shook her head on a bewildered, belligerent chuckle. "You *should* have been a diplomat. You'd hog-tie anyone in a net of platitudes and persuasions so thick, they wouldn't see the way out and would soon stop wanting one. But it's too late with me, so save it."

His gaze lengthened in turn. She could swear he was struggling not to smile again. At last he exhaled, like a man bound on tolerating a nuisance for life, leveled that supernatural gaze on her. "You believe you have reason to hate us. Tell me."

"I'm telling you nothing. As far as I'm concerned, you're no better than my kidnappers. You're actually far worse. My enmity with them was incidental. I was just the source of damaging info to their hereditary enemies. But with your family, my enmity is very specific. And don't play the 'I took a bullet saving you' card. I now realize why you did. You want what they wanted. And my answer to you is the same one I gave them. You can go take a flying leap from one of your capital's world-record-high skyscrapers."

"Is that how you always reach your verdicts, Talia? You judge by symptoms that have many differential diagnoses and insist on the first one that occurs to you and explains them?"

She gritted her teeth against the urge to punch him again. The man made perfect sense every time he opened his mouth. Was there no provoking him into making his first mistake? "Oh, don't start with the professional similes. You know nothing about me."

"I may not know the facts about you, but I know a lot about the truth. I'm certain of everything I know, through the proof of your actions in the worst possible conditions.

You're brave and daring and capable and intense. You're passionate in everything you do and about everything you believe in, most of all your sense of justice. Be fair with me now. Give me a chance to defend my family. Myself. Please, Talia, tell me."

His every word expanded in her heart like a compulsion trying to spread out and take hold of her. She resisted his influence, slammed him with her frustration. "I told you not to call me that. But since you're breath-depleting and you can talk me under the sand, just call me T.J. if you must call me at all. Everyone does."

This time he let that smile spread on his lips again. "Then something's wrong with everyone you know, if they can look on your beauty and think something as sexless and characterless as T.J., let alone articulate it. I'm calling you nothing but Talia. Or *nadda jannati*. It's impossible for me not to. Deal with it."

She gave a smothered screech. "For Pete's sake, turn off your female-enthrallment software. It won't work anymore. It's making me so sick that I'd rather you use your fists like my captors did."

It was as if she'd hit a button, fast-forwarding his face from teasing to ominous. He rasped, "They hit you?"

She instinctively rubbed the lingering ache in her gut, which had been swamped by far more pressing urgencies. "Oh, a couple did, just for laughs. It wasn't part of the interrogation, since those jerks weren't cleared to engage in that, and I bet their orders were not to damage me. But they couldn't resist bullying the smaller man they thought I was. One made it sound as if it's some duty a true Zohaydan owes any foreigner messing in the kingdom's business."

His teeth made a bone-scraping sound. "I wish I had used something other than tranq darts to knock them out. Something that would have caused permanent damage"

She gave an impressive snort. "Stop pretending to care."

"I can't stop something I'm not pretending. And I would have cared had you been a man, even the spy with the multiple agenda I thought you to be. Nothing is more despicable or worthy of punishment than abusing the helpless. Under any pretext. Those men aren't patriots as they pretended, they're vicious, cowardly lowlifes who can't pass up a chance to take their deficiencies out on those who can't retaliate."

"Right. Like you're the defender of the weak and the champion of the oppressed."

He gave a solemn nod. Then, as if he was renewing a blood oath, he said, "I am."

And she couldn't hold back, blurted it all out. "Like you defended my brother? Like you championed him against the bullies in your family who abused their power and threw him in jail?"

Four

Harres had thought he'd been ready for anything.

He had made peace with the fact that he would never know what to expect next from Talia Jasmine Burke.

But this was beyond unexpected. And he wasn't ready for it.

He stared into her eyes. They were flaying him with rage. But now anxiety muddied their luminous depths. It fit what he knew of her, that his first sighting of the debilitating emotion there wouldn't be on her own account, but on a loved one's.

Her brother.

So that was it. Why she was here.

He knew she'd been determined not to tell him, hated that she had, was madder than ever, at herself. But it was out.

At least, the first clue was. He realized she was talking

about the same T. J. Burke he'd investigated. There couldn't be another one who happened to be in jail, too.

That still didn't tell him why she'd implicated his family in her brother's imprisonment. And it was clear he had another fight on his hands until she gave him anything more.

After a long moment of refusing to give an inch, her whole body started shaking from escalating tension, her eyes growing brighter as pain welled in them. His insides itched with the need to defuse her agitation. But he was the enemy to her now. She wouldn't let him console her while she considered him—however indirectly—the cause of her brother's suffering.

Struggling not to override her resistance and to hell with the consequences, maybe even letting her vent her surplus of anguish by lashing out at him, he let out a ragged exhalation. "You've come this far. Tell me the rest."

She glared defiance at him then echoed his exhalation. "Why? So you can tell me I got it all wrong again? You've said that a few times already. I'll cut and paste on my own."

"*Oqssem b'Ellahi,* I swear to God, Talia, if you don't start talking, I'll kiss you again."

Outrage flared in her eyes. And, he was certain, unwilling remembrance and involuntary temptation, too. That only seemed to pour fuel on her indignation. He would have been thrilled that her attraction was so fierce it defied even her hostility. *If* the grimness of the situation wasn't mounting by the second. Then she thrilled him anyway.

She hissed, "My earlier 'feminine' threat of chomping a part of you off stands. It'll just be your lips instead of your hand."

He inclined his head at her, suppressing the smile spreading inside him. He couldn't exhibit any levity. She'd only

put the worst possible interpretation to it. "Why bother
when you'd only end up fixing it? Talk, Talia. If I'm to
be punished for it, at least face me with the details of my
charge."

Her scowl darkened. "I again remind you I'm not the
police. I don't owe you a reading of the charges against
you. I'm the family of the victim, and you're the family of
the criminals."

"So what did my family of criminals do?" he prodded.
"Don't leave me in suspense any longer."

She huffed some curses about his being a persistent pain
in the posterior under her breath, then finally said, "My
brother—my *twin*—" she paused to skewer him with a glare
of pure loathing "—was working in Azmahar two years ago.
He's an IT whiz, and international companies have been
stealing him from each other since he turned eighteen. He
met a woman and they fell in love. He asked her to marry
him and she agreed. But her family didn't."

So a woman was involved. Figured. Not that he'd
expected it.

"The woman's name is Ghada Aal Maleki." She watched
him as she pronounced the foreign-to-her name in perfect
precision, her eyes probing, shrewd. Then she smirked. "Do
turn down the volume of the bells ringing in your head.
Very jarring now that the desert seems to have turned in
for the night."

He contemplated the implications of the new information
even as his lips twitched at her latest bit of lambasting.
"Excuse the racket. Bells did go off quite loudly. The woman
in question belongs to the royal family of Azmahar. I know
she's long been betrothed. But what caused the jangling is
to whom. Mohab Aal Shalaan, my second cousin and one
of the three men on my retrieval team tonight."

Her mouth dropped open. Then she threw her hands

in the air, looked around as if seeking support from an invisible audience as she protested the unfairness of this last revelation. "Oh, great. Just super dandy. So now I'm supposed to owe *him* my life, too?"

He shook his head, adamant. "You don't owe anyone anything. We were doing our duty. As for Mohab and Ghada's betrothal, it was family-arranged, but I have a feeling both have been working together to sabotage their families' intentions. She first insisted on obtaining her bachelor's degree, then she wanted to finish her postgraduate studies and he gladly agreed, granting her year after year of postponement. I think both want to escape marriage altogether and are using each other as an alibi for as long as they can put off their families. As of hours ago, there's been no sign of a wedding date being set."

She digested this then raised her chin, trying to seem uninterested. "Well, maybe your second cousin doesn't want to marry Ghada, but your family wants him to, at any cost. Must have some huge vested interest in the marriage so they'll do anything to see it comes to pass. When Ghada told them she was breaking it off with your cousin and marrying my brother, they drove him away from Azmahar. But when Ghada said she'd join him in the States, they decided to get rid of him altogether.

"They fabricated a detailed hacking-and-embezzlement history implicating him in major cyber raids. They somehow got the States to arraign him and put him on trial. He was found guilty in less than two months and sentenced to five years. After the first couple of weeks there, they even arranged for him to be attacked. When he defended himself, he became ineligible for good behavior. So now he'll serve the full sentence without possibility of parole. In a maximum-security prison."

Silence detonated after the last tear-clogged syllable

tumbled from her lips. Only the harsh unevenness of her breathing broke the expanding stillness as her eyes brimmed then overflowed with resurrected anguish, outrage and futility.

And she was waiting for him to make a comment. He had none.

She on the other hand, had plenty more. "T.J.—yeah, that's his name, too, Todd Jonas—looks like me, Prince Harres. I'm tall for a woman, but imagine a five-foot-eight man who doesn't have much on me in breadth and who's got my coloring and the eternally boyish version of my features. Do you have any idea what prison is like for him? I die each day thinking what his life is like on the inside. He's got four years and seven months more to serve. All thanks to your family."

He could only stare at her. He knew in gruesome detail what she was talking about. A prison full of the lowlifes he'd just described, preying on the weakest of the herd. With her brother as an easy, eye-catching target.

She went on, a fusion of terrible emotions vibrating in her voice. "But no thanks to all of you, he's safe. For now. I…buy his safety. I probably won't be able to afford it for long, as the premium keeps going up. In the past three months it has already tripled."

This time when she fell silent, he knew she'd said all she was going to say.

It was endless minutes before he could bring himself to talk. "Nothing I say could express my regret at your brother's situation. If it's true any member of my family was responsible—"

"If?" Her sharp interjection cut him off. "Oh, it is true, Prince Harres. And I've been given the chance to prove it. And to do something about it."

He couldn't help coming closer with the urgency her fiery

conviction sparked in him. "What exactly? And given? By whom?"

She looked at him as if he'd told her to jump out of a plane without a parachute and he'd catch her. "As if I'd tell you."

"It's vital that you tell me, Talia," he persisted. "If I know all the details, I can help. I will."

"Sure you will. You'll help prove your own family guilty of fraud, send those involved to jail instead of my brother."

"I can't say what will happen, since I don't know the specifics, but if there's anything I can do to help your brother, I will do it."

She smirked at him. "*That's* more like it. Be inconclusive, make insubstantial promises. Until the silly goose gives you what you bothered to come after her for."

He leveled his gaze on her, tried to convey all the sincerity he harbored in this specific situation and the rules he lived by. "I again say I don't know the specifics. But I will. And when I do, I will act. And I can and do promise you this. I deal with my family members the same way I do strangers when it comes to guilt. If they're guilty, they will pay the price."

"Oh, give me a break."

"You think I can keep the peace in a kingdom like Zohayd by playing favorites? I am where I am, as effective as I am, because everyone knows my code and believes beyond a shadow of doubt that I would never compromise it. And I never do."

Her eyes flickered before they hardened again. "Good for you. But I'm not telling you anything more. What will you do? Force it out of me like those thugs intended to?"

He ached with the need to erase that doubt, that fear, once and forever. He couldn't bear that she could be uncertain of her fate with him. "I again swear that you are safe with me, in every way, no matter what."

His gaze bored into hers, as if he'd drive the conviction inside her mind with the force of his, until she gave an uncomfortable shrug.

He knew that was all the concession he'd get now.

He exhaled. "With that settled, let's get to other vital points. Now that I know you're not the reporter you were...reported to be, and not the spy I suspected you to be, I am wondering if all this isn't a case of catastrophic misinformation on all sides, if you weren't kidnapped for the wrong reasons."

She gave him an exasperated look. "Is that your round-about way to get to the reason I was taken, the same reason you came to extract me? Okay, let's get this out of the way. I came here following a lead that can prove my brother's innocence. And I stumbled on information terminally damaging to the Aal Shalaans. I have no idea how your rival tribe, or you for that matter, got wind of that, and so quickly. Maybe when I emailed my brother's attorney with the developments. So yes, I know why I was kidnapped. Your rival tribe wants the information I have to destroy you. You want it to avoid being destroyed."

And though she was looking at him as if she'd like nothing more than to see him and his family "destroyed," another wave of admiration surged inside him for this golden lioness who was here risking everything for her twin.

He at last sighed. "At least one thing turned out as I believed. But you said you were 'given' the chance to prove your brother's innocence and refused to tell me who gave it to you. Don't you realize that someone is orchestrating all this?"

A considering look came into her eyes. "Sure. Your point?"

"My point is, that someone cares nothing about you or your brother, you're just one of the instruments they're using to their end of causing the most chaos and destruction."

She gave a slow nod. "I never thought they were doing this out of the kindness of their hearts."

"Did they give you anything that might exonerate your brother yet?" She glared at him, then gave a grudging headshake. "Don't you find it suspicious they only gave you information that will hurt the Aal Shalaans?"

Her eyes spat blue fire. "According to them, it will end your reign."

He gritted his teeth at the very real danger of that coming to pass. "Didn't you ask yourself how they intend you to use that information? How using it will help your brother?"

She shrugged again, her eyes losing their hard gleam, the first flicker of uncertainty creeping there. "I didn't have time to think. I just got the info this morning, and within a couple of hours I was snatched. But I came to one decision. I wouldn't give my kidnappers anything. For every reason there is. I knew I wasn't walking out of that hole. So not only wasn't I about to be party to your tribal feud, I sure wasn't helping my abusers become the rulers of Zohayd and the abusers of millions."

He stared at her. There really was no end to her surprises. Almost anyone in her place would have said and given anything for a chance to walk away from the situation. But he'd pegged her right in those first moments. She *would* rather die in defiance, for a cause, than beg for her life from someone she despised and have her survival mean untold misery to others.

He fought the need to pull her into his arms, chide her for being such an obstinate hero. The one thing that stopped him, besides the settling weariness of the whole thing, was that he knew she'd resist. Spontaneous expression of emotion was something he'd have to work on re-earning.

He at last said, "You seem to realize the gravity of the information you have and what having it fall into the hands of the wrong people can mean. Have you decided what you'll do with it?"

Her shoulders drooped. "If I get out of this in one piece, you mean? I'll solidify my facts first. Then I'll think long and hard how best to use it." She shot him a sullen glance. "I may announce it to the world, maybe paving the way for Zohayd to become a democracy at last."

He raised both eyebrows, answering her surliness with sarcasm. "Like one of the so-called democracies in the region? *That* is the epitome of peace and prosperity, in your opinion? You want to save Zohayd from its current wealth and stability, from the hands of a royal family who have ruled it wisely and fairly for five hundred years and place it into the hands of hungry upstarts and militia warlords? And that's only Zohayd. Do you have the first inkling what the sprouting of such a 'democracy' among the neighboring monarchies would do? The unending repercussions it would send throughout the whole region?" He waited until he again found evidence of his points sinking home, in the darkness of grim realization in her eyes, the tremor of ominous possibilities in her lips. Then he went on, "Even if we're deposed tomorrow, and that doesn't plunge the region into chaos, it still doesn't help your brother. Or would you settle for avenging him, seeing his abusers punished, and leave him in prison for the rest of his sentence?"

"I don't know, okay?" she cried out, her eyes flaring her confusion and antipathy. "I told you, I had no time to think. And it's pointless to start right now. I'm in the middle of nowhere where I'm neither help nor threat to anyone. Ask me again, if I get out of this mess in any condition to be either."

Before he could assert that he would do anything to see her to safety, she winced, almost doubled over.

His heart folded in on itself, mimicking her contortion.

Before he could move, she keened, lurched back, and a ball of panic burst in his gut.

He'd taken her word that she was fine. What if he'd left an injury she'd sustained unseen to that long?

He pounced on her, disregarding the pain the careless move shot through his side. He raised her face to his, feverishly examining its locked-in-pain features.

It was only when she tried to escape his solicitous hands that he could rasp, "Talia, stop being stubborn, not about this. Are you injured?"

"No." He firmed his hold on her shoulder, on her head, detaining her with support and solicitude, demanding a confession. She groaned, relented. "It's those punches. Guess I was too distracted to focus on anything my body was feeling till now. But suddenly it…cramps with every breath. You know, like being cripplingly sore the morning after too many sit-ups." Something feral rolled out of his gut. Her eyes shot wider. Then she gave a huff that segued into a moan as her eyes slid down his body to his abdomen then back to his eyes. "What am I saying? It's sit-ups that are probably sore after a stint with your six-pack."

She was distracting him. Even thinking she owed him nothing but hostility, even if she wasn't acknowledging the sincerity of his outrage on her behalf, she was still trying to defuse it.

Before he kissed her, compelled her to carry out her earlier threat, he said, "Talia, I'm going to take off those layers of clothes…"

"Oh, no, you're not!" she squeaked.

"Then you do it. But I will have them off. Then you're going to lie down against me. You're going to stretch those muscles, or they're only going to get worse. I'll massage them with anti-inflammatory ointment."

She remained stiff in his hands for a moment longer before she capitulated, nodded and unzipped her coat.

He followed those capable hands as they undid the layers of clothes beneath it. And when he realized she wore a corset under her man's undershirt, he felt blood desert his head, his heart seeming to pump it only to his loins. He'd been in enough trouble when he'd believed her figure was as uneventful as a boy's. She'd been subduing a very... eventful one.

When she'd moved things around to expose only her midriff, she looked at him awkwardly. She tensed again when he began to turn her, and he whispered in her ear, "Let me take care of you. Don't resist me."

A breath shuddered out of her as she let him manipulate her body onto his lap. "Resistance is futile, huh?"

He smiled down at her as he opened the ointment tube. "Oh, yes. You're in no shape for it right now. Resist me all you like when you're no longer in pain."

She murmured something, a cross between grudging consent and whimpering pain/pleasure as he carefully began to examine her, then spread the ointment he'd warmed first between him palms over her aching flesh. His own flesh ached, too, all over.

Then, as she relaxed into his touch, arched up into his soothing hands, he saw the outline where the impact had bruised her paleness.

All blood was back, shooting into his head.

He heard the viciousness in his voice as he growled,

"Just thinking they had their hands on you at all, let alone in violence, makes me contemplate murder."

She fidgeted at his intensity, her eyes scanning him from her upside-down position. "You mean you don't do that on auto?"

He gave her a chiding glance. "Murder isn't even in the same solar system as manipulation or framing innocents for fraud. Don't you think you're taking your enmity too far?"

She sighed as she relaxed again under his cosseting hands. "I don't know. Maybe you think killing someone a suitable punishment for abusing their power, as an ultimate example for others. As for taking my enmity too far, let me throw one of your brothers in jail for five years, ruin his future and destroy his psyche, and then we'll discuss the exaggeration of my beliefs and reactions."

He stopped his massaging movements when she started to quiver. She could be getting cold or tender…or aroused. He was all of that. And though all he wanted was to rip off his clothes and hers and remedy all the causes of their distress, he knew that must remain a fantasy for now.

With what stood between them, maybe forever.

He kept his hands pressed lightly into her flesh for a few more defusing moments, his gaze tangling with her turbulent one.

Then he removed his hands, helped her up. She declined his help straightening her clothes. Then, with her eyes still wrestling with his, she nestled into the farthest part of the cockpit from him, against her door.

He'd thought he could postpone this until she was less raw, until he'd decided how to go on from here. But her withdrawal snapped something inside him. He had to settle this score. Now.

He pressed closer, showing her he wouldn't take her

categorizing him as the villain and shunning him. "Let's get one thing clear, Talia. *I* was not a party to what happened to your brother. So I have no more to say on this matter. And nothing to apologize for." Satisfaction surged as he saw that sense of fairness of hers flickering in her gaze, admitting his point. "So, until I'm in a position to learn more, and do something about it, I won't let you bring it up again. The subject of your brother is closed for now."

He held her eyes until she gave him a resentful if conceding huff.

He gave her an approving nod, as if sealing their treaty.

Then he said, "Now, to the only subject we should concern ourselves with for the duration. Our survival."

Five

"What do you mean *our* survival?"

Harres frowned at Talia's glower. His was of confusion. Hers seemed to be equal measures that and a revival of anger.

"What kind of a question is that? We're in the middle of nowhere, as you pointed out. The most hostile nowhere on the planet."

"Yeah, sure. So?"

He shook his head, as if it would shake her words into making sense. "You were worried about getting out of this alive. I thought you understood the danger we're in."

"I thought *I* was in danger. The only danger I thought I was in was human-induced."

His exasperation rose to match hers. "You mean *me*-induced."

She shrugged, unfazed by his displeasure. "Yeah, you-induced. I was thinking you'd use my being out here with you as the only way of rejoining humanity, as…persuasion to get me to spill. And that once you were certain I wouldn't give you anything, you wouldn't be too gung ho about my well-being, maybe even my survival."

Blood bounded in his arteries until he felt each hammer against the confines of his body.

He forcibly exhaled frustration before he burst with it. "I thought we got this ridiculous—and let me add, most dishonoring, injuring and aggravating—misconception out of the way."

Her eyes seemed to be giving him a total mind-and-psyche scan before she gave a slow nod. "I guess so. But since that only happened in the past few minutes, I had no time to form an alternate viewpoint. I sure didn't consider for a second that you were in any danger. After the escape, the gunshot and the crash, that is. After you survived all that in one glorious piece, I thought you were home free."

"How is it even possible you think so?"

"Oh, I don't know." Her voice drenched him in sarcasm. "Maybe my first clue was how glib about the whole situation you were. You know, being so cheerful and carefree that you spent most of the past hour laughing and lobbing witticisms in between pestering me for my gender, interrogating me for my agenda and trying to deluge me with testosterone."

And he had to. He laughed again. "It's your effect on me. You make me cheerful and carefree, against all odds."

Her lips crooked up in a goading smile. "Next you'll say I made you kiss me."

"In a fashion. You made me unable to draw one more breath if I didn't. You made me thankful. That I found you, that I saved you, that you saved me, that you exist and that you're with me. And you did make me do it in the most important way, the way all of the above still couldn't have made me. Because you wanted me to."

She gave her lips, which had fallen open, an involuntary lick, her eyes glittering as if she felt his there, tasted him. Then she gave a smothered, chagrined sound before her eyes sharpened again and she thrust both hands at him in a fed-up gesture. "See? Is it any wonder I couldn't even conceive that you had anything to worry about? Who talks like that if he's in any kind of danger, let alone a potentially life-threatening situation?"

He sighed, conceding her point. "Apparently, I do. With you around. But when you talked about my needing your scalpels again, I thought that proved you were aware that I shared your danger."

She waved a hand. "Oh, I was just pointing out that if you held me here at your mercy, you'd be at mine, too."

He huffed a stunned chuckle. "We're sitting inside a crashed helicopter, *our* as well as *my* only way out of here. How can you consider that I'm not right with you at the mercy of the desert?"

Her shrug was defensive this time. "Why should I have considered that? So the helicopter crashed. But you're the one, the only, Prince Harres Aal Shalaan. You must have all sorts of gadgets on hand and can contact your people to come pick you up whenever you want."

He gave a regretful nod. "I do have gadgets, every one known to humankind. And all useless, since we are in a signal blackout zone. The nearest area with possibility of transmitting or receiving anything is over two hundred miles away."

Her eyes widened with each word until they'd expanded to a cartoonish exaggeration. "You mean your people have no way of knowing where you are?

"None."

After a moment of wrestling with descending dread, she seemed to come to a conclusion that steadied her. "Well, that alone will have your armies combing the desert to find you."

"Sure it will." He sighed in resignation. "And they'll find me. In maybe a week. We have water on board for a couple of days."

"They can't possibly take a week to find you!" Her protest came out a squeak. "With all the high-end tech stuff at their disposal, and the whole country out looking for its precious prince, I bet they find you within a couple of hours from the moment they realize you're missing!"

He wanted to press her into his flesh and absorb her worry. But he owed her the truth. He would see her to safety, but he had to prepare her for the grueling experience that he couldn't spare her before he did.

Bleakness clamped his heart, erasing any lightness as he forced himself to decimate her hope. "They have no way of knowing where to start looking. Once my men go back home and realize I didn't precede them, they'll go back to where we originally landed as a starting point to search. But they'll have no way of knowing which way I headed, or how far in which direction I crashed."

"So they'd take longer, maybe a day or two," she still argued. "Surely they'll crisscross the area with enough aircrafts, one of them is bound to spot us within that time frame."

He shook his head, needing to erase any false expectations. Those were more damaging than painful reality. "Relying on visual search over an area of a hundred thousand square miles? With some of the dunes around here over one thousand feet high? Apart from a stroke of luck, I was being optimistic when I said a week."

Silenced howled after his last word.

She stared at him with horror gathering in her eyes.

Then it burst from her lips. "Oh, *God.* You're stranded here with me."

He couldn't hold back any longer. He reached out and cupped her velvet cheek in soothing cherishing. "And I couldn't have dreamed of better company to be in mortal danger with."

Her mouth opened, closed, then again. She couldn't have looked more flabbergasted if he'd said he was actually a plant.

Then she slapped his hand away with a furious sound. "How can you joke about this now? About anything?"

"I'm not joking in the least." He reached out to her again and she snapped her teeth at him like the infuriated feline she was. He withdrew his hand with a sigh. "You can chomp any part of me you like, but it won't change the fact that what I said is the truth. Apart from not wishing you to be in any discomfort or danger, there's no one else I'd rather have with me now."

Tears suddenly eddied in a swirl of silver in her eyes, had his blood churning in his heart before two arrowed down her cheeks.

Then she choked out, "Oh, shut *up!*"

He hooted with laughter. "And you take me to task about being cheerful? I'd be mute if you had your way, wouldn't I?"

She shot him a baleful glance, even as her lips twitched, too. "You've said enough, don't you think?"

"Actually, I was getting to the interesting part."

"What interesting part? How after a few millennia they'll dig our bones from this desert and put them in an exhibit and have scientists hypothesizing that we were actually Adam and Eve?"

He dug his fingers into his seat so he wouldn't yank her to him and claim those lips under his. "How...anthropologically imaginative of you. But I have no intention of becoming a fossil just yet. To this end, we'll have to get out of this hunk of twisted metal and have us a desert trek."

She said nothing. Then she shifted, came closer and patted her lap. "You should lie down again. It's clear you did hit your head and everything you've said and done so far has originated from a swollen brain."

His eyes laughed into her in-doctor-mode ones. "You mean you don't think I have one by default?"

"Sure, as is no doubt expected of your princeliness. But when you start suggesting we take a two-hundred-mile stroll in 'the most hostile nowhere on the planet,' it's time for medical intervention."

"Actually, it's only a fifty-mile stroll. That's the distance to the oasis I was taking us to when we had this little diversion."

He winced inwardly at the hope that swept her ultra-expressive features, rearranging them into the image of relief, then reprimand. "Why didn't you say so? That's not too far."

"That's two marathons' worth. In the desert. With temperatures reaching 120 degrees Fahrenheit at midday and 20 at night. And that's if we're talking a linear path to our destination, which we're not. Not with the seas of dry quicksand in the way."

She raised her chin defiantly at him. "If you're trying to scare me, save it. I didn't come to Zohayd from an air-conditioned exam room in a five-star hospital, but from an understaffed and hectic emergency room in a teaching hospital and a couple of aid stints in Africa. I've been steeped in discomfort all my working years and I've rubbed shoulders with danger and despair quite a few times, by choice."

He had to pause to admire her for a moment before he

said, "I'm only trying to prepare you. I'll see that we get through this, in the most efficient way possible, but I need you to be aware of the facts. So far, we've gone through the easy part. Now we face the desert."

He could see her defiance and determination wavering, uncertainty and fear skirting their protective shell, scraping against it for chinks, for a way in.

But the good thing about challenge was that it kept one focused. Maybe he should escalate it, keep all her faculties locked on it, and on him.

He crooked his lips, knowing by now that would stoke her ready flames. "Anyway, great to know I won't have a swooning damsel on my hands."

"As long as I don't have a swooning dude on mine!"

There she was. Ricocheting right back at him. And he laughed again, shook his head at his helpless reaction.

They were in a demolished multimillion-dollar helicopter in what might as well be another planet for all the area's desolation. He was going to brave the desert's mercilessness in his weakened condition to ensure her safety. She seemed to wish him and his whole family erased from the face of the earth.

And yet, he had never enjoyed anything as much, never looked forward to anything more.

But though he did, and had said they'd focus on their current predicament, he couldn't forget the beef she had with his family. An unjustly imprisoned sibling was the stuff of undying grudges.

This *was* worse than anything he'd imagined. He'd thought he'd be bargaining with a news bounty hunter or an intel black marketer. But he couldn't have imagined this. Imagined her. What she was, how she affected him, what she had against his family.

Even the response he wrenched from her was one more strike against him.

Not that he'd let this, or anything, stand in his way.

He wanted her to give him everything. The info. And herself.

He always got what he wanted.

And he'd never known he *could* want like this.

Everything she knew, felt, was, had to be his. *Would* be his.

He cocked his head and her gaze slid unwilling admiration and sensuality over the hair that fell to his shoulder.

Pleasure revved inside his chest. "Now we're squared on that, how about shelving your enmity until we survive this?"

"*You're* only playing nice because you need *me*. Primary closure of a wound of that caliber is in four to ten days."

He knew that. He also knew she needed to provoke him to keep her spirits up. He let her. "And *you* need *me*. You won't find any passersby here to hitch a ride with to the nearest oasis. So how about *you* be nice to *me?*"

Her eyes stormed through vexation, futility and resignation before she harrumphed. "Okay, okay. I concede the need is mutual."

"It is. In every way. Even if you're too mad right now to concede that."

She blasted him with a glare of frustration. He only grinned and dueted her exasperated, "Oh, shut *up*."

Six

No one could know how absolutely majestic and humbling night could be until they'd been in the desert at night.

Problem was, it was also downright petrifying and alien.

Talia had known they were in the middle of nowhere. But before she got out of the helicopter, that had only been a concept, a figure of speech. Now it was reality. One that impacted her every sense and inundated her every perception. As she at last had the chance to appreciate.

And what a vantage she had to appreciate it from.

Harres had crash-landed them about five dozen feet from the top of one of those thousand-foot dunes he'd spoken of. From this spot she had an almost unlimited view of the tempestuous oceans of sand that seemed to simmer with their own arcane energy, emit their own indefinable color and eerie illumination. At the edge of her vision, they pushed in a scalpel-sharp demarcation against a dome of deepest eternity scattered with stars, the unblinking shrapnel of the big boom. Under their omnidirectional light, each steep undulation created occult shadows that seemed to metamorphose into shapes, entities. Some seemed to look back at her, some seemed to beckon, some to crawl closer. It made her realize how Middle Eastern fables had come to such vivid and sometimes macabre life. She certainly felt as if a genie or worse would materialize at any time.

Then again, she'd already met her genie.

Right now, he was taking apart the mangled rear of the helicopter to get to the gear and supplies they'd need before they set off on their oasis-bound trek.

She shuddered again, this time complete with chattering teeth, as much from expanding awe and descending dread as from marrow-chilling cold aided by a formidable windchill factor.

Though he was making a racket cutting the twisted metal with shears he'd retrieved from the cockpit, and the wind had risen again, eddying laments around them, it seemed he'd heard her.

He straightened with a groan that reminded her of his injury, made her wonder again how he ignored it, functioned—and so efficiently—with only the help of a painkiller shot.

He reached out to her face, cupped her cheek in the coolness of his huge, calloused hand and frowned. "You're freezing. Go back to the cockpit."

She shook her head. "I'm cold, yes, freezing, no. You're the one who's half-dressed."

Her last word got mangled by another teeth-rattling shiver.

His scowl deepened. "We need to set some ground rules. When I say something, you obey. I'm your commanding officer here."

She stuck her fists at her waist. "We're not in your army and I'm not one of your soldiers."

He fixed her with an adamant glare of his own. "I'm the native around here. And I'm the leader of this expedition."

"I thought we agreed we have equal billing."

"We do. In our respective areas of expertise."

"And you're the desert knight, right?"

He gave her a mock-affronted look, palm over his chest. "What? I don't look the part?"

"You sure do." *With a capital T in "the,"* she added inwardly. "But we established that looks can be deceiving."

"I thought *I* established they can't be."

"So you're the real thing. But you could be the prototype and this would remain *my* area. I'm the one qualified to judge which one of us is in danger of hypothermia. And until you get bundled up in thermal clothing like I am, that's you. So now you've done your Incredible Hulk bit and torn away debris and cleared a path to our supplies, you go back to the cockpit. I'll get the stuff we need."

He took a challenging step, crowding her against the mangled hull. "You'd spend hours trying to figure out what is where. I'm the one who knows where the stuff we'll need is, and can get it in minutes. If you can stop arguing that long."

"So I'm the uninjured, suitably dressed one, and your doctor, but you're the expert on this lost-cause aircraft and on survival in the desert. See? We end up with equal billing. So we both stay, work together and cut the effort and time in half."

His eyes had been following her mouth, explicit with thoughts of stopping it with his lips. And teeth.

Then he raised them to hers and captured her in that

bedeviling appreciation she was getting dangerously used to. "You're a control freak, aren't you?"

She let her shoulders rise and drop nonchalantly. "Takes one to know one, eh?"

His lips widened in a heart-palpitating grin. "You bet."

And even though she'd been and still was in mortal danger, and the emergency light at his feet cast sinister shadows over his hewn face, as if exposing some supernatural entity lurking inside him, she couldn't remember a time when she'd felt more...energized.

Strange how the company made all the difference when the situation remained the same.

I couldn't have dreamed of better company to be in mortal danger with.

Yeah, what he'd said.

Not that she'd agreed to it then. Or could credit it now. But there it was. She was actually looking forward to the grueling and possibly life-threatening time ahead. She'd always thrived on challenge and hardship to start with, but she'd never been anywhere near that level of danger. With Harres by her side, anything felt possible. And doable. And anything was...enjoyable?

She shook her head, as if she could dislodge the ridiculous thought. How could anything be enjoyable in their situation?

She had no idea how. But having no rationalization didn't change the fact that being with him was turning this nightmare into the most stimulating experience of her life.

She watched as he bent the last strip of protruding metal, widening the makeshift hatch, then stepped back, gestured to her.

"Report to packing duty, my obdurate dew droplet."

Her heart punched her ribs. No one, not even her parents,

had ever come up with such endearments for her. Nothing anywhere as ready and inventive and…sweet. A woman could get used to this.

And this woman shouldn't. For every reason there was.

She bit down on the bubble of delight rising inside her, popped it.

"That's your retaliation for pigheaded, mulish ox and my assortment of other insults?" she tossed over her shoulder as she preceded him into the cramped space, kneeled on the uneven floor of what remained of the cargo bay and awaited his directions.

He came down facing her, started reaching for articles as if he knew exactly where they were. And he clearly did. Prince Harres seemed to be hands-on in his operations' every level and detail.

After he hoisted on a thermal jacket, he answered her previous barb. "I am sabotaging myself by telling you this, since you might now stop them, but those aren't insults. From you, they have the effect of the most…intimate caress."

His eyes left her in no doubt of what that meant. She almost choked her lungs out imagining his body stirring, hardening, aching in response to her words, to her…

She pretended to cough, waved a hand at him. "Try another one. You're just insult-proof, as you said early on."

"You remember?" He looked disproportionately pleased that she did. "*Aih,* I've never had a hair-trigger ego. And then, most insults are falsehoods or exaggerations, attempts to get a rise. My best payback to insults is to let them slide off me, inside and out."

She gasped in mock stupefaction. "You mean people actually dare to attempt to insult you?"

"I have an older brother. A very…aggravating one. And three younger ones. I'm no stranger to insults. But you will insult me only if you fear me or distrust me."

Her heart hiccuped at the sudden seriousness in his eyes. The cross between warning and entreaty there had the mocking comeback sticking in her throat. She instinctively knew he was telling the truth. That this was the one thing he wouldn't laugh at. The one thing that would hurt him.

And even if she told herself Todd's ordeal balanced out everything Harres had done for her, that he'd only done it for the person who held the vital info he wanted to extract and to keep hushed, her fairness again intervened. He'd been right when he'd said he had nothing to do with Todd's imprisonment. And she didn't believe in guilt by association, even if she made it sound as if she did. And if she went a step further into truthfulness, she had to admit something else.

She didn't want to hurt him. Not in any way.

Lowering her gaze in indirect agreement and swallowing her barbed tongue, she helped him drag out backpacks then cut off the safety belts that still secured crates in the debris.

He dragged one between them, popped the lid open before looking at her with teasing back in his eyes, to her relief. "There's one thing I can't get over. How you don't take words lauding your beauty and effect as your due—my jasmine dew."

She followed his lead, loaded water bottles and packets of dry food into the backpacks. "Next you'll call me Mountain Dew."

A chuckle rumbled inside his massive chest. "Oh, no. You get your own brand names. But we do have canned relatives around."

She stuffed a compartment into one backpack, turned

to the other one, which she noticed was much smaller, as he pulled out another crate. "How nutritionally sloppy of you."

He opened the crate, produced guns, flares, flashlights, batteries, compasses and many other articles, which he distributed between the two backpacks. "I assure you, I never come within a mile of anything canned, except in emergencies. For easily stored quick fixes of hydration and calories, they work in a bind."

"Let's hope we don't have to resort to them. I'd rather drink detergent. But then we won't have to, since you have it all figured out, being the desert knight that you are."

He gave her a stoking glance. "That's right. And this desert knight says close your backpack and let's move on to packing our accommodations."

"You mean this tiny thing is mine?" She eyed his backpack. It was almost as big as her. "And this behemoth is yours?"

He nodded matter-of-factly. "I am twice as big as you are, and can carry four times as much or more."

"Listen, this is getting old. I won't stand by while you bust my sutures."

"I thought they were mine." Before the urge to smack him transferred from her brain to her arm, he added, "If I can't handle it, I'll tell you."

"Yeah, right. Right after you tell me you've sighted the first flying pig."

"But I'm the mulish ox here, therefore perfectly qualified for hefting and towing." Before she could plow into a counterargument, he cupped her face in both hands. The gentleness in his grasp made everything inside her crumple, pour into those palms. "Thank you for worrying about me, for braving exhaustion to spare me. But I've been through worse, have trained to weather the worst conditions for over a quarter of a century." His lips quirked. "Probably longer than you've been on the planet."

That shook her out of her hypnosis. "What? When I told you I've been practicing medicine for years? You think they grant babies medical licenses now?"

"They do, to prodigies."

"Well, I'm not one. I'll be thirty next August."

"No way." He looked genuinely stunned.

"Yes way."

"See? No end to your surprises."

"Stick around. They're bound to end sometime."

"Oh, I intend to. And I bet they never will."

"Didn't take you for a betting man."

"I'm not. But I'll bet on you anytime."

Only then did she notice he still held her face in his palms. And that she was shaking all over again. And that he knew that he turned her into a live wire, knew she was struggling not to succumb. He was also certain she would.

She glared back. *Never again.*

"Don't be so sure," he murmured, his tone a sweeping undertow, his exotic accent sliding over her, enveloping her.

She gasped. He'd heard her thoughts, was taking the challenge.

She shook her head, reclaimed her face from his possession.

With a last molten look of challenge, he resumed packing.

Afterward, he fashioned a sled from the helicopter's remains, using ropes for a harness. On it he loaded a folded tent, their quarters, as he called it, and piled on blankets, sleeping bags and mats.

She matched him move for move, followed his directions,

anticipating his needs as if they'd been working together for years in perfect harmony. And she felt that overwhelming in-sync feeling again, just as she'd felt when he'd assisted her in treating his wound, always reading her next move, ready for it with the most efficient action.

It wasn't only that. She felt her body gravitating toward him, demanding his closeness. She resisted the compulsion with an equal force until she felt she'd rip down the middle.

It's survival, she told herself. Seeking the one person around. Being out here would have been unsettling enough in controlled conditions. But she'd just learned that her predicament was far worse than she'd thought. And with him generating that field of reassurance and invincibility, who could blame her if all she wanted was to throw herself into his haven?

And since when did she indulge in self-deception?

This man had jolted things inside her, like electric cables forced life into a dead battery, from the second she'd turned to face him. Ever since, his nearness, everything he said or did, revved that life into something almost…painful. An edge that scraped everything aside. A knot of hunger that—

"You're hungry."

She jerked at the dark compulsion of his voice, and glared her resentment at him. Couldn't he have the decency to have one crack in his imperturbable facade? It might be self-defeating to wish that her one chance at survival be less than the absolute rock he needed to be to get them out of this, but she still wished it. No one could be *that* unflappable, could he?

He only looked at her with that boundless tranquility that she felt traversed his being. She answered her own question.

Yes, someone could be. And his name was Harres Aal Shalaan.

And he'd just read her mind. Again.

Before mortification choked her, he let her off the hook. "Like you, your stomach snaps its teeth." And she realized it was. She hadn't eaten in over twenty-four hours. "So here's the plan. We eat, prepare our gear then move out. It's 1:00 a.m. now. If we move out in an hour, we'll have around eight hours before things get too hot. When it does, we'll set up camp, hide out the worst of it, then set out again before sunset. The schedule throughout will be two hours on, one hour off. More off if you need it. At a rate of about five miles every three hours, we'll make it to our destination in about three days. If we ration ourselves, our supplies should last."

"If they don't, I'll use the IV fluid replacement. We have a few liters still."

"See? You *are* the best I could have hoped to be with in this mess."

"I'm sure you could have managed on your own," she mumbled, thrilled, annoyed, feeling things were about to get real at last, and struggling not to throw herself into his arms and cling.

"You're admitting I'm not a useless nuisance? I'm deeply honored."

She studied him for a moment, a suspicion coming over her.

Was he doing this on purpose? Every time she felt her will flagging, he teased her or provoked her and it brought her out of her funk and right back in his face.

Whatever it was, it was working. She grabbed at it with both hands. "It remains to be seen what exactly you are. You might still take us in the wrong direction and we'll end up lost. And fossilized."

He laughed. Rich, virile, mind-numbing laughter. Made all the more hard-hitting as it mixed with a guttural groan of pain. "I don't take wrong directions. It's a matter of principle."

Yeah. She'd bet. And she was willing to gamble her life on that. She was going to.

Then again, what choice did she have?

None.

But then again, why should she even worry?

He'd gotten her this far, through impossible odds.

If there was anyone in this world who could get them through this, it was him.

But what if there was no getting through it…?

He suddenly grabbed her hand and yanked her against him.

This time she met him more than halfway. As he'd told her she would.

And whether it was survival, magic, compulsion, or anything else, she needed it. He needed it. She let them have it.

She dissolved in the maddening taste of him deep inside her, with the thrust of his hot velvet tongue as he breached her with tenderness and carnality and desperation. She surrendered to his domination and supplication, all-consuming and life-giving.

Then he wrenched away, held her head, her eyes. "I said you were safe with me, Talia, in every way. I'll keep you safe, and I'll see you safe. This is a promise. Tell me you believe me."

She did. And she told him. "I believe you."

Seven

Talia wondered, for the thousandth time since she'd been snatched from her rented condo at gunpoint, if any of the things that had happened since could be real.

One thing was certain, though. Harres was.

And she was following him across an overwhelmingly vast barren landscape that made her feel like one of the sand particles shifting like solid fluid beneath her feet.

They'd set out over six hours ago. Before they had, during the hour Harres had specified for preparations, he'd studied the stars and his compass at length, explaining how he was combining their codes with his extensive knowledge of his land's terrain and secrets to calculate their course. He'd said he needed her to know all he did. She thought that impossible when she couldn't imagine how he fathomed different landmarks when sameness besieged them. Yet he'd insisted it was vital she visualize their path, too, and somehow managed to transmit it to her.

They'd just embarked on their third two-hour hike. He still walked ahead, seemingly effortlessly, carrying his mammoth backpack and towing the piled sled while she stumbled in his wake with her fraction of their load. Which was still surprisingly heavy. He'd been keeping them on paths of firm sand, so it wasn't too hard. At first. She'd soon had to admit anything heavier would have been a real struggle.

She still continuously offered to carry more. Each time he'd answered that silence would boost their aerobic efficiency and increased the steps he kept between them no matter how hard she tried to catch up with him. It wasn't only adamant chivalry, it felt as if he was making sure he would be the first to face whatever surprises the seemingly inanimate-since-creation desert brought, wouldn't let her take a step before he'd ascertained its safety, testing it with his own.

Acknowledging his protection and honoring it, she treaded the oceans of granulated gold in the imprints of his much larger feet, feeling as if she was forging a deeper connection with him with each step, gaining a more profound insight into what made this unprecedented—and no doubt unduplicable—man tick.

It had been hours since dawn had washed away the stars and their inky canvas, the gradual boost in illumination bringing with it an equally relentless rise in temperature. While that had made each step harder than the last, it had given her a new distraction to take her mind off counting them, off the weakness invading her limbs.

He'd shed one layer of clothing after another, was now down to the bandages she'd changed an hour ago and the second-skin black pants fitted into black leather boots. With his back to her, she was finally free to study him, to realize something.

He was perfect.

No, beyond that. Not only couldn't she find fault with him, but the more she scrutinized, the more details she found to marvel at.

He seemed to be encased in molten bronze spun into polished satin ingeniously accentuated by dark silk. His proportions were a masterpiece of balance and harmony, a study in strength and grandeur. She'd never thought a man of such height and muscular bulk and definition could display such grace, such finesse, such poise. How could such a staggeringly physical manifestation combine such power and poetry of motion? And that was when he was half-buried under the backpack and tethered with the sled's harness. *And* that was only his body.

His face was a testimony to divine taste, hewn beauty in planes and slashes of perfection. In the dimness, his eyes had dominated her focus, but now, as she saw his face from every possible angle, she found something new to appreciate with every self-possessed move of his head. Between the intelligence stamped on the width of a leonine forehead, the distinct cut of razor-sharp cheekbones, the command in the jut of a sculpted jaw and nose and the humor and passion molding sense-scrambling lips, she couldn't form an opinion on a favorite feature. Not when so many other things vied for her favor. The eyebrows, the lashes, the neck, even the ears.

And then there was the hair.

Since dawn's first silvery fingers had touched it, she'd become fascinated with it. But it had taken full exposure to the desert's merciless sun to highlight its wonders.

The color seemed to have been painted from a palette of every earth color in creation, forged from resilient gloss and blended with trapped solar energy. As he walked ahead, the undulating silk seemed an extension of his beauty and virility, transmitting the same power and purpose. Every few minutes, when he turned to check on her, the mass seemed to beckon to her numb fingers to come revel in its pleasures for themselves.

Just then he turned to her again, and that curtain of luxury swished around, catching the nine-o'clock sun, leaving her gulping down her heart. And that was before he gave her that look, that amalgam of encouragement, solicitude and challenge that injected willpower into her veins and pumped it to her limbs. And she realized something.

This was what the Prince of Darkness should look like. To seduce without trying, to enslave into eternity, to induce all sorts of unrepentant sins. To have a woman believe her soul was a trivial accessory.

And she must be starting to hallucinate from exhaustion.

Maybe she should call another time-out before she collapsed.

Problem was, she was exhausted, but nowhere near collapse. Which meant all those thoughts were originating from an unwarped mind.

She tore her eyes away from his hypnotic movements, tried to document the subtle yet rich changes every mile brought to the awesome desert terrain. This place might be a trekker's nightmare, but it was any geologist's, artist's, or nature-lover's dream.

There was so much to delight in as the landscape shifted from magnificent sand dunes to endless gravel-covered plains to sinuous dry lakebeds and stream channels and back again to dunes. The sky, too, transformed from a fathomless ink canopy studded with faraway infernos to a stratus-painted, multicolored canvas to a blazing azure void as the sun rose and incinerated all in its path.

As the heat and glare intensified, she felt so thankful

for the sunglasses he'd had on board—the one undamaged pair that he'd insisted she have—and the cool cotton cloth he'd fashioned into a head cover for her.

At 10:00 a.m. sharp, he stopped.

Though all she wanted was to sit down and never rise again, when he turned to her she rasped, "I can go on."

He shook his head and took off his harness and bag. "No use going farther only to exhaust you so you'll need longer to rest. Or worse, be unable to go on altogether."

"You're the one with the gunshot wound. And I'm used to being on my feet for days on end in my work."

He only took her bag, his smile adamant. "You've gone through the equivalent of four of your grueling days in the last twelve hours." Before she could protest again he overrode her. "But since it's against your principles to be catered to, you can help me set up the tent."

She nodded reluctantly. She was dying to rest, but she wanted to get this trek over with more.

He handed her the tent. Then she found out why he'd offered it to her. Because he knew there was nothing for her to really do. Once she unfolded the thing, it sprang into existence with very little adjustment.

After gathering supplies for the next hours, he led her inside and she was even more impressed. It was big enough to accommodate ten people, and he could stand erect inside it. The sand-colored fabric was tough and cool, the floor's insulation total, the openings sealed once zipped and the ventilation ingenious.

But it was still hot. Too hot. And most of the heat was being generated by her smoldering hunk of a companion.

She looked up from gulping water and found him staring down at her with eyes that flared and subsided like fanned coals.

"Take off your clothes."

She jerked at his dark murmur, a geyser of heat shooting from her recesses to flood her skin.

His eyes left hers, traveled down, as if looking for the origin of the flush that rose to take over her neck and face.

And that was before he added in a will-numbing whisper, "All of them."

She stared at him, at a loss for the first time since she'd seen him. This was the last thing she…she…

Then his lips twitched, one corner twisting up devilishly, belying the seriousness in his voice when he elaborated, "If you don't, you'll sweat liters we can't replace."

Oh. Of course. She bit her lower lip, nodded, dispersing the ridiculous alarm and temptation that had slammed into her.

Problem was, in a usual "all of them" clothes-removal scenario she would have kept her underwear on, which would have amounted to a conservative bikini. But with only a man's undershirt over her now undone corsets, she'd be down to her boxer shorts. And she didn't know what mortified her more. That he'd see her topless, or that he'd see how ridiculous she looked in them.

Oh, right. And that was grounds for risking dehydration?

She nodded, exhaled a tremulous breath. "Any hope you'll turn your back?"

He gave her a mock-innocent look. "Why?"

Then he began to take off what little clothes he had left. He started with yanking off his boots, then straightening to undo the fastening of his pants. Her eyes were glued to his every move, her tongue darting to moisten suddenly desiccated lips. It was only when she realized her eyes were sliding lower with her mouth open as she anticipated the big revelation that she felt fury spurt to douse her mortification and abort her daze.

She met the master-tormentor's gaze defiantly, then started to undress herself. If he thought she'd swoon at the sight of his endowments, that she'd turn around for modesty or try to shield her nudity with virginly arms, he could think again!

As she prepared to yank off the short-sleeved undershirt, Harres stretched and manipulated something at the ceiling. A heavy cloth partition snapped down between them.

She froze, staring at the opaque surface inches from her eyes, until his amused drawl from the other side roused her.

"I did say 'quarters,' plural."

And she cried, "You…you…weasel!"

"Now we move from the farm to the animal kingdom at-large."

The mixture of relief and chagrin choked her as she threw off the rest of her clothes to the sound of his teasing chuckles and tackled her thin matttress as if it were him.

But if she'd thought she'd toss and turn with him inches from her with only flimsy fabric between them, she was mistaken. She felt nothing from the moment she became horizontal, to the moment she came to. To his caresses.

She blinked up in confusion. He was kneeling beside her, running his hands gently over her hair and face and arms.

For a long moment she could only think what a wonderful way this was to wake up.

Then the wonder factor rose exponentially when he smiled down at her. "I called. And called. I even poked you through the partition, to no avail."

She blinked again, looked down, found herself covered in a light cotton blanket. But since he was the one who'd covered her, he must have seen everything. Still, he had covered her so that he wouldn't infringe on her. She struggled with the urge to throw her arms around him and bring him down to her, thank him for being so thoughtful. And more.

Instead, she croaked, "What time is it?"

"Sunset."

She jackknifed up in alarm. "But we were supposed to move out two hours ago!"

"You needed to rest. Now we'll move faster." Before she could reprimand him for not sticking to their schedule on account of her alleged delicacy, he ruffled her hair and winked. "Hop to it, my dewy doc."

She huffed as her heart fired against her ribs. He was suddenly treating her like his kid sister. And it *still* turned her insides into a mushy mess.

As she began to reach for her clothes, he turned back to her.

He took her undershirt away from a hand gone lax. He pulled it over her head, guided her flaccid arms through it, managing not to drop the blanket from where it covered her breasts. He drew it away only once the undershirt was securely in place.

Just when she thought she might suffer a coronary, his intent and serious expression turned incandescent with a surge of something dark and driven. Then he leaned down, opened his lips over the junction of her neck and shoulder.

The feel of his tongue and teeth there was like being prodded by lightning. She lurched under the force of sensations that thundered through her. Then he made it worse.

He glided to the tip of her shoulder, scraping her flesh

with his teeth, gathering the sweat beaded on it with his tongue.

He growled against her skin, sending a string of shock waves through her with every syllable.

She thought he said, "A reward...an incentive..."

Then he pulled back and disappeared into his compartment.

She flopped onto her back, gasping, before she forced herself up and into her clothes. Then she crawled to his side to check his wound before they resumed their grueling trek.

She'd have hours to contemplate the meaning of his words.

And the feelings he'd ripped from her depths.

By the end of the second day, their water supply had dwindled even though they drank only when absolutely necessary. They were losing gallons in this weather and with the exertion.

After midnight they stopped for their hour's rest.

As she drank, she noticed he didn't. She stopped, insisting he drink, that he was the one losing the most fluids handling ten times the weight she was. He only insisted on taking her up on her offer of IV fluids.

He hung the saline bag on his jacket so that she wouldn't have to stand and hold it for him. She protested the inefficiency of this maneuver, and he calmly unrolled a mat from the sled, propped it against the sloping edge of a dune, tossed a few blankets beside it, then caught her hand and pulled her down on it with him.

Before she knew what hit her, Harres was lounging with his back to the dune, his endless legs open with her between them, her hips in their V, her back to his chest, her head on his right shoulder. Then he cocooned them both in the blankets and crossed his arms over her midriff, plastering her to him.

After the first stunned moment, she tried to fidget away.

He tightened his hold, groaned in her ear, "Relax."

Relax? Was he insane?

And he wasn't only that, he was rubbing his lips against the top of her head, inhaling her and rumbling enjoyment as he talked. "Rest. Get warm. It's far colder than yesterday."

"W-we have enough blankets," she protested weakly. "We can roll in them separately."

"This *is* the best method of body temperature preservation."

"And to think I reminded you of that!"

His chuckle, reverberating beneath her ear, sent more waves of distress crashing through her. "Conserve your energy, my Talia. Sleep, and I'll wake you up in an hour, maybe two."

"I—I don't want to sleep."

"I don't either. I'd rather be awake, experiencing this with you."

And though she was far from cold, a tremor rattled through her.

He'd just put into words what she felt.

Though his arms were pressing beneath her suddenly aching breasts and her buttocks were pressed to what she suspected, if couldn't credit, was a massive erection, it wasn't sexual. Or not only so. She'd never felt this close to anyone. This intimate. Even during her now almost-forgotten sexual encounters, she hadn't been any closer to experiencing what she did with Harres than she was to one of the stars above.

She sighed, feeling as if her bones had turned to warm

liquid and the rest of her senses had melted in the sluggish heat of her blood. "Stars. They *are* still up there."

He nuzzled her cheek with his lips. "You don't see them much where you live, eh?"

She sighed in deeper contentment. "Make that don't see them at all. Not for years. But even when I did, I never saw so many. I didn't think there *were* so many. Scientifically speaking, I know there are endless numbers of them in our galaxy alone. But I never thought we could actually see them. There are millions of them."

Her voice sounded intoxicated to her ears. And she was. With the overpowering mixture of the virility enfolding her and the desert's magnificent menace.

His voice poured directly through to her brain, frying more synapses. "Actually, only about eight thousand are visible to us poor earthlings in any given hemisphere, no matter how clear the skies are. And you won't find any clearer anywhere in the world."

That piece of info she hadn't known. She turned in his arms languidly, looked up at him. "Don't tell me you counted them."

"I tried. Then had to borrow good scientists' findings."

"They seem so much more. But I'll take your word for it. I'm just glad they all showed up tonight."

"I ordered them to be present especially for you."

Coming from any other man, that would have sounded like an outrageous—and annoying as hell—line. But somehow, from Harres, this force of nature who seemed to be as one with the powers of this land, *his* land, it didn't seem far-fetched. She did feel as if he had an empathy, an understanding with their surroundings, as if they let him divine their secrets and share their strengths. And then, coming from the man who'd risked his life to save her, who'd lavished such care on her, showed her such admiration and restraint and solicitude, she could easily believe his wish to please her, to gift her. So even the sentiment behind the claim seemed right, sincere. Profound.

And if an inner voice told her it was his need to learn her secrets that fueled all of the above, she couldn't listen. No one could be that good at hiding ulterior motives. And she had experienced him through the worst that could be thrown at a person. He'd shone through with gallantry and resourcefulness, with kindness and control.

She at last sighed again. "I wouldn't put it past you. So they're your subjects, too?"

"Oh, no. They're just old friends. We have an understanding."

Just as she'd thought. "I sort of believe you."

"I could get used to hearing you say that."

The rolling *r*'s of the accent that caressed his perfect English thrummed that chord of ready desire that seemed to have come into existence in the core of her being. Instead of agitating her, it lulled her. She suddenly wanted to sleep. Like this. Ensconced in his power and protection.

She yawned. "You're comfy."

"*I* certainly am not comfy." His chuckle vibrated through her. But it was the powerful jerk against her buttocks, what she could no longer doubt was his hardness, seeming to be getting bigger, if that was possible, that lurched her out of her stupor.

He pulled her back against him. "Don't move."

"But you're…you're…"

"Aroused? Sure. I've been hard as steel since I laid eyes on you. And no, I'm not like that by default. But I don't mind."

"I thought men didn't mind anything more."

"I'm not 'men.' And even though it started out as uncomfortable, veered into painful and is now bordering on agonizing, I've never enjoyed anything more. I've never felt so alive."

She squirmed with his every word, only to be struck still when she realized it only made him harder. She'd never known mortification like this. Or arousal.

Her heart rattled her frame, until he pressed her closer to his body and whispered against her cheek, "I'll never do anything you don't invite me to, Talia. Beg me to."

She believed him. And she sagged back, savoring the way their bodies throbbed in unison. She'd probably be horrified later. But who cared about later when now was here? And like this?

She melted into him, felt her breathing and heartbeats match to his.

Endless minutes of shared tranquility and silent communion later, he kissed her forehead and sighed. "See that star? The one winking azure-blue? I'll call her Talia."

She nuzzled into his kiss, inviting a few more down her cheek, her core now so hot, so drenched and cramping she was breaths away from inviting more. Begging for it.

She pressed her thighs together, alleviating a measure of the pounding, and choked a thick murmur. "It must already have a name."

"I don't care. It reminds me of your eyes."

She giggled. "Maybe you should call it Talia's Eyes."

"Since it's only one, better yet Talia's Eye. So which will it be, *ya nadda jannati?* Talia's Left or Right Eye? I can foresee the myths that would one day be woven around such a name."

"Hmm, if I were a Cyclops, we wouldn't have this dilemma."

"If you were a Cyclops, they'd be the sexiest creatures to ever dominate men's fantasies."

She snorted. "And among all your skills, you acquired a black belt in far-fetched flirting?"

"You're right. I should have stuck with the truth. That it would dominate *this* man's fantasies. The two-eyed, sexy bundle of cuteness I'm wrapped around right now already does."

"I bet you wouldn't say that if you saw me in bloodstained scrubs with my hair spiked like a porcupine. Yeah, that 'atrocious' haircut wasn't for my disguise's sake. That's how I keep my hair out of my way and off my mind."

"You're talking to the man who found you overwhelmingly arousing when you were sporting a beard. I'd find you sexy if you were covered in mud. Oh, wait…now *there's* an idea."

"Mud-wrestling fantasies, huh? How mundanely male of you."

"I don't have those, no. But if it involves you and me, I'll definitely add them to my inventory of fantasies." She twisted around to glare up at him and he only whistled. "Whoa. Maybe I'll call it Talia's Glare."

"Since it's harsh and cold, huh?"

"Far from being either, this star, like your glare, is compelling, hypnotic, resolute, indomitable."

She almost did something stupid. Like kiss the aftertaste of those delicious words off his lips, or swirl her tongue in that solitary dimple that winked in his left cheek when he grinned.

She gave him a pseudo-self-important glance instead. "I'll have you know this glare has my interns and junior residents in the E.R. jumping and remaining in the air until I say down."

"I believe it." Suddenly he gathered her tighter. "Would you consider doing that here?"

Her heart veered in her chest. She struggled to spin

around further in his arms, came to lie sideways over him so she could more easily look into his eyes. "You mean work in an E.R. in Zohayd?"

"Actually, I'd love for you to consider training my men and women in field and emergency medicine."

"Oh…" The idea of remaining in Zohayd after they got through this, the fact that he esteemed her enough to offer her a responsibility like that, and elation at the thought of being where she could see him regularly erupted inside her.

Without thinking of the feasibility of such a scenario, she grinned up at him. "That sounds incredible!" It was only when his eyes blazed in return that she faltered. "I mean, we'll have to, y'know, talk this through when this is over…see if it's even plausible given why I'm here and all and—wait…women? You have *women* in your special forces?"

Impatience spurted in his eyes, probably since she'd changed the subject without giving him an answer. Then they softened again, perhaps in acknowledgment of the difficulties of their situation beyond the real and present danger. "Not many, since it doesn't seem to be one of the career options Zohaydan women prefer."

"I'm staggered that it *is* an option in Zohayd. That you have any."

His smile turned whimsical. "There *is* a difference between being a pigheaded, mulish ox and being a male chauvinist pig."

She rolled her eyes. "I'll never hear the end of that, will I?"

"Do you want to hear it?" he teased.

She thought for a moment. Then grinned impishly. "Nah."

With that, they both fell silent and snuggled deeper into each other as if by agreement.

After an hour of being melded together in deepening companionship, during which she'd simultaneously managed to remain molten and he to remain hard, they set off again.

The third day came. And passed.

At the end of the fourth day, their supplies had been all but exhausted. And there was no sign of the oasis.

On the fifth day, after sunset, as they'd set out on their cycle of hikes and rests, Harres had done something that had dread and desperation taking hold of her.

He'd dumped all their gear.

When she'd protested, he'd fallen silent for a long moment. Then he'd looked at her solemnly.

He'd said that she had no reason to believe he knew what he was doing anymore. But he could no longer afford to go at that pace. Would she trust him to know what they needed to survive, to reach the oasis?

And she'd trusted him.

But they hadn't reached the oasis.

Ten hours later, she'd been unable to go on.

She'd collapsed. Harres had managed to catch her before she hit the ground. He'd laid her down with utmost gentleness, held her in his solid embrace, raining on her soothing kisses and pleas for forgiveness.

She'd succumbed to unconsciousness thinking those would be the last things she felt and heard in her life.

But she woke up to find herself wrapped in the two blankets left with them. And Harres's jacket. She was parched and frying alive in the blistering heat of midday. Emphasis on *alive*.

And she realized another thing.

She was alone.

She struggled out of the tight cocoon, sat up. Harres was nowhere in sight.

He'd left her?

No. She knew he never would.

But what if something had happened to him? What if their enemies had found them? Would the prince of Zohayd be a bigger hand to gamble with in their quest for the throne? How would they use him? What would they do to him?

She sobbed. No tears came from her dehydrated eyes. She drifted in and out of consciousness. And even in waking moments, nightmares preyed on her. Showed her Harres, abused and worse, and all because he'd come for her....

Oh, God, Harres...please...

Then, as if in answer to her plea, he was there. She knew he wasn't *really* there. She was hallucinating with dehydration.

For this Harres was not the sand-car-and-helicopter-riding modern desert knight, but one on a white horse. Galloping her way as if he rode the wind, as one with the magnificent animal, made of the same energy, the same nobleness and fierceness and determination. Her knight coming to save her.

But there was no saving her. This was the end.

Not that it was too bad. She had only two regrets. That she hadn't saved Todd, and that she had let everything stand in the way between her and Harres.

If she had her time with him to live again, if she had more time with him, she would disregard it all and just be with him, experience all she could of him, while she could.

Now it was too late, and she would never know his passion for real.

What a waste.

Her dream Harres leaped off his horse before it came to a halt, spraying sand in a wide arc with the sudden abortion of its manic momentum. Harres descended on her, the wings of his white shroud spread like a great eagle's, enveloping her in peace and contentment. She was so thankful her intense desire had given her such a tangible last manifestation of the man she loved…yes, *loved*….

She could barely whisper her bliss to the apparition. "Harres…you feel so good…"

"Talia, *nadda jannati,* forgive me for leaving you."

"S'okay…I just wish…you didn't have…to leave, too."

His regal head, covered in a sun-reflecting white *ghotrah,* descended to protect her from the glare, his magical eyes emitting rays of pure-gold anxiety.

She sighed again. "You make…an incredible…angel, Harres. My guardian angel. Too bad you're here now…as that other angel guy…the death guy…"

"What?"

Talia winced. She'd been floating in the layers of Harres's voice, so deliciously deep and emotional. Now it boomed with sharpness and alarm.

"You're alive and you'll be well. Just drink, *ya talyeti.*" She found nectar on her lips, gulped it without will or question, felt life surging into her as she sank in the delight of his crooning praise and encouragement to her, pouring hoarse explanations. "If I'd carried you, I wouldn't have been able to reach the oasis. So I left you, ran there. It took me six more hours, and two to ride back. I died of dread each second away from you. But I'm back, and you're alive, Talia."

"Y-you're sure?"

His face convulsed in her wavering focus. "Sure I'm sure. Now please drink, my precious dew droplet. Soon you'll be as good as ever."

"Don't you mean a-as bad?"

She felt herself gathered into arms that trembled, pressed against a chest that heaved, her depletion probably shaking up her perceptions. "There you are. My snarky gift from *Ullah*."

"You say…the most wonderful things. You are the most w-wonderful thing…that ever happened…to me…"

Then she surrendered to oblivion in the safety of his arms.

In the dreamscape that claimed her at once, she thought she heard him say, "It's you who are the most wonderful thing that ever happened to me, *ya habibati*."

Eight

Harres ignored pain, smothered exhaustion.

He had to last until he got Talia back to the oasis.

Those who'd ridden with him offered again to take care of her, of both of them.

He couldn't let them. Wouldn't. He had to be the one to carry her to safety. As he'd promised.

He asked a few of them to go back in his and Talia's tracks before they were wiped away by the incoming sandstorm, to retrieve what he'd ditched. The medical supplies most of all. He let those who stayed with him help secure Talia astride the horse, ensconced in his arms like he'd had her during their rests between the punishing hikes.

The ride back to the oasis took longer. Too long. Each moment seemed to expand, to refuse to let the next replace it, bound on prolonging his ordeal, on giving him more time to relive the hell of being forced to leave her behind.

He'd gone further out of his mind with each bounding

step away from her. He'd struggled to force himself to focus
so he could see his path to the oasis, their ticket to survival.
But the sight of her bundled up in blankets and ensconced
in the barricade of a steep dune had been branded on his
brain. He'd lost chunks of sanity with each hour, knowing
the blankets' protection would turn to suffocation once the
desert turned from an arctic wasteland to a blazing inferno.
He'd prayed the message he'd left her in the sand wouldn't
be wiped away by the ruthless winds, that she'd heard his
plea before he'd left, to please, please wake up soon, read
it, unwrap herself and use the blankets as shelter with the
tent prop he'd kept.

But the message had been obliterated. And she'd unwrapped herself but hadn't taken refuge from the baking
sun. After more than five days of ordeals almost beyond
human tolerance, it had been a miracle she'd lasted that
long. The only reason he had was because he was bound
on saving her.

He gathered her tighter to his body, his heart draining
of blood all over again as he imagined her waking up alone
and finding no explanation for his disappearance.

It had been his miscalculations that had led to this
situation. The terrain had changed beyond recognition from
the last time he'd been there, and fearing the lethality of
the quicksand areas that were the major factor behind the
segregation of the oasis, he'd taken a much wider safety
margin around their now obscured boundaries. He'd ditched
their supplies too late, when doing so no longer meant
quickening their progress, with irreversible exhaustion
setting in.

He'd stumbled into the oasis's outer limits a few stages
beyond depleted. He'd seen how he'd looked in the horrified
expressions of those who'd run to him with water and efforts
to spare him another step. Their horror had only risen when

they'd realized he was bleeding. In his mad dash, he'd torn Talia's meticulous sutures.

He'd let the oasis people bandage and clothe him in weather-appropriate clothes, gulped down reviving drinks only because he knew he'd be no good to Talia if he didn't get repaired and refueled. He'd still given it all only minutes before he'd jumped on their most powerful endurance horse and exploded out of the oasis with their best riders struggling to keep up with him.

It had been another eternity until he'd gotten back to her.

He groaned. Even in the face of death, his Talia had been the essence of composure and grace. And wit. A chuckle sliced through him as her words echoed inside him again. Until he replayed her last ones before she'd surrendered to oblivion in his arms.

You are the most wonderful thing that ever happened to me….

He shuddered, pressed her closer as if to absorb her into him, where he'd always protect her with his very life.

She might have meant those words for her savior. But he'd reciprocated them, had meant them, for her.

After one more interminable hour, he brought his horse to a stumbling stop at the door of the cottage that had been prepared for them.

He only let others support Talia's weight for the moment it took him to sway off the horse. Then he reclaimed her, folded her into him as if he feared she'd evaporate if he loosened his hold.

Once inside the dwelling that he couldn't register beyond it being a roof over their head and a door cutting them off from the rest of the oasis, he coaxed the mostly unconscious Talia to drink again, glassfuls of both water and a high-calorie, vitamin and mineral drink the locals had concocted for conditions of extreme dehydration and sunstroke.

With utmost care, crooning encouragement and praise, he undressed her down to those ridiculous men's underwear, bathed her in cool water, fanned her dry and then sponged her down again, cooling her raging heat. When he finally judged her temperature within normal, he dressed her in one of the crisply clean, vibrantly colorful nightdresses the oasis women had provided.

Throughout, though her consciousness rose and fell like waves in a tranquil sea, she surrendered to his ministrations, unquestioning, unresisting.

He finally laid her down on the soft *kettan* linen sheets freshly spread on a firm mattress on top of a wide, low platform bed. As he withdrew, a distressed sound spilled from her suddenly working lips, her brow knotting as if in pain.

She couldn't bear separation from him. As he couldn't from her.

He came down beside her, cocooned her with his body. She burrowed deeper into him with each ragged breath until he felt she'd slid between the layers of his being, making him realize again that he'd had so many vacant places inside of him, ones she'd exposed. Ones only she could fill.

He stilled, savoring the imprint of each inch of her, vibrating to her every tremor, his rumbles harmonizing with her unintelligible purrs of fatigue and pure contentment.

Then she went limp and silent, her breath steadying, indicating her descent into replenishing sleep.

But he couldn't take that for granted.

At the tattered periphery of his awareness he thought he should seek the oasis elder and ask if there was still time before the sandstorm to have envoys sent to his brothers. Maybe if they moved fast enough, they'd get ahead of it.

But he couldn't bring himself to leave Talia. His only concern was to see to her health and comfort. Until she opened her eyes and her beloved personality shone at him through her heavenly gaze, he could think of nothing but her. Even the fate of Zohayd came second.

He'd do nothing but watch over her until she woke up....

Talia woke up.

For long moments after her eyelids scraped back over grit, she couldn't credit the images falling on her retinas.

She was ensconced in gossamer off-whiteness, drenched nerve-tingling spiciness and sourceless light.

Her surroundings came into sharper focus. She was actually surrounded by a fine mosquito net, lying in a gigantic bed on the smoothest linens she'd ever touched. She'd smelled the scents more than once since she'd come to Zohayd, seemingly a lifetime ago, incense of musk and amber and *ood*. The light was seeping from openings below a low ceiling blocked by arabesque work so delicate it must be almost as effective as the net.

She hadn't turned her head yet. She couldn't. But she saw enough to fascinate her on the side she could see. A wall of whitewashed mud-brick, a palm-wood door and window with shutters, cobblestone floors, two reed couches spread with wool cushions handwoven in a conflagration of color and pattern, with the same distinct Bedouin design gracing a rug and wall hangings. Oil lamps and incense burners hung on the wall, made of hand-worked bronze, simple, exquisite and polished to a dazzling sheen.

Was this another world? Another era?

She should know where she was. The knowledge just evaded her. She also knew she'd woken up many times before. If she could call the hazy episodes waking up. Now fragments of recollection clinked and bounced around like a rain of beads on the ground of her awareness.

Then as moments of wakefulness accumulated, the jittery particles settled, coalesced, stringing together to form a timeline. And she realized what had happened.

Harres had come back for her. Her desert knight had ridden back on a white horse, leading the cavalry. But not before she'd compounded dehydration and heat prostration with sunstroke.

No wonder distortions and abridgments stuffed her head. Yet one thing possessed hyperreality in the jigsaw of the haziness. Harres. Caring for and healing her. Looking so worn-out, so anxious, she would have wept had she been able to.

"Are you awake for real this time, *ya habibati?*"

His voice was as dark and haggard as she remembered from her delirium.

She twisted around, homing in on it. She found him two feet away on her other side, sitting on the floor with one knee bent, primed, slightly above her level with being so tall and her bed so low. He was wearing a white *abaya*.

So she hadn't imagined it.

She closed her eyes to savor the sight of him in his land's traditional garb. He looked regal in anything, but in this, he looked…*whoa*.

Yeah. *Whoa* should become a sanctioned adjective to describe the indescribable. Him. The ultimate in mind-blowing virility. Especially adorned in what he was born to wear.

He stood in one of those fluid moves that never ceased to amaze her, considering his size and bulk. Before her eyes could travel up to his, he swept the net surrounding her away and his *abaya* fell open.

Her gaze snagged on his chest. But for his bandages it was bare, a bronzed expanse of perfection and potency.

This was where she'd sought refuge from jeopardy and exhaustion, the haven that had turned their nightmare into a dream she'd cherish for the rest of her life.

His bandages were now narrower than she'd made them, exposing more of the ebony silk that accentuated each slope and bulge of sheer maleness. If that wasn't bad enough—or good enough—the tantalizing layer arrowed down over an abdomen hewn from living granite, guiding her eyes to where it began to flare…before it disappeared beneath string-tied white pants straight out of *Arabian Nights*. Those hung low, dangerously so, on those muscled hips, their looseness doing nothing to hide the power, the shape and size of his formidable thighs and manhood.

She couldn't breathe. Her insides contracted with a blow of longing so hard, she moaned with it.

Which was good news. If she could go from zero to one thousand in seconds at the mere sight of him, all her systems were functioning at optimum.

"Don't, *ya talyeti*. I beg you, don't close your eyes again."

She hadn't realized she'd squeezed them shut. His ragged plea and the dipping of the mattress jerked them open and up to his. And she moaned again.

The urgency in his eyes, in his pose, doused the heat spiraling through her. Even though his expression made him look more imposing, intimidating even, and even more arousing….

Enough. Say something!

She tried. Her throat was sore and as dry as the desert from disuse and the aftereffects of dehydration and exhaustion.

Her voice finally worked in a thready whisper. "I'm a-awake. For r-real."

He loomed over her, his eyes singeing her with the intensity of his examination and skepticism. "You said that before. Too many times. My sanity can't take much more false hope." He looked heavenward, stabbed his fingers through his hair. "What am I saying? If you're still sleep-talking, this won't make you snap out of it."

She struggled to sit up, managing only to turn fully toward him. "I a-am awake this time. I sort o-of remember the false starts. But I'm not only awake, I feel as good as new." His eyes darkened. "No, really. I've self-diagnosed since coming around, and I'm back to normal. I'm just woozy, which is to be expected, and sore from the exercise of my life and lying in bed too long...."

Her words petered out as she tried to sit up again and took her first look down her body.

She was in a low-cut, sleeveless satin nightdress in dazzling blues and greens and oranges, echoing the exuberance of the room's furnishings.

Heat rose as she imagined him taking her out of her clothes and dressing her in it. Her imaginings scorched her as they veered into vivid, languorous enactment of him taking her out of it again....

To make it worse, he was coming nearer, his anxiousness to ascertain her claim trapping her breath into suddenly full lungs, making the nightdress feel as if it had come alive, sliding over her nipples, slithering between her legs with knowing, tormenting skims, intensifying the heavy throb within.

She wriggled, trying to relieve her stinging breasts, squeezed her legs together to contain the ache building between them. She looked up at him with eyes barely open with the weight of desire. "Say…h-how long have I been out?"

He snapped a look at his watch, before looking back at her, his eyes losing their bleak look. "Fifty hours, forty-two minutes."

"Whoa!" she exclaimed, her voice regaining power and clarity with each syllable. "But that's a very acceptable time frame to get over a combo of dehydration and sunstroke. Good thing I'm a tough nut, eh?"

Elation dawned in his eyes, intensifying their vividness and beauty. "That you are, along with being an in-evaporable dew droplet. And *shokrun lel'lah*—thank God into infinity for that."

Her lips managed a tremulous smile. "So what have you been doing while I was sleep-talking?"

His lips quirked, the old devilry she knew and adored reigniting his eyes. "I took care of you, sent envoys out to my brothers, took more care of you. Then, oh, I took care of you."

She slapped his forearm playfully in response to his teasing then patted it in thanks for his effort to paint his grim vigil in lightness. "Did you take care of *you* at all? Did you get any sleep?"

He gave her a delicious look of mock contrition. "Not intentionally, I assure you."

She now saw the strain and exhaustion traversing his face in lines that hadn't been there even during their worst times. Her heart compressed even as it poured out a surplus of gratitude and admiration. "Oh, Harres, you're such an intractable protector." She caressed his forearm, basking in mixing their smiles. Then she gasped. "What about your wound? Did you get someone to look at it? How is it?"

He gave a perfect impression of a boy mollifying his

teacher before he revealed something that would send her screaming. "Uh—I have good news and bad news."

Her eyes flew over him, feverishly assessing his condition. No. Whatever his news was, it couldn't be terrible. Apart from the evident fatigue, he looked fine.

Her heart still quivered in her chest as she said, "Hit me with the bad."

He gave a pseudograve look. "Your sutures were very good."

"Past tense?" she squeaked. "You busted them!"

He nodded, holding his hands up. "Good news is, there's no sign of infection. See?" He moved his left arm up with minimal effort and no apparent discomfort. "What's more, the oasis people retrieved our medical kit, so you can sew me up again."

"You bet I will!" She subsided in relief at the proof that he was okay. Her eyes darted away from him for the first time and took in the whole room. She could see the rest of the place through the open door behind him. "This place is incredible."

"It is a very special place," he agreed. "It was the previous oasis-elder's dwelling. He died two years ago. Elders' houses remain uninhabited, as a tribute to their lives and leadership. It is an honor to be given this place during our stay."

Her smile trembled again. "Only the best for Zohayd's Guardian Prince."

He shook his head, his eyes bathing her in warmth. "It's not that. Any refugees they claimed back from the desert would have been given the same treatment. I also have a relationship with the people here that has nothing to do with me being their prince. I'm not sure they consider the Aal Shalaans their ruling family, or if they do, that they give the fact much significance."

"Why not?"

"The oasis and its people are considered off-limits to the outside world they live independent of. They are…revered by the rest of Zohayd and all the region, almost feared as a mystic nation who will always exist outside others' time and dominion."

She digested this, the feeling of being in another world and time intensifying, validated. "A nation? How many are they?"

"Around thirty thousand. Yet their refusal to join the modern world in any way makes them unique. Uniqueness is power beyond any secured by numbers."

"Not if they lack the modern methods of defending themselves against intruders, it isn't."

His face closed. "There will never be intruders. Not on the Aal Shalaans' watch. Not on mine."

She believed him. Harres the knight whose honor dictated he protect the helpless against the bullies of the world.

Suddenly, she felt she'd suffocate if she didn't feel him against her.

She held out trembling arms. "So, do I get a welcome back to the land of the awake?"

His face clenched with what looked like pain. For a heart-bursting moment, she feared he'd been placating her about his wound. Then his eyes filled with such turmoil, she thought she'd imposed on him.

Just before mortification caused her arms to slump to her sides, he groaned and sank into them.

The enormity of the reprieve, after thinking she'd lost her chance of having him like that, of everything, had her hands quaking as they slid over the breadth of his back, the leashed power of his arms. Her fingers caressed his vitality, his reality, committed every detail of him to tactile memory, felt him being integrated into her perceptions and senses.

Then she reached his face and translated into awareness what she'd been looking at and not fully registering.

"You shaved."

He smiled into her nuzzling, letting her singe her lips with the pleasure of coasting them over his perfect smoothness. "It was the first thing I did the moment a blade and disposable water were available."

She rubbed her lips over the underside of his jaw. "You know...I've never seen you clean shaven. When I first saw your face in that bathroom, you were already sporting a mighty ten-o'clock shadow."

He rubbed his chin over her cheek, giving her further demonstration of his silkiness. "So you approve?"

"I far, far more than approve."

Her lips traveled up until they glided hesitantly over his, her tongue tentatively laving them in tiny licks, still disbelieving the reality of experiencing this, of their texture and taste.

A rumble poured into her mouth, lancing into her heart just as it spiked her arousal to pain with its unadulterated passion.

Then he broke away from her quaking arms.

She had no power to drag him back into them. And no right, if this wasn't where he wanted to be.

He sat up, severing their connection. Then he rose off the bed altogether.

He stood above her, his heavy-lidded eyes obscuring his expression for the first time since...ever.

Then he drew both hands through his hair and exhaled. "You might be awake, but you're not really all there yet. And you are—fragile, in every way." His shoulders rose and fell on another exhalation. "So now we get you back to fighting form."

Was that why he'd pulled back? He wanted her back to

full health, physically and mentally, before he'd consider changing their status quo?

It made sense. And made her even more grateful to him, if that was possible.

She was a cauldron of seething emotions and needs right now, had no control over any of them. And she needed to know if what she felt melting all resistance was the ordeal talking, the days of inseparable proximity and total dependence, or if the feelings originated from her.

Now that stress and danger were over, would the physical and emotional pull remain this overwhelming? Would he remain the same man who'd done everything to keep their spirits up? It had niggled that he might have exaggerated his attraction to her for many worthwhile ends. Survival, smoothing over a bumpy beginning. And maybe not so worthwhile ones. Gaining his objective—the secret to secure his family and their throne.

So many things hung like a sun-obliterating cloud over the whole situation. Todd's ordeal, the Aal Shalaans' role in it and their current danger, the info she'd stumbled on, Harres's duty as guardian of his family and people.

So he'd done the right thing by drawing away. She'd follow his lead, recover her health and clarity. Until she figured out what was real. Inside her, around her, about him, between them. Or until this mess, this assortment of *messes,* was sorted out.

If they possibly could be.

Nine

A string of eruptions reverberated in Talia's bones.

She would have taken instinctive cover if Harres's arm hadn't been around her shoulder.

He gave her a reassuring squeeze, chuckled in her ear. "No, that's not a firing squad."

Gulping down her heart, she let him resume leading her through the hurrying crowd, still not sure where their destination was, where the feast was being held. "A gun salute for the Guardian Prince of Zohayd, then?"

His grin widened. "That's just how they announce the beginning of their entertainment."

"With an aerial blitz?"

He threw his magnificent head back and laughed before looking his pleasure and merriment down on her. "The extra zeal is in honor of your recovery and your gracing of their feast tonight."

She raised him a wider grin, her heart zooming again

with elation, with anticipation. But mostly, with his nearness.

She'd been up and about for three days now, had recovered fully. But what relieved her was the condition of his wound. Her sutures had been very good. And had remained mostly intact, with only a few needing reapplication. The healing had been spectacular. She'd never known humans could heal that fast. She kept teasing that he must have mutants or local gods in his ancestry. Which wouldn't surprise her.

And during the idyll of recuperation and recreation, they'd remained in the cottage or its garden, with the oasis people coming periodically to check their needs and replenish their supplies. She hadn't wanted to go out, to see more.

She'd had Harres with her.

She now knew that the bonds of harmony and sufficiency they'd forged during their desert trek hadn't just been crisis induced. It hadn't been the isolation or the desperation. It all originated from their unpressured choices, their innate inclinations, their essential selves, and flowed between them in a closed circuit of synergy and affinity.

Being with him *was* enough. Felt like everything.

Tonight was the first night they would join the oasis people. She felt so grateful to them, so humbled by their hospitality. But earlier she'd felt embarrassed, too.

The oasis-elder's wife and daughters had come, bringing her an exceptionally intricate and stunningly vivacious outfit to wear to the feast. As Harres had stood beside her translating their felicity at her recovery and her thrill over their magnificent gift, the ladies had eaten him up with their eyes. She'd wanted to jump to their side and indulge in the pleasure of *oohing* and *aahing* over the wonders of him with those born equipped to appreciate them. Which was every female with a pulse.

But it had been when their eyes had turned to her with knowing tinged with envy that she'd realized. With her and Harres's living arrangement, they must think they were… intimate. And if she was truthful, and she was, they hadn't been only because of his consideration and restraint.

Not one to let misgivings go unvoiced, she'd asked. Was their situation compromising him, a prince in an ultra-conservative kingdom? Now that her staying with him was no longer necessary, couldn't she move elsewhere until his brothers came for them?

He'd said that the oasis people didn't follow any rules but their own. Being one with nature, living outside the reach of politics or material interests, they didn't police others' morality and conduct, lived and let live. But even if they hadn't, he cared nothing for what the world thought. He cared only about what she wanted. Did *she* want to move out?

Her heart thudded all over again at the memory. He'd been so intense, yet indulgent, not taking it for granted that she didn't want to. And she didn't. She couldn't even think how fast the day was approaching when she would move out of his orbit, return to a life that didn't have him in it.

She couldn't think, so she didn't. Plenty of time later to. Her lifetime's worth.

Now with her heart thudding, she investigated the external source of pounding.

In the dual illumination of a waxing moon and raging fires, she saw it was coming from the direction of the biggest construction she'd seen so far in the oasis.

Silvered by moonbeams and gilded by flickering flames, a one-story circular building rose among a huge clearing within the congregation of dwellings. It was made of the same materials but could accommodate probably a few thousand. It had more windows than walls, and flanking its

single door, older women in long-sleeved flowing dresses
with tattoos covering their temples and chins were squatting
on the ground, each with a large wooden urn held between
bent legs, pounding it with a two-foot pestle.

He smiled into her eyes. "When it's not used as a per-
cussion instrument, the *mihbaj* doubles as a seed grinder,
mainly coffee, and…" A storm of new drumming drowned
out his voice, coming from inside the building, making
him put his lips to her ears. "The whole rhythm section has
joined in. Let's go in."

As they did, she felt as if she'd stepped centuries back
into the ancient orient with its special brand of excesses.

The ambiance was overpowering in richness and depth
and purity with an edge of mystic decadence to it. Heavy
sweet-spicy *ood* incense blended with the distinctive smell
of fruit-mixed tobacco that many smoked in their water-
filled *sheeshas*. The fumes undulated like scented ghosts,
twining through the warm, hypnotic light flickering from
hundreds of polished, handcrafted copper lanterns.

The huge circle of the floor was covered in handwoven
rugs, the whitewashed walls scattered in arabesque windows, most thrown open to let in the desert-night breeze
and the rising moon rays.

All around, multitudes of exuberant cushions were laid
on the floor and against the walls, with *tableyahs*—foot-
high, unpolished wooden tables—set before them for the
banquet.

On the unfurnished side, a three-foot-high platform
hosted the dozens of drummers producing that blood-
seething rhythm.

"The tambourine-like instrument is the *reg*. The *doff*,
the large one with no jangles, acts as the bass drum." She
followed Harres's pointing finger, eagerly imbibing the
info. "But it's the *darabukkah*, the inverted vaselike drums,

whose players keep up the hot rhythm. Usually they wow the crowd with some impossibly complex and long routines before the other instruments join in."

They sure wowed *her*. She felt the rhythm boiling her blood, seeping into her nervous pathways, taking hold of her impulses.

She let Harres guide her to the seating arrangement. But with every step she swayed more to the rhythm, her every cell feeling like popcorn, ricocheting inside her with the need to expend the surplus energy gathering in them in unbridled motion.

Suddenly Harres took her hand and spooled her away then back into his arms, all while moving as one with the beat. "Dance, *ya nadda jannati*. Celebrate being alive and being in paradise."

And being with you, she wanted to shout.

She didn't, let her eyes shout it for her. Then she danced, as if she'd been released from shackles that had kept her immobile all her life, riding the compelling rhythm, moving with him to the primal beat, her heart keeping the same fiery tempo.

Somehow, they wound up in the middle of a dancing circle that he'd either led her to or had formed around them.

The young tribe members swirled around them in intricate routines, the males swooping like birds of prey, bounding and stomping in energetic courtship and persistent demand, the females twirling around like huge flowers, gesturing and tapping in practiced coquetry and eager acceptance.

Harres led her in emulating them, then in improvising their own dance of intimacy and delight in each other.

And for an indeterminate stretch, she felt she'd been transported to another realm where nothing existed but him. She felt him, and only him, as his eyes and touch lured her, inflamed her, shared with her, joined with her, as he moved with her as if they were connected on all levels, as if the same impulses coursed in their nerves, the same drive powered their wills and limbs.

She surfaced from the magical realm to everyone singing. In moments she found herself repeating the distinctive, catchy melody and lyrics, without understanding a word.

Suddenly Harres pulled her to him, turning the energy of their dance into a slow burn of seduction, his lips at her ear shooting more bolts of stimulation through her. And that was before she heard what he whispered.

"Everything before you passed and went to waste."

Her whole frame jerked with the shock, the emotions that surged too fast, too vast to comprehend, to contain.

He pressed her nearer, his voice deeper, darker, the only thing she heard anymore. *"Koll shai gablek addaw daa."*

That was what she was singing along.

Harres was just translating.

But no. He wasn't. He meant it. Even if the magic of those moments, of their situation and surroundings was amplifying his emotions...

The music came to an abrupt end. The silence that exploded in the next moment felt like a freezing splash, dousing her fire.

No. She wanted this time out of time to continue, to last.

But she knew it wouldn't. None of it would.

She could only cherish every second, waste none on despondency.

She looked up at Harres, found him looking back at her with eyes still storming with stimulation. She teetered from his intensity, from the drain of energy. He bent and lifted her into his arms.

People ran ahead, indicating the place of honor they should occupy. She tried to regain her footing, but he only tightened his hold on her. She struggled not to bury her face in his shoulder in embarrassment, to be carried like that, and after the whole tribe saw her dancing like a demon, too.

At their place, he set her on the cushions, sat down beside her and fetched her water and *maward*—rose essence. Then he began peeling ripened dates and feeding them to her.

She fought the urge to do something to be really embarrassed about. Grabbing his hand and suckling the sticky sweetness off his fingers. Then traveling downward...

Going lightheaded with the fantasies, with holding back, she mumbled around the last mouthful, "You do know I'm fully recharged and in no need of coddling, right?"

He shook his head. "You used up your battery with that marathon jig."

She waved her hand. "I'm just saving up for the next one."

He smiled down at her, poured her some mouthwatering cardamom coffee in a tiny, handblown, greenish glass and brought it to her lips. "A sip with each bite of dates is the recommended dose."

She did as instructed, her eyes snapping wider at the incredible blend of aromas and flavors, of bitterness and sweetness, at the graininess of the dates dissolving in the rich heat and smoothness of the coffee.

She sighed, gulped the rest. Sinking deeper in contentment, she turned to adjust her cushions. He jumped to do it himself.

She leaned back on them, quirking her lips at him. "When will you believe you don't have to keep doing stuff for me, that I've never been in better shape? No emergency doctor could have done a better job on me."

"I know, my invincible dew droplet, but would you be so cruel as to deprive me of the pleasure of pampering you?"

Now what could a woman say to *that?*

Nothing but unintelligible sighs, evidently. That was all that issued from her as the oasis elder rose to deliver a word of welcome before waiters with huge trays holding dozens of plates streamed out to serve dinner.

More sighs accompanied the fantastic meal. The food at the oasis was the best she'd ever had. Tonight it rose to ambrosia level.

Harres fed her, cut the assortment of grilled meats, told her the names and recipes of the baked and grilled breads and the vegetable stews. He introduced her to date wine, which she proclaimed should replace nectar as the drink of the gods. But it was *logmet al gadee* that was truly out of this world. The golden spheres of fried dough, crunchy on the outside, soft on the inside and dipped in thick syrup were so good there should be—and probably there was—a penalty for it.

After dinner they danced again, then she shook hands with hundreds of people, thanked them all for the best night of her life. On their stroll back to the cottage, she decided something.

Everything in this place was pure magic.

But she knew that wasn't an accurate assessment. Had she been with anyone else, she wouldn't have enjoyed it a fraction as much. She'd been to idyllic places for vacations before, but had never enjoyed one after her parents died, had stopped trying to years ago....

"What are you thinking, *ya talyeti?*"

She shook off the surge of melancholy, smiled up at him. "This means my Talia, right?"

He nodded, sweeping a soothing hand over her hair, now

supple and sparkling from a miraculous blend of local oils. "Your Arabic is getting better every day."

"I find it fascinating, so rich and expressive in ways so different from English. I'd love to learn more."

"Then you shall."

It was always like that. She wished for something, and he insisted she'd have it. She knew he *would* give her anything, if at all possible.

Feeling her skin getting tighter with emotion, she answered his previous question. "I was thinking of my parents."

His eyes grew softer. "You told me they died. I didn't want to probe. Not a good idea bringing up death and that of loved ones in our situation back then."

"But you want to know now."

"Only if it doesn't pain you to talk about them."

"No, no. I love to talk about them. I hate it that people avoid bringing them up, as if it will remind me of their loss. As if I need to be reminded. It's actually not mentioning them that makes me feel their absence even more acutely."

His eyebrows knotted. "People can be misguided in their good intentions." His brow cleared, his lips quirking. "What I find amazing is that you didn't set them straight."

"Oh, I did."

He chuckled before gentle seriousness descended over his face. "Were their deaths recent?"

"It *feels* like yesterday. And like a few lifetimes ago."

"I know what you mean."

Her heart kicked. "You've lost loved ones, too?"

He shook his head, his gaze heating. "I meant knowing you. It's so vivid it feels perpetually new, yet so powerful it feels as if you have been there all my life, a part of my being." Now what could she say to something so—indescribable?

And worse, that sounded so spontaneous and sincere? Good thing he didn't let her struggle for a comment, but went on. "But I don't have a comparable experience when it comes to losing someone that dear. My mother died when I was five, so I hardly remember her. So tell me, *ya talyeti,* talk to me about your loved ones."

"I feel I lost them simultaneously, even though they died seven years apart. Okay, let me start at the beginning." She let out a shuddering exhalation, let him draw her closer into him, then began. "I never knew my biological father. I knew *of* him, but he didn't want a wife and a kid, let alone two. We had our mother's family name until she married the man I consider my father when Todd and I were two. As I grew up and learned the whole story, I thought my mother the luckiest woman on earth and my father—the man whose name I carry now—the best man in existence. I never saw anyone more in love or right for each other than they were.

"The only problem was, my father was almost thirty years older than my mom. He'd never been married before, always said he'd been waiting for her. For all of us. When I was in my second year in med school, right before his eightieth birthday, he passed away in his sleep, beside my mom. She never recovered. Seven years later, she overdosed on a concoction of the prescription meds I'd been begging her for years not to take. I could have saved her if I was there, but only Todd was home. By the time the ambulance arrived, it was too late."

For long moments after she fell silent, Harres said nothing. Then they entered their cottage, and he pulled her into his embrace, pressed her head against his endless chest.

They stood like that, sharing, savoring, her body throbbing to the tempo of the powerful heart beating below her ear.

Then he kissed the top of her head. *"Ana aassef, ya nadda jannati.* I'm sorry."

He said nothing more. Then they went about their bedtime routine. Once in bed, hearing him moving in the other room, she had a sudden realization. Why she'd always given up on any attempt at a relationship so early, so easily.

With her parents' example, she'd set her own bar high. Every connection she'd attempted had fallen miles below it. She'd soon given up on trying, had been resigned that she'd never have anything like they'd had, and that if she couldn't, she'd rather be alone. She'd become content with a life full of activity and purpose.

Now there was Harres.

"It's…huge."

At Talia's exclamation, Harres pressed his hard body to her back, murmured in her ear, "Yes, it is."

She nestled back against him, cast her gaze over the depression of *el waha*—the oasis that sprawled below them.

It had taken the past four days to cover the place on horseback. Now, on top of Reeh—or Wind, the white horse Harres had ridden on his charge back to save her—she had the best vantage point yet to appreciate it all from.

It seemed the explosion of life among the barrenness of the desert fed the conditions that fueled its proliferation in an endless cycle of balance and symbiosis. Date palms and olive trees numbered in the hundreds of thousands. Wildflowers and cacti were impossible in beauty and abundance. Farmed fruits and vegetables, especially figs, apricots, berries and corn, were astounding in size and taste. And besides horses, camels, sheep, goats, cats and dogs, there were innumerable representatives of the animal kingdom, all like the residents, unstressed and unthreatened.

Deer and foxes let her walk up to them, a few let her pet them. Even reptiles and birds humored her when she cooed to them and presumed to offer them food and seek their acquaintance.

She sighed her pleasure again. "Scratch huge. It's endless. It goes on forever."

Harres chuckled as he unwrapped her from his arms, jumped off the horse and reached up to carry her down. His effortless strength and the cherishing in his glance and touch as she slid down his body sent a current through her heart.

"We can see about three miles to the horizon if we're on the ground, farther the higher up we go. Since we're three hundred feet up, we can see for about twenty miles. And since the oasis measures more than that on its narrowest side, you can't see its end from any point, making it look endless."

She whooped, loving his explanations. "You should consider a career as a tour guide, if ever princes are no longer in demand...." She bit her tongue. Not something to joke about with a dethroning conspiracy going on in his kingdom. He only grinned at her, showing her he knew she'd meant nothing, enjoyed her joke. Grinning back in relief, she said, "I can now see how this place earned its mystical reputation."

"So it's worth the ordeal I put you through coming here, eh?"

"I would have welcomed a trash dump if it had water and shelter. But it isn't because this place meant life to us that I find it amazing. It is a paradise, like you said. Mostly because of its inhabitants. Everyone is so kind and bright and wise."

She left out the main reason why she found this place enchanting. The present company.

For minutes, as sunset expanded its dominion over the oasis, boosting the beauty to its most mind-boggling, he guided her to a spring of crystalline water enclosed within a canopy of palms. The air was laden with sweet plant scents and heady earth aromas, its temperature seeming to be calibrated for perfect comfort, all year round as he'd told her.

As they stopped by the spring, she said, "It would be so easy to live here forever."

If Todd was with her, she amended inwardly, or at least out of prison.

Harres spread a rug at her feet, looked up. "Wouldn't you go out of your mind without modern conveniences?"

She sank down on the rug, reached for their food basket. "Sure, I'd miss a few things. Hot showers for one. And the internet. Uh…I'm sure there's more I'd miss, but I'm drawing a blank right now."

He got out glasses. "How about medicine?"

"Oh, I'd practice it here like I have been so far. I'd probably do far more good in the long run than I do patching up people who go out and drive recklessly or OD again."

He raised a slice of apricot to her lips. "But you're a very complex being, *ya nadda jannati,* a product of dozens of centuries of human evolution. I am best qualified to judge how sturdy and tenacious you are, but beyond the comforts you'd substitute with the pleasures of healthy living and labor, you'd itch for what the people here can't conceive, need challenges they can't provide."

He knew her too well. And she could say the exact same of him. She nodded. "Probably. It's just the simplicity, the contentment and tranquility that breathes in this place is enchanting. If I had my way, this would be normal life and the bustle of the twenty-first century would be the vacation."

"Then you will have your way."

It felt like a pledge. As if he never meant this to end.

Yet she had no illusions, no hopes. Oceans of harsh realities, mountains of obstacles existed between them.

She was a commoner from another country and culture and he was a prince with a binding duty to his people. Then there was Todd's ordeal. She had no idea what securing his freedom would mean, to Harres, to his family. Even if there could be a solution that didn't end up harming them and making her Harres's enemy, he was probably—like that woman her brother had fallen in love with—intended to marry for king and kingdom.

Not that she'd ever put Harres and marriage together in a linear thought where *she* was concerned.

She now watched as he braided palm leaves into an ingenious basket for her fruits. Then she said, "You know, I came here thinking all of you Aal Shalaans were pampered perverts, mired in excess, useless at best, and helpless without your guards and gadgets, that all there was to you was unearned wealth and inherited status."

His nimble hands had stopped midway through weaving his own basket, his eyes becoming somber, contemplative. Then he inhaled. "So what did you think of me specifically?"

She owed him the truth, no matter how ugly it was. Feeling shame surge into her cheeks, she said, "When I first heard the tales of your valor and victories? I thought you were the most obnoxious of the lot, playing at being a hero, taking credit for the achievements of the true but faceless heroes, or at best relying on the safety net of your men's lives and your endless resources to play the role of Zohayd's Guardian Prince. I thought you'd show your true colors when you were stripped of your force field of assets."

He put a palm over his heart. "Ouch. And now you

think all that plus a few more choice put-downs and denigrations?"

She cast him a reproachful glance. "You know what I think now."

"Tell me."

The way he'd said that. The way he looked at her. As if he couldn't live without this vital knowledge.

Breath left her. "You know what you are. You have a whole kingdom who revere the dirt beneath your feet."

He sat up slowly. "Reverence doesn't matter to me. I never do anything in anticipation of anyone's thanks or admiration. I surely don't expect either, or care if I get them."

Her lips twitched. "Too bad. You'll just have to keep your chin up and take shiploads of both like the worshipped prince you are. Judging by the way the oasis inhabitants treat you, you're far more than that to them. And it *is* only you, not the whole royal family. You personally have done so much for them."

"I only do what I am in a position to do. I don't deserve credit or gratitude for doing my duty, but I would have earned disrespect and disrepute if I didn't."

"As you say around here, 'squeeze a lemon on it,'" she teased.

"So I can stomach the queasiness of adulation? Do you at least believe I never expect, let alone crave, any of it?"

"Oh, yes. I saw you squirming when they told tales of your glories last night. You sure don't crave anyone's adulation."

"I didn't say *that*."

Her heart punched her ribs. "You...crave mine?"

His nod was solemn. "I crave your acceptance, your approval."

"Uh…you have been around the past two weeks, right?"

He rose until he was on his knees, towering over her. "I need to hear it, *ya nadda jannati,* in your inimitable words. What you think of me is the only validation I have ever craved."

She struggled with an attack of arrhythmia. But he'd demanded. And the truth was his due, the least she could give him when she owed him her very life.

She gave it to him. "From the first moment, you forced me to reassess you. With every action and word, you showed me you are all that's advertised and far more. Stripped from all the trappings of your power, you proved to be the total opposite of what I thought, with stamina and resourcefulness and bravery that constantly awe me. You showed me you take your duty to protect anyone weaker than you, at whatever cost to you, more seriously than I thought possible in this day and age. I believe you're one of a kind, Prince Harres Aal Shalaan."

His gaze lengthened, heated, until she felt she'd burst into flames. Just when she was about to whimper, *please, enough,* he took her hand, buried his face in its palm for a long moment.

Then raggedly, still against her flesh, he whispered, "You honor me with your opinion. I will always strive to deserve it."

From then on, the atmosphere seemed charged with emotion, intensifying each sensation into near distress.

As if by agreement, they barely spoke as they had their meal. She was thankful for the silence. It gave her the chance to deal with her upheaval and face herself with more truths.

There were Aal Shalaans who hadn't hesitated to destroy Todd's life to gain their ends, but she could no longer dip the whole family in the bile of her anger and prejudice. And just as she didn't know who exactly among the Aal Shalaans and Ghada's family were culpable, there could be sides to the story that would change her perspective. Whatever *that* became, she now believed, from Harres's example, that the Aal Shalaans weren't an evil regime that deserved to be deposed.

Which led her to more realizations. And a decision.

Soon it got chilly and they rode through the now sleeping oasis back to the cottage under the blaze of a full moon.

Inside, they took turns bathing.

The moment he came out into the sitting area, she began. "I decided something when I thought I was dying."

His smile froze, his face slamming shut. "Don't say that again. Don't even think it."

"I need to tell you this." She waited until he gave a difficult nod, then went on. "When I thought it was over, I thought that if I had a chance to do things over, or a second chance to put things right, I'd do what I really wanted to do, with no thought to obstacles or misgivings or consequences. Then you saved me. And I got cold feet."

He didn't ask her to elaborate. He just stared at her, seriousness seizing his face fully for the first time.

She knew this would lead nowhere. And it made no difference.

She loved him. A love that permeated her soul and traversed her being. A love forged in shared danger, fortified by the certainty of mutual reliance. And she was no longer letting anything stop her from expressing that love, from taking what she could with him, of him.

She rose from the low couch, her steps impeded by the ferocity of her emotions. She stopped before him, looked up into the eyes that meant everything to her. Then she made the leap.

"You told me you'd never do anything I didn't want you to, didn't beg you to do. So here I am, begging you. I want you, Harres. I want nothing but you."

Ten

So this was temptation.

Unstoppable, irresistible. To die for.

This golden virago who'd invaded his being, occupied his mind and heart, conquered his reason and priorities.

She stood before him, open, offering everything. He could feel, in every nuance of his essence, the totality of her offer. It wasn't only of her body and pleasures. She was bestowing all she had, all she was, on him.

And if he closed the gap between them now, he'd take all of her, consume her.

But how could he when he couldn't give his all in return?

She *did* have all of him, Harres, the man, the human being. She had since that first night in the desert, when they'd been stripped to their essentials, when their souls had mingled in the most profound ways possible. If he'd had any concerns that the ordeal had augmented his feelings,

influenced their depth and direction, the past ten days
had erased them, had replaced them with certainty and
wonder.

Added to how she'd awed him with the way she'd handled
their trials, stood up to and beside him. She'd delighted him
with every second of their stay in the oasis. After only a
week, even with the language obstacle, she was already the
more favorite among the inhabitants.

The day after the feast, she'd set up a clinic, offered
her services. He'd thought those who'd relied on healing
practices passed down through generations would shy away
from her and her modern medical practices and instruments.
But she'd anticipated that, offered only her medical skills
and whatever the oasis provided of supplies and medicines.
After a slow day, she'd been called to an obstructed labor,
where she'd saved both mother and twin babies.

Then she'd become a legend. People had flooded in.
They'd stood in queues from morning till sunset, when he,
who acted as her assistant, insisted the doctor needed rest.
She kept proving how she, too, needed nothing beyond her
diverse skills to survive and excel anywhere, under any
conditions. He told her she was the epitome of the Arabic
proverb "A skilled woman weaves with a donkey's leg" and
teased her about being Dr. MacGyver.

She wasn't just a healer, but a warrior and a protector like
him. She shared his soul in all its breadth and peculiarities.
He wanted, *needed* to share the rest of himself with her,
for the rest of his life. There was no doubt in him anymore.
Harres, the man, was hers. Forever.

And though Harres the prince had divided loyalties, that
wasn't what stopped him from proclaiming his love, his
devotion. Only one thing did. Her grievance against his
family. If everything she'd told him was the truth, she had
legitimate reason to want to bring his family—which she

perceived as a unit that worked to the same end of retaining power—to her brand of justice. What if he couldn't secure her brother's release and redemption? How could he take her, when he couldn't promise that in return?

Turmoil ripped the bindings of his heart. And that was before she closed her eyes, her chin trembling as two crystalline tears escaped her luxurious lashes.

Then she raised glistening azure eyes and he nearly had a heart attack. "I thought you wanted me, too...."

He couldn't bear it. *Elal jaheem* with the obstacles between them. He *would* obliterate them.

With a sob, she began to turn away. He grabbed her hand, placed it on his chest, felt as if his heart would ram through it to feel the touch of that hand that healed so many, that had saved him.

Her hand shook under his, each tremor an electric shock. Her words' effect was more brutal.

"Just forget I said anything. I've put you in an awkward position, what with all the things that remain unresolved. And then you've probably been flirting with me with no intention of taking it any further, and I understand your motivation, totally—"

"Oh, shut *up*."

Her mouth fell open at his growl, her eyes snapping wide, those eyes that glowed an unearthly blue in the vividness of the honey tan the desert sun had poured over her.

He looked down at her in that satiny dress that hung from her shoulders in relaxed pleats to the floor, another that the oasis women had given her in a shade that attempted to emulate the eyes that so fascinated them. The dress was by no stretch sexy. Not on anyone else. On her, it was the ultimate in eroticism.

She fidgeted, tried to escape his gaze. He wouldn't let her, his other hand capturing her delectable chin.

"Do I have your attention, *ya nadda jannati?*" He waited until she raised moist eyes to him and gave a hesitant nod. "First, yes, ultimately major issues are unresolved." She gasped, tried to wriggle out of his hold. He clung tighter, his hold growing gentler until she subsided in it, gave him her wounded gaze. He groaned. "But not where I'm concerned. My father once told me a man is granted one certainty in his life, one perfection. And it's up to him to recognize it, to seize it, to let it bless his life. He wasted his, for reasons that seemed imperative at the time. My younger brother Shaheen just found his certainty, and learning from our father's mistake, didn't let anything stop him from seizing it. I thought *my* certainty was that I'd never have such perfection. I lived at total peace with that. At least, I did until I found it. Found *you*. So no, Talia, I don't *want* you."

The eyes that had been misting with an escalation of emotion jerked with stricken confusion. Eyes to bring a man, willingly, eagerly, to his knees.

They brought him to his before her.

She gasped, swayed, then a hot sound of protest broke from her as she tried to pull him back up.

He only brought her hand to his lips and pledged it all to her. "*Ana ahebbek, aashagek ya talyeti, ya noor donyeti*—I love you, worship you, and more, my Talia, light of my world."

She went totally still. Her tremors stopped. Her breathing. Her stare emptied of all but shock.

Then she shook her head. "I—I don't—you don't have to say that…I just want to be with you while I can…so don't… don't…"

He rose, gliding his aching body against hers, catching her around her hips and raising her up until she was blinking her surprise down at him. His heart quivered at the incredible sight and feel of the treasure filling his arms, his lips spreading with the pleasure. "I am getting good at getting you to shut up and listen. And yes, *ya talyeti,* I do have to say this, because it's what I feel, *all* that I feel."

She wriggled in his arms until she made him put her down. He smiled all his love down at her, willing her to read into his heart. But when the flabbergasted look in her eyes, the distress didn't waver, uncertainty crept up on him.

Had he seen and felt more from her than there actually was? She wanted to act on the desire that had raged between them from the first moment, but that was all?

The unbearable doubt with all its ramifications hit him like a barrage of bullets in his gut. He swayed back under its brunt.

At last, he rasped the most difficult words he'd ever uttered in his life, "If you don't reciprocate, just walk away, and we'll forget *I* ever said anything."

With his certainty shattered, the expressions that wove in her eyes tangled in his mind. He stopped trying to analyze them, too afraid to hope, too scared she'd end hope.

"You won't take me up on my offer?" she said, slow and husky.

His heart contracted. "Not if you don't feel the same."

Suddenly, something he'd never thought to see in her eyes almost had him flat on his back. A look of unadulterated seduction, so hungry and demanding and erotic, he could swear he heard hormones roar in his arteries.

His arousal jerked painfully. And that was before she gave him a reason-numbing body rub with her hot firmness.

"Sure I can't change your mind about that?" she purred against his neck before sinking her teeth in his jaw.

"Talia…" He growled his agonized stimulation, his

whole body turning to rock with the need to crush her to him.

Before he could push away, her hands tangled in his hair and dragged his head down.

He knew if she kissed him, he wouldn't be able to stop. And he'd rather not have her at all than have her in every way but the one that mattered.

He turned his face away, felt her scorching lips latch on to his cheek, open, moist, devouring. "Don't…"

"Oh, shut *up*."

Her aggressive growl ended with a sharp tug on his hair. Then before his overcharged nerves could fire one more impulse, her lips sank onto his, paralyzing him with their hunger, with their softness and fragrance and taste.

Before the pain of it all could travel to his core, shatter it, she moaned inside him, "I thought it was impossible, but I can love you more. You just made me."

He jerked back, she clung. His whole system was going haywire from the mixed signals. He groaned. "You love me?"

She spread nips and nibbles over his jaw, detonating depth mines of pleasure and ferocity in his blood. "Down to your last pore. I'm sure I'd find even your cellular structure pant-worthy."

The image her words painted, their import, struck him. And just like that, everything inside him surged with jubilation.

He squeezed her off the ground, held her up high, guffawed. "Only you. Only you would say this, my unique dew droplet. I did have to go fall in love with a doctor."

She braced her hands on his shoulders, her eyes burning with desire dueling with challenge dipped in insecurity. "Of all the women you wade in, huh? I did hear the Guardian Prince was also the sultan of a worldwide harem."

He put her down, caught her face in an adamant grip. "Only one woman for me. Ever. You. And I would say everything before you went to waste, but it didn't. It did serve a great purpose. To make me recognize the certainty of your perfection for me faster, appreciate it with everything in me."

She only nodded, her eyes now inundating him with everything in her. She believed him. With just his word. And she was making him believe, too. That he had all of her.

He now truly had the whole world.

He bent, breathed her in, angled his lips against hers. Then he sank. He felt life rush through him, passion cresting in dark, overwhelming waves, crashing inside him. Magic. And love. More. Adoration and beyond. His Talia.

"Talyeti, enti elli, wana elek," he growled in her mouth, between tongue thrusts that breached the sweetness she surrendered with such mind-destroying eagerness. "You're mine. And I'm yours."

"Yes, yes…" She snatched at his lips, hers rising in heat. "How do I say 'my Harres'?"

"Harresi," he groaned.

"Harresi. My guardian knight."

And he did feel hers. Owned. And delirious to be so.

He sank to his knees before her again, bunched her dress in his fists, raised it up in inches, replacing it with his lips, tongue, teeth, coating her velvet firmness in suckles and bites, skimming and tantalizing her, lingering and tormenting himself. Her moans echoed his groans, became keens, then pants.

When he could no longer bear it either, he exploded up and took her dress with him. She flung up her supple arms in a sweep of eagerness and surrender, helping him, urging him. He snatched the garment away as if it was his worst enemy. But before he could step back and look on the treasure he'd uncovered, her hands were attacking his clothes with the same vehemence.

She tore the *abaya* off his shoulders and down his arms. Then with him still entangled in its tethers, she devoured him, her tongue painting him in ravenous greed, her teeth sinking into his flesh in delicate bites, each nip a new lash of arousal. He lurched under the power of each one. Then she moaned, "You taste and feel as magnificent as you look. I want more of you, all of you."

He roared. The pressure in his loins was becoming unbearable. He had to stop her, pull back from the precipice or this wouldn't be the languorous seduction he'd planned it to be. Any more and it would be like a dam breaking the moment he thrust inside her.

No. He wouldn't let her first intimacy with him be less than perfect bliss. He would show her he craved her pleasure far more than he craved his, that his pleasure would always stem from hers.

He tore away from her, snatched his fetters away then stopped. Stood transfixed. Stared at her.

He'd struggled to respect her helplessness when he'd covered her nakedness in the tent. And when he'd tended her in her sickness, his male hormones had been buried under gallons of stress. *Now* he looked.

She'd wrenched an unprecedented response from him when she'd been disguised as a man. He'd thought her the most beautiful creature in creation when he'd seen only her exquisite head and hands. She'd had him balancing on an edge both distressing and intoxicating with glimpses at her assets. But now...

Now he could see himself truly devouring her.

Encased in golden, glowing skin, taut and tight every-where, her breasts were turgid and peaked, her thighs and hips full and firm, her waist impossible amidst her voluptuousness.

And he could no longer just look, he needed to experience all that, claim it, wallow in it.

"Rao'ah, jenan…" He growled, filling his hands with sunlight and gold and honey made woman. *His* woman. "A marvel, madness—beauty like this shouldn't have been sanctioned by the heavens."

"Look who's talking," she moaned as he took the mounds of her breasts into kneading hands, yearning for their weight and feel.

He felt he'd blow an artery without a taste. He bent to have it, laved their peaks, answered their demand for the pull of his suckles, the grazing of his nips.

"Elahati, my goddess." He swept her up into his arms, didn't register the journey to the platform bed. He laid her on it, arranged her limbs as if they were flowers, tracing every line demarcating her tawny tan from her still-creamy areas with his tongue. "We'll sunbathe naked from now on. I want to see your inner lioness fully manifested. We'll do anything and everything."

A peach flush evened out her color and her eyes turned almost black as she writhed. "Yes…please, anything… everything…"

The totality of her hunger and trust shot to his heart, tampering with its rhythm. He anchored her as she began to buck beneath him, his fingers lost in the mindless pleasure of spanning her sharp concavity, digging into her taut flesh.

She whimpered a white-hot tremolo that attested to a pleasure she couldn't breathe for its power. "Harres, take me…*daheenah.*"

Hearing her say *now* in his mother tongue felt like a giant hammer shattering the last pillar of his control. He would later swear he'd heard the shrieking snap of his mind giving way, the howling implosion of restraint's end.

A rumble rolled inside him like distant thunder as he snapped her turquoise panties down her silken legs. She was golden down to her last secret. Rising on his knees, he barely pushed his drawstring pants down enough to release an arousal that was beyond rock now.

The look of feverish hunger, of shocked intimidation on her face made him want to hold back, take it infinitely slow and gentle. And they made him want to ram into her, ride her, grind his flesh into hers until she wept with the closeness, broke with the pleasure, dissolved in the fusion.

Feeling the world receding in a white noise of incoherence he grabbed her thighs, would have pressed them apart if they hadn't fallen wide-open.

She arched, writhed, tried to drag him to her, inside her.

He pulled back, tried to regain control. She was tampering with his sanity, at the verge of destroying it. He could hurt her. Even if he knew he'd pleasure her, too, he had to hold back.

He opened her folds, forged a path between their molten heat, but denying her the full entry she craved. She came off the bed at the first touch of their most intimate flesh. He laved his hardness in her nectar, rubbing her in escalating rhythm, until she was sobbing. He alternated between shallow nudges and circular strokes, over and over and over, teasing without fully taking.

She rose on her elbows, lips open with distressed gasps, her eyes spewing azure wildness and invitation of anything at all he would do to her.

Then he moved in a tighter rhythm until she fell back

on the bed, legs shaking wide, her back bowed deep as she convulsed into wave after wave of a screeching orgasm.

Seeing her lost to pleasure, pleasure he'd brought her, made his heart thunder with pride, with relief, with uncontrollable lust for more. He was already addicted to the sight, to the experience. He wanted it again. And he set about having it.

He stroked her swollen flesh, soothing it, desensitizing it. Drenched in tears and satiation, yet darkening with a deeper hunger, a wilder need, her eyes seethed as she watched him perform those ultimate intimacies on her, owning her flesh, manipulating her responses, extracting her ecstasy.

Soon, her pleas were a litany. "No, no more…more, you…you…take me, take me, *daheenah,* now, *now…*"

"*Aih*, now. I will take you now, finish you, claim you, brand you. I will plunder you and pleasure you until you weep with the satisfaction, *ya talyeti.*"

He rose onto his knees, kicked off his pants, cupped her buttocks in his hands, tilted her, opened her petals. He started to invade her…and it hit him like a sledgehammer.

He *couldn't* take her.

He almost keeled over her with the realization.

He did slump over her, his head to her breasts, his whole frame shuddering.

She cried out, tried to drag him up, but he resisted her, raised his head, the words cutting him on their way out. "When we get back to the capital. I can only take you fully then." He smoothed the look of distress off her brow, rasped, "But I'll pleasure you now, in so many other ways."

Understanding dawned in the pieces of heaven she had trapped in her eyes. Then a slow, sensuous smile spread her lips. She clamped her legs around his back, pulled him up. He acquiesced, slid over her slippery ripeness, mingling their moans and shudders and sweat.

Once he reached her lips, she gave a throaty moan of scorching seduction. "You *can* take me now. It's safe. For at least a week. You can trust me. I'm a doctor."

So it was a safe time for her. He almost wished it wasn't, and he'd take her knowing that.

If it was up to him, he was sure. He wanted it all with her, now, no waiting. He needed her to know, everything.

"I trust you, *ya habibati,* with my life. And more. And I only cared, for you." She nodded, her eyes adoring him into oblivion, the perfection of her belief pouring fuel on his conflagration. He filled his hands with her, unconditional love made flesh of his flesh. "And I'm safe, too."

She nipped his chin, as if chastising him for needing to voice this. She believed he would never endanger her in any way, didn't need to be told.

And she was opening her arms for him to fill, her beloved body quivering, her every cherished feature emanating her need in bludgeoning waves.

It was too much. He wanted too much. All of her. At once.

His growl sounded frightening in his ears as he sank his teeth anywhere in her flesh on a blind swoop. They dug in where her neck flowed into her soft, strong shoulder like that time during their ordeal when her nearness had meant life. She jerked and threw her head back, giving him a better bite. He took it.

He was a hairbreadth from going berserk. He tried to rein in the frenzy.

Then she made rationing his passion impossible.

"Show me how much you want me." Her voice reverberated in his brain, dark and deep. Wild. "Give me everything, take everything, ride me, finish me. I can't bear the emptiness...*fill* me."

With a growl of surrender he stabbed his fingers into

her short locks, pulled her head back for his devouring. She bombarded him with a cry of capitulation and command. He drove her into the thin mattress with a bellow of conquering lust. And on one staggering thrust, he embedded himself all the way to her womb.

They arched back. Backs taut, steep curves. Mouths opened on soundless screams at the potency of the moment. On pleasure too much to bear. Invasion and captivation. Completion. At last.

His roar broke through his muteness as he withdrew. She clutched at him with the tightness of her hot, fluid femininity, her delirious whimpers and her nails in his buttocks demanding his return. He met her eyes, saw everything he needed to live for.

He rammed back against her clinging resistance, his home inside her. The pleasure detonated again. Her cry pierced his being. He thrust, hard, harder, until her cries stifled on tortured squeals. Then she bucked. Ground herself against him. Convulsed around him in furious, helpless rhythms, choking out his name, her eyes streaming with the force of her pleasure.

He rode her to quivering enervation. Then showed her the extent of his need, her absolute hold over him.

He bellowed her name and his surrender to her as he found his life's first true and profound release, ecstasy frightening in magnitude, convulsing in waves of pure culmination, jetting his seed into her depths until he felt he'd dissolved inside her.

But even as he sank into her quivering arms, instead of being satiated, he was harder, hungrier than before.

Which didn't matter. He had to give her time to recover.

He tried to withdraw. She only wound herself tighter around him, cried out, clung to him.

"There will be more, and more, soon, and always." He breathed the fire of his erotic promise into her mouth. "Rest now."

She breathed her pleasure inside him, thrust her hips to take him deeper inside her. "I can only if you stay inside me. I can't get enough of you, *ya harresi*."

"Neither will I of you…ever." She was driving him deeper into bondage. He loved it. He drove back into her and she pulsed her sheath around him until he groaned. "Tormentress. But just wait. I, too, will drive you to insanity and beyond."

In response to his erotic menace, she tossed her arms over her head, arched her vision of a body, thrust her tormenting breasts against his chest and purred low with aggressive surrender.

Still jerking with the electrocuting release, he turned her around, brought her over him, her shudders resonating with his.

"Give me your lips, *ya talyeti*…" he gasped, needing the emotional surrender to complete the carnal abandon.

She groped for his lips, fed him her life and passion. Then her lips stilled, still fused to his, as sleep claimed her.

Only then did he let go. And he slept. Truly slept for the first time since he'd gone to rescue her.

She wanted to lie on him forever.

For the past four days she'd gone to sleep like that, after nights of escalating pleasure and abandon.

She propped herself up to wallow in his splendor.

Unbelievable. That just about summed him up.

Just looking at him, her heart tried to burst free of its attachments and her breath wouldn't come until she bent closer to draw it mingled with his beloved scent.

He smiled in his sleep, rumbled, *"Ahebbek."*

I love you. She caught his precious pledge in an open-mouthed kiss. He instantly stirred, dauntingly aroused, returned the kiss then took it over, took her over.

"Ahebbak," she gasped her acute pleasure and total love, as he swept her around, bore her down and thrust into her, knowing he'd find her ready and unable to wait. Their hunger was always too urgent at first, it took only a few greedy tastes of each other, a few unbridled thrusts, to have them convulsing in each other's arms, their pleasure complete.

After the ecstasy he drove her to demolished and re-formed her around him, he twisted again to bring her over him.

He sighed in contentment. *"Aashagek."*

He'd explained what that meant. *Eshg* was a concept that had no equivalent in English. More comprehensive than love, too carnal for adoration and as reverent as worship. It fit perfectly.

"Wana aashagak." She rose over him, took a deep breath. "And I can't believe I thought of this only minutes ago, but I wasn't in any condition to think of anything beyond you." She knew this would intrude on the perfection. But she had to say it. "I want you to know everything."

Harres stiffened beneath her. She frowned in alarm as he disentangled himself from their fusion, sat up. It was one of the few times she'd seen him totally serious.

"This time is ours, *ya nadda jannati*. We will not bring anything or anyone into it. Plenty of time for that when we rejoin the world. Now only you and I matter, *ya malekat galbi*."

Talia shivered at the intensity of passion that permeated his voice. He'd just called her the owner of his heart. By now, she was certain she was.

She was also certain it wouldn't matter.

When they rejoined the world, it would tear them apart.

There was only one thing to do now. Cling as hard as she could to her remaining time with him. And tell him what he needed to know. "I need to tell you."

His golden eyes were explicit with his aversion to letting the world intrude on them now instead of later. But he finally squeezed them shut, giving his reluctant consent.

And she started. "A month ago, I got a letter. It was addressed to Todd. He'd been living with me since he came back from Azmahar, before his conviction. All his mail comes to my house, and I take it to him when I visit. But something made me open this one. Two things. That all mail so far carried only more bad news, and I decided that this time, I'd try to do something about it and tell him only if I failed. The other reason was that it had Zohaydan stamps."

His eyes went dark. He just nodded for her to go on.

"I didn't know what to expect, but it certainly wasn't what I found." She shuddered again with the memory of the explosive emotions the letter had elicited. "The writer said he knew who was involved in framing Todd, that he could expose them, exonerate him. He asked that Todd come to Zohayd, where he'd supply him with the information. He had a huge stake in exposing them, too, but he needed it to be at a stranger's hand. And who better than someone they'd so deeply wronged?

"I realized only after I'd read the letter a dozen times that the writer didn't know Todd was in no position to fulfill his demand. There was an email included, so they could drum out details of the 'mission,' as he called it. I wrote an email explaining the situation, but accepting their mission in Todd's place. Then, right before I hit Send, I reconsidered.

If the writer knew Todd was already convicted, he might give up on the whole thing. And from Todd's reports on the region, I thought he would balk at doing business with a woman. Not to mention that a female foreigner on her own would draw too much attention, all of the unwanted variety. And my plan formed.

"If this person didn't know Todd was in prison, then I could go as him. I had his passport, and I could pass for him with some disguise. I created a new email with Todd's name, emailed him with my acceptance. I got a response within an hour. All I had to do was buy a plane ticket to anywhere in the world to get into the airport's departure gates. Someone would meet me with a pass to a private-jet flight, so I could slip into the region without record of my entry. That worried me, about my departure, but I rationalized they would want me to leave, to carry out their exposé for them. I thought I could also run to the American Embassy if I got into trouble.

"They brought me here. I demanded the info I came for, and my contact told me it was bigger than I thought, that 'my' problems were a part of something that could not only exonerate 'me' but that would destroy the Aal Shalaans, as they deserved to be. Then he called on the cell phone they'd given me. He used one of those electronic voice distorters, said he couldn't afford to ever be linked to what he was about to reveal, wouldn't leave anything to be tracked back to him. And he told me about the stolen and counterfeited Pride of Zohayd jewels, and the consequences that would have for the Aal Shalaans and their regime. I asked how that would help 'me' and he only said I was a bright lad, would work out how to use that info to my benefit. When I started to protest, he said he was in a very sensitive position, had to go now or risk exposure, but that he'd call me later with more info.

"I emailed Mark Gibson, Todd's lawyer and our child-hood friend, to ask his opinion. I didn't specify what my contact had told me, just that I possessed info that could bring the royal house of Zohayd down. Two hours later, I was snatched from my rented condo. The next thing I remember was waking up in that hole in the desert. The rest you know."

Then she felt silent. And realized that tears were streaming down her face. Reliving those past events and anticipating even more anguish and hopelessness, not only for Todd but for her and Harres in the future, broke her heart.

Harres's bleak eyes were eloquent with his acknowl-edgment of the validity of her trepidation. He said nothing, just pulled her back into his arms. Soon, he was kissing her, inflaming her, taking her with a new edge of recklessness, of desperation.

The dread that their time together was counting down to a crushing end made their hunger explosive, their mating almost violent, their ecstasy almost damaging.

Afterward, she lay curved into his body, quivering with the enormity of it all. He pretended to be asleep. She knew he wasn't.

She couldn't sleep, either.

She wondered, once she lost him, if she'd ever sleep again.

As night deepened, the oasis's unique environment somehow warded off the bitter cold of the desert. Even if it had been as bone-chilling as it had been during their trek, Harres wouldn't have felt a thing. He was burning up, from the inside out.

She'd finally fallen asleep. He'd left her side, gone out to try to find air to breathe.

He couldn't find any in the vastness around him.

He stumbled to a stop at the far edge of the cottage's garden, stared up at the preternaturally clear and steady stars. They blurred, swam. The heat seething inside him was filling his eyes with the moisture of frustration and despondence. Just as he'd seen in hers. It had hurt, still did, like a knife in his gut.

What hurt more was that he couldn't wipe those feelings away. He couldn't promise her what he wasn't certain he could deliver. Promises now would torment her with hope. That was even more agonizing than resignation, and if for any reason he failed to keep them, the crash to despair would be far more devastating.

He *would* do whatever it took to secure her happiness. But until he did, he had to keep silent, had to suffer her suffering. And love her with all of his being.

He only prayed it wouldn't come down to a choice between him and her brother.

He couldn't afford to lose her. He wouldn't survive it.

Eleven

Talia lurched awake, the ferocity and satisfaction of Harres's last possession humming in her blood, in her bones.

She stretched, moaning at the delicious frisson of soreness zigzagging through her. He *had* kept his promise of driving her to insanity and beyond. She now thought sanity, like the soul she felt he'd claimed, was a highly overrated and mostly inconsequential trimming.

He wasn't there. But he would be any second.

She rose, freshened up. Just as she finished, she heard the steady clatter of Reeh's hooves at the back of the cottage.

She rushed to the door. The moment she stepped out, gazing up into the twilight of the skies she'd come to depend on seeing, a meteor flashed bright then faded, as if it had never been.

It felt like their time together.

But they didn't behave as if it would ever fade. They both pretended this was forever.

He rode around the cottage, approached her with the smile that was everything worth living for. She rushed to him and he pulled her up on Reeh's back, molded her back to his front, enveloped her within his hot, hard body.

After a while of trotting leisurely in their daily excursion to *al ain,* Talia sighed, snuggled back into the cherishing heat and protection.

"I've come to a conclusion," she announced. He kissed the top of her head, held her more securely, waiting for her revelation. "Getting kidnapped was the best thing that ever happened to me."

He chuckled, hugged her exuberantly. "What a coincidence, since it turned out to be the best thing that ever happened to *me.*"

She sighed, knowing he meant it, nuzzled back into his embrace, soaking up his feel, assimilating it into her being along with his scent, mingled with those of the pristine nature.

Then she teased, "Do you think it's possible I'll get to ride my own horse one day?"

"I have issues with seeing you in danger."

"What danger? Horses here, like the rest of the inhabitants, human or otherwise, are wonderfully understanding of inept foreigners."

"Then I have issues about keeping you in my arms for as long as possible…." He stopped, groaned, amended. "Having you in my arms at every opportunity."

She knew he must be kicking himself for phrasing it that way, for even hinting that their time together would come to an end.

She swerved from the subject, turned lips tingling with the numbness of fear into his neck. "A noble cause."

She felt a ragged breath empty his lungs as he gave her a tighter squeeze, as if to thank her for circumventing the emotional landmine. "None higher. I got addicted to holding you like this, ever since I rode back to the oasis with you."

"Buttuli." She tilted her head back to smile up into his eyes and caught the bleakness there.

Tenderness replaced it, making her wonder if she'd even seen it. But she had. And she wouldn't bring it up.

What was the point of worrying about the future but to taint the purity of happiness they shared in the present?

She rubbed the hair he'd told her he adored, called spun gold milled from sunshine, against his bare chest. Now that he no longer wore a bandage but a local dressing over his fast-healing wound, she'd been wallowing in the sensory nirvana of touching his sculptured perfection at every opportunity. Which was almost always.

"Harres…"

"Yes, Talia, say my name like that, like you can't draw another breath if you don't have me inside you. As I will be, here and now."

The blow of arousal at the thought of him carrying out his intention, here, was paralyzing. And not just because it was a fantasy she'd thought would forever go unfulfilled. They were out in the open, with the oasis people in the distance.

She thought he was only stimulating her, that he'd wait until they were by the *ain,* where they'd shared more than one explosive if hurried mating, but then he lifted her, dragged her voluminous dress from beneath her, let it flow over his lap.

Then, as one hand held the bridle, the other slid around to dip below the folds of the neckline, seeking her breasts. Fire forked to her core as his fingers manipulated her nipples. It burst into flames when he sank his teeth in her nape, like a lion securing his mate.

She swooned back, her already open thighs falling apart wider, moisture dampening her panties.

"Do you know what scenting your arousal does to me?" He growled in her ear as his hand slid inside her panties, his palm gently squeezing her for a moment, winding the rhythm of the throbbing there into a frantic pounding. "I want to taste you again, but I'll have to settle for feeling your heat and your satiny flesh as it softens and melts for me. Show me how much you crave my touch, *ya talyeti*."

Beyond caring that they might be seen, she bucked back against him, widening her thighs, giving him full access. "I'm out of my mind craving anything you do to me, all the time. Touch me, feel for yourself, do everything to me."

With a groan of male possession, he dipped a finger along the molten lips of her sex, sliding its thickness and power on a mind-numbing path to and fro, each pass tightening the coil of agonizing pleasure inside her. She writhed, whimpered, turned her face up to his. He thrust his tongue inside her mouth as he replaced his finger with his thumb and plunged his middle finger inside her. The coil snapped, and she unraveled around him, in his arms on bucking keens. He stroked her inner trigger, stoked it until the climax drained her of the frenzy he'd built inside her.

"Having you lost to pleasure is the most magnificent thing I've ever experienced," he rumbled against her mouth as his fingers still stroked her, avoiding her sensitive bud, until he soothed her, then he changed direction and rhythm, had her climbing to mindlessness again.

Once she was begging, she felt him release himself, his hard length slamming against her buttocks. He whispered in her ear, "Rise up with your thigh muscles like I taught you in the trot."

He was really going to take her here. Like this. The idea almost drove her over another edge.

She rose up and he positioned himself at her opening.

He was saying, "Settle down on me," when her muscles jellified. She crashed down on him.

He forged through her inner folds like a hot lance. She thought she'd gotten used to his length and girth, but it seemed that every time felt like the first time, felt as if he filled her more.

Now the pressure reached an edge of pain, of domination that redefined all her concepts of physical intimacy and pleasure. She was addicted to the impossible fullness, the feeling of total occupation, of trapping such a vital part of him so inescapably inside her and drawing both their pleasure from depths she—and he insisted he, too—hadn't known existed.

By the fourth or fifth buck and fall of the trot she was a mass of tremors, fully at his power, breached to her core, invaded, occupied, pleasured, taken, maddened.

"Ride me...ride me..." was all she could say anymore, all that was left in her mind. She was enervated with an overload of sensation, the pressure becoming beyond her endurance. She needed him to thrust her to release. Before anyone passed.

He only lay back into the trot, let its rhythm layer even more sensation. All the time, he said things that drove her deeper into bondage. "Filling you this way, invading you, being captured by you is all I can think of, I want to be home, inside you, pleasuring you, always...."

And she found another word. *"Please."*

She felt him jerk inside her, grow bigger. She keened, writhed, and he growled, nudged Reeh, pounded into her with all the fury of the gallop. Just when she thought her heart would stop and she would dissolve around him and be no more, his fingers massaged her bud in escalating circles, his teeth sinking into her neck again, his growls a carnal current knotting her heart and core. And she detonated.

A scream welled from her depths, too frenzied to form. The next one would have but he caught it in his palm, gave her his flesh to vent her agonized pleasure on.

She bit into the side of his palm, over and over as breaker after breaker of release crashed through her, receded, built only to smash into her again, scattering and reforming her for the next incursion. The convulsions radiated from the deepest point within her body, which he caressed, spread in expanding shock waves, each building where the last began to diminish. Then he plumbed a new depth in her, seeming to impale her to her heart, releasing his ecstasy there. Feeling him fill her to overflowing sent her thrashing once more. She wished…she wished…

She regained lucidity with a jerk. They'd reached *al ain*. He was still inside her. The pleasure was a continuous flow now, a plateau of contentment. Her head rolled limply over his heart.

"You should have told me you won't just drive me insane, you'll regularly knock me out, too."

He chuckled, a sound of profound male smugness. "I live to please."

She shuddered as he separated their fusion. "And how."

He adjusted his clothes and jumped off the horse, holding out his arms for her. "And no one saw us."

She closed her eyes in mortification. She couldn't believe she'd risked that. He did drive her insane.

His smile became pure bedevilment. "Let's hope for better luck next time."

* * *

There was no next time.

It was almost sunset the next day when she felt a bass drone reverberate in her bones.

In moments the distant yet approaching thunder became unmistakable. A helicopter.

Harres's people had come for them.

Their idyll had come to an end.

Harres turned to her, his eyes eloquent with the same sentiments. But he attempted a smile. "They'll be here in minutes. Do you want to leave immediately?"

She didn't want to leave at all.

She only said, "Yes."

He nodded. "Let's gather the stuff the oasis people gave us."

"I only wish I had something to give them, too."

"You gave them far more than souvenirs, made a lasting difference in so many lives. Many told me they were blessed the day the desert 'yielded you to them.' And you can bring them whatever you want later." She gasped. Then he articulated her wildest hope. "We'll be back here, *ya nadda jannati*. I promise."

In fifteen minutes, she was standing with Harres a hundred feet from the clearing where the helicopter had just landed.

Four men jumped down, walked toward them with movements made of power and purpose, not even acknowledging the brutal wind buffeting them from the still-storming rotors.

As they strode closer, Talia was left in no doubt they were Harres's blood.

Apparently Aal Shalaan men all descended from a

line that had originated the oriental fables of supernatural beings.

The men were close enough to be classed in the same level, yet different enough as to be totally distinct from one another.

But it was the man who'd been in the pilot's seat who captured and kept her focus. And not because she recognized him as Zohayd's crown prince.

Amjad Aal Shalaan had an aura about him that lashed out across space and punched air from an onlooker's body. He reminded her of a majestic black panther, perpetually coiled for attack, complete with startling, searing, soulless emerald eyes. And he had those eyes trained on hers. She could swear she felt her eyeballs about to combust before he turned his attention to his brother.

But that brief eye-lock had been enough for her to have no doubt. He was nothing like Harres. That perfect body housed a dangerous, merciless entity. No one got a second chance with Crown Prince Amjad Aal Shalaan. She doubted anyone got a first one.

For the next few minutes she watched as those male manifestations of the forces of nature descended on Harres with relief and affection. All but Amjad. He held back, his gaze on her.

She felt him slicing through the layers of her character like a mental CAT scan, cutting to her essence like a psychic laser.

Harres introduced the others, Munsoor, Yazeed and Mohab—the latter Ghada's reluctant fiancé—as the cousins who'd been with him for her retrieval operation. They shook hands with her, expressed their pleasure to see her well, if not exactly who they'd signed on to save. They exchanged with Harres dozens of questions and reports about what had happened since they got separated twenty days ago.

Suddenly Amjad spoke. "Enough with the reunion. You can all debrief each other, or whatever you do in this secret-service game you play, later." He focused on Harres. "After Shaheen spent the last three weeks tearing the kingdom apart with me looking for you, he couldn't waste one more moment away from his bride coming to fetch you and has jumped back into her embrace. He sends his 'love' from its depths."

Harres's lips twisted at him. "You tore apart the kingdom looking for me? I'm so touched. I hope we can now glue it back together."

Amjad shot him a look of demolishing sarcasm. She was sure a lesser man than Harres would have shriveled up. "The trials and tribulations of the oldest brother and all that. And then I couldn't let you get lost in the desert with my vital info, now could I? You can glue things back together yourself. Cleanup detail is why a man puts up with younger siblings."

Talia's mouth fell open. Harres only hugged her to his side and guffawed. "*Aih,* I love you, too, Amjad."

Amjad's gaze clamped the unit she and Harres formed.

Then he grimaced, rolled his eyes before leveling them on Harres disgustedly. "Not you, too."

Harres only laughed. "Oh, definitely me, too. And I hereby echo Shaheen's words. I can't wait until you make it three."

Amjad dismissed him like one would an insignificant annoyance, turned to her. Then, as he looked directly into her eyes, he talked about her in third person. "So what does she have over the rest of the women in the northern hemisphere? Since you went through them all, I'd be very interested to know what extra features she has installed that made you shed your sanity."

Harres nudged Amjad's shoulder, pointing to his own eyes with two fingers. "Eyes here, Amjad."

Amjad ignored him, kept looking at her, yet talking about her, not to her. "The way she's glaring back at me. Fascinating. Fearless, is she? Or is she just so perceptive that she read you right, knew she could pretend fearlessness knowing she has nothing to fear, and that would be what gets to you?"

This time Harres sort of punched him. "Quit your snide mother-in-law routine, Amjad, or prepare to eat some sand."

Amjad's sculpted lips twisted, the provocation in his gaze only rising as he looked down at her. "First you let Shaheen sink into Johara's thrall without throwing so much as a cursory rope and now you're eagerly rushing to join the collective of beached men. Is she pregnant, too? At least, was she any good…" Amjad allowed a beat for her to start to seethe, for Harres to take offense for real before he continued smoothly. "…for any info we can use?"

Okay. All right. The verdict was in.

They hired this guy to teach goading in hell.

The other three men had slipped away midconfrontation, went back to the helicopter to prepare it for the return flight. And, no doubt, to give the brothers a chance to have at it.

Though Amjad was formidable, Harres was clearly the more physical one and there was no doubt who would win in a fight. That was, if Amjad didn't fight dirty. Which she was sure he would, and did.

Keeping her hand clasped in his, Harres said with Amjad's same lethal tranquility, "I'll say this once, Amjad. Talia is my woman, my princess." Talia almost collapsed. Harres was saying what he wished for, wasn't taking into account the implausibility of it all. It felt like heaven. And like hell. And he was going on. "I owe her my life, and I have no life without her from now on. Deal with it. Nicely. Or else."

Suddenly Amjad addressed her. "See this? Your man, your prince, hits a snag, and he threatens, and may I add, employs, physical violence. Tut, tut. A bleak prognosis for a future with him, don't you think, doctor?" Then he swung his eyes to Harres. "And I had such high hopes for you. Have fun in your new life of mind-numbing sameness and soul-destroying emotional servitude."

Before she could finally set him straight, on so many accounts, before Harres could elaborate on his gag order, Amjad turned away, gave the oasis people who'd come to say goodbye a whimsical wave and headed back to the helicopter.

Then, as Talia hugged everyone who came to see her off, crying rivers with Harres beside her promising their return, the aggravating man had the nerve to honk.

Talia's return to the capital was the total reverse of her departure from it.

Going back in a royal helicopter surrounded by princes was certainly something she couldn't have even dreamed of when she'd been kidnapped twenty days ago. But being next to Harres as the real world approached made her realize the depth and breadth of the lifetime they'd lived together during that time.

After they landed in the princes' private airport, Talia changed into the clothes Harres had had delivered there, while he changed, too, before they drove to the palace in separate limos.

He told her they couldn't afford to have her tied to him. Apart from those who knew the truth, everyone thought he'd dropped off the radar on a mission as usual. But the traitors in the palace would know what this mission involved. If she were seen with him, they'd work out her true identity. So she'd arrive at the palace as a friend of Laylah, his cousin. Once that was established, he'd pretend to hook up with her, and it would seem natural to everyone that he'd be interested in the blonde beauty.

She told him she'd reconnect with her informant, get the rest of the promised info. And he forbade her to. He wouldn't risk her in any way, not even if the kingdom hung in the balance. He would find another way to discover the truth.

Then, reluctant to leave her but having matters to attend to, he gave her a cell phone so they could call each other until he could start seeing her again. Which he intended to be as soon as possible.

It took arriving at the palace—which was right up there with the Taj Mahal, just far more extensive—to take her mind off the turmoil of their situation, off feeling bereft at being away from him.

When she'd researched Zohayd before coming there, she'd read that the mid-seventeenth-century palace had taken more than three decades to build, and thousands of artisans and craftsmen to build it. But it was one thing looking at detailed photos, no matter how stunning they'd been, and something totally different treading this place with her own feet, feeling the history and grandeur saturating the walls and halls surround her, permeating her senses.

Just being there explained so much about Harres, how such a powerhouse had come into existence. The nobility and power and distinction, the ancient bloodline that had forged this place coursed through him. From what she'd seen of his relatives, it also did in them.

And no matter what he said, she had to do all she could to protect this legacy. Even if she hadn't fallen in love with him and would therefore do anything to protect him and his loved ones, Harres had been right. The whole kingdom was steeped in peace and prosperity. She'd been prejudiced when she'd thought that it would be better off without the royal family that had clearly done so much to produce and maintain that.

But if she played her cards right, she might help bring the danger to Harres and his family, to the kingdom and the whole region, to an end.

Just as she began to call her informant, reinitiating contact, her alibi for her long absence rehearsed, the phone came alive in her hand.

Knowing it was Harres, she pounced on the answer button.

His beloved voice poured into her ear. "I have news, *ya habibati*. The investigations and negotiations I had my family do while we were in the oasis bore fruit. Your brother will be released from prison. There won't be a retrial, just the charges dropped and he will be given a public apology in every international newspaper and anything he demands in compensation."

To say she was overcome would be to say her love for him was a passing fancy. She began to babble her shocked elation and thanks when he said, "I beg your forgiveness, *ya nadda jannati*. There is another pressing thing I have to attend. I'll call again the second I can. Until then, congratulations, *ya mashoogati*."

She stared at the phone, reeled. Todd. Released. It was over. Really over. She'd have her brother back. He'd have his life back. It was too much to take in. Harres hadn't told her that he'd been working to exonerate Todd already. But he had been, and he'd succeeded. And she knew it had all been for her.

She fell on the bed and curled into a tight ball. She

felt she might explode from too much love and relief and gratitude otherwise.

Then she burst up in a frenzy of purpose, dialed the number of her informant. She was told the number was no longer in service. She tried again, just to make sure she hadn't dialed it wrong. She hadn't. It must have been a temporary number so it couldn't be tracked. On the same thought, she went online, shot him an email, listing her phone number.

Moments after she hit Send, the phone's distinctive three-tone ring shot through her again. Harres. He must have more info.

Her flailing hand dropped it twice before she could answer. Then she almost dropped it again.

It wasn't Harres. It was a distorted voice that scraped her every nerve raw. Her informant's.

She hadn't dreamed he'd get back to her that fast. But it wasn't that that shocked her mute. It was what he'd said.

"Hello, Dr. Talia Jasmine Burke."

She squeezed her eyes. So their precautions hadn't worked. She didn't know how, but her cover was blown.

"Don't worry, doctor. I still want to do business with you. You're now in an even better situation to do the most damage. Harres is doing all he can to stay on your good side, to exploit you, so I hope you aren't falling for his charm and forgetting your original goal to redeem your brother." At her gasp, the distorted voice gave a macabre chuckle. "Yes, I know everything. That's why I went after you in the first place. Because I wanted someone with a cause, and because you are a woman. It suits me to have the Aal Shalaan's downfall be at the hands of someone who has a vendetta against them, and who better than a woman to bring all those mighty men to ruin.

"And now, I'll tell you who the mastermind behind the

conspiracy is. Yusuf Aal Waaked, prince of the neighboring emirate of Ossaylan."

Talia at last found her voice. "But why expose him and risk having the Aal Shalaans stop the conspiracy in its tracks once they learn who they have to fight and where they need to look for their missing jewels?"

"Oh, there's nothing the Aal Shalaans can do with his identity. My exposure will actually guard against him changing his mind. It will guarantee he'll see this through to the end."

Suddenly there was a long silence then the voice became uglier, scarier. "You idiot! You'll use the info to help Harres, won't you? He *has* gotten to you. I should have known, with a woman in the legendary playboy prince's clutches for so long. He must have you willing to sell your soul for him by now. But I'll prove to you that he and his family don't deserve your help, but your vengeance."

The line went dead.

She didn't know how long she'd stayed there, staring into space, shaking with agitation.

At last she roused herself. She had to call Harres, give him the new info. No matter what her informant said, she was sure Harres *would* do something with it, maybe solve this whole mess.

As she began to dial his number, two masked men burst into the room from the French doors that opened to a patio leading to the gardens. The gun in the first's hand made sure she didn't attempt a scream or a struggle.

"We won't harm you," the armed man said, "if you don't try to expose us. We just want you to come with us. There's something our master wants to show you."

They took her from the French doors, swept her around the palace through the extensive grounds.

They entered through another open French door into

a room. It was empty. Before she could say anything, she heard Harres's voice.

Her heart fired with hope, then dread crashed right on its heels. What if he walked in here, and they panicked, shot him?

But then she realized he wasn't moving. He was in an adjoining room, talking to someone. On the phone.

"...and how many women have you seen me take and discard? You think this American means more than any of them? The others at least were pleasant pastimes I remember with some goodwill. She, on the other hand, almost cost me my life. Can you even imagine the distaste I suffered as I catered to her for so long, struggled to save her miserable life, to get her to trust me and spill her secrets, and to change her mind about exposing them? Do you realize how enraged I was when I found out she knew practically nothing? But I had to continue to play along. I knew she could still renew her mission and secure the rest of the promised info."

He was silent for a moment, then he drawled, his voice pitiless, "Why do you think I gave her the trivial incentive of setting her brother free? She trusts me with her life now, will do anything to get me my coveted intel. I went so far as to proclaim my love, would have even offered to marry her if necessary."

He was silent for a moment more as the person on the other line interrupted him. Then Harres gave an ugly laugh, a sound she'd never thought could issue from him. "I might have afforded a measure of chivalry and human compassion in other circumstances. But anyone is expendable in my quest to fulfill my duty to protect this kingdom. So if she's useless to me on that front, do you really think I care if she lives or dies?"

Twelve

"Did you hear enough, *ya ghabeyah?*"

Ghabeyah. Stupid.

She'd been far beyond that.

She was beyond devastated.

The nightmarish voice continued. "That's what your prince says when he's having a private conversation with his crown prince, who's taking him to task over you. That's the ugly truth of his feelings. Still want to run to him with the information? Or will you now finally take the revenge you're owed?"

Talia stared at the phone on the bed. Who'd turned it on? How had she made it back to this room?

Her eyes panned around, unseeing. She was alone.

Her escorts must have led her back, turned on the phone's speaker. Their master, her informant, was pulling at the hook embedded inside her, shredding her insides.

Then at some point, the mutilation stopped. And silence decimated what was left intact of her.

She found herself on her side on the bed, a discarded body paralyzed with pain too huge to register yet. Her eyes were open and bone-dry. Harres's words revolved like a serrated wheel inside her skull, mashing her brain to tinier fragments.

He didn't mean it. Whimpers of denial spun in a countering direction. *There's an explanation. He was placating Amjad, his odious brother, to get him off his back, off my case. Or something. It must have killed him to say those things. He'll explain why he did. He loves me. I won't believe otherwise...*

"Talia."

Harres. Here? Or in her feverish hopes?

She jerked up. He *was* here. Looking down at her.

Please, my love, take it back, explain it away. Just look at me with love in your eyes and it will all go away.

But for the first time since she'd laid eyes on him, his were empty.

No. Give me something.

He gave her nothing, his face as expressionless as his voice. "Sorry to interrupt your rest, but my private jet is ready."

"Ready for what?" She heard her bleeding whisper, wondered how she could still talk.

"To take you home."

She stared up at him, the void emanating from him engulfing her. Then she found herself rising, as if a closer look would make her see inside him, decipher the truth.

She saw nothing. Only the abyss of uncaring he'd professed to feel for her.

And it all crashed down on her, the full weight of his betrayal, of his heartless exploitation. It crushed her.

But she realized one thing. Even hurt beyond expression or endurance, injured beyond healing, she couldn't retaliate in kind. She wouldn't. This was the one thing her informant hadn't taken into consideration in his quest to destroy the Aal Shalaans.

Harres had systematically destroyed her, for his duty, his family. But even had she wanted to exact revenge on him, she wouldn't destroy the royal family and the whole kingdom along with him. And she *didn't* want to avenge herself. She just wanted to curl up and die, far away from this land where she'd lost her heart and her faith in anything forever.

One thing was left in her wreckage. "What about Todd?"

"The procedures of his release are ongoing as we speak."

She saw the truth of this at least in his eyes. Or maybe she imagined it as she'd imagined everything between them so far.

And she gave him what he'd ruined her for. "The conspiracy's mastermind is Yusuf Aal Waaked, prince of Ossaylan."

His eyes flared. But she'd lost the ability to read them. She'd never had it. And she no longer cared. She just wanted out of his orbit. Wanted to go somewhere far to perish in peace.

"I know," he finally said in the same expressionless voice.

He did? How?

One thing explained everything. He'd monitored her phone call and got his coveted information the moment she had.

So the master secret-service man had adjusted his plan on the fly every second since they'd met, according to her reactions and based on an unerring reading of her character. She'd fallen in step with his every undetectable nudge. His masterstroke had been that last bit of reverse psychology. While indirectly stressing the danger Zohayd was in, he'd forbidden her to reinstate contact with her informant, knowing the first thing she'd do was just that. As the coup de grâce, he'd secured Todd's release. It clearly had required no effort or sacrifice on his part, had been insurance to make sure she would do anything for him.

Now her purpose to him was over. He couldn't wait to get rid of her.

It made sense. Far more sense than this all-powerful prince falling in love with her, so totally.

With this last shard of rationalization tearing into her heart, it was like a dampener dissolved and every memory of the past twenty days bombarded her, rewritten in the macabre new perspective.

Agony mushroomed to unmanageable levels, humiliation inundating her. She felt she'd suffocate, shatter.

She lashed out with all her disillusion and devastation. "So you know. But you can't say I didn't give you something in return for my brother's freedom and redemption. Now that I have them, I can't wait to leave this godforsaken land."

There was no mistaking what slammed into his eyes now. Shock.

Of course. He must have thought she'd simper and fawn and beg for him to keep her on any degrading terms he wished to impose. As he'd reassured his brother, he was an old hand at using and discarding women. He must have fully expected the dumping to be one-sided.

Before he could say anything, Amjad stuck his head around the door. "What's taking you so long?"

Harres tore his stunned eyes from hers, turned them to his brother. He still said nothing.

Then he shook his head, as if trying to credit what she'd said. She could only imagine how she'd sounded, looked as she'd said it. If a fraction of what was stampeding inside her had been apparent, he must be flabbergasted at the seemingly out-of-the-blue change that had seized her.

He stood aside, staring at her with eyes crowded with so many things it made her sick trying to fathom them. She gave up, on everything, preceded him out of the room.

Amjad was leaning on the wall outside the door in an immaculate sports jacket, his arms folded over his chest.

As she passed him, his eyes gleamed ruthlessly. "Give my...regards to your brother. He's to be congratulated for having a sister like you."

She stared at him, felt the urge to ask for an explanation. It fizzled out as it formed.

Feeling ice spreading from her center outward, she turned away, let Harres steer her outside the palace.

He sat beside her in his limo, the eerie silence that had replaced their animated conversations, his feigned interest and indulgence, deepening her freeze.

They arrived at the private airport they'd landed in only hours ago. What a difference that time had made.

He rushed out of the limo before it came to a full stop. He materialized on her side in seconds, handed her out of the limo, led her to the sleek silver Boeing 737 purring like a giant alien bird on the pristine tarmac.

His movements were measured, his hold the epitome of composure. The vibes emanating from him were the opposite.

At the stairs he turned to her. But though the move was controlled, his eyes were anything but, storming with emotions barely held in check. His voice sounded even more agitated. "What was that back at the palace?"

It couldn't be just his displeasure at her rewriting his expected dumping scene, could it?

Stop it. She *must* stop casting anything she felt from him through the prism of nobility and sincerity. She'd heard the truth with her own ears. What was she waiting for? To have it said to her face?

She wouldn't survive that. *End this.* Now.

She shrugged, started to turn away, to run away.

His hand snagged hers. But it was the confusion and hurt she thought she saw eclipsing the twin suns of his eyes that stopped her, captured her. "You're saying it was all for your brother? To manipulate me into setting him free?"

How could he still sound so genuine? How could she still be so pathetic that she wanted to believe him, melt into his arms, to answer her walking orders with proclamations of undying love?

Ghabeyah. Stupid. That was what her informant had called her.

No. She wouldn't give him the satisfaction of seeing her weep for him. She was so far beneath him, so disadvantaged, in every way, but especially in the depth of her involvement. She could only try to leave him on equal ground in at least that.

She heard the acid that now filled her arteries drip from her voice. "That wasn't too far to go to make you help an innocent man prove his innocence, don't you think?"

She'd seen him get shot. He hadn't reacted this spectacularly then. After his recoil, he stilled, seeming to loom larger, his vibe darkening until it was deeper than the night enveloping them.

Then he finally snarled, "It is *I* who has gone *far* farther to help a guilty man get away with his crimes."

For a moment she didn't get his meaning. Just as it dawned on her, he gritted out, "I guess committing fraud runs in your family, after all."

She staggered out of his hold. "I didn't think even you would go that far."

"*Even* me? What is that supposed to mean?"

"Nothing. None of it meant anything." She'd crumble at his feet any moment now. *Get away from him.*

She groped for the rails. He caught her back, twisted her around to face him. His face was a conflagration of every distraught emotion humanly achievable.

You're seeing what you want to see.

Pain skewered her, tearing the last tatters of her sanity.

"What is it?" she rasped. "Is your ego smarting? You want me to go but still want me to beg to stay? Or maybe you want another payment for Todd's freedom? On board your jet? I can give you one last go if you want to cross another fantasy off your list, with a reluctant woman this time."

For an eternity, it seemed, horror froze his features. Then his phone rang. He lurched, looked down as if not understanding where the sound was coming from, or its significance.

She broke away from his now loose hold, ran up the stairs. She wanted to keep running, out of her very skin.

Then she had to stop, heaped on the farthest seat in the jet. She begged the first person who came offering her services to please, leave her alone. She wanted nothing.

She only wanted to let the pain eat her up.

And for the duration of the flight toward a home she'd forgotten, a home no longer for now she'd remain forever homeless, she let it.

"Talia! You did it!"

Talia slumped against the door she'd just closed.

Todd.

She swung around, and there he was zooming toward her, his eyes filled with tears as he pounced on her and snatched her into a crushing embrace.

She shook, her battered mind unable to grasp the reality of his presence, here, so soon. How…?

She must have voiced her shock. He pulled back, held her at arm's length, his eyes, so much like hers, unsteady and avid over her face. "How did you do it? Mark told me you were trying to get me out, but I didn't dare hope that you would actually do it."

She almost told him, *I sold my soul to the devil for your freedom.* But that wouldn't be accurate. She'd given her soul of her own free will to said devil. And she'd asked for nothing in return. Todd's freedom hadn't been the price of her soul, just another strand in a convoluted, undetectable web of manipulation.

Yet to see him, free, here, was worth anything.

Not that she could bear more turmoil now, or contact, with even the brother who'd always felt like a physical part of her. Every nerve in her body felt exposed.

She pushed away, shrugged. "It doesn't matter what I did. What's important is that you're free and exonerated."

"How can you say that? I need to know if you got yourself in trouble for me."

"What's important is you're out and can resume your life."

"Oh, God, you did do something terrible, didn't you?" He caught her by the shoulders, his agitation mounting, shaking his whole slight frame. "Whatever you did, undo it. I'll go back to prison, serve the rest of my sentence."

"Don't worry, Todd. I'll deal."

But the lie must have been blatant on her face. Todd's

tears flowed down his shuddering, flushed face. "Please, Talia, take it back. I'm not worth it."

"Of course you are. You're my brother, my twin. And the most important thing is that you're innocent."

"But I'm *not*."

She'd thought she'd depleted her reserves for shock, that all that was left in her was oceans of grief and agony.

She stared at Todd, denial still fighting to ward off comprehension. His next words ended its struggle.

"I—I committed all the crimes I was convicted for. I hacked into accounts I found out about when Ghada once let me fix her computer. She was just a good friend, and I made up the whole thing about us to give you a story you'd believe and sympathize with. I embezzled millions, sold dozens of vital secrets. I did far more than what they found out. But I couldn't admit it to you. It was part shame, part needing you to stand by me, to help me get out of this nightmare. I feared that if you knew I deserved what I got and worse, even with loving me, your sense of honor would stop you from trying. But I no longer care. I'll go back so you can stop paying the price for the freedom I don't deserve. I only hope you can one day forgive me."

She stared at him. This was too much.

It was all a lie.

The two men she loved more than life had both used her and exploited her unconditional love for them.

She tore herself away from Todd's pleading hands.

He sobbed as she staggered away. Before she stumbled into her room, to hide from the world and never exit again, she turned numbly. "Just don't get yourself in trouble again. I don't have any more in me to pay. And what I paid is forever gone."

The heart, the soul, the faith, the will to live.

All gone.

* * *

Seemed she was more resilient than she thought.

At the crack of dawn she was up, crackling with an unstoppable need. To confront Harres.

She'd thought she'd die rather than do it. But when she'd slept, her dreams had crowded with faithful replays of their time together. The contradiction between what she'd lived firsthand and the words she'd heard him say was so staggering, she knew something didn't add up. She hadn't been in any condition to realize that yesterday, too worn-out in every way, too shocked, too ready for bad news, too insecure, too you-name-it, that her mind hadn't functioned properly.

Now she was back to her scientific, logical, gotta-have-answers-that-fit self. More or less. And she would settle this, would ask the question she'd been too raw to ask before.

Why had he said those things?

She'd take any chance that he'd have a perfect explanation and remain the man she loved with all her soul, the memory of whom would enrich her life even if she could never see him again. Far better than believing he had no reason but the obvious one, and was the monster she couldn't bear living believing he was.

So she called him. For six hours straight. His phone was turned off.

Going crazy with frustration, she went back to work. Might as well do something with all this energy that others would benefit from.

She headed to the doctors' room, running on auto. But as she approached, she felt…something.

She shook her head. *Stop daydreaming, T.J.* What would that "something" be doing here?

She squared her shoulders, readying herself for the

storm of interrogation over her sudden month-long leave of absence when she'd never missed a day of work.

The...premonition expanded with every step. The pull became irresistible. She knew she'd feel like the stupidest person in the galaxy in seconds when it turned out to be all in her mind, but she didn't care. She ran.

She burst into the room.

And there he was.

Harres.

She hadn't been imagining it. She had *felt* him.

Which meant she had an infallible sense where he was concerned.

Which meant she might have the man she loved back after all.

He'd been leaning against the table that acted as the doctors' meeting/dining/sleeping surface, pushing his tailored jacket out of the way to dip his hands deep into the pockets of molded-on-him pants, his feet crossed in deceptive relaxation at the ankles.

He'd always looked incredible. But here, among mundane surroundings and everyday people, he looked unequivocally godly. The potency of the ancient pride and the birthright of power emanating from him swept over her.

He waited until she entered and got a load of him dominating the place, being gaped at by all present, before he pushed to his feet, oh, so slowly, his eyes lashing out solar flares.

She imagined herself breaking into a sprint, charging him, pushing him flat on that table and losing her mind all over him. A mind that flooded with images and sensations, of tearing his clothes off as his magical hands rid her of hers, before raising her as she straddled him, then lowering her on his...

She swayed with the power of the fantasy. She felt as if

he was transmitting it directly into her brain, generating it, sharing it.

But it was his eyes that snared her in a chokehold. A tiger's. Crackling with scorching...rage? Pain? Both?

One thing was unmistakable. Searing challenge.

He straightened fully, cocked his head at her. "You called?"

"Saw my missed calls, huh?" She turned to her colleagues, who were watching her and Harres like they would their favorite soap. She wouldn't be surprised if someone ran out for popcorn. She twisted her lips at their audacious interest, poked sarcasm at all present, starting with herself. "I accumulated over two hundred. Must be why Prince Harres found a transatlantic visit to be the only suitable way to see what the hell was so pressing."

Taking her cue, showing her that he was embarrassment-proof, he walked up to her with seeming indolence. When he was within arm's length, he lashed out like a cobra, caught her to him, his gaze snaring hers in a fiercer grip.

"So, Dr. T. J. Burke...are you congratulating yourself how I, who could always smell the slightest trace of fraud, ate up your lies and am still back for more?"

She stood in his grip, her heart quivering with unfurling hope. "I never lied. In fact, like you once said, I can't lie. Just ask those guys." Grunts of corroboration issued from everyone around who'd been singed by her inability to hide the truth of her feelings. Suddenly, the pain she'd experienced yesterday welled up inside her. And she pinched him, in the sensitive underside of both arms. Hard. "But *you* lie like a bird can fly."

His frown cracked on a twitch of surprise at her unexpected action, at its sting, on a jerk of humor at her rhyme, before resuming full force. "I never, *ever* lied to you. And if you never did to me, as I would have staked my life on till yesterday, why did you say what you said? Or did you really think you needed to seduce me to get me to help Todd? If you did, didn't you know I would have helped the very devil to make you happy? That you didn't need to say you felt anything for me, because it's enough for me that *I* feel everything for you?"

His words washed over her in healing waves, wiping away all the pain and doubt in swell after swell.

Then she remembered Todd's staggering confession, and her heart compressed. Harres had probably done a host of illegal things to get him off the hook. All for her.

She soothed the flesh she'd abused, her heart brimming with sorrow and remorse. "I was just lashing out in shock and misery."

"Why?" He had the look of a man who was watching his sanity ebbing before his eyes.

She pinched him again, harder this time, dragging a growl from his depths, a mixture of pain and aggravation and arousal. "Because I *heard* you. Saying you don't care if I live or die. So you *were* lying, to someone. That's why I called you. To ask you who you were lying to, and why." She pushed out of his arms, stuck her fists in her waist. "So?"

Harres felt the mountain that had been crushing him since yesterday lifting. This explained everything.

She'd heard him.

"*Ya Ullah.* It's a wonder you didn't kill me and ask questions later." He laughed, with all the discharge of his confusion and agony. "So, the reason I said those things—which, by the way, made me so sick that I haven't been able to put a thing in my mouth since—is I got a phone call, someone telling me they know who you are, what you mean to me, and if I don't back off, they'll harm you. I had to say you meant nothing to me, to make you invalid as a target.

"After I said what I did to my extortionist, I had to keep playing it cool with you since I knew we had traitors in the palace, and your room was probably bugged. I would have explained things to you the moment we were outside monitoring range, but you hit me with that delightful surprise about never feeling anything for me. I couldn't believe it, but you seemed so distant, so different, until I began to lose my mind thinking it might be true. I wouldn't have let you go if Amjad hadn't called at that moment. As it was I sent a dozen men as your security detail just in case."

"So that explains all those *GQ* specimens suddenly hanging around outside my house. Way to go picking guys only I in my condition couldn't see for the elite secret-service agents they are." A smile, sheepish and adoring, trembled on her lips, still echoing pain. He wanted to devour them, soothe away the remainder of her agitation. She bit them, making him feel her teeth had sunk into his own flesh. "I can't tell you how sorry I am for...Todd. I should have suspected something, but I guess I am too stupid when it comes to him."

"I'm not sorry. In fact, I owe your misbehaving brother a debt I can never repay. Your misplaced belief in his innocence drove you to Zohayd and into my life. Amjad and Shaheen pulled some major strings, but I personally paid back with interest everyone he defrauded, and it feels like such a tiny price for having you."

Then she was in his arms, burrowing deep into his chest and deeper into his being and bawling her eyes out.

He filled his aching arms with his every reason for life, every source of happiness. When he'd thought he'd lost her, had never had her... He shuddered. He couldn't even think of those soul-gnawing hours. And he had to tell her something else.

"I'm not here because you called, *ya talyeti*. I was on my way here. That's why you amassed those missed calls. But I am ecstatic that you didn't give up on me, even after hearing the horrors I was forced to utter about you, that you still called, still gave me the benefit of the doubt."

She looked up from the depths of his embrace, her heavenly eyes brimming with love. "How could I not, when I sobered up and remembered what we shared?" She told him about her own phone call, and they both realized at the same moment. She articulated the realization. "My informant masterminded everything. Threatening my safety to you, forcing you to say what you did and forcing me to hear it."

"But that's where he went wrong." He gathered her to him more securely, feeling his heart stagger with the blessing of having her belief, so deep it had withstood that brutal test. And he had no doubt, would stand a lifetime of tests, come what may. As would his. "He didn't count on you being too ethical to lash out by doing his dirty work for him, and loving me so much that you'd give me a chance to exonerate myself."

The adoration in her eyes enveloped him, made him feel invincible. "And he didn't count on you being unable to believe I could use you that way, that you'd come after me, and that we'd talk, get past the doubts and hurt and find each other again."

He suddenly swung her in the air around and around. Her unfettered laughter echoed his overwhelming relief and elation, fell all over him like pearls tinkling off crystal.

He finally put her down, cupped her beloved face in his hands. "And now we have. And with your brother free and no doubt planning to atone, and with us being on the final leg of aborting the conspiracy now that all the pieces are in place, and now that I'm certain the threat against you was just a ploy to get you to hear me and lash out, all our obstacles have been removed." He kneeled in front of her. "I have nothing to give you while I make this offer but everything I am. So will you now take me, *ya talyeti, ya ghalyeti, ya noor donyeti,* all of me? Will you marry me and make me whole?"

Talia would have fallen if Harres hadn't caught her by the hips.

She stared down at him as he kneeled before her, shock and overwhelming joy twisting her tongue as she choked out, "Y-you're not—not promised to some m-marriage of state?

He smiled up at her, that annihilating smile that vaporized her mental functions at a hundred paces. "I'm not. I am free to marry the wife my heart chooses. And my heart, and everything in me, chooses you."

And she threw herself all over him, sobbing her love and relief. "Considering I'm yours forever, too, it's wise of you to make use of the fact."

From somewhere far away, she heard clapping and hooting.

Her infernal colleagues. They were still here?

Well, doctors in the E.R. didn't have much of a private life. She'd seen most of their revealing and embarrassing moments. They'd witnessed many of hers, too. Let them now share her most incredible one.

As she lost herself in Harres's fate-sealing kiss, one of her male colleagues said, "There's a very nice-size supply cabinet just around the corner, dude."

They both turned on him with a simultaneous, "Oh, shut *up*."

Then, exchanging a conspiratorial look with Harres, she grabbed his hand and they rushed out of the room.

On their way out, a female colleague asked, "What if the Chief sees you signed in but nowhere around?"

"Tell him I have a gunshot victim to tend to," she said.

"Yes," Harres added. "Someone who's so impressed by her uncanny medical skills, he's going to donate any number of millions she sees fit to your department in gratitude."

They left the room to an explosion of excitement.

Once they reached that supply cabinet, he dragged her inside, pushed her against the wall. "And to this golden virago who owns my heart by awakening it, my life by saving it, my faith by inspiring it, what would you see fit I donate?"

She dragged him down to her, begged in his mouth. "Just your love. Just you."

And he pledged to her as he made her whole, "You have it, and me, always. Forever."

* * * * *

Sheikh, Children's Doctor...Husband

MEREDITH WEBBER

Meredith Webber says of herself, 'Some years ago, I read an article which suggested that Mills & Boon® were looking for new Medical Romance™ authors. I had one of those "I can do that" moments, and gave it a try. What began as a challenge has become an obsession—though I do temper the "butt on seat" career of writing with dirty but healthy outdoor pursuits, fossicking through the Australian Outback in search of gold or opals. Having had some success in all of these endeavours, I now consider I've found the perfect lifestyle.'

CHAPTER ONE

HE'D send for her!

No, he'd go himself.

Shouldn't there be someone else to handle things like this? Monarchs of their country shouldn't have to check out women who'd intruded themselves into the royal family.

His father certainly hadn't checked out Clarice.

Perhaps if he had, things would have been different…

His Supreme Highness Sheikh Azzam Ghalid bin Sadiq, newly anointed ruler of Al Janeen, groaned and buried his head in his hands as the random thoughts whirled around inside his head.

As if his father could have done anything to prevent his twin brother's marriage. Bahir had fallen in love with Clarice the moment he'd laid eyes on her, not noticing that Azzam had already lost his heart to the beautiful woman. But it was the way Clarice had transferred her attention from him to Bahir that had staggered Azzam, and her behaviour since, the pain she'd caused his brother, had left Azzam with a deep distrust of women.

That is a ridiculous bias, the sensible part of his brain told him. You're judging all such women by one example—totally unacceptable!

Yet deep inside he knew the hurt had never really healed—Clarice's betrayal had cut deep, leading to him shunning most female company over the last few years and seeking solace in his work.

Which didn't solve the problem of the stranger in their midst!

He'd see her himself. *He'd* handle it.

He left his office, his mind churning as he entered the wide colonnade surrounding the courtyard gardens, striding towards his mother's favourite sitting area.

Striding—but reluctantly.

He'd met his mother off the plane on her return to Al Janeen, but in the cluster of chattering women disembarking with his mother he hadn't noticed a stranger among them.

Had she deliberately hidden herself among the other women?

He tried to ignore the alarm bells ringing in his head but the parallels with Clarice's arrival in his country were just too strong to be ignored. Back then, it had been him, not his mother, Clarice had accompanied, him she'd fussed over on the flight, convincing him he'd need a massage therapist once the cast was off the leg he'd broken in a skiing accident.

Not that he'd needed much persuasion. He'd been attracted to the golden beauty from the first moment he'd set eyes on her, fallen in love with her within days, only to find that once she'd met Bahir and realised *he* was the heir, Azzam had been dropped like a smouldering coal.

Azzam couldn't say for certain his sister-in-law was responsible for his brother's death, although he knew her continual and extravagant demands had weighed his brother down. Then there was the talk of fights and arguments that was surfacing among the staff—one story in particular of a loud and bitter altercation before Bahir had driven off in his car that fatal day...

It could all be rumour-mongering, but Azzam had to admit that recently Bahir had been patently unhappy, though he, Azzam, had been too busy with his own interests—with his passion for the new children's hospital—to seek too closely into the cause.

The pain this knowledge caused outweighed all other—to have failed his brother, his twin, his other half! Although, could he have done anything? Interfered in his brother's marriage?

Azzam knew he had to stop groaning. Groaning achieved nothing. In fact, it was weak and wimpish—he was behaving like a fool!

He had to pull himself together and behave like the ruler of the country.

He had to check out this woman, for a start. His mother was particularly vulnerable at the moment, and he didn't want anyone taking advantage of her then upsetting her further by letting her down. That, too, had happened in the past...

Straightening his shoulders, he strode on towards the shaded area where his mother sat each afternoon with her friends and female relations.

What was she doing here?

How *had* she let herself be persuaded to fly off at a moment's notice to some foreign country?

What about her *jobs*?

The hospital had assured her, when Alex had phoned them, that they would always have her back. Doctors willing to work nights in emergency rooms were always welcome. But how long would the clinic keep her second job open? She'd thought maybe they'd pay her while she was away, as technically Samarah was their patient, but that idea had been slapped down, the manager telling her if she took time off to accompany Samarah back to her home, it would be without pay.

Pay she desperately needed. But when Samarah had wanted her help, she hadn't had the heart to refuse.

Alex pondered the situation for the hundredth time as she lay back on the silk-quilted bed. No answers were forthcoming so she looked around the sumptuous surroundings, trying to take it all in so she'd remember this part of the dream in which she found herself.

She was in a room with dark red walls, hung with what looked like very fine carpets—tapestries perhaps—woven into fascinating patterns with jewel colours of emerald, ruby and sapphire, and the shadows on the silk coverlet on which she lay were formed by fretwork across open windows, what looked like marble carved into patterns as intricate as those in the carpets on the wall. More carpets were layered on the floor, so when she stepped off the bed her feet sank into softness. Above her, silk sheets like those on which she lay were draped from a central point in the ceiling so she had the impression of being in an extremely luxurious tent.

Her journey had taken on the aspects of a magic-carpet ride to a fabled world, for here and there around the rooms were huge brass urns like the ones in Ali Baba's story, and strange-looking lamps Aladdin would have recognised!

It's an adventure, she told herself.

Enjoy it.

Work will wait.

Oh, how she longed to believe that—to relax and enjoy the thrill of the new—to see something of the world beyond this room, the wide, empty desert, the rising red dunes, the colour and scents of the markets and the noisy delight of the camel auctions Samarah had spoken of with such vivid words and obvious love.

Impossible, of course, Alex knew that much! The reason she worked two jobs wouldn't wait—not for long. Bad enough that her brother had cheated his bosses, but how could he have been so stupid as to get involved with dodgy money-lenders? With people who would have no qualms about threatening his wife and vulnerable daughter?

Alex sighed, then turned her attention to practical matters, like getting out of this country she was yet to see.

Apparently Samarah had a niece who was a doctor. As soon as she returned from overseas, Alex would be free to leave. Samarah's son, the king, was also a doctor, but Samarah was adamant it was not his highness's job to look after her.

In the meantime?

For a start, she should get up off the bed, find her way outside, possibly dropping breadcrumbs on the way so she could find her way back, and have a look around. Arriving in the dark of very early morning, she'd gained nothing more than the impression of an enormous building, more like a walled town than a house. She'd been led along dimly lit corridors, past shadowy rooms, then seen Samarah settled into bed, sat with her a while until she slept easily, then slept herself. Now daylight was nearly done and she'd seen nothing—

'Please, you will come.'

The young woman who'd been fussing over Alex since she'd woken up halfway through the afternoon was hovering in the doorway.

'Samarah? She's sick again?'

Alex shot off the bed as she asked the question, looked around for her shoes then remembered she'd left them in the doorway the previous night. She brushed back the stray hairs that had escaped her plait, and followed her guide.

'Samarah is there but it is the prince who wishes to see you.'

'The prince?'

'His new Highness.'

It was all too confusing, so Alex kept walking, trusting that a conversation with this august personage would sort out a lot of things, not least of which was when she could return home.

Her carer led her out of the building, into a covered colonnade that joined all the houses around a beautiful central courtyard, with fancifully shaped trees, and massed roses in full bloom and fountains playing tinkling music, the cascading water catching the sunlight in a shimmer of such brilliance Alex felt her breath catch in her throat.

What a beautiful, magical place...

'Come, come,' the woman urged, slipping on her sandals and motioning for Alex to do the same, but although Alex responded, she did so automatically, her mind still lost in the delight of her surroundings.

That all this lush beauty should be hidden behind the high walls she'd glimpsed last night!

They walked around the colonnade, passing another dwelling, eventually reaching the end of the rectangular courtyard. In front of her, Alex could see carpets spread, with fat cushions and a low settee placed on them. Samarah was there, and some of the women who had been in Australia with her, their low-voiced chatter reaching out to Alex, making her feel less apprehensive about this meeting with the 'new highness'.

But as she drew near, the women moved away, drifting lightly down into the courtyard, Samarah among them, so only a man in a white robe remained on the plush red velvet settee on the vivid carpets.

* * *

Azzam looked at the pale, tired woman who appeared in front of him. Not a golden blonde, more a silver ghost, slim and insubstantial, the shadows beneath her grey eyes the only colour in her face.

Was it the strain he read on her neat features—a strain he knew was visible in his own face—that made him pause before he spoke? Or did he have some fundamental weakness—some predilection for blondes—that clouded his judgement?

That suspicion, though he instantly denied it, strengthened his will.

'I am Azzam,' he said, standing up and holding out his hand. 'My mother tells me you have been good to her and I wish to thank you.'

'Alexandra Conroy,' she replied, her voice soft but firm, her handshake equally solid. 'And I've done no more for your mother than any doctor would have done. Adult onset asthma is not only very distressing for the patient, it can be extremely serious.'

She paused and the grey eyes, made paler by their frame of dark lashes, studied his face for a moment before she added, 'But of course you'd know that. You're the doctor, your brother was the lawyer.'

Another pause and he saw her chest rise as she drew in a deep breath.

'I am sorry for your loss. It is hard to lose a sibling, doubly hard, I would imagine, to lose a twin.'

The simple, quietly spoken words pierced his soul, the pain of losing Bahir so acute that for a moment he couldn't speak.

Had it been the wrong thing to say? Alex wondered. She found the man's silence discomforting, but more distracting was the glimpse she'd had of his eyes—a startling green, gleaming out of his olive-skinned face like emeralds set in old parchment.

'Please, sit,' he eventually said, his voice cooler than the evening air, making Alex certain she'd breached some kind of protocol in mentioning his brother's death. She eyed the cushions, then the settee, which had taken on the appearance of a throne as she'd approached. But he waved his hand towards it, so she sat, then regretted it when he remained standing, putting her at an immediate disadvantage.

'My mother's asthma? It came on suddenly?'

If a discussion of his mother's health was all he wanted of her, why was she feeling uneasy?

Because there's an undertone in his voice that sounded like—surely not suspicion...

She was imagining things.

Yet the sense that this man was judging her in some way persisted, making her feel uncomfortable, so her reply was strained-hurried.

'I work for a clinic that does—I suppose you'd say house calls—to hotels on the tourist strip of the Gold Coast. About four weeks ago, the clinic had a call from the hotel where your mother was staying. I was on duty and I found her breathless and fatigued, and very upset, which wasn't so surprising as it was her first such attack.'

'You treated her?'

An obvious question, yet again she heard some underlying emotion in it.

Putting her silly fancies down to tiredness, not to mention an inbuilt distrust of men as handsome as this one, she explained as concisely as she could.

'I started with an inhalation of salbutamol, then a corticosteroid injection. Her breathing became easier almost immediately, but I put her on oxygen anyway, and stayed with her. The next day, when she was rested, I talked to her about preventative measures she could take to prevent another attack. I explained about having a management plan for the condition.'

'I can imagine how well she took that,' the man said, and Alex thought she caught the suggestion of a smile lifting one corner of his lips. Unfortunately, it drew attention to his lips, so well shaped an artist might have drawn them. Something that *wasn't* apprehension fluttered inside her. 'Not one to take even a mild painkiller for a headache, my mother.'

Alex nodded, and forgot her suspicions, *and* the flutter, enough to smile herself, remembering the battle she'd been waging with Samarah to convince her that prevention was better than suffering the attacks.

'You're right, although after the second attack I think I was gaining some ground.'

Her smile changed her face, Azzam realised. It lifted the tiredness and smoothed out the lines that creased her brow, making her not exactly pretty but—

She was speaking again. He had to concentrate.

'Unfortunately, when the news of her son's death came, it triggered the worst attack. She was desperate to return home, but I couldn't in all conscience let her travel without medical care. A competent nurse could have handled it, but Samarah had come to know me as I'd called in most days over the weeks since I first saw her. I suppose she felt safer with me beside her, so I flew here with her and her friends. As you know, we broke the journey in Singapore, stopping over for the night so she could rest.'

'And now?'

Azzam knew he'd spoken too abruptly, his voice too cold, too remote, but once again the past seemed to be colliding with the present—Clarice's insistence she fly to Al Janeen with him—this woman coming with his mother.

The woman's smile gave way to a frown as she responded.

'February is our most humid month at home. Although your mother was in a hotel, she'd had the air-conditioning turned off in her suite and she insisted on walking on the beach beside the surf every day. I am assuming it was the humidity that triggered the attacks and now she's back in the dry air here, she should be all right, although with adult onset, the asthma could persist, and she did have a mild attack on the first stage of the flight.'

Again Alex paused. A woman who thought before she spoke...

'I believe she has a niece who is a doctor and who normally takes care of her health, but apparently she is away.'

Was she angling to stay on?

His mother would like her to—he already knew that—but previous experience suggested the sooner the stranger was gone the better. His mother would settle down with her friends, he'd get on with the mammoth task of learning his new role, and everyone would be happy.

No, happy was definitely the wrong word, but life could begin to return to normal—a new normal, but still...

'So?'

The word came out like a demand, unintended, but she was disturbing him in ways he couldn't understand. So quiet, so shadowy.

Insidious?

But if his mother needed someone to keep an eye on her, which she obviously did, then this woman...

'I suppose it's up to you,' she said. 'But I won't leave

Samarah without competent care. Is there someone else who could keep an eye on her until her niece returns?'

Alex wanted to suggest he do it himself, despite Samarah's protestations, but there was something forbidding in the stern features of this man.

And what features! They drew her mesmerised gaze as a magnet drew iron filings—the high sculpted cheekbones, the deep-set eyes, the slightly hooked nose—a face that looked as if the desert winds she'd heard of had scoured it clean so the bones stood out in stark relief.

Hard as weathered rock...

She was still cataloguing his features when he replied so she missed the early part of his sentence.

'I'm sorry?' She was so embarrassed by her distraction the words stumbled out and seemed to drop like stones onto the carpet where Azzam was pacing.

'I asked if you feel my mother should stay on preventative medication now she has returned home.'

Was it suspicion she could hear in his voice? Was *that* the note bothering her?

Or was it pain? He'd lost his brother, his twin—his world had been turned upside down...

Realising she should be speaking, not thinking, and relieved to have an easy question to answer, Alex now hurried her reply.

'Probably not in the long term, but for a while perhaps it would be best if she continued to take leukotriene modifiers. I've been monitoring her lung capacity with a peak-flow meter daily and prescribing preventative medication as needed, but she is reluctant to use the meter herself and to take control of the illness.'

To her astonishment, the man smiled. Smiled properly, not just a lip quirk. And it was a smile worth waiting for, because it lip up his stern face the way sunrise lit the highest peaks of a cold mountain.

Alex gave a little shake of her head, unable to believe the way her mind—not to mention the fluttering thing inside her chest—had reacted! Sunrise on a mountain indeed! She was losing it!

Tiredness, that was all!

She looked at a point a little above his right shoulder so she didn't have to see his face again, and concentrated on his words.

'You are asking her to do something against what, she believes, is meant to be. She would see, and accept, her illness as the will of God. Can you understand that?'

Alex nodded, then, for all her determination not to even look at him, she found herself returning his smile as understanding of Samarah's opposition became clear.

'Ah,' she said. 'I did wonder why she was so adamant about it, but if she feels that way, of course she doesn't want to interfere in what she feels should be beyond her control. Can *you* persuade her? Could *you* convince her that she is better off taking mild medication than having to take the really heavy-duty stuff when she has an attack?'

His smile had slipped away, and he looked darkly grave, as if, in his mind, *he'd* slipped away, and to a not-very-happy place.

'My brother could have,' he said quietly, and this time she heard the pain distinctly. 'My brother could have charmed the birds from the trees so my mother was easy work for him.'

He paused, looking out over the delights of the garden courtyard, and Alex imagined she could feel his pain, throbbing in the air between them.

'I will try,' he said, 'and in the meantime you will stay, care for her, until Maya, her niece, returns?'

Although the invitation sounded forced, as if the man felt he had no alternative but to ask, Alex's immediate reaction was to agree, for she'd grown very fond of Samarah and certainly wouldn't leave her without competent medical support, particularly while she was grieving for her son. But money, something Alex had never thought she'd have to worry about, reared its ugly avaricious head, and she hesitated.

As the full extent of Rob's indebtedness had became obvious, she'd promised her dying mother she'd repay his debts, clearing the family's name and restoring its honour, but beyond that promise was the fact that her sister-in-law, unable to work herself because of her daughter's special needs, was relying on her. No way could Alex let these much-loved people down.

An image of the money-lender's henchman rose up in her mind, clashing with memories of the promise. She'd met him only once and that had been enough. There was no way she could allow that man to terrorise her sister-in-law or her frail little niece.

Alex drew in a deep breath. It was useless. No breath could be deep enough for what she was about to ask, so she blurted out the words she hated having to say.

'I can stay. I'd be happy to, but personal reasons mean that I can't stay unless—'

She balked! She couldn't do it!

'Unless?' he prompted, and she knew the coldness and suspicion she'd imagined she'd heard earlier had returned to his voice.

She stood up and did a little pace of her own around the carpet, avoiding the man who now stood close to the steps that led into the garden.

'Look, this is an embarrassing thing to have to ask and I am ashamed to have to ask it, but if I stay, could I talk to you about some wages? Originally it was just to be two days—fly over with Samarah and fly back—then the stopover and now her niece isn't here to take over... We'd become friends, Samarah and I, and I was happy to be able to help, but I've this obligation—money that is paid out of my bank account regularly—and if I'm not working, not earning, if the money's not there—'

He cut her off with a wave of his hand, an abrupt movement that seemed to ward her off, although she was back on the settee now, embarrassed—no, utterly humiliated—by having to discuss money with a stranger.

'Money!' he snapped. 'Of course there'll be money. Do not worry, Dr Conroy, you will be well paid!'

He stalked away, his white robe swirling around him, and what felt like disgust trailing in his wake.

Not that Alex could blame him—she was pretty disgusted herself, but what else could she have done?

Anger pushed Azzam away from the woman. No, not anger so much as an irritated discomfort. At himself for not realising she *wasn't* being paid? No, the sensation seemed to have been triggered by the fact that she'd been so obviously uncomfortable at having to discuss it.

By the fact he'd made her uncomfortable?

Of course she should be paid, he'd arrange it immediately. Yet as her words replayed in his head he heard the strain behind them, particularly when she'd said 'obligation'. Now more questions arose. If the money for this obligation was paid automatically from her bank account, what good would cash be to her here?

He wheeled round, returning to find she'd walked into the garden and was moving from one rose bush to the next, smelling the blooms. The rose she held to her face now was crimson, and it brushed a little colour into her cheeks. For a moment he weakened—his irritation slipping slightly—because there was something special about the sight of that slim, jeans-clad woman standing among the roses.

'You might give your serving woman your bank details. If, as you say, payments are taken regularly from your account, it is best I transfer the money direct into it rather than give you cash.'

'If, as I say?' she retorted, stepping away from the crimson rose and facing him, anger firing the silvery eyes. 'Do you think I'd lie to you? Or are you just trying to humiliate me further? Do you think that asking a stranger for wages wasn't humiliating enough for me? Do you think I wouldn't care for Samarah out of fondness and compassion if I didn't have financial obligations? Believe me, if I'd had an alternative, I'd have taken it.'

She stormed away, her body rigid with the force of her anger as she slapped her feet against the paving stones.

There'd been a ring of truth in her words, and the anger seemed genuine, and for a moment he regretted upsetting her. But Bahir's death had brought back too many reminders of Clarice's arrival in their midst, and suspicion was a bitter seed that flourished in pain and grief.

She shouldn't have asked, Alex told herself as, on shaking legs, she escaped the man.

She should have told him she had to leave immediately!

But how could she leave the gentle Samarah when she was grieving and ill? How could she, Alex, just walk away from a woman she'd come to admire and respect?

She'd *had* to ask, she reminded herself, so she may as well stop getting her knickers in a twist over it. So what if the man thought she was a mercenary female?

She kicked off her shoes with such force one of them

flew across the paving, disturbing the neat rows of sandals already there. Muttering to herself, she squatted down to restore them all to order and it was there Samarah found her.

'You will eat with us this evening?' she asked in her quiet, barely accented English. 'I am afraid we have neglected you shamefully, but I was tired from the flight and slept until late in the day. In our country we pride ourselves on our hospitality. It comes from the time of our nomad ancestors, when to turn someone away from a camp in the desert might be to send them to their death.'

'I would be honoured to eat with you,' Alex told her, standing up and studying Samarah's face, then watching her chest to check it was moving without strain. 'You are feeling all right?'

Samarah inclined her head then gave it a little shake.

'Hardly all right when my first-born is dead, but it is not the asthma that affects me. Only grief.'

She reached out and took Alex's hands.

'That you will understand for I read grief in your face as well. It is not so long since you lost someone?'

Alex turned away so she wouldn't reveal the tears that filled her eyes. It was tiredness that had weakened her so much that a few kind words from Samarah should make her want to cry. Weakness was a luxury she couldn't afford— like the pride that was still eating into her bones over her request for wages.

Samarah took her hand and led her into the building.

'I know I gave you little time to pack, but you will find clothes in the dressing room next to your bedroom and toiletries in the bathroom. We will eat in an hour. Hafa will show you the way.'

Alex thanked Samarah and followed Hafa, who had

appeared silently in front of them, back to the splendid bedroom.

Clothes in the dressing room?

Alex looked down at her serviceable jeans and checked shirt, then caught up with her guide.

'Samarah mentioned clothes,' she said to Hafa. 'Are my clothes not suitable here?'

Hafa smiled at her.

'Because you are a foreigner no shame attaches to you, but I think Samarah has chosen clothes especially for you—a gift because she likes you—and she would be pleased to see you wear these things.'

'Very diplomatically put,' Alex responded, smiling at the woman, worry over her request to the 'new highness' pushed aside by the kindness of the women she was meeting.

Not to mention the thought of a shower and getting into clean clothes. Packing in a hurry, she'd grabbed her passport, a small travel pack, underwear and two clean shirts, thinking her jeans would do until she returned home. At the time, all she'd intended doing was accompanying Samarah home, but the older woman's asthma attack on the flight had frightened both of them, and Alex had realised she couldn't leave.

So she'd *have* to send her bank details to the prince, though her stomach twisted at the thought, and she felt ill remembering the contempt she'd seen in his eyes.

The same contempt she'd seen in David's eyes when she'd told him about Rob's debt and offered him back her engagement ring, certain in her heart he wouldn't take it— certain of a love he'd probably, in retrospect, never felt for her.

His acceptance of it had cut her deeply—the one man

she'd been relying on for support backing away from her so quickly she'd felt tainted, unclean in some way.

But David was in the past and she had more than enough problems in the present to occupy her mind.

Inside her room, fearing she'd lose the courage to do it if she hesitated, she dug a notebook out of her handbag and scribbled down the information the prince would need to transfer the money. At the bottom she added, 'Thank you for doing this. I am sorry I had to ask.'

'This note needs to go to the prince,' she told Hafa, who took it and walked, soft-footed, out of the room, the roiling in Alex's stomach growing worse by the moment.

Forget it. Have a shower.

The thought brought a glimmer of a smile to her face and she pushed away all her doubts and worries. If the bedroom was like something out of the *Arabian Nights* then the bathroom was like something from images of the future. All stainless steel and glass and gleaming white marble, toiletries of every kind stacked on the glass shelving and a shower that sprayed water all over her body, massaging it with an intensity that had been delicious after the long flight.

She stripped off, undid her plait and brushed it out, deciding to try some of the array of shampoos that lined the shelves and wash her hair. The shampoo she chose had a perfume she didn't recognise, yet as she dried her hair she realised she'd smelt the same scent here and there around the palace, as if the carpets or tapestries were permeated with it.

She sniffed the air, liking it and trying to capture what it was that attracted her.

'It's frankincense,' Hafa told her when Alex asked about the scent. Frankincense—one of the gifts carried by the wise men! Again the unreality of the situation hit her—this was truly a strange and fascinating place.

By this time she was showered and dressed, in long dark blue trousers and a matching tunic top—the least noticeable set of clothing she'd found among an array of glittering clothes in the dressing room—and Hafa had returned to take her to dinner.

'I've heard of it, of course, but I don't think I've ever smelt it,' Alex said, and Hafa smiled.

'It is special to us,' she replied, but didn't explain any more than that, simply leading Alex out of the suite of rooms and along new corridors.

What seemed like a hundred women were gathered in a huge room, most of them seated on carpets on the floor, a great swathe of material spread across the floor in front of them, the material loaded with silver and brass platters piled high with fruit and nuts.

Hafa led Alex to where Samarah sat at what would be the head if there were a table. Samarah waved her to sit down beside her, greeting Alex with a light touch of her hands, clasping both of Alex's hands together.

'Tomorrow we will bury my son, my Bahir,' Samarah told her, her voice still hoarse with the tears she must have shed in private. 'You would feel out of place in the traditional ceremony so Hafa will look after you, but tonight we celebrate his existence—his life—and for this you must join us.'

'I am honoured,' Alex told her, and she meant it, for although she'd only known Samarah a short time, she'd heard many tales about this beloved son.

Serving women brought in more silver plates, placing one in front of each of the seated women, then huge steaming bowls of rice, vegetables and meat appeared, so many dishes Alex could only shake her head. Samarah served her a little from each dish, urging her to eat, using bread instead of cutlery.

'We do eat Western style with knives and forks as you do,' she explained, 'but tonight is about tradition.'

And as the meal progressed and the women began to talk, their words translated quietly by a young woman on Alex's other side, she realised how good such a custom was, for Bahir was remembered with laughter and joy, silly pranks he'd played as a boy, mistakes he'd made as a teenager, kindnesses he'd done to many people.

It was as if they talked to imprint the memories of him more firmly in their heads, so he wouldn't ever be really lost to them, Alex decided as she wandered through the rose garden when the meal had finished.

She'd eaten too much to go straight to bed, and the garden with its perfumed beauty had called to her. Now, as she walked among the roses she thought of Rob, and the bitterness she'd felt towards him since he'd taken his own life drained away. At the time she'd felt guilt as well as anger about his desperate act. She'd known he was convinced that finding out the extent of his indebtedness had hastened their mother's death from cancer, but Alex had been too shocked by the extent of the debt and too devastated by David's desertion to do more to support her brother.

Forget David—subsequent knowledge had proved he wasn't worth being heartsick over—but now, among the roses, she found she could think of Rob, remembering rather than regretting. Here, in this peaceful, beautiful place, she began to reconstruct her brother in her mind, remembering their childhood, the tears and laughter they had shared. Here, among the roses, she remembered Rob's ability to make their mother laugh, even when the burden of bringing up two children on her own had become almost too heavy for her to bear.

'Oh, Rob,' she whispered to the roses, and suddenly it didn't matter that she'd had to ask the prince for money. She was doing it for Rob, and for the wife and daughter he'd so loved—doing it for the boy who'd shared her childhood, and had made their mother laugh...

CHAPTER TWO

THE last person Azzam expected to find in the rose garden was the stranger, but there she was, tonight a dark shadow in the moonlight, for her fair hair was hidden by a scarf. He watched her touching rose petals with her fingertips, brushing the backs of her hands against the blooms, apparently talking to herself for he could see her lips moving.

He stepped backwards, not wanting her to see him—not wanting to have to talk to anyone—but fate decreed he missed the path, his sandal crunching on the gravel so the woman straightened and whipped round, seeming to shrink back as she caught sight of him.

'I'm sorry, maybe I shouldn't be here,' she said, and her voice sounded muted—tear filled?

'There is no reason why you shouldn't be here,' he told her, and although he'd been certain he didn't want to talk to anyone when he'd sought the solitude of the courtyard, he found himself drawn towards her.

'You like the roses?' he asked as he came closer.

'They are unbelievable,' she said, voice firmer now. 'The perfume overwhelms me. At home it's hard to find a rose with perfume. The new ones seem to have had it bred out of them. Not that we can grow roses where I live—not good ones—the humidity gives them black spot.'

Azzam found himself smiling. How disconcerting was

that? Was it simply relief that all the details of the funeral were completed that he found a conversation about perfume and black spot on roses a reason to smile?

'The same humidity that triggered my mother's asthma?' he said, coming closer, smelling the perfume of the roses for himself, breathing in the scented air, releasing it slowly, relaxing, but only slightly, made wary by this unexpected shift in his mood...

She returned his smile as she said, 'That's it,' and made to move away.

He was about to put out his hand to stop her—though why he couldn't say—when she paused, turned back towards him.

'I had dinner with your mother and her women friends a little earlier,' she said quietly. 'I found it very moving that they all offered her their memories of Bahir, as if giving her gifts to help her grief. He must have been a very special person.'

Azzam knew the women gathered at this time, but offering gifts of memories? He hadn't thought of their behaviour in quite that way. He studied the woman in front of him, surprised by her perception, and caught, again, in his own memories of his twin.

'Bahir, the dazzling, the brilliant.'

The words slipped almost silently from his lips, while pain gripped his heart.

'The dazzling, the brilliant?'

The woman echoed the words and Azzam hauled his mind back into gear. He should have walked away, but perhaps talking to a stranger might ease his pain, whereas talking to his family forced him to carry theirs as well.

'It is what his name means in our language,' he told her, and saw her shake her head as if in wonder, then she looked up at him, her eyes a shining silver in the moonlight.

'And your name?' she asked. 'Azzam?'

'My name is less lofty, Azzam means determined, resolute.'

Her lips curled into a smile, and it was his imagination that the ground seemed to move beneath his feet.

'I am sure you are that,' she said. 'When your mother spoke of you, she made it sound as if you were the one who got things done—as if your brother might have had the vision, but you were the practical one who could make things happen. She spoke of a hospital you were building— a hospital for children.'

She was beguiling him—though it couldn't be deliberate, for how could she have known he'd seek refuge in the rose garden?

He set his suspicions aside as his disappointment about the hospital flooded his being and forced words from his lips.

'It was to be a special hospital for children, built to accommodate the families so they do not have to be separated from their sick child. It must be a frightening place, for a child, a large, impersonal hospital, although I know these days all hospitals try to make the children's wards bright and special. In my mind it needed to be more—low set for a start, maybe two or three levels, not a towering, impersonal, corridor-littered monolith.'

'It sounds a wonderful idea,' the woman said. 'But surely you can still achieve it.'

He hesitated, uncertain why he should be discussing his dream with a stranger.

Or was it because she *was* a stranger that he found it easy to talk to her?

'I had hoped to make things happen quickly with the hospital—to make my vision come true—but having to take my brother's place as ruler will put a stop to that.'

She touched his robe above his arm and he felt the heat of her fingers sear through the fine cotton material.

'You will do it,' she said quietly. 'Determined and resolute—remember that—and although I'm sure you'll have a lot of pressing duties for a while, surely once you're used to the job, you'll find time for your own interests.'

'Used to the job!' He repeated the words then laughed out loud, probably for the first time since Bahir's death. 'You make it sound so prosaic and just so should I be thinking. I have let all that has happened overwhelm me.'

He took her hand and bowed to kiss it.

'Thank you, Alexandra Conroy,' he said. 'Perhaps now I shall sleep.'

Definitely weird, Alex thought as she watched him move away, the swaying robes making it seem as if he glided just a little above the earth.

Not the burning on her hand where he'd dropped the casual kiss, although that *was* weird, but the way the man had treated her, like a friend almost, when earlier his voice had held a distinct note of suspicion, and later, when she'd asked about the wages, there'd been a faint note of contempt.

Yet out here in the moonlight it was as if the afternoon's conversation had been forgotten.

Poor man, he'd be devastated by his brother's death, and now to have to shoulder the responsibilities of the ruler—no wonder he was confused.

'*And* confusing,' she added out loud as she lifted her hand to her lips and touched them with the skin he'd kissed, the warmth his touch had generated still lingering in her body.

She smiled to herself, delighting, for a moment, in the fantasy in which she'd found herself, alone in a rose garden in a foreign country with a rivetingly handsome sheikh talking to her of his dreams...

What was she supposed to do? Alex had eaten breakfast in her room, checked on Samarah, who'd been pale but stalwart, then returned to what was coming to feel like a luxurious prison cell. Not wanting to get inadvertently caught up in the funeral proceedings, she'd stayed in her room until Hafa had explained that the ceremonies were taking place back in the city, nowhere near the palace.

Now she escaped, drawn by the compulsion of their beauty and perfume, to the rose garden. But wandering there, smelling the roses, reminded her of the strange encounter of the previous evening.

When he'd spoken of his brother, she'd felt Azzam's pain—felt it and seen it—recognising it because she'd carried a fair load of pain herself over the past few years.

Had that recognition drawn her to the man that he'd stayed in her mind, his almost stern features haunting her dreams? Or was it nothing more than the strange situation in which she found herself, making her wonder about the man and the country he was now ruling?

She wandered the courtyard, drinking in the lush beauty of it, freeing her mind of memories and questions she couldn't answer. One of the fountains spurted its water higher than the others, and she left the rose gardens to go towards it, ignoring the heat burning down from the midday sun, wanting to hear the splashing of the water and see the rainbows in its cascading descent.

As she approached it seemed to shimmer for a moment, or maybe she was still tired, for her feet faltered on the ground. Soon cries echoing from the buildings surrounding the courtyard and figures emerging out of the gloom suggested that whatever had happened wasn't tiredness or imagination.

'An earth tremor,' Hafa told Alex when she found the woman among the chattering crowd of servants who had remained at the palace. 'Sometimes we have them, though not bad earthquakes like other countries. Ours are usually gentle shivers, a reminder to people, I think, that there are powers far greater than humans can imagine. For this to happen today…well, there are people who will tell you it is the earth's response to Bahir's death—the death of a loved ruler.'

Alex considered this, wondering if it was simply accepted form that every ruler would be a loved one, or if Azzam's brother had been as dazzling and brilliant as his name.

Certain any hint of danger had passed, the women all returned to the buildings, Alex following Hafa.

'Samarah has returned,' the young woman told Alex. 'The women's part of the proceedings is done.'

'I should check on her. I still get lost—can you show me to her rooms?'

Following Hafa along the corridors, Alex felt a surge of regret that she'd probably never get to know her way around this fabulous place. Soon she'd be gone, and Al Janeen would be nothing more than a memory of a story-book bedroom and a white-robed man in a scented rose garden.

Samarah welcomed her, and although the older woman looked exhausted, her lung capacity was surprisingly good.

'See, I am better in my own land,' Samarah told her, then, to Alex's surprise, she turned and introduced a young woman who'd been hovering behind her. 'And now here is my niece, Maya. She arranged her return as soon as she heard of Bahir's death so she could care for me. But although she is now here, I would like you to stay for a while as my guest. I would like you to see something of this country that I love, and to learn a little about the people.'

Alex acknowledged the introduction, thinking she'd talk to Maya later about Samarah's condition, but right now she had to deal with her own weakness—the longing deep inside her to do exactly as Samarah had suggested, to stay and see something of this country. It was so strong, this longing, it sat like a weight on her shoulders but she couldn't stay if she wasn't needed—well, not stay and take wages, that wouldn't be right.

And she *had* to keep earning money!

Her mind was still tumbling through the ramifications of hope and obligation when she realised Maya was speaking to her.

'Adult-onset asthma?' Maya asked, holding up the folder with the information and treatment plan Alex had prepared.

'It could have been the humidity in Queensland. We've had a very hot summer and the humidity has been high,' Alex explained.

'That, and the fact that she's been debilitated since her husband's death a little over twelve months ago. I ran tests before I went away but found nothing, just a general weakening,' Maya replied. 'It was I who suggested a holiday somewhere new—somewhere she hadn't been with her husband. She was excited about it, and though I suggested a doctor should accompany her, she believed having a doctor in the group would worry her sons and, of course, *they* must be spared all worry.'

The edge of sarcasm in Maya's voice made Alex smile. Someone else wondered at Samarah's attitude towards her sons—the unstinting love that probably hid any imperfections they might have had.

An image of Azzam's striking features rose unbidden in Alex's mind.

'And now?' she asked, determinedly ignoring the image. 'Do you think she's strong enough to get through whatever will be expected of her in the weeks ahead? Is there much for her to do? Will she have duties she has to carry out?'

'More than she should have,' Maya replied, moving Alex away from the lounge on which Samarah rested. 'It is traditional that the wives of the dignitaries who have come for the funeral call on the widow, but this particular widow will make some excuse to avoid anything that might seem like work to her and Samarah will feel duty bound to take her place.'

'Perhaps the widow is just grieving too much,' Alex offered, surprised by a hint of venom in Maya's soft voice.

'Perhaps!' Maya retorted, more than a hint this time. 'But Samarah will find the strength to do what must be done. She is a very determined woman.'

They talked a little longer about the various preventative treatments available, until Alex sensed it was time to leave. She said good-bye to Samarah, promising to see her in the morning, knowing it would be a final good-bye because staying on would be impossible.

The only bright side was that she could send a note to Azzam telling him to forget about the wages, although she'd already been gone three days and if it took a day to arrange a flight and another day to fly home, that made six by the time she got back to work. One week's wages lost, that was all.

She sighed, thinking how little importance she'd once have placed on one week's pay. These days she knew to the last cent how much was in her account, her mind doing the calculations of credit and debit automatically. Knowing what went in each week and what went out made it easy, but losing a week's pay from the two jobs would eat into the small reserve she'd been carefully hoarding.

If the clinic *did* take her back, all would be well.

And if it didn't? If they'd replaced her?

She sighed and knew she wouldn't send a note to the prince. If the job was gone, she'd need a little extra to tide her over until she found something else…

Damn it all! Why was money such a difficulty?

Gloomily Alex followed Hafa back to her room. It wasn't only for the money she had to return home. Simply put, there was no reason for her to stay. But the thought of leaving the place Samarah had spoken of with such vivid words and so obvious a love without ever seeing more of it than a highway and the high-walled building in which she was staying caused disappointment so strong in Alex that it shocked her.

Not that she *could* go home! Not right now anyway. The prince—Azzam—had said it would be arranged, but he'd hardly be organising her flight home while attending the all-day ceremonial duties of his brother's funeral, and the state visits that Maya suggested would come after it.

Needing to escape to consider these contrary reactions—wanting to stay yet knowing she couldn't—Alex retired to her room. But once there, she was uncertain what to do. She didn't want to sleep again. All the rules of air travel suggested fitting into the local time patterns as quickly as possible, so she'd go to bed at the regular time—Al Janeen time—tonight.

Now the women and maybe the men as well were back at the palace. If she went outside again—to walk around the beautiful courtyard—she might unwittingly offend. So exploration within the walls of her suite was all that remained to her. She opened cupboard doors, discovering a small writing desk, and behind another door a television set. Wondering if the funeral procedures might be televised, she turned it on, not understanding any of the words but guessing from the serious expression of the news-reader that he could be talking of the ceremony.

Huge photos of a man so like Azzam he *had* to be Bahir appeared to have been erected all along the street, and shots of them were flashing across the screen, interspersed with images of a crowd, no doubt lingering from the funeral. White-garbed men and women, a sea of white, filled the screen, and their cries of grief echoed from the television set, filling the room with their pain.

With the voice droning on in the background, Alex sat at the desk, taking up a pen and finding paper, determined to jot down her meagre impressions of this country she had yet to see.

And probably never would!

She'd barely begun to write when a change in the tone of the talking head's voice had her turning back towards the screen. Once again she couldn't understand the words, but now a map was showing on the screen, apparently a map of Al Janeen. The capital—given the airport and the lights, Alex assumed they were somewhere near it—was shown in the bottom right of the picture, and arrows pointed to an area to the north.

'Great! They're probably being invaded!' she muttered to herself. 'Don't coups usually happen when the monarchy is unstable—when there's a change of ruler? Just my luck to be caught in a war in a foreign country! What else can happen?'

Wanting to know more—the timbre of the man's voice suggested shock and panic—but still worried that if she wandered beyond the building she might end up where she shouldn't be, Alex left her room, wondering where Hafa disappeared to when she didn't need her.

Hafa was sitting outside the door, legs crossed, head bent over some intricate embroidery.

She smiled as she stood up and tucked the piece of material into her pocket.

'I wonder if you could explain something else to me,' Alex asked. 'I turned on the television in my room and the announcer sounded very excited about something happening in the north of your country. Is it a war?'

'A war?' the young woman repeated, looking more puzzled than anxious by the question. 'I do not think war. We are a peaceful country and we like and respect our neighbours.'

'Come and see,' Alex invited and led her back to her room where the television still showed a map of what Alex assumed was Al Janeen, with arrows pointing to a place in the north.

Hafa listened for a while, a frown gathering, marring her fine, clear skin.

'It is not war but an earthquake,' she said, still frowning. 'This is not good. The town is a not big one, more a village really, but it is a very old place of history in the north, between the mountains, and the reports are saying the quake was very severe.'

'That must have been the tremor we felt here,' Alex remembered. 'I was in the garden.'

The young woman nodded but she was obviously too engrossed in what she was hearing from the television to be taking much notice of Alex.

'Many people have been injured,' Hafa explained. 'There is a school that has collapsed with children inside. The town is in the mountains and landslides have closed the roads in and out, so it will be hard to get help and supplies to it.'

She paused as a new figure appeared on the screen, a familiar figure.

'It is His Highness, His new Highness,' she pointed out, her relief so evident Alex had to wonder at the man's power. 'He has left his brother's funeral. He says he will go there now. If the helicopter cannot land, he has been lowered from one before. He will assess the situation and arrange to bring in whatever is needed. He can also give immediate medical help.'

'Where will he go from?' Alex asked, as new excitement stirred inside her. This was what she'd been trained for, but it was some time since she'd done this kind of work, the need to earn as much as possible to repay Rob's debts taking precedence over all else.

'He will fly from here—his own helicopter is here at the palace. It is used for rescues as well as his private business so it has medical equipment on board. Sometimes it takes people to hospital if there is an emergency. It brought the other Highness, Prince Bahir, to the hospital after the accident.'

Alex had heard enough. What she had to do was find Azzam and offer her services—explain her training and expertise, not to mention her experience.

But finding Azzam might not be the best way to attack this situation. Better by far to find the helicopter and get aboard. Samarah was in good hands with Maya. The hospital would already be on full alert. Arrangements would be under way for other medical staff to get to the stricken area, but she knew from experience that such arrangements took time, while the sooner trained people were in place, the more chance there was of saving the injured.

She wrapped a scarf around her head—downdraughts from helicopters caused havoc with even braided long hair. The helicopter, if it was used for rescues, would have emergency equipment on board, but she grabbed a small plastic pack out of her hand luggage. In it she had water-less hand cleaner, a small toothbrush and toothpaste, a spare pair of undies and a tiny manicure set—experience in emergencies had taught her to be prepared. The pack fitted easily into the wide pockets of her loose trousers. Then she ran out the door, calling to Hafa to show her the way.

CHAPTER THREE

'You are doing what?'

Azzam stared in disbelief when he saw Alex already strapped into the back of the helicopter, adjusting a helmet over her pale hair.

'Coming with you to the earthquake region,' she answered calmly, adding, too quickly for him to argue, 'and before you get uptight about it, it's what I'm trained to do. As well as clinic work, I'm an ER doctor, mostly doing night shifts these days, but I'm a specialist major emergency doctor with experience of triage in cyclones, fire and floods. I also know how long it takes to get hospital personnel mobilised, and right now, for the people in that village, two doctors are better than one, so let's go.'

Was she for real?

Surely she wouldn't be lying about experience like that, and if she wasn't lying, she'd certainly be useful.

'Maya is with your mother, so she is in good hands.'

She *sounded* genuine, and he knew from his mother that she appeared to genuinely care, but he must have still looked doubtful for she hurried on.

'I've been lowered from helicopters. I've done rescues off ships. I *am* trained.'

'Cutting my legs out from under me—isn't that the expression?' he responded.

She smiled and he realised it was only the second time he'd seen a proper smile from her, but this one, in daylight rather than the dim light of the rose garden, was something special. Her generous lips curved in what seemed like genuine delight, while silver flashes danced in her eyes.

Disturbed in ways he didn't want to think about, he turned away from her, gave a curt order to his pilot, nodded to the navigator, who would act as winchman if necessary, and climbed into the front seat. He hoped there'd be a patch of flat land where the helicopter could land, but if there wasn't they'd have to be lowered on a cable.

'You say you've been winched down on a cable?' he asked, speaking through the microphone in his helmet as the engines were roaring with the power needed for lift-off.

'Onto the deck of a ship pitching in sixty-knot winds,' she told him, and he felt an urge to grind his teeth.

'Wonder-woman, in fact?' he growled instead.

She glanced his way and shrugged.

'No, but I believe if you're going to do something you should do it well.'

He believed the same thing himself, so it couldn't be that causing his aggravation. Was it nothing more than the presence of the woman in the helicopter?

Impossible question to answer, so he turned to practical matters, taking care to keep any hint of sarcasm out of his voice as he said, 'Well, you've probably had experience of this before, but unless the chopper lands a fair distance away, dust from the rotors can cause more problems for people who have been injured, or buried beneath the rubble. Dropping in a short distance away is usually safer and if we can establish a drop zone, medical supplies and water can be lowered into the same place as well.'

Azzam realised he'd mostly done training runs and

learnt from books and lectures the latest ways to handle mass disasters. He'd even written the hospital's policy papers for the management of such things. But he'd never really expected it to happen—not in his own country.

Driven by his need to see for himself, and his fear for the people of the northern village, he'd left the funeral feast and rushed straight back to his rooms, issuing orders through the phone to the hospital as he went, speaking to the police department and army officers as he changed into tough outdoor wear, making sure the emergency response teams he had set up, but never yet used, were all springing into action.

'I don't know how long the flight will take, but you should try to snatch some sleep.' Her voice broke into his thoughts as he went over the arrangements he'd already put in place.

'Sleep?'

He heard the word echo back in his helmet and realised he'd spoken a bit abruptly.

'I've found these emergency situations are a bit like being back in our intern years, and the rule is the same— snatch what sleep you can when you can.'

He realised she was right. There was nothing else to do until they were on the ground, where, together, they would assess the situation and call in whatever help was needed.

He wanted to tell her she was right and that he was grateful to her for being there, grateful that he'd have someone with whom to discuss the situation and work out best options, but it had been a long time since he'd shared any feelings with a stranger—and a female stranger at that.

Yet—

'I *will* sleep.'

At least he'd acknowledged her presence, Alex thought

as she looked around the interior of the helicopter. She sat in one of two seats fitted against the fuselage, a door beside her and another one opposite it. In the seat behind the pilot, directly opposite her, was another man, who apparently didn't speak English for he hadn't been involved in the conversation Alex had had with the pilot when she'd persuaded him to allow her to join the flight.

Alex assumed this second man would play multiple roles—second pilot, navigator, and winchman.

She hoped he was good at his job!

Secured to the walls were familiar-looking equipment backpacks. Some would hold emergency medical supplies, one a special defibrillator and vital-signs monitor. Next to them were two collapsible stretchers, also in backpacks, and she could see where these, once opened out, could be secured to the floor of the aircraft.

'I understood this was your personal chopper, so why the emergency equipment?' she said, forgetting she'd told her companion to sleep.

'It *is* the prince's aircraft, he flies it himself at times,' the pilot replied, 'but he believes it should have more use than a convenience to get him to and from work in the city, so he had it specially fitted out.'

Knowing how much money was needed to keep the emergency helicopter services afloat at home, Alex could only marvel that one person could have a private aircraft like this at his disposal. Her wages would be chicken feed to him, although even thinking about her request for wages made her stomach squirm.

Forget it! she told herself, and she did, turning instead to peer out the window, seeing for the first time what a desert looked like.

It was like flying over the sea at sunset, something she'd been lucky enough to do, seeing the ocean turned to red-gold, the row upon row of waves like the dunes beneath them now. But shadows were already touching the eastward sides of the dunes and the blackness of those shadows made the colours more vivid.

Up ahead she could see mountains rising from the sands—red mountains with deeper shadows below them, what appeared to be a road or track of some kind disappearing between two ranges.

Used to flying over coastal scenes and greenery and water, the endless red conjured up the magic-carpet image yet again, the patterns of the windswept sand and shadows like the patterns in the carpets back at the palace or whatever it was to which she'd been taken.

'Ayee!'

The cry came from the man behind the pilot and Alex peered forward, shocked by what had caused his cry. From the air it looked as if large white blocks had been tumbled down a hill but, as they drew closer, Alex realised they were houses.

'It is a narrow ravine,' Azzam explained, his bleary voice suggesting he had slept at least for a short time. 'It was a guard point on an ancient trade route—the frankincense trade, in fact. It was settled because of the oasis there at the bottom, the houses built on the sides of the hills because the *wadi*—the river bed—floods after rain.'

His voice faded from her earphones but not before Alex had heard shock and deep sadness in it.

Now Alex could see where the mountain looked as if it had sheared in two—as if some giant with a mighty sword had sliced through it. She was trying to make sense of it when the helicopter lifted in the air, turning away from the shattered remains of the town and heading back along the narrow valley.

'We could cause more disruption with the noise so we

will winch down further along the valley,' Azzam said to her. He had climbed into the back cabin and looked directly into Alex's face.

'There is no need for you to do this,' he said, the dark eyes so intent on hers she felt a shiver of apprehension down her spine.

'I didn't come along for the ride,' she told him, unbuckling her seat belt and standing as steadily as she could. 'Which backpack do you want me to take?'

His eyes studied her again, assessing her.

'The medical supplies and stretchers can drop safely, but I would appreciate it if you would take the defibrillator. I don't anticipate needing it but the monitor could be handy. The pilot will drop us in, lower what gear he can, then return to the capital to bring back more personnel and supplies. He will find a safe place to land further down the valley and the rescuers can walk in. For now I—we—need to assess the damage and get word out about the amount of damage done and the kind of help we will need.'

Alex took the small backpack he passed her.

'Strap it on your front,' Azzam told her. 'We will be winched down together.'

Alex stared at him.

'I've *been* winched down before, I *know* the routine!'

'Together,' the infuriating man repeated, while Alex added 'bossy and obstinate' to the meanings of his name.

It was an exercise drop, nothing more, she told herself as Azzam's strong arms closed around her. And she was only annoyed because he didn't trust her to do it on her own!

More annoyed because she felt uncomfortable about the way he was holding her, as if dangling on a line above an earthquake-wrecked valley was some kind of romantic foreplay!

Yet annoyance couldn't mask the responses of her body, which, through clothes and backpack straps and webbing, still felt the hardness of the man who held her clamped against him.

Still reacted to it, warming so inappropriately she wondered if she was blushing.

Would she have felt this reaction with David holding her? Or was it because she'd known him so well she'd never felt these tingling, tightening sensations along her nerves, or a strange heaviness in her muscles, when *he'd* held her in his arms.

David had only ever kissed her, nothing more. Anything extra was what he'd kept for the string of other women who, unbeknownst to Alex at the time, had drifted in and out of her fiancé's life.

'Ready to roll if we need to?' Azzam asked, his chin brushing her ear, the words so close she felt as well as heard them. She drew up her knees, unconsciously pressing closer to him so they'd roll together as they hit the ground. But the roll wasn't needed, the helicopter pilot holding the craft steady and the winchman easing them onto the ground so they stepped from the loop in the cable without even the slightest jar.

Azzam released the line and moved away from his companion, disturbed by the fact his body had responded to hers, not boldly or obviously but with a flare of awareness that was totally inappropriate. He'd not been with a woman for some time, preferring to keep his life distraction free as he'd pushed ahead with his plans for the children's hospital—*his* hospital. At first it had been little more than a wild idea—a hospital purely for children, staffed only by specialist paediatric doctors and nurses. He could have, as

Bahir had pointed out many times, simply built a special wing onto the existing hospital, but Azzam was certain the new hospital would provide a more peaceful and positive atmosphere for families from a culture that had an inbred fear and dread of being separated from their children.

The woman who'd been the source of his body's betrayal was looking up towards the cradle stretcher being lowered from the chopper, the basket laden with more medical supplies. She lifted her arms to catch it as it drew close and he stepped up beside her, taking it from her.

'Stand clear, I will do it,' he said—or maybe ordered.

She snapped a salute at him and said, 'Yes, sir!' in a derisive tone that would have earned instant retribution in his army. Did she not realise who he was?

The thought had no sooner swung into his mind—as he swung the stretcher to the ground—than he had to shake his head at the impertinence of it. There *were* some women in Al Janeen's army now, and he supposed it *was* his army, but *this* woman was here to help his country. He could hardly bust her for insubordination!

'I am grateful to you for coming here,' he said, straightening up and looking directly at her. 'I may not have said that before.'

She smiled, the smile that had struck him as unusual once before, and he caught the glint in her eyes again.

'No, you may not have,' she agreed. 'Now, shall we leave most of this gear here until we've seen what we're up against? I think even the defibrillator could stay and I'll carry the second pack of medical supplies.'

He took the defibrillator from her and fitted it onto his chest, then held the pack of medical supplies as she put her arms through the straps. He adjusted them for her slight frame and was about to secure them across her breasts when the inappropriate heat he'd felt earlier returned.

Tiredness, grief, concern over what they would find in the village...

No wonder his head was no longer in control of his body. And if he was going to be attracted to a woman, it certainly couldn't be to this woman. His brother's experience of marriage had been enough to convince Azzam to seek a wife—something, given the circumstances, he'd have to do before long—from his own country, someone who knew what would be involved in her duties and would carry them out without a fuss.

'Right, let's go,' said the woman to whom he wasn't attracted, the pack securely strapped across the breasts he'd come close to touching.

The downdraught from the helicopter as they were lowered had loosened her head scarf and she was retying it as she spoke. He watched as she covered the pale hair and wondered about a woman who would voluntarily come to help people she didn't know.

Of course, she was a doctor, but would all doctors have reacted in this way?

Might not some have offered to help out at the hospital?

What motivated such a woman?

She was here to help and then she'd leave, so all he could do was wonder.

He finished strapping his two backpacks into place and looked up, realising she was well ahead of him, striding out along the old track at the bottom of the valley.

And for some obscure reason the fact that he wouldn't get to know her well caused a twinge of something that felt very like regret deep inside him.

None of the buildings had been very big, Alex realised as she drew closer to the scene of devastation that lay before her, but as they'd tumbled down the steep-sided hills on either side of the valley they'd crushed the buildings below them.

Azzam joined her and she read on his face the same pain and horror she was feeling, although for him, she knew, it must go deeper, for these were his people.

'Daytime,' he groaned. 'The school would have been operating. It was there, tucked beneath the cliff on the lower level.'

He pointed across the rift.

'And the market, a little further on, would have been full of men and women, traders and customers.'

They were close now, opposite where he'd pointed out the school, and they could see dust-covered figures working in the rubble and hear the cries of panicked men and women, no doubt parents of the children who lay beneath the shattered walls and roof.

'You go on ahead,' Alex said. 'You need to see the whole picture before you can radio out for more help. I'll stay here and tend the rescued.'

He turned and frowned at her, as if he couldn't understand her words.

'Go!' she ordered. 'The sooner you report back to the services in the city, the sooner we'll have more help.'

'But I cannot expect you—'

Azzam was trying to work out which was the most important reason for his not leaving her—safety, danger from an aftershock, her lack of understanding of the language—when she spoke again.

'Go,' she repeated, and, knowing she was right, he went, his heart growing heavier and heavier in his chest as he saw the extent of the destruction and heard the wailing cries of the injured and bereft.

The village headman came to greet him, blackened

streaks of tears tattooed by grief and horror on his cheeks.

'Highness, you have come,' the man said, taking one of Azzam's hands in both of his, then, speaking quickly, he explained what was already being done, pointing to where a line of men and women lifted and passed back jagged rocks and pieces of mud-brick wall from the top of the debris, digging down to find the injured.

Azzam walked what was left of the village with him, before radioing back to the hospital at Al Janeen, which he'd already established as the control point for all services. The first necessity was for a helicopter to drop bottled water and more medical supplies, also paramedics and the small group of trained army rescue specialists. Heavy equipment should be sent along the road to clear the landslide there, so ambulances and supply vehicles could get through. In the meantime, they'd airlift out the most seriously injured people, but night was closing in quickly in this deep valley, the darkness making it too dangerous for a helicopter to come in low, so no more help would be arriving tonight.

The cries of the children beneath the rubble tore at Alex's heart and she dug into it, working as fast as the men and women already there, tearing away the rocks but careful all the time that they didn't cause any further collapse for the cries told them the children—at least some of them—were alive.

'Aiyiyi!'

The high-pitched wail startled her, but it had the quality of happiness rather than grief. She hurried to the man who was crying out, and saw him squat, pointing downward.

'Doctor—I'm a doctor—medico,' she said, hoping one of the words would ring a bell with someone in the group.

It must have, for the man moved to squat a little farther

away, passing Alex a torch so she could shine it into a gap that had appeared beneath a huge slab of wall.

The torchlight picked up two shining eyes, a grubby face and lips twisted in pain or fear.

'Talk to the child,' she said to the man. 'Do you understand me?'

'I know little English. I talk. What more?'

'Ask if there are other children there.'

The man took the torch and moved into her place, and Alex mentally congratulated him as his voice was calm and soothing as he spoke into the darkness.

'More children,' he reported back to her, 'but they can't get out.'

Alex studied the pile of stones and rubble they would need to shift, wondering just how stable it might be. Once they pulled more rocks off the top, might that not alter a precarious balance and cause the lot to collapse on the children?

Tentatively she moved a rock that was beneath the slab but not supporting anything, then another, until she had a hole she knew she could slide into.

'I will go down and pass the children up to you,' she told the English-speaking man.

He wailed in horror, throwing up his hands then passing on the information to the gathered men and women, who now clustered closer to Alex, speaking rapidly but whether in delight that she was going to rescue their children or warning her not to do it, she didn't know. She only knew they accentuated the danger.

'Tell them to keep right back—right off the rubble—and don't move any more stones until I get the children out.'

She wasn't sure if his English was good enough, but the man not only understood but obeyed immediately—waving the people back onto firm ground, yelling at those who hesitated even momentarily, moving them all back to a safe distance.

She removed her backpack and opened it, showing the man whom she'd appointed as her helper what was in it. She unwrapped the webbing from the pack, knowing the backstraps could be used as a rope, and indicated she would take one end down the hole as she went.

'I'd prefer to pass the children up to you,' she said. 'The rope might help the older ones climb. When they come out, there are three things you must check, ABC, airways, breathing, circulation. Clear the mouth and nose of dust or debris, make sure the child is breathing, or breath for him or her.'

Alex used a rock to demonstrate breathing into a child's mouth and nose.

'Then check the heartbeat and find any blood. If it's pumping out—' she used her hands to illustrate a spray of blood '—apply a tight pad and bandage over it.'

The man nodded, repeating 'ABC' as if the concept was familiar to him.

With the medical supplies set out and the agitated crowd safely out of the way—if there *was* a collapse she didn't want anyone else injured—she had to figure out the easiest way into the space where the children were trapped. Feet first for sure, but on her back or on her belly?

'Do not even think about it!'

Azzam's voice came from directly behind her, and she turned, sure he must be speaking to her because who else would speak such perfect English?

'You cannot go down there.'

'Of course I can,' she told him, irritated by the waste of time an argument would cause and knowing from his voice that argument was looming. 'Look at the hole—I'm the only one who will fit. Besides, you'll be more useful up here tending the injured—you can ask questions and understand the answers the injured people give you, which is more than I can do.'

She didn't wait for his response, opting to slide in on her belly, thinking she could remove any impediments beneath her without compromising what was above. Tremors of fear vibrated along her nerves as she knotted the wide trousers around her ankles so they wouldn't impede her. She reminded herself that one of the reasons she'd become involved in rescue work had been to overcome her fear of small, enclosed spaces—a fear she refused to acknowledge as claustrophobia.

Wriggling down a short tunnel that seemed to have the dimensions of a rabbit burrow, she finally reached a place where most of her body was dangling in the air, only her head still in the hole, with her arms above it, braced against the sides so she wouldn't plummet to the floor and injure some small child.

Above her she could hear Azzam's voice, still grumbling and growling, but her entire being was focussed now on what lay below.

Were there older children in the space? Would they have the sense to keep the younger ones out of her way when she fell?

She was still wondering about this when small hands grasped her leg and she found her feet guided onto something. A rock? Perhaps a desk?

Praying that it would take her weight, she released the pressure of her arms against the rock tunnel and eased herself out, turning on the torch she'd thrust into her pocket before starting her journey. She was standing on what must have been the teacher's table, a solid wooden piece of furniture that right now seemed like an enormous piece of luck.

Shining the torch around, she saw dark eyes, most red with tears, peering at her out of dusty, blood-streaked faces. She dropped down off the desk and held out her arms. The little bodies crowded against her, so, for a few seconds, they could feel the safety of an adult hug.

'English?' she asked, but there was no response, so she eased herself away from them and lined them up, running the torch over each child, checking for serious injury. She had reached the end of the line of nine when she saw the others on the floor, some sitting, some lying down, perhaps unconscious.

She was drawn towards these children that needed help, perhaps immediately, but instinct yelled at her to get the others out. Perhaps she could do both.

Checking the line-up, she chose the smallest child and, lifting the little girl onto the table, she climbed up, tied the webbing around her, and lifted her higher into the hole. Alex tugged the rope and felt an answering tug. The little one would suffer scrapes being hauled up the short but rough tunnel, but at least they were fixable.

Next she chose a sturdy-looking boy and, as soon as the feet of the small girl disappeared from view, she pointed to the tunnel and made climbing motions with her hands. The boy understood and as soon as she held him up, he grasped at stones on the sides of the escape route and climbed nimbly out of sight.

The children, realising what was happening, began to clamour, no doubt about who would be next. Another big child climbed onto the table as the rope slithered back down. He gesticulated to the hole and to the children then pointed at Alex and at the patients in the corner.

Without words Alex understood he would do her job of lifting the children while she tended the injured, so she climbed down, passed him a small child, and, not wanting him to think she didn't trust him to save his friends, turned her attention to the children on the floor.

Not all of them were children, she realised, for a man in a long, dark robe lay there as well, his body curled protectively around the smallest of the injured. He was dead, Alex saw at once, but the child beneath him was alive. He'd saved that child!

She'd left her torch on the desk so all the children had some light to lift their fears, and couldn't see what injuries these—four, she counted—had suffered. Not wanting to deprive the children of the light, she'd have to go by feel, and trust her hands to do the basic diagnosis. Chest first to check on breathing and heartbeat—rapid movement. This child was alive. Her hands felt their way to the head, seeking a tell-tale shift in the bony skull, feeling for blood spurting or seeping. No head wound but further exploration revealed this first child had an open fracture of the humerus, no doubt the pain of that contributing to the child's lack of consciousness.

Aware there could be spinal damage but more concerned about further injury should an aftershock bring down the wall above where they lay, she lifted the child and carried him across the small space, placing him beneath the table in the hope—possibly false—that its solidity might provide some protection.

One of the children waiting to be lifted out began to cry and knelt beside the child. No doubt a sibling, a bond so strong the able child was obviously insisting she stay too, settling beneath the table to hold the little boy's hand.

No time to argue! Alex shrugged at her helper on the table and passed another child up to him. Five to go, then him, then the injured ones. She'd need to work out how best to get them out.

The next child was conscious, anxious eyes peering at

her in the dim light, lips moving as he tried to tell Alex something. His breathing was okay, heart rate rapid but not dangerously so, no sign of bleeding, but when Alex pricked the small foot with a sharp shard of plaster she'd found on the floor, the little boy didn't flinch. Spinal injury. How was she supposed to handle that?

She crossed to the table again and took the torch.

'Sorry, kids,' she said, although she knew they wouldn't understand, and she swept the torchlight around the small space, searching for anything that might do to stabilise the injured boy's neck and spine. A tall stick stood in one corner. With these steep hills, maybe the teacher had used it as a walking aid. She grabbed it and returned the torch to the table so the evacuation could continue, but before she could break the stick, she heard a voice yelling down the tunnel.

'That was an aftershock! Are you all right? Come up out of there—we'll extend the hole.'

CHAPTER FOUR

AZZAM held his breath. How could he have been so stupid as to leave Alex on her own? Although he could hardly have known she'd decide to go down through an impossibly small hole into the ground below. She was either incredibly brave or incredibly foolish, but he could no longer hover here above her while she risked her life in an unstable hole beneath the ground.

Surely they could enlarge the hole.

'Nothing shifted,' she called up to him, sounding so calm and composed he regretted the momentary panic he'd felt as the ground had shuddered once more. 'But there is something you could do. There are no children in the tunnel right now so could you drop down some bandages, and a small neck collar if there's one in the pack, a couple of splints if you have them. Most of those men are wearing intricate turbans—could you drop a few of them down too so I can use them as bindings to protect the injured children as you pull them out?'

Calm and composed? She was more than that. Thinking ahead and thinking clearly—thinking medically.

'And another torch,' she called. 'That should provide weight for the other things as you drop them.'

'Get out and let me come down,' he ordered.

'As if you'd fit,' she retorted. 'Just get that stuff down

here so I can get the rest of these kids out. This space could disappear if there's another aftershock.'

The image she'd offered him stopped his heart for a moment, but he organised what she needed, grumbling to himself all the time, frustrated that this stranger was doing so much for his people—that *she* should be the one risking her life. She was a visitor to his country—a guest—and she had put her life in danger.

It wasn't right!

And yet it was. As she'd said, she'd trained for it—it was what she did—but the courage it must have taken for her to slide down that hole…

'Some time soon,' she prompted, and he bundled up the things he'd been putting together as his mind raced with worry. Thinking ahead, as she had, he realised she might need more than a few turbans. He slid off his gown and wrapped that around the bundle, and dropped it down.

Alex heard a lot of grumbling from above but eventually a bundle came down the hole, wrapped not in black turban material but in dirty white cloth which she suspected had once been Azzam's pristinely perfect gown. An image of the man ungowned—broad chest, toned abs—flashed into her head but was quickly banished. For all she knew, he could have a pigeon chest and a beer gut.

Obviously her brain was using these irrelevancies to stop her worrying about the situation. She lifted a little girl who had become hysterical and was flailing in her arms, making it obvious she had no intention of being thrust up into the hole above their temporary shelter. Using the dark turbans, Alex wrapped the little limbs so the child's arms were close to her body and her legs bound together, not too tightly but not loosely enough for the child to kick or hit out and injure herself against the tunnel wall.

Using the webbing, she tied her bundle securely then called up to Azzam.

'As far as I can tell, this child is uninjured but she's panicking so I've wrapped her in a bundle. Can you haul her gently? Are the children's parents out there? Is there someone who can soothe the poor wee thing?'

Azzam felt the tug on the webbing rope and pulled gently, finding, indeed, a bundle on the end of it. Alex had managed to swaddle the little girl so completely that even her face was covered with a thin layer of cloth through which loud shrieks of fear and anger could still be heard.

Anxious hands took the bundle from him, the child passed back from man to man until it reached the parents waiting on the solid ground at the base of the *wadi*. The loud wailing cry of a woman told him the child had found her mother, but again his attention was drawn back to the hole.

The work continued, bigger children scrambling out on their own, smaller ones wrapped and tied to the webbing.

'The boy coming up next is a hero,' Alex called to him. 'It is he who looked after the other children and then passed them up to the hole so they could get out. But I think he's close to exhaustion so if you could reach in to help him out, I would be grateful.'

'*You* would be grateful!' Azzam muttered, but mostly to himself as he flattened himself on the rough ground and eased his head and arms into the hole, hoping to feel for the boy's hands and haul him out.

The hands were smaller than he'd expected, a child still, this lad.

'You are all right. You have been very brave to help the others. You are only a boy but the doctor says you did a man's job down there.' He urged the boy upward, drew him out then held him close, soothing him as he spoke, because now he was out of danger the scared child inside the lad had begun to shake and cry.

'But I need more help from you,' he added as the boy calmed down.

Hearing the conversation, a woman called from the *wadi*.

'Help the man, Dirar. He is your prince.'

The boy looked up at him.

'You are the prince?'

There was so much wonder in the boy's face, Azzam had to smile.

'But I am only a man,' he said, 'and once I was a boy like you, but I doubt I was as brave. Now, tell me, Dirar, how many people are still trapped and what is the doctor doing down there?'

'Our teacher is there but I think he is dead,' Dirar whispered, tears sliding down his cheeks again. 'And Tasnim will not come because her brother is hurt. He is under the table. The woman put him there.'

Great! Just wonderful! Azzam thought to himself. The mountain could collapse and that insane female thought a school table might provide protection.

Yet inside the anger he acknowledged respect, for she was doing the best she could under incredible and horrific circumstances. It was frustration that he couldn't be down there himself that made him want to snarl like a wild leopard.

Leopards!

Night was coming and the leopards would smell the blood of the dead and injured...

He'd think of that later. Now he had to concentrate on what the boy was telling him. Four injured children and a loyal sister. Would he and Bahir have been less foolish over women—over Clarice—if they'd grown up with sisters?

'So you must get them out now,' the boy was telling him, easing out of Azzam's arms and running nimbly over the debris of the buildings towards the waiting arms of his mother.

A tug on the rope reinforced his decision to concentrate on one thing at a time.

'I've splinted this one's arm as best I could. I notice you sent morphine down but not knowing if the child has head injuries I didn't want to use it. He's unconscious anyway. Perhaps when he comes up, you should get my English-speaking helper back there and do some doctoring.'

Did she not want him here? Azzam wondered as he gently pulled the rope. He felt so drawn to stay—so held in place by the fear he had for her—he doubted he could move, although what she'd said made sense.

The child, again bundled like a mummy, emerged, and after the bundle a small girl scrambled out, glaring at Azzam as he unwrapped the turban from the injured child's face so he could breathe more easily.

'My brother!' she said, in such a possessive voice Azzam put out his arms and drew her into a hug.

'You are a good sister,' he told her in her own language as she wept against him. 'Your brother will be all right. I am going to pass him over to safe ground and I want you to go with him.'

The little girl nodded against his shoulder but even after she eased away he felt the imprint of her frail body.

Would the day ever come when he could put the past behind him, and hug his own children?

It would have to come. The country would need an heir...

'It'll be a while before I can move the rest,' a soft voice called, recalling him yet again to his duty. And loath though he was to leave the top of the escape hatch, he waved to the man who'd held the position earlier and they crossed paths as he made his way down to the *wadi* to see the injured child. Dr Conroy—he'd think of her that way—was right. There were already too many injured people to be tended by one doctor. He'd had no business to be wasting time in the rescue effort.

The villagers were lining the injured up on a grassy bank near where the *wadi* had been deepened and widened to form an oasis. On this section of the northern side there'd been no buildings to collapse so the area was safe from anything but a rock fall and he had to pray that wouldn't happen until the road was clear and all the injured evacuated.

Men had walked back to the helicopter drop and carried the cradle with supplies, and some of the women were carrying bottles of water to the men still lifting debris. Azzam concentrated on the victims, seeing first the little boy with the broken arm, checking the rough way Alexandra had positioned the splints and wrapped them, realising she'd been trying to immobilise the arms so the movement up the escape route wouldn't cause further damage.

What to do? The child was conscious now, asking for his mother, his sister by his side. He was breathing easily and didn't seem to be in much pain. He could be dealt with later—decisions made then about setting the arm.

He wanted to tell the little girl to find their mother, but what if their mother was trapped? Did he want to send the child on a search that could cause her heartbreak?

He patted her head instead, telling her to watch her brother—an unnecessary statement as she seemed to have attached herself to his good hand and had no intention of moving.

Azzam walked towards the other injured villagers, thinking only of lifesaving measures, knowing he needed to prioritise who would be lifted out first and who could be cared for here.

'Sir, sir!'

A call from the man at the school. Azzam hurried back and was handed a small form wrapped in his once-white gown. The child's pulse was faint, so Azzam carried him swiftly to the *wadi* and put him gently on the ground, carefully unwrapping the little form, finding not only a brace around the child's neck but three lengths of stick ingeniously bound into a firm stretcher, the little body tied to it with lengths of turban.

Azzam grabbed a torch from the pack and opened one of the child's eyes to shine the light into it. No response. Neither was there any response when he pinched a finger or a toe.

A woman dropped to her knees beside the child, demanding that he sit up, refusing to accept the child might be badly injured, berating Azzam for not helping her son to sit.

'Spinal injury or brain, internal injury, it's hard to tell,' a soft voice said, and he realised the rescuer had been rescued. She was filthy, her clothes torn and her hands streaked with blood, yet his heart gave a leap that he knew was relief that she was safe, for all it was an unusual response. 'I think he is the most severely injured, although there's a little girl who's comatose as well. I brought her out. Her father is with her.'

She hesitated, then added, 'The school teacher and another child are both dead. It would be good to get them out so they can be laid to rest by their families, but I thought I might be needed here.'

He could hear the anxiety in her voice and understood she'd fought a battle with herself before leaving those two souls behind.

'You did the right thing,' he assured her. 'And you saved the other children as well, remember that, although—' his voice deepened to a growl '—your behaviour was incredibly foolhardy.'

Not that she took the slightest notice of him, turning to wash her hands with water from a bottle then kneeling beside a woman who'd been pulled from the rubble.

Alex checked and re-checked the injured, one by one, doing what she could for each of them in these appalling circumstances, aware, all the time, of the presence of Azzam, not because the local people were treating him with such deference but because some kind of awareness— definitely unwanted and totally bizarre—was tweaking at her body.

Had it started in the rose garden, this attraction? Had she been drawn to him when he'd revealed just a little of his grief for the brother he'd so obviously loved?

Surely it couldn't be the bare chest. His lower half was decently garbed in what looked like a once-white sarong-type thing, though in the ingenious way of these people it was now fashioned into, yes, Sinbad-type trousers.

But it *was* the bare chest, olive skin, streaked with ash and dust, over heavy slabs of muscle, the chest of an athlete, not a doctor or a prince, that was causing her uneasiness. Not that she knew what princes' chests *should* look like but not many doctors she knew had time to work out sufficiently to keep such well-defined muscles.

What was she doing?

How could her mind be wandering like this—
she who prided herself on her focus and professional
competence?

She moved to the next patient, focussing all her attention
on the injured.

Until she heard the cry.

'That's a baby.'

She looked over towards where the school had been,
sure of what she'd heard.

'It was a bird,' Azzam told her, but already the little girl
who had sat beneath the table beside her injured brother
was stumbling across the wrecked buildings towards the
hole.

'There couldn't have been a baby in the school,' Azzam
said, patient common sense accentuating the denial. But
already Alex was following the child.

'Ask her,' she called back to Azzam. 'Ask her why she
knows the cry.'

Alex caught the child and passed her back to Azzam,
who, although she struggled and objected loudly, held her
gently and easily in his arms, calming her with his voice.

'She says her mother always came to meet them after
school. She brought the baby. She says her father is away—
he is gone, she says, although I don't know what she means
by that.'

'They could have been outside the school—the mother
and the baby. I'm going back down,' Alex told him, then
saw the fury in his face as he thrust the child into someone
else's arms and stepped towards her.

'I will *not* leave an infant down there!' Alex told him,
hoping the defiance in her voice was visible in her face for
there was no time to be arguing with this man.

'You know you won't fit and neither will any of the men
I've seen here,' she added, before he had time to open his

mouth for his objection. 'If you want to be useful, you can hold the rope.'

Alex eased herself feet first into the tunnel, dreading a return to the hole beneath, but hearing the baby's cries more clearly now. She'd pocketed the torch and when she dropped onto the table, she shone it around, shuddering as the light passed over the body of the school teacher and the child, wishing, as she had earlier, that she didn't have to leave them down here in the darkness.

The indignant shrieks of the infant, no doubt hungry and wondering why its demands were not being met, seemed to come from the opposite corner. Alex played the light around the area, seeing a twisted frame of what might once have been a door, still with sufficient strength to shore up the debris above it, making a kind of cave.

Approaching cautiously, Alex shone the torch into the depths, but although she knew she was closer to the baby because the cries were louder, she could see nothing.

'Come up, we'll widen the hole,' Azzam commanded from above.

'And bring the whole lot down?' Alex retorted, pulling carefully on a piece of broken masonry, praying the doorframe would still hold. The masonry came away, another rock, a piece of wall—slowly she widened the gap behind the doorframe until eventually she felt the softness of a person. Not the baby, the hand she grasped was too big for a baby's, and the wrist she held had no pulse.

Tears of grief and fear spilled down Alex's cheeks and deep inside her anger stirred as well. She didn't know this woman, but two children up above, and the baby if she got it out, would now be motherless. How did fate choose whom to harm? Was it just on a whim that the earth threw open a great chasm and caused this devastation?

Aware she was raging against the fates to stop herself

thinking about the possibility of not being able to rescue the infant, she set to work again, pulling out small stones, always checking, no matter how tiny her target, that moving it wouldn't cause a collapse.

The infant's cries ceased, and Alex moved more swiftly now, still careful but aware that time might make the difference between life and death, and suddenly, what she wanted most of all, was for this child to live.

She felt a small hand—even better, felt the tiny fingers move and grip her thumb. More tears flowed, but now Alex cursed them. This was no time for emotion. She had to concentrate—she had to somehow ease the baby out from beneath its mother.

Edging closer, she slid her hand along the ground, easing it beneath where she now knew the infant lay. It whimpered at the movement—was it injured? Had she hurt it?

But she *had* to get it out!

Her hand had met resistance. The baby was somehow tied to the mother. Alex closed her eyes and tried to picture the different types of slings a mother might be wearing to hold her baby close to her body.

All she could think of were the kind of things sold in baby shops at home, and this would surely be a less complicated arrangement. But whatever it was, she needed some way to cut the baby free.

Backing out of the space, she hurried to the table beneath the hole and called up to Azzam.

'I need some scissors or a sharp knife. The baby is in some kind of sling, tied to the mother, who is dead.'

Azzam heard the waver in her voice as she said the last word and wondered at Alex's strength of character that she'd even gone back down the hole in the first place, let alone be determined enough to remain and cut the baby free. He found a sheathed knife and knelt beside the hole, frustrated by again playing a secondary role in this rescue but wanting to help however he could.

'Mostly, our women tie their babies in a criss-cross fashion, their scarves dangling from their necks then crossing in front and tied at the back. Can you picture that?'

'Clearly,' came the reply, 'and thanks for that. I can cut at the back of the neck and not risk stabbing the baby.'

Azzam shook his head. He'd teasingly called her wonder-woman earlier, but that's what she was proving to be. And he'd had doubts about her? He felt ashamed, not only about those doubts but about the poison he'd allowed to spread through his heart and soul, infecting his whole body not only with pain but with suspicion.

'I have the baby, I've wrapped it well—can you pull really gently?'

The woman he no longer doubted sounded exhausted and he worried that *she'd* be able to get out.

He *had* to get her out!

'Azzam?'

Once again, her voice reminded him of the immediate task.

'I'll be gentle,' he assured her. 'Tug when you're ready.'

He felt the tug and hauled slowly and steadily, the weight so slight he had to force himself not to hurry lest he injure the baby in his haste. Then suddenly it was there and he pulled the wrapping from the little face and saw wide brown eyes staring up at him and the tiny mouth open in a wail of protest.

'It's all right, little one,' he murmured, then realised he was speaking English and translated, although he was reasonably sure it was his tone of voice, not the words, that had hushed the baby.

But with the baby held against his chest he again felt

that rush of longing he'd experienced earlier. Children were the future—Alex had been right. The baby *had* to be rescued.

But for now, perhaps he should be concentrating on the baby's saviour.

'Alex? Can you climb up?'

'I guess I'll have to,' she said, injecting a laugh into her voice, although he suspected she was using it to cover if not fear then definitely apprehension.

'I'm going to squirm down as far as I can so reach up and grasp my hands and I'll haul you out,' he said.

Quite how he'd manage it he wasn't sure, but he feared she might not make it on her own. He'd sent everyone off the rubble to make the situation safer so now he set the baby down and wriggled as far as he could into the hole, forcing his shoulders between the boulders and building fragments, praying everything would hold. Two small hands grasped his, and a jolt of lightning seemed to pass right through him. He could not fail her now.

Fear for her lent him strength as he drew his knees up under his body to get some leverage. With one almighty heave he pulled her out, collapsing back onto the ground, the woman held securely in his arms, the warmth of her transferring itself to his body, his mind in turmoil as he tried to make sense of myriad reactions—relief, some anger still that she had risked so much, and—surely not—but, yes, definitely sexual attraction.

His arms tightened, and for an instant he imagined she'd snuggled into his embrace, but before he could process the thought she moved, almost abruptly, picking up the baby, and though Azzam kept a hand on her shoulder, he knew he shouldn't be holding her. Already people might be wondering why he'd held her at all, but she'd been so close to collapse, he'd had to.

'I *had* to get her out!' she whispered as she held the baby against her body. 'The mother is dead but for those two to lose a sibling as well, I couldn't bear that.'

If she was aware of Azzam's hand on her shoulder she gave no sign of it, simply rocking the baby against her chest.

'Family!' she whispered. 'Family ties are strongest, for good or ill. I *couldn't* let the baby die.'

And he wanted to hold her again. The words, he was sure, were spilling from her subconscious, but she was uttering the thoughts he'd had himself—thoughts that were ingrained in him through breeding and upbringing.

But now, looking down at her filthy, straggling hair— had she used her scarf as wrapping for the baby?—and watching as she dripped water on her little finger and held it to the infant's mouth, he wondered if it had been pain he'd heard when she'd talked of family, and what had happened to her in the past that she'd risked her life a second time to reunite the children with their sibling.

CHAPTER FIVE

REACTION to what she'd been through. That was all it was that compelled Alex to sit very still on the rubble and drip water into the baby's mouth. She was aware of Azzam squatting beside her, making her feel extremely uncomfortable about giving way to emotion against his bare chest a little earlier.

She tried to tell herself it was his fault, because the gentleness with which he'd held her after he'd hauled her out of that dark hole had broken through her reluctance to show any weakness.

Any weakness!

But the stoicism of the trapped children, the way the little girl had stayed beside her brother—these things had already cracked the protective shell she'd built around her heart and soul to prevent further damage. The man's arms had just widened the cracks and let feelings in...

'You must move from here. You are able to stand, to walk?'

Azzam would have liked to lift her in his arms and carry her and the baby to safety but she'd shied away from him earlier, thrusting her body apart from his as if being held in his arms was an affront of some kind.

Not that he'd wanted to keep holding her—well, not that he *should* have wanted to keep holding her...

She stood up and he reached out to grasp her elbow as she stumbled. She didn't pull away, allowing him to guide her to a safe area of the *wadi*, where the little girl remained, a silent sentinel beside her brother.

Azzam watched as the woman knelt beside the girl, holding the baby for her to see. He saw the questions in the child's eyes—the big question—and knelt on the other side of her.

'We will keep looking for your mother,' he said gently as the child took the baby, tucking the infant against her chest as if she was accustomed to looking after it.

Did the baby recognise its sister that a little hand reached out and grasped the girl's finger?

Azzam found he had to swallow hard and turned to find Alex had also looked away, her fingertips brushing at tears that were leaking from her silvery eyes.

She recovered first, standing up and looking around her.

'Where can I start?'

'Prioritise,' he replied. 'These high mountains mean up-draughts that would make night-flying in a helicopter very dangerous. So, we won't be airlifting patients out tonight, and need to consider shelter.'

She looked bemused.

'Shelter? Is it likely to rain? Do you have heavy dew? Will it be cold?'

'No to the rain, but yes to the dew. The village headman is organising the survivors. Those able enough will con-tinue to move rubble from the areas where it's most likely people are still trapped, particularly around the market. The children? With the teacher gone, I have arranged for some of the mothers to take them to a safe area until night-fall. There's a date palm grove a little way along the *wadi*.

They will be sheltered there, away from the rubble should aftershocks occur.'

He paused, unreasonably pleased when she nodded agreement to his suggestions.

'You and I—if you feel strong enough to continue to be involved—will stay with the injured. We have some emergency packs of fluid and I've already started IV drips in five people, but I haven't examined any of the children closely. If you could examine them again, and work out what we need to keep them comfortable, I would be grateful. The headman has a generator and he is setting up lights for us to work by.'

He wondered if he should mention the leopards and for a moment regretted that he and Bahir had nagged their father into setting up the protected national park area for them and instigating a breeding programme.

No! He wouldn't mention the leopards—not yet.

Alex began with the unconscious child, again feeling all around her head for some displacement in his skull and finding, this time, a small swelling behind her ear, as if something had struck her there.

She looked up to find a man who'd been squatting a little distance away had moved closer.

'You are her father? Daddy? Papa?'

The man nodded, anxious eyes asking questions Alex couldn't understand, let alone answer. Although she could guess at their content—would she live, his daughter? Was she in pain? Why did she lie so still?

The girl had been awake earlier, she remembered, just unresponsive, but feeling the lump she realised that whatever had struck her had hit her hard enough to cause external swelling, which meant that internally her brain would have been jolted against her skull and the likelihood was that her intracranial pressure was raised. Alex thought with longing of all the tools she'd have at her disposal in a hospital to assist in a diagnosis, but this was emergency medicine at its most basic.

Azzam was setting up a children's hospital! Did it follow he was a paediatrician?

She called his name and he was beside her within seconds, kneeling to examine the little girl, feeling as Alex had felt, around the skull.

'We need to handle her carefully,' he said, and she knew he was talking to himself as much as to her, running through the protocols for head injury. 'I'll lift the head a little and we need to keep it straight to decrease pressure on the jugular veins.'

Although it was some time since she'd worked with children, Alex knew what he was thinking—the sticks she'd used to make a neck brace could be adding pressure to the blood vessels, so she unwrapped them, making a pillow out of Azzam's now-filthy gown instead.

'Slip it under her head when I lift it, then pad some of the material against her temples so she can't turn her head,' Alex told her.

The father, seeming to understand what she was doing, put his hands beside the little girl's head, holding it steady.

Azzam spoke quietly to the man, no doubt explaining the injury and what they would have to do.

'Should we intubate her to keep her airway clear?' Alex asked, her mind moving through the stages of what was little more than first aid—all that could be offered here.

'She's breathing well herself but if you can find a small face mask, we'll deliver oxygen through that.'

How could he be so calm when her fingers were shaking as she delved into the medical supplies, seeking the smallest mask she could find? She'd been in situations like this before and surely her hands hadn't shaken?

Now, consciously steadying them—thinking only of the task in hand—she fitted the mask over their patient's face, relieved to find it sealed well. Azzam had already adjusted the flow on the oxygen tank's small dial and now he secured the outflow tube to the mask, the father watching every move they made, the anxiety he was feeling evident in his anguished eyes and the tension of his body.

Thinking medically to block out all other thoughts, Alex's mind raced through different scenarios. But she wasn't alone here—she had Azzam!

'Swelling in the brain—should we restrict fluids?'

'The child needs *some* fluid,' he responded. 'Let's try thirty per cent of a maintenance dose for a start. She'd weigh, what? She's so slight. Twenty-five kilos?'

Alex understood he was asking her as a colleague, a fellow professional, and the idea steadied her, although why she'd imagined he wouldn't she had no idea.

'I'd say twenty-five kilos,' she responded, doing the sums in her head. 'You've started five drips—how much fluid do we have?'

'Enough,' he told her. 'We have to give her diuretic drugs to relieve the pressure on her brain and we can't do that without giving her some fluid. I think you'll find another bag of fluid in the kit by that tree. I'll find some mannitol in this bag and we can titrate it into the fluid.'

He paused, then said quietly, 'She'll need to be watched through the night. If the pressure builds, we might have to release it manually.'

Manually?

Alex shuddered as she stood up to fetch the fluid. Manually meant boring a hole into the child's skull, not exactly the kind of operation you wanted to carry out in the dark on a bare patch of earth that was likely to tremble any time.

Had the father understood some of the conversation that he was looking more anxious now?

This was a child—a loved child. She deserved a chance at life, so of course if they had to operate they would do it.

Alex watched as Azzam, with infinite gentleness, swabbed the little hand, found a vein, and eased a cannula into it, attached a tube, fitted the other end to the bag of fluid, calibrated it to drip in slowly and added the mannitol to filter slowly into the girl's blood.

He passed the bag to the father, picked up a hunk of masonry and spoke to the man, obviously indicating he should build a small stand for the bag, but the father shook his head and held it high, understanding what was needed but determined to do this small thing for his daughter.

'In a hospital we'd be measuring fluid output as well,' Azzam said quietly, the rest of the sentence, *but we're not in a hospital*, left unspoken.

Alex moved on to the next child, one she hadn't found an injury on earlier, although the child had been huddled by the teacher. He'd been totally unresponsive, this little boy, and he was still limp, now held across his mother's lap, her fingers moving restlessly against his skin, smoothing his face and hair, her dark eyes filled with despair.

Alex touched the woman gently on the arm before beginning her examination, and the woman nodded to her.

The boy's stomach was distended, his pulse racing now, his breath coming in shallow gasps.

Internal bleeding?

Alex moved his mother closer to the light so she could see the child more clearly but could find no sign of bruising on his skin. She was pressing gently on his ribs when

the little body went into a violent spasm and she knew
he'd died, drowned in his own blood perhaps, or his heart
compressed by the fluid inside him to the stage where it
stopped beating.

Azzam was by her side in an instant, no doubt having
heard the woman's wail of despair. He took the little boy
and laid him on the ground, his finger checking the mouth
was clear of obstruction, listening for breathing, blowing
two quick breaths into the child's open mouth, before his
hands moved to the small chest, delivering thirty quick
compressions before breathing for the boy again.

'Let me do the breathing,' Alex told him, shifting to the
child's head, vaguely ashamed she hadn't acted faster, but
she'd been so struck by Azzam's immediate reaction that
she'd watched instead of moving.

They worked together, Alex counting the compressions
out loud now, willing the little boy to live, but eventually
the mother moved, taking Azzam's hand, speaking urgently
to him, all but pushing him away from her son.

'She says it is the will of God,' he whispered to Alex,
and she heard the despair of defeat in his voice.

Standing up, she took his hand, squeezing it as she
helped him to his feet, keeping hold of it as the woman
lifted her son into her arms, rocking him against her body
as she swayed back and forth, moving to her harsh cries
of grief.

Azzam removed his hand and walked away, and Alex
could only watch him go, aware of the burden he was carrying but not knowing what to say or do to ease it.

'You did try,' was all she could offer. 'And even if we'd
got him breathing again, with no facilities to operate and
fix whatever was injured inside him, he would surely have
died before reaching hospital.'

Azzam ignored her words, walking on to where most of

the injured adults had been assembled, close by a gnarled old tree.

Alex watched him for a moment then moved on to the next child—the boy with the broken humerus. Beside him sat his sister, the baby in her arms. The baby was asleep but would surely wake hungry. How to tell the girl to take it to where the uninjured villagers were gathered so they could both get some food?

Using sign language, bringing her hands to her mouth to indicate eating, then pointing towards the palm grove, she urged the girl away, but the child had no intention of deserting her post. Alex bent and kissed her head, thinking of her own brother—Rob—whom she had loved just as devotedly, and whom she couldn't hate no matter how much he'd hurt their mother, or how much chaos he'd left behind him.

But it was *this* child she had to treat—*this* boy she had to consider! He was in shock, trembling all over, and she found the scarf she'd discarded after coming out of the hole with the baby and wrapped it around him, carefully avoiding his arm, which she'd bound against his body earlier.

'I've thirteen serious injuries, patients who, if they survive the night, will have to be airlifted out.'

Azzam had returned and his words sent shivers down her spine. Two, maybe three, people could be lifted out at a time, the helicopter flying back and forth, maybe two helicopters, but would they have the support staff, paramedics, necessary to staff two?

'So I should splint and bandage the boy's arm to hold the bone aligned until he can be taken in an ambulance?' She looked up at Azzam as she spoke.

His face was shadowed, the light behind him, but she'd heard the horror of what they were experiencing—and the death of the child—in his voice and knew that, as these were his people, he would be feeling the pain of the disaster even more deeply than she was.

'We'll only airlift out the most severely injured,' he agreed, then knelt beside her, her response to his presence gratitude that he'd returned to share the decisions that had to be made, nothing else.

Or so she told herself!

'I will help you with the boy,' he said. 'It's easier with two, and there is nothing I can do until more survivors are brought out of the rubble.'

The little girl scuttled sideways to make room for him, but now watched both adults, her gaze switching from one to the other, a pint-sized guard ready to defend her brother should they attempt to do him any harm.

'Can you tell her where to go to get some food, and if possible some milk for the baby?' Alex asked him, nodding at the child. 'Maybe do your prince thing,' she added, smiling at him, although there was little to smile about in this place of devastation.

Azzam saw the smile and felt his heart lift, the hopelessness that had been creeping on him dissolving like desert mist before the sun.

He didn't question what the woman had that could make him feel this way, just accepted the gift of optimism she'd handed him.

'Prince thing?' he queried.

'My helper by the school was most impressed by your standing, repeating your name and saying "He is the prince" in tones of absolute awe.'

'I would rather be a doctor,' he muttered at her, but he did speak to the little girl, telling her to take the baby to the date grove.

The child left, reluctantly.

'You can't be both?' Alex asked as she unwrapped the

cloth—her scarf, he noticed—from around the boy's fractured arm.

'I doubt it,' he answered, although a simple 'No' would have been more truthful. 'Maybe, later on, when I know the duties expected of me and can see a path forward—maybe then I can give some time to the project of my heart.'

Project of his heart? Was it the circumstances in which they found themselves that he was telling this stranger—this female stranger—something he'd never said aloud, not even to Bahir? Oh, Bahir had known his brother was obsessive about the new hospital, but hadn't understood it was for people like these mountain folk, who feared the city and its ways, that he'd wanted to build the special hospital for children—a place where the whole family could stay beside their sick child—a place where they would not feel intimidated by machinery and uniforms and strangers tending their child.

Fortunately Alex didn't hear the phrase, or, if she did, she forbore to question it. She'd found some morphine in the kit, worked out a dose and administered it to the child while Azzam's mind had drifted far from the job in hand.

Concentrating now, he took the boy's arm, aligning the bone as best he could by feel, Alex holding the splints in place while he bound it.

She looked up at him and smiled again.

Alex—a woman he'd met less than, what, forty-eight hours ago? Yet her smile—several smiles now—had shifted his world...

The exhaustion still dogging him had caused the shift, not the smile! He had trained himself to not respond to female smiles, the hurt inside still too raw to want to trust his feelings.

Although was the hurt still there?

He tried to think when he'd last felt that stab of pain.

Maybe his lack of interest in seeking out female company lately had been more because of his immersion in his work than the fear of new heartbreak.

Heartbreak?

Did he really believe that?

Hadn't his pain been hurt pride more than anything else?

Azzam shut off the stupid thoughts racing through his head, concentrating instead on the job in hand. He finished binding the boy's arm and fashioned a sling to hold it against his chest, his mind still muddling over motives and reactions—in all honesty, it would be easier to be considering the leopards.

'We should keep watch tonight.'

The words brought him out of his thoughts and he looked up to see the headman of the village had approached them. Welcoming the distraction, Azzam stood up to talk to him and to listen to tales of recent leopard sightings near the village and how the villagers now kept their animals inside at night to prevent attacks.

'I've been thinking about the leopards,' Azzam told him, unconsciously using not the local word, *nimr* but the English word so that Alex looked up, repeating it.

'Leopards? Leopards out here? You can't be serious? Don't leopards live in Africa? Don't they sprawl on the limbs of trees ready to drop on unsuspecting passing animals? Where are trees here?'

She sounded so indignant he had to smile.

'Arabian leopards live in the mountains—they climb rocks and cliffs to drop on their unsuspecting prey. They were close to extinction twenty years ago, but a good breeding programme means the mountain areas have been restocked with them.'

'Great!' she muttered. 'Here I was thinking that the worst thing that could happen was another earth tremor and the mountain would fall on us, but now you tell me a very large and probably hungry cat could cart me off into the night!'

Azzam found himself chuckling now, then he translated her words to the headman who also laughed, though he quickly added, 'But she is right, they'll smell blood and could prove a danger.'

'We'll set a watch. Keep everyone together, light fires if we can find fuel, and do whatever is necessary to keep the people safe. I don't want to move the injured, so perhaps we should set up camp close by where they are, although the date grove would provide better shelter.'

'We can make shelters,' the headman told him. 'We have tents for the goat and camel herders who move the animals to different pastures. We have not lost our traditional ways, not all of us.'

The man departed and before long the uninjured began to gather on the grassy area, close to where the injured lay but not too close.

Alex watched the survivors drift like shadows through the night, heard the quiet chatter as they settled around the area where she sat with the children. Some men, and possibly some women, were still removing debris and she could hear their voices, warnings sounded and sometimes cries that told of joy—another person rescued.

'Who will protect the workers on the rubble from the leopards?' she asked Azzam when he returned with the headman and began to organise the erection of temporary shelter over the area where the wounded lay.

'I will call them in shortly,' he told her. 'It is too dangerous both for them and for anyone who might still be buried underneath for people to work at night, and the generator only has so much fuel, so it's best to conserve it for emergencies.'

'And these three children—the boy and his sister and the baby? Isn't it strange no adults have come looking for them? In a village, wouldn't someone be related to them?'

Azzam frowned down at the little boy.

'Of course there should be someone who would care for them. I will ask.'

You didn't have to be a prince to be efficient, Alex thought to herself as he walked away. But did the aura of the ruler add weight to his suggestions and advice? Did him being here bring solace and comfort to people who had lost everything, including, in some cases, a loved one?

Men and women seemed to share the chores, erecting tents, finding food, lighting fires, and now the scent of the frankincense she'd first found in the shampoo perfumed the night. Was it special, as Hafa had said, because it protected the people? Or because it was from some plant native to this country?

The little girl returned, the baby in her arms and a baby's bottle, miraculously found somewhere, full of watery-looking milk. She settled beside her brother, and once again Alex's heart ached for the three children—the little that remained of the family. The child lay down beside her brother, obviously exhausted for her eyes closed and the baby slipped from her grasp.

Alex picked up the infant, awake but uncomplaining, and used her now-filthy scarf to tie it to her chest. She could work among the injured knowing the baby was secure, but she didn't want to move too far from the children either—not until someone had claimed them.

Azzam, too, returned.

'You should sleep, but first you must eat. I have brought

some bread. It isn't much, but with water it will make your stomach think it's been fed.'

Once again Azzam had appeared beside her as if teleported there, for she'd heard nothing of his approach, but how he'd reached her paled into insignificance against the effect the man's presence had on her. Was it the sight of the light from the fire dancing on his bare chest that sent shivers up her spine? Or was it nothing more than the maleness of him, she who hadn't known a man intimately, who hadn't even kissed a man since David's defection? The man smell—sweat and dust and something deeper. She probably smelt pretty bad herself, but this smell was—

Idiot! Of course it wasn't intoxicating! She was tired, that was all, and in a strange country with leopards stalking the night it was only natural her instincts would tell her subconscious to seek out a protector.

She took the bread from him and bit into it, finding it so tough she had to tug at it to free a bite. He passed the water bottle, his fingers brushing against hers, an accidental touch that caused much the same reaction as the smell of him had only minutes earlier.

'I think the little girl's ICP has decreased slightly,' she said, reminding herself she was a competent medical practitioner, not a weak and needy—and possibly slightly hysterical—female.

Azzam heard the words, but they seemed so strange, out here in the mountain pass with tumbled houses all around them and coming from a dirty, dishevelled woman standing there, a baby strapped roughly to her chest, and shapely ankles showing beneath the hem of her trousers.

'That's good,' he said, because something was obviously expected of him, but beneath the words he sensed another conversation going on. Was she afraid? Was it fear he could feel in the air between them?

She *should* be afraid! Alone in an isolated place, in a country she didn't know, surrounded by strangers, she certainly had cause to be a little fearful if not downright terrified. Yet he didn't want to diminish the courage she'd shown earlier by saying something—by asking her if she'd like him to stay close to her, to protect her through the night.

No matter how much he'd like to do it!

'The children? Did you find out anything about them, find anyone who would take care of them now they are apparently orphaned?'

He shook off the strange thoughts he'd been having, thoughts related to being close to this woman through the night.

'It seems they are incomers, a family who arrived here a few days before the baby was born. They have been living in an abandoned cottage. The father took off within weeks of their arrival, leaving the mother and the three children.'

'And no one has befriended her?'

Even as Alex asked the question she thought of country towns back home where newcomers might be treated with suspicion but surely not totally ignored.

'Our connections are tribal,' Azzam explained, 'and although the link might be generations in the past, the people of the tribe are all related. Some tribes naturally affiliate with others, but maybe these people were...'

He paused and Alex guessed he was wondering how to explain.

'Not enemies, exactly, but from a tribe that didn't inter-marry with the locals.'

'But surely children don't carry any stigma from their breeding? Wouldn't someone want to take care of them?'

'I am guessing here and will continue to ask,' Azzam

told her, 'and maybe we will find someone, but you must realise these people have lost everything. To take on three extra children when you have nothing...'

He didn't need to finish. Alex nodded, thinking the villagers had probably been poor before the earthquake had struck, taking away what little they'd had. But she held the baby more tightly against her chest as her heart ached for the children no one wanted.

Azzam was talking again and she stopped thinking ridiculous thoughts of taking the children home with her and listened.

'I must go,' Azzam said, though he didn't want to leave the woman, who looked so vulnerable as she held the baby against her chest. 'I will take a shift with the men who are patrolling. Someone has found a rifle so don't be alarmed if you hear a shot. It will probably be someone firing at shadows, but if a leopard should approach, a shot will frighten it away.'

She sank down onto the ground, one arm still held protectively against the baby.

'I'll be all right,' she assured him, but he heard the quiver of alarm in her voice and remembered the tears that had slid down her cheeks earlier.

He knelt beside her and put his arm around her shoulders, drawing her close against his body.

'You have been incredibly brave, you have done more than should be asked of any human for people you do not even know. It is all right to be afraid, even to cry, now the worst of it is over. It is also right to grieve for the ones we couldn't save.'

'The mother of the children is dead, and the school teacher and two of the other children, too—one that I rescued and the one I left behind,' she whispered.

'But many are alive because of you,' he reminded her,

feeling the softness of her in his arms, the fragility of her small bones—feeling her as a woman so once again his body stirred.

She shook her head as if denying herself the praise and the comfort of his words then shifted so they were no longer touching.

'You must go—there are things you should be doing.' Her voice was husky—tears or just exhaustion? He couldn't tell and didn't want to think about it as either would strengthen his desire to stay close to her. 'I'll be all right on my own.'

'I *must* go,' he agreed, knowing his duty lay outside this shelter, organising, making arrangements to see them all safely through the night. Yet his body was reluctant to move—the softness of the woman a temptation he hadn't felt for a long time.

Not *this* woman, his common sense warned.

He rose and left the shelter, not looking back.

Although he would have to return—he knew that. It would be unacceptable to leave Alex and the children on their own throughout the night.

'You still intend to sleep here with the children?' Azzam asked, finding Alex much as he had left her two hours earlier, sitting by the children in the makeshift shelter.

'Of course,' she said. 'The boy is still unwell and the baby will need feeding during the night. I can't abandon them.'

Neither could he abandon her, Azzam realised. Apart from anything else, she was a guest in his country, his mother's friend. And he'd heard not fear but distinct uncertainty in her voice as she'd told him of her plans. She wasn't stupid and would realise that this tent, on the outskirts of the little tent village now set up, would be the first visited by a leopard should one come prowling, yet she'd asked nothing of him.

On the other hand...

How to explain?

'While it is understood that all people will sleep close to each other for warmth and safety, they will do so in family groups, as that is our way,' he began, aware he sounded far too tentative but unable to explain the customs that dictated this. 'The families are already settling into tents but if we share a tent, you and I, it would be...'

'Remarked on? Unseemly? Not done? There's been an earthquake, for heaven's sake. We have to do the best we can.'

He had to smile at the incredulity in her voice, especially when she added, 'Anyway, if people want to get picky, we can point out we have the children with us as chaperones.'

There was a pause, taut and expectant, before she added, 'Not that I need you to share the shelter with me. You said people will patrol the camp. I'll be quite safe.'

If she'd sounded a little less defiant—defiance hiding uncertainty—he might have let it go, but duty to this woman who was helping his countrymen insisted she be protected.

'The children would not count, neither can I leave you unprotected. I am sorry, but my position—it must seem ridiculous in your eyes, I can see that, but in this village it would be seen as...'

He turned away, battling to find the words he needed, English words that would convey the extent of dishonour him sharing a tent with her would bring, not only to his name but even more so to this woman who was innocent of anything other than a desire to help.

But there were no words—well, none he knew—in English to cover such a situation.

'It would be impossible!' He settled for simply dismissing the idea, before bringing up a solution. 'However, there *is* a way that we can do this. If you would sleep easier with my company—and I would certainly feel happier about your safety if I was with you—then we can make a marriage.'

'A marriage?' Incredulity didn't cover it—this was stark disbelief! 'We get married so you can share a tent with me? In an earthquake-stricken village where the choice of shelter is non-existent?'

'It is an old arrangement, usually made for the convenience of both parties but without the obligations of a real marriage. It is legal to do this, to make a *misyar* marriage for both our convenience so the people do not think that I am shaming you, or that are you a shameless...'

'Hussy is the word we'd use,' she said, actually chuckling as she said it. 'I can't believe this. It is just too weird. I know other cultures have their boundaries and it's the difference between people that makes the world the fascinating place it is, but...'

Laughter swallowed up the words and now instead of fanciful smiles in the night air, Azzam felt the stir of anger.

'Is marrying me so ridiculous?' he demanded. 'Many women would be gratified to—'

'Be proposed to by a prince?' The words were accompanied by a further gurgle of laughter. 'Oh, dear, I have to stop laughing but you must admit it's funny. Here I am, given a choice of facing a stray leopard on my own or marrying a prince, and I'm dithering over it. And on top of that there's the fact that you have this convenient kind of pseudo-marriage, which sounds to me as if it's there to cover men who might want to cheat on their wives.'

'It was not intended for that.' He sounded far too stiff and formal, but that was because he knew it *was* used in that way from time to time. Though not to cheat, for the wife would surely know of it. 'It is also convenient for older women, widows even, who might be happy on their own but sometimes desire male company.'

He completed his explanation, his voice so cold Alex realised she'd have to stop joking about the situation, although the only way she'd been able to handle the uneasiness inside her that had followed his strange proposal had been with humour. She was wondering if she should apologise when he spoke again.

'It was intended too, for times like this, for when a woman might need the protection of a man but is without a brother or a father. If it has been made a convenience of by some people, that is by the way. For tonight and however many nights we need to remain here, would you be willing to go through with it?'

'Marriage or the leopard—it's really not a choice,' Alex said, deciding this was just one more bizarre memory she would have to take home with her. 'What do we have to do?'

'Agree, have two witnesses and the headman, who will be the local marriage official. I'll go and see him now.'

Within thirty minutes they were married, it seemed, although her husband had departed with the headman as soon as the ceremony, if it could be called that, was over. He was checking the arrangements for keeping watch, he'd said, and would talk to people about the possibility of someone taking the children into their own family.

Married so they could share a tent?

Forget that—it was nothing more than a formality. She must concentrate on what needed to be done.

Alex fed the baby, cleaned him as best she could, wrapped a bit of cloth around his nether regions then set him down, asleep, beside his sister. She wished she had something to cover them with, but all the available materials had been used.

With the siblings asleep, she moved across to the next tent where the unconscious girl lay, her father still holding the bag of fluid. The girl's pupils were still unresponsive to light and her limbs failed to react to stimuli. Despair crept into Alex's heart as she began to think this child, too, might die, but when she felt the child's fontanelle, nearly but not entirely closed, she found the small gap between the bones at the top of the skull was no longer bulging. It meant the pressure in the child's brain had decreased, and she smiled at the girl's father, hope lightening her heart.

She returned to the children—her children, as she was beginning to think of them. Azzam had left a bottle of water in the tent, and, using her bra as a washer, she wet it with a little of the precious fluid to give herself a quick wash, thankful she'd had the forethought to bring her emergency pack with the spare pair of undies in it, although she hadn't thought ahead enough to bring nappies for a baby!

The baby—he'd stir, probably wake during the night. Best he sleep next to her. But as she'd retrieved him, she'd felt the little girl's skin, had felt how cold she was, although the night was still young. She *had* to find some cover for them.

Her clothes, of course, were filthy, but the tunic top she wore came to just below her knees. She could slip off the long cotton trousers and still be as decent as a woman in a dress at home. There was enough material in the wide trousers to cover the children for the night, and in the morning, before anyone was around, she could pull them back on.

She settled down beside the children—not hers at all but three who needed someone to show care and perhaps a little love towards them. With the baby wrapped against her chest, she curled her body protectively around the siblings, resting her arm across them so they were all snuggled up together.

Azzam stood his shift on watch then walked back to where the children were, looking down at the woman in the light shed by the fire outside the tent. While he'd been gone, she'd lost her trousers, the sleeves of her tunic had fallen back and the hem of it had ruffled up, so shadows of dark and light played across her pale, slim limbs, highlighting scratches that made him angry for some reason.

Angry that she'd been hurt...

He blocked the image and the thought from his mind, seeing the way she had placed herself between the edge of the shelter and the children. She may have been afraid of leopards but that fear hadn't blotted out her protective instincts.

He lay beside her now, adding another layer of protection for the children, but it was the warmth of *her* body that stirred him, thoughts of *her*, not the children, drifting through his mind until sleep claimed him.

CHAPTER SIX

THE baby stirred against her chest and gave a feeble whimper. Not wanting it to cry and wake Azzam or the other children, Alex slid out from between them. She unwound the scraps of material with which she'd bound the baby to her chest, found the bottle of milk, and held the teat to the infant's lips. She tried not to think where the milk—or the bottle—might have come from, and dismissed all thought of sterility from her mind.

Which wasn't that hard, as thoughts of the man who'd slept beside her were clamouring for attention.

She'd woken to the feel of his warmth and the solidity of his body, and had felt her own warmth build in response to his closeness. Not sexual warmth—or she didn't think it was—more just a feeling of security, a sense of shared responsibilities.

He was her husband…

Nonsense, he wasn't a real husband—not in any sense. It was convenience, nothing more.

Definitely not sexual warmth!

The baby sucked avidly, reminding her of where her attention should be. Holding the bottle and baby with one hand, Alex searched through the medical supplies until she found another sling, and, padding it with cotton wool, fashioned a nappy for the infant.

'There,' she said to him as he finished the milk and snuggled against her chest, 'now you'll be more comfortable.'

She checked his sleeping siblings then tucked the baby in between them, so she wouldn't be hampered, and he wouldn't be disturbed, if she had to move to tend another patient during the night. In fact, now she was awake she should check on all the patients.

Or was she looking for an excuse to escape the man who lay, sleeping so soundly, right beside her?

An excuse to escape her thoughts?

She smiled to herself as she realised that to someone who'd battled on alone as she had recently, the warmth of shared responsibilities might be more alluring than sexual warmth.

Well, almost…

Although it had been such a long time since she'd felt any stirrings of a sensual nature, she couldn't really judge. She'd stopped feeling them long before David had opted out her of life so precipitously. When first they'd met, his insistence they not make love until they married had seemed so quaint and old-fashioned she'd admired him for it—even felt special in some way. But why had it never occurred to her to wonder why the decision didn't irk her?

Because being with David hadn't stirred her body and her senses the way this man's presence did?

Because she'd never felt much physical frustration over his decree? Maybe a quiver or two when they'd kissed, but even that had stopped long before they'd parted. In fact, in retrospect, she had to wonder if David had remained engaged to her to protect himself—to avoid a permanent commitment to another woman. Any woman!

So, if she was to feel strange stirrings now, would it be so surprising? Even in the dim light of the dying fire, the man who lay beside her was clearly something special. His face had struck her earlier, outlined against the bright whiteness of his headdress, then his body—his naked chest—so well developed.

Now the heat of him, so close…

She sat and looked at him, aware this wasn't quite right, to be studying a stranger while he slept.

Except he was her husband—didn't that excuse her?— even if he had only married her to save her name. Although he *had* made out it was equally to protect his own good standing that he'd taken the step of marrying her.

His own good standing as prince, or as a man?

She had no answer to that or to any of the questions that taunted her.

What would it be like to be truly married to such a man? To feel his body held against hers? To know him intimately?

Now the warmth she felt had nothing whatsoever to do with security. It burned along her nerves, awakening responses between her thighs, reminding her she *was* a woman and this was what all her friends would consider a very beddable man.

A beddable man? Was she becoming addle-brained? How could she think such a thing?

She stood up and slipped away from the sleeping children—and Azzam—moving to the next temporary shelter where the man who had stayed beside his daughter had attached the fluid sac to a stout stick he'd stuck in the ground, and he now lay sleeping, one hand on the little girl.

Alex moved quietly on, into the shelter where the generator hummed, providing dim light for the people caring for the wounded adults. It was the first time Alex had seen them all lined up together, and she wondered how some of them had survived, so severe were their injuries. A woman moved between them, moistening lips with water, answering cries of pain.

'I am nurse,' she said to Alex. 'I have a little English from school and university. I am doing the work of doctor in the village. Our new Highness, before he was the prince, organised health centres in all villages and I run the centre here.'

Alex nodded her understanding and was impressed by the caring way the woman worked among her patients. They were in good hands and she could return to her children, for dawn was lightening the sky and she didn't want them waking and not finding her there beside them.

Her children?

The unresponsive little girl had her father, the mother of the boy who'd died had carried her son away, and all the other children she'd rescued must be with their families. Leaving her with the three motherless ones.

Her children…

Azzam woke to the roar of an engine and the clatter of rotor blades, sounds that told him the sun was up and the helicopter had returned. He stirred and groaned as his muscles told him it was too long since he'd slept on bare earth.

He looked around, aware of an emptiness he didn't understand.

Inner emptiness?

No, that was surely hunger.

But Alex *was* gone, the baby also, although the little girl remained steadfastly by her brother's side.

'I've been foraging for food.'

Alex returned as he sat up, shaking his head to clear it of the fog that sleep had given it. Part of the fog was an image that had lingered, of this woman's slim, pale limbs, but thankfully she was now fully covered again, except for her hair, which was so dirty she was no longer recognisable as a blonde.

She had a slab of flat bread in one hand and a flask of what looked like milk. The baby, he noticed, was once again strapped against her chest. Was it instinct that she carried the baby as the local women carried their infants? Or practicality?

Probably the latter, to keep her hands free, he was deciding when she spoke again.

'I need most of this for the baby, but you need to drink something and I couldn't find any water.'

Couldn't find any water? Last night, in all the confusion, he'd heard men talking about water—about the oasis in the *wadi*—but he'd taken little notice, intent on doing what had to be done.

'There should be water,' he told her. 'It might be dirty from the debris but this is an oasis.'

She shrugged.

'Well, this is all I could find.'

He took the bread, his mind fully focussed now. Had the debris from the earthquake completely filled the oasis, or had the earthquake itself opened up the ground sufficiently for it to leak away? He'd need to set men digging further up the *wadi*—the survivors would need water, and soon.

He took a gulp of the milk—camel milk, he'd forgotten the strange taste—and ate some bread, touched the baby on the head and left the shelter before he reached out and touched Alex as well. Maybe not on the head, but on the shoulder, although every instinct told him touching her was madness.

He'd slept too soundly, that was the problem.

Now, focus on the present.

Focus on the next move.

Focus!

It sounded as if the helicopter had landed, so the most seriously wounded would have to be carried down the valley to it. So much to do, so many things to think about, but as he left Alex said his name.

'Azzam!'

He looked back at her, standing straight and tall in her dirty clothes, a baby that she didn't own strapped to her chest.

His wife, albeit a *misyar* one...

'The unconscious little girl should go on one of the helicopter trips,' she said to him, 'but can they take her father as well? I don't know for sure but it seems to me they are all that are left of their family for wouldn't the mother be here if she was alive?'

Azzam knew what she was saying and understood the father would not be separated from his daughter. Of course he would be clinging to the one remaining member of his family. Wasn't this why he, Azzam, was building the special hospital?

Yet the father would take up the space where one of the injured could be, and would add weight in an aircraft where weight had to be considered carefully.

'I will try to arrange it,' he told her.

She nodded as if understanding all the permutations of his thinking, and returned to the next shelter to examine the child once again. He watched her sign to the man before leaving the little girl and moving on to help the nurse with the adult patients, the two women tending them as best they could while they waited for their turns to be carried down the valley to the helicopter.

'That's it for today but at least all the badly injured have been airlifted out.'

Azzam appeared as night was closing in. Alex had seen

him at various times during the day, although he'd spent most of his time helping carry the injured to the helicopter, remaining there with them until they were airlifted out.

Alex had stayed at the village, helping move rubble, tending survivors who were still, miraculously, being found, and keeping an eye on the three children. As better tents, flown in by helicopter, were erected, to be used as housing until the village could be rebuilt, the local nurse tried to fit the children into other families. One woman offered to take the baby, another family was willing to care for the boy and girl, but the little girl stubbornly refused to have the family split up, remaining where she was, caring for the baby when Alex was busy elsewhere.

'There are still injured people being found beneath the rubble,' Alex reminded him, using the bottom of her tunic to wipe her face.

'The helicopter will return tomorrow and keep returning as long as it is needed,' Azzam replied. He slumped onto the ground beside where she was sitting, outside the small shelter that she thought of as 'hers'.

Theirs?

'This village is at the border of my country,' Azzam continued, tiredness making his words sound gruff and strained. 'Our neighbours in the big town further down this old trade route have been affected as well. The town is not as badly damaged but because it had a bigger population there have been more injuries. Their rescue services are at full stretch so we couldn't ask them for help, but by tomorrow evening our road to the village should be clear and we can bring in heavy machinery not only to clear the rubble but to dig a new well for the village.'

'The rescue people who've already flown in have made a difference,' Alex told him. 'They've given all the villagers a break from the digging and rubble shifting, and brought optimism as well as their strength.'

'Not to mention food and water,' Azzam said, swinging the backpack he'd been carrying onto the ground and delving into it. 'Abracadabra—isn't that what your magicians say?'

'Your magicians too, surely? Or was it "Open sesame"?'

She was more disturbed by his presence at the moment than she'd been since she'd first met him, finding herself uneasy and a little at a loss because she couldn't understand her uncertainty. Not that he appeared to notice for he was delving into the backpack.

'Aha! Just for you!' He produced a pack of wet tissues, handing them to Alex.

'Can you manage a bath with just these?' he asked her. 'I'd have liked to ask someone to pack clean clothes for you but necessities like food and water seemed more important.'

'These will do just fine,' she managed, then, clutching the treasures to her chest, she retreated into the tent. The little girl was sitting by her brother, apparently telling him a story, the baby asleep on her knees.

'Look,' she said to the girl. Talking to the child had become a habit, although Alex knew she couldn't understand. 'Wet wipes.'

She knelt beside the children, pulled out a wipe, and wiped the boy's face, then with a clean cloth wiped the baby, finally handing three wet tissues to the little girl, who looked at them with delight before using them to scrub her face, hands and arms.

Deciding to keep the wipes for the children, Alex retreated further into the small tent, where she used the waterless cleanser from her emergency pack to wash her hands, arms and face. Then, aware of how grubby she was, she slipped off her clothes and, once again using her bra as a washer, washed the rest of her body as best she could.

Her clothes might be filthy but at least now she was kind of clean underneath. Her hair, hanging in a dirty braid down her back, didn't bear thinking about, but, deciding this was as good as it was going to get, she dressed and went back out to find that Azzam had, miracle of miracles, produced a packet of disposable nappies for the baby.

'Are you more delighted by those than by the food I'm preparing?' he asked, and she realised he was heating something in a small pot over a tiny gas stove.

'Definitely more interested in the nappies,' she told him. 'I was running out of things to use to keep him dry. As for food, I found bread and milk for the children earlier, so they're okay, but now I can smell whatever it is you're cooking there, my stomach is more than interested in the food.'

She squatted beside him and Azzam looked at her face, pale but clean, although rimmed with dirt around her hairline. A truly remarkable woman, he realised, uncaring of her own needs as she helped the strangers among whom she found herself.

Why?

She was a doctor, it was natural she should respond by helping, but surely going down that hole to rescue the children had been beyond the call of duty?

He switched his mind from the mystery of this woman to practical matters.

'When all the injured have been airlifted out, we will be able to leave, probably some time tomorrow,' he told her. 'A paramedic will come in on the first flight in the morning and he and the nurse should be able to cope with the less severely injured, who are staying here. Most of the personnel we'll fly in next will be people to continue digging and others to get services set up so the village can function while it's rebuilt.'

'And the children?' she asked, nodding her head towards the inside of the tent.

The children? He found himself frowning at her question.

'I thought the headman was arranging for other villagers to take them.'

'The boy is feverish, probably with an infection, and the girl won't leave him, or the baby, and no one in the village can manage all three.' She hesitated, then frowned as she asked, 'Do you know what has happened to the father? I know you said they were from a different tribe but there's something more. The nurse couldn't explain when I asked her, but it seems to me as if these children are—well, some kind of outcasts? Could that be? Does that happen? Could their father have done something bad? And if so, would that mean that if the children remain here, they might not be treated as kindly as they should be?'

'I will ask,' Azzam told her, 'but for now forget the children and eat.'

He tipped half the rations into a bowl and handed it to her, offering a plastic spoon he'd scavenged from the helicopter, thinking she'd find it easier than using flat bread to scoop up food.

'I wouldn't like to think they'd be unhappy—unhappier than they must already be with the loss of their mother. And it seems strange that they are so alone when your mother said it was a long-held tradition to welcome others to the camp. So there must be some definite reason they *weren't* welcome.'

He turned towards her.

'Are you always this persistent?'

She smiled and once again he felt something move inside him, although he knew it couldn't be attraction.

Gratitude, perhaps, that she'd done so much for his people.

'Only when it concerns the welfare of small children,' she said, 'and possibly patients who aren't very good at standing up for themselves.'

'And elderly women who are against a management plan for their asthma,' he added. 'I read the way you worded my mother's plan, making it simple for her yet emphasising the importance of prevention rather than cure. I know she is unwilling to take drugs unless it's absolutely necessary. That is why you were concerned for her?'

She glanced up from her meal but as night had fallen and he'd turned off the stove he couldn't read the expression on her face.

'I liked her,' she said, and he believed her, though it brought into his mind once again the disparity that kept niggling at him about this woman. Here he saw unselfishness of spirit as she gave generously of herself in the devastated village, so why did he still see the faint shadow of Clarice behind her, the shadow of a woman who'd come to his country to get as much as she could out of it?

He knew, instinctively, that Alex was different, so why couldn't he get Clarice out of his mind?

And suddenly it came to him—the answer so simple he could have laughed out loud. The betrayal he'd felt hadn't been heartbreak at all—pique maybe but nothing irretrievable. His pain had come from the physical side of things, from the fact that Clarice had been able, without a second's hesitation, to go from his bed to Bahir's. That, to him, who had believed in fidelity, had been the ultimate betrayal.

He was shaking his head at the fact that he'd let it poison his life for so long, all because he hadn't seen his own reaction clearly, when Alex's voice recalled him to where he was.

'That meal was delicious,' she said, setting down the empty bowl. 'Thank you.'

Then she chuckled, a warm, rich sound that seemed to fill the night with smiles.

'A meal cooked by a prince,' she teased. 'Not everyone can boast of such a thing.'

But the laughter didn't linger, her voice serious as she added, 'You haven't answered me about the children. I wouldn't like to leave here not knowing what will happen to them.'

'Arrangements will be made,' he said, speaking firmly so the subject could be dropped and he could go back to considering where such a fancy as a night filling with smiles could have come from. He was a practical man, always had been. Bahir, now, he might have thought such a thing, for at heart he'd always been a romantic dreamer. Yes, his brother was still with him—just a little…

Alex moved, standing up, thanking him again for the meal and the things he'd brought, saying good night…

More unsettled than ever by Azzam's presence, Alex escaped into the tent. He would stand a watch, surely, and she could be asleep before he came in to sleep, and if that was regret she was feeling, she needed her head read!

Proximity, that's all it was, and being alone in a strange place—of course she'd feel drawn to a man who wanted only to protect her.

Protect her body *and* her reputation, she thought, smiling to herself, although the nurse had told her of leopard sightings during the previous night and protection of her body wasn't such a joke.

Yet, remembering how it had felt the previous night, the warmth she'd drawn from his body, she felt a shiver of apprehension, admitting to herself how easy it would be for his body to seduce hers.

Not that he'd have the slightest interest in her that way, which made her reactions even more shaming.

Except that humans were designed that way for the continuation of the species. Without attraction between men and women, the race would have died out centuries ago.

Having thus excused herself for her wayward thoughts and feelings, she lay down, curled around the children, her arm across them once again.

The children!

Thinking about them would take her mind off her other wandering thoughts.

If she was married, could she adopt the children?

Though how could she work the hours she did and bring up a family?

If Azzam would agree, perhaps, to provide enough money to keep the children, she could take them home with her. No, it wouldn't work. Bad enough for them to lose their parents, but to lose their country? How could she consider bringing them up in a strange land, she who didn't even understand them when they spoke?

Her arm brushed against the lamp she'd found earlier in the rubble, a beautifully shaped brass lamp that the little girl had claimed as hers.

Now it reminded Alex once again of the fairytales that kept recurring to her throughout this whole adventure and she had to wonder whether, if she rubbed the lamp, a genie might appear. A fantasy, of course, but there was no harm in dreaming. She could ask the genie for a home for all of them. A second wish would be for money—not a lot, just enough to cover the debt—and she'd keep the third for when it might be needed. With Rob's debt paid, she could stay here, in this strange and fascinating land, and bring up the children with their friends...

She chuckled as she held the lamp, laughing at herself because she couldn't bring herself to rub it. The whole experience she was going through was so unbelievable a genie *might* just appear.

'You are laughing again? Surely not still at our marriage?'

Azzam had entered the tent as silently as he always appeared, and she rolled over and looked at the dark shadow that was him, hunkered on the floor beside her.

'No, now I'm laughing at my own silly fancies,' she said. 'Working out what three wishes I would ask for should a genie emerge when I polish my Aladdin lamp.'

She passed the little lamp to him, and Azzam ran his hands over it, wanting to ask what she would wish for but already too confused about this woman to be hearing of her wishes for the future.

The less he knew of her the better. He'd decided that while walking the perimeter of the camp with the headman. Already he knew he'd have a problem with the children who were, he'd discovered, not exactly outcasts but from a family held in disrepute by their own tribe and therefore not likely to be exactly welcome in a family here.

He'd have to take them home with him. There were plenty of staff to care for them and they would give his mother a new interest. His family had a tradition of taking in lost or orphaned children running right back through the centuries, and his mother would take a personal interest in them.

Yet as he sat down on the rock-hard earth and felt the proximity of the woman who was now his wife, he wanted more than anything to know her wishes, and to hear her talk and laugh again. Well, maybe not more than anything, because somewhere deep inside a desire to hold her was also building up within him, and if that wasn't stupidity, he didn't know what was.

He went for the easy option.

'What would you wish for?'

'You can't tell wishes,' she told him, her voice, and her face as far as he could tell in the dim light, deadly serious. 'Otherwise they don't come true.'

And now the urge to hold her had changed to an urge to give her a hug, for the words had had a wistful quality about them, and this strong woman who'd crawled into a dark crevice to rescue children, and who had worked with the men shifting rubble, sounded...vulnerable!

'Money can make most wishes come true,' he pointed out.

She shook her head.

'I've never had enough to know if you're right or wrong, but while I agree it could help—that it could make some things easier in a person's life—I wonder if it's true, generally speaking? Can it buy happiness, for instance? Can a designer handbag or a brilliant diamond bring true happiness? And can money guarantee the people you love won't die?'

As soon as the words were out of her mouth, Alex regretted them. She turned to Azzam and rested her hand on his arm.

'I'm sorry, that was a totally insensitive thing to say. You must miss your brother terribly.'

He was looking away from her, but she felt him move, and he put one hand over hers where it lay on his arm, holding it there.

'Will you sit with me outside for a short time? The stars are out and everyone should see a night sky in the desert.'

Sit under the stars with him?

Let starlight work its magic when she suspected she was already on the way to being in love with this man?

Of course she couldn't!

'Please?' he added, and she knew she would. She stood up and walked in front of him, stopping just beyond the door to their shelter and looking up at the magic of a billion bright stars in a black-velvet sky.

He took her hand and led her to a smooth rock not far from the tent, then used gentle pressure on her hand to ease her down beside him. Her hand felt safe in his.

How peculiar!

When had hands felt unsafe?

And was her mind wandering down this obscure alley so she wouldn't think about the profile she could now see clearly in the bright starlight? The clean, strong profile that would be etched forever in her mind?

'I felt such anger at first,' he said, speaking so quietly she had to strain to hear the words, but even straining it was hard to miss the pain behind them. 'It was such a use-less waste of life—and of a life that had so much to offer. Anger blotted out the grief, and now the situation—not the earthquake but being thrown into a role I wasn't trained for, and certainly never wanted—that has taken all my attention.'

Alex squeezed the fingers of the hand that still clasped hers.

'Grief will come when you are ready for it,' she said quietly. 'I know this for a fact. Some people find it there immediately, and find release in it, but others need to get through that fog of disbelief—and anger too, that's a le-gitimate reaction—that follows sudden death before they can remember the person they loved and truly grieve their loss.'

He moved the hand that had held hers imprisoned, freeing her fingers.

Was she sitting too close?

Had her words been too personal?

He didn't shift away, or remonstrate, instead using his freed hand to touch her cheek, turning her head towards him in order to drop the lightest of kisses on her lips.

'My good wife,' he whispered, as he drew his head back just a little. 'Offering comfort and wisdom to your husband.'

Alex was still coming to terms with the kiss, attempting to still the commotion in both her brain and her body, when he added the compliment—and with it added to the commotion...

'I'm not a real wife, remember,' she said lightly, hoping to relieve the tension in the air around them.

'You're very real to me,' he said, then he pointed to the stars, naming the constellations they could see, different names from the ones Alex knew, although apart from the Southern Cross she'd never been able to identify stars.

'This is Alchibah,' he said, pointing upwards where she strained to pick out one particular star from all the others. 'His name means tent, and over there, beyond that bright constellation, is Adhara, the maiden. So I am sitting here, outside the tent, with Adhara, the maiden. How fortunate can a man be?'

He slid one arm around her shoulders and held her close as they both continued to gaze in awe at the magic of the night sky, but the warmth Alex felt, being held so casually, was out of all proportion to the situation. Somehow, the words, and being pressed against his side, had raised a firestorm of reactions in her body—rapid heartbeat, heat racing along her nerves and a heaviness in her blood that made her want to let go of all her cares and, just for a while, experience nothing but feeling and emotion.

Could he feel it? Did it have to be two-sided, this intense attraction that stroked against her skin, even brushed her breasts, making her nipples tingle? But she didn't want to move, for to do so might spoil the moment, might break the web of sensation his body was spinning so effortlessly around her.

She *had* to move!

She *had* to rub her hand across her chest to stop the ache that started there and zeroed down between her thighs.

'You feel it too?' he murmured, then he was kissing her, kissing her properly. 'Is it nothing more than the magic of the night, do you think?' he continued murmuring against her lips, 'or something very special that involves just the two of us?'

She answered by initiating the next kiss, and when she drew away to catch her breath found herself admitting ignorance.

'I've no idea,' she told him honestly, revelling in the arms that held her firmly against his chest, revelling in the feel of his hard body against hers. 'It probably is the night—moon magic or starstrike, perhaps—because it's nothing I've ever felt before.'

She'd offered him a gift with that confession, Azzam realised. A gift he would hold close to his heart.

But it was a gift that prevented him from taking this attraction further—not here and now anyway. Yes, she was ripe for seduction, he could feel desire thrumming in her body, but would it not be a betrayal of her innocent admission, to take advantage of her? And what of later—back in the real world—what of the consequences of such an action?

Having finally sorted out the reasons the pain of Clarice's

defection had lingered so long, he knew he couldn't go into an affair with this woman lightly. It was something he needed to think clearly about, and his mind, right now, was beyond clear thinking.

He kissed her once again, but gently this time, and equally gently disengaged himself from her.

She looked at him, questions in her eyes, then must have read something in his face that made her offer him a rueful smile and a little nod before she rose to her feet and went inside their little shelter.

CHAPTER SEVEN

THEY flew back to the palace at about midday, Alex, Azzam and the three children the only passengers in the helicopter.

After a relatively sleepless night—he shouldn't have kissed her or mentioned the attraction, he shouldn't have seen her face by moonlight, the pale, ethereal beauty of her remaining in his head to haunt his dreams, he shouldn't have unburdened himself to her or talked about the stars or held her close—Azzam was happy to be returning home.

Until the helicopter landed and he stepped out to realise Clarice was there to meet them. For all her earlier protests that she was too distraught to handle her duties as the ruler's widow, mourning had obviously passed her by. The traditional white that was the colour of mourning had been set aside and she was dressed in the bold, vivid blue she knew set off her eyes, her skin and her hair tones, the tunic and the bottom of her loose trousers elaborately bejewelled so she dazzled in the sunlight.

The draught from the rotors had blown the head-scarf—something she'd never secured too well—back from her golden locks, so she came hurrying towards him, all bright and golden, crying out his name.

'I have been so worried for you,' she said, ignoring the staff gathered there *and* the other passengers and flinging her arms around him. 'Had anything happened to you on top of Bahir's death, I would have had to die myself.'

Her lush body pressed against him and for a moment he was a young man once again, meeting this golden beauty for the first time. She had dazzled him then in a way he'd never felt before and he'd fallen headlong into love, only to discover, once she met Bahir, that he, Azzam, was not the man for her.

The chatter of the children as they disembarked reminded him of where he was, and he turned to see Alex carrying the baby and herding the boy and girl away from the rotors of the aircraft. He eased away from Clarice, suspicious now of this unexpected welcome. Clarice, he had long since learned, always had an ulterior motive.

He reached out to Alex, took her hand, and drew her forward, aware that what he was about to do was wrong, yet unable to resist. He told himself it wasn't payback for that long-ago rebuff, and in truth it wasn't. This was instinctive, preparation for something that lay ahead, although he wasn't quite sure what.

'Clarice, this is Alex, my wife.'

Alex stared at the vision of golden beauty in front of her, frozen in place by the words Azzam had uttered. She realised this was some kind of ploy, one she didn't understand, and anger at being used this way began to grow inside her.

'I need to get the children inside, to bath and feed them and find a bedroom for them,' she said to Azzam, removing her hand from his grasp. 'Then I must get the boy to a hospital so his arm can be x-rayed.'

'I will organise it,' he said quickly, perhaps registering, even regretting, that he'd upset her. 'I will find a woman who will care for them. As for the boy, I shall take him myself. If the break is well aligned, we can put a cast straight on it.'

The woman, Clarice, made a protesting noise, but Alex's problem was with the man, not her.

'The boy is injured,' Azzam told Clarice, then he turned again to Alex.

'I will find someone also, to help you. You, too, need food.'

'Not to mention a bath!' she snapped, disturbed in ways she didn't understand by the tension she could feel in the air.

Who *was* this woman?

His girlfriend?

And if so, why aggravate her by introducing his 'wife' when she, Alex, wasn't a real wife at all?

Clarice?

Had she heard the name before?

She was far too tired to think right now, and getting the children bathed and fed was a priority. Several servants had appeared, Azzam rattled off some orders, and one young girl came forward, talking gently to the children, another stepping forward to take the baby from Alex.

'No, I'll take him. Just lead me back to my room,' Alex said, remembering this young girl as one she'd seen helping serve at dinner with Samarah about a hundred years ago. Could it only have been three days?

She followed the two young women and the children from the helicopter pad into a rear entrance to the palace, then along a familiar corridor to her room, where Hafa was waiting for her.

'We had word from the helicopter that the children were coming,' she said. 'The room next to yours is prepared for them and Ghaada, who loves all children, will be looking after them. I will help her bath and clothe and feed them, and His Highness will take the boy for X-rays, leaving you free to have a bath yourself.'

Brooking no argument, Hafa took the baby from Alex's arms and went with the children to the room next door, now talking in their language and waving her free arm, apparently assuring the little girl that Alex would be nearby.

Another young servant was waiting in Alex's bedroom, and to Alex's delight she, too, spoke English.

'I will help you,' she said simply, then she moved forward and as Alex raised her arms, the woman drew the filthy tunic over her head. Then she released the band around the plait and teased out Alex's hair, murmuring at the state of it.

'I have run a bath for you,' she said, ushering Alex into the bathroom, where there was a foaming tub with the scent she now knew so well rising from the bubbles with the steam.

Stripping off the rest of her clothes, Alex stepped into it, lying back in the warm water and feeling fatigue, as well as grime, ease from her body.

The young woman had followed her, and now she proceeded to wash Alex's hair, ignoring Alex's feeble protest that she could manage. Instead, she gave herself up to the luxury of it, and lay there, relishing the woman's fingers massaging her scalp—relishing the simple pleasure of being clean.

She eventually emerged from the bath and had a quick shower as well, washing off the grime she was sure would have lingered in the bath water. As she stepped out, the young woman wrapped her in a thick, warm towel, patting her dry.

'Enough!' Alex finally told her. 'I can look after myself now, but thank you anyway.'

'No, I am to see you eat and rest,' she said, polite but

stubborn. She held out a white towelling robe for Alex to put on then led her to a table by the window in the huge bedroom. An array of food was laid out there, with jugs of fruit juices and pots of coffee as well. Suddenly aware of her hunger, Alex sat down at the table and began to pick at what was on offer—sliced fruit, flat bread, meat and cheeses of different kinds, all things chosen to tempt a very tired woman's appetite.

Once fed, she realised sleep had become a priority, and she explained to the girl that she really needed a short rest. The short rest became three hours, and she woke with a start, unable to believe she could have slept so long and so deeply.

'Where are the children? Are they all right? The boy, how is his arm?'

Hafa had returned and must have been watching over Alex as she slept, for she came forward, assuring her all was well and that the older children had been playing in the garden once the boy's arm had been set.

Now she waved her hand towards the dressing room.

'When you are dressed, I will fix your hair,' she said. 'His Highness wishes you to bring the children to his mother in half an hour. We do not have much time.'

Alex found herself smiling for the first time since her return to the palace.

'I'm a doctor,' she said. 'I can be dressed and ready to move in two minutes. Half an hour is a luxury.'

Hafa returned her smile.

'But today you need not hurry like that,' she said, leading Alex, still clad in the cotton robe, across the dressing room and opening the doors to reveal that Alex's meagre wardrobe had been supplemented by at least another dozen outfits, far more exotic looking than the plain tunics and trousers that had been there originally.

Before Alex could protest the children returned, the boy and girl now dressed in pristine white clothing, the baby swaddled in a soft white muslin cloth. The little girl, Tasnim, Alex remembered, stared in awe at the clothes in the closet then pointed to a pale, silvery tunic and trouser set, pointing next at Alex.

Laughing at the child's delight, Alex stooped and hugged her, then turned to Hafa.

'I know she is Tasnim, but could you find out the other children's names, and tell her mine is Alex? I have tried with sign language but we both get muddled.'

Excited conversation followed and in the end Alex knew the boy was Zahid, the baby Masun.

Ghaada removed the children, promising to wait in the colonnade just outside the door until Alex was ready to take them to meet Samarah. Alex dressed in the outfit Tasnim had chosen, although she felt self-conscious about donning such beautiful clothes. The material was the finest silk, the palest blue-green colour shot through with silver. She had no make-up, but Hafa produced a box of lipsticks and a beauty case of unused cosmetics.

Shaking her head at such unimaginable luxury—that a guest room should come complete with new, expensive cosmetics—Alex chose a pale pink lipstick and used that on her lips before brushing her hair, tugging at the tangles, then covering it with a scarf that matched her outfit.

'I'm done,' she said to Hafa, who looked concerned that anyone could pay so little attention to her toilet, but Alex waved away the protest she began to make, saying, 'Samarah wishes to meet the children. She already knows me, although she might not recognise me in these beautiful clothes.'

She came towards them like a silvery ghost, carrying the baby and herding the two little ones in front of her.

Azzam knew he was staring, but he couldn't stop himself. He, who'd always thought golden beauty unsurpassable, was now struck dumb by this delicate, silver wraith.

'You have brought me children to love,' his mother cried, holding out her arms and speaking now to the two little ones in their own language. They came to her, as children always did, and she held them close then looked up at Alex, standing there with the baby.

'You will let me hold him too?' she asked, and Alex passed the white bundle to Samarah then knelt to put her arms around the children as well, so all three of the orphans were enclosed in the loving embrace of the two women.

The scene was burning into Azzam's eyes, like a painting seen and never forgotten, when he realised Clarice was speaking to him—Clarice, who had never been far from his side since his return, objecting when he turned her away from his own quarters so he could wash and dress.

'I have been thinking about Bahir,' she was saying, and Azzam had just restrained himself from demanding to know what else she should be thinking about so soon after his death, when she continued.

'And what he might wish for me.'

Ah, that was more like the Clarice he'd come to know. She was concerned about herself, not about her dead husband—concerned about her place in things now.

'He would not wish for me to be sad and lonely,' Clarice continued. 'You, his brother, must know that's true.'

Unfortunately, Azzam did. Bahir had been so besotted he'd have given Clarice the world, had it been at his disposal. He'd certainly lavished her with riches—palatial homes back in the U.S., which she visited regularly, a ski lodge in Switzerland, an apartment in London, not to mention jewellery worth more than the GDP of many small countries. She was hardly going to be cast out into the world as a poverty-stricken widow.

Yet she was after something more. He knew her well enough for that to be more than a suspicion.

'*Are* you sad and lonely?' he asked.

'Of course I am,' she snapped. 'That's why we're talking. I think we should be married. It is within the bounds of propriety in your country for a man to marry his brother's widow, I've read about it.'

A rage he'd never felt before rose up in Azzam.

'How can you be thinking of marriage to another man when my brother has been dead little more than a week? How does your mind work that you are putting this pressure on me? Have you no feelings? No propriety? No sense of right or wrong?'

She turned to face him, the beautiful golden hair lit from behind by the sun so she seemed to gleam with light, her perfect features beautifully made up, her blue eyes shining at him. And as he watched she slid the tip of her tongue along her lower lip, wetting it so it, too, shone.

It was a gesture she'd used on him many years ago and now he wanted to turn away from her—to never see that face again.

'You would have married me all those years ago had Bahir not come along,' she reminded him, making him feel ashamed at the truth she spoke.

'I cannot think of this now, let alone talk of it. It is beyond anything anyone could imagine, that you would talk of marriage now. Bahir is barely dead. At least respect the rules of mourning if you're throwing rules at me.'

'Three months and eleven days?' She all but shrieked the words at him. 'You expect me to be without a man for all that time?'

The crudity of it, on top of the lack of respect she was

showing his brother, angered Azzam so much he had to turn away from her lest he say something he would later regret.

'We will talk again,' he managed to say, through teeth clenched tight to keep in words that would do more harm than good.

'Soon!' she retorted, and he heard a threat in the words.

He spun towards his own quarters, knowing she wouldn't follow him there, then remembered he'd left Alex with his mother, and in a kind of limbo, for she'd be uncertain what her role was now, and would no doubt be thinking of returning to her home.

A stab of something he hoped was only regret slashed through him, but what would hold her here?

The children?

For a while—until they were settled in the palace. He thought he knew her well enough now to understand she wouldn't just walk away because they had shelter, food and clothing. She was the adult they'd clung to after losing their mother—she would understand that.

He returned to the open part of the wide colonnade where it was the habit of the women to gather every afternoon. Alex was seated on carpets by his mother's knee, the little boy this time on her lap, while the little girl, Tasnim, chatted to his mother, who still held the baby in her arms.

The thought of marrying Clarice had made him feel nauseous, while the sight of Alex by his mother's knee had him feeling very different—and unlikely—things.

Bahir, I need you!

The inner cry went up, so heartfelt he could feel it rip right out of his chest, but Bahir was gone and he had to solve the riddles on his own. It was his job to make decisions, not only for the country but for this family...

Alex listened as Samarah and one of her aides, Afifa, translated snippets of Tasnim's conversation. She felt strangely at ease—peaceful—here at Samarah's knee, Zahid dozing on her lap, listening to the chatter of the women and the wondering questions of Tasnim.

It was nothing more than a reaction to the last few days, she understood that. The tension she'd kept hidden beneath the surface as she'd helped the earthquake survivors was now gone, and in its place not emptiness, just a feeling of contentment.

Which would, she knew as she watched Azzam return from his assignation with the beautiful Clarice in the garden, soon be over, for once the children were settled, she would return to Australia and this little interlude would be as much a fairy story as Aladdin and his magic lamp.

'You will stay while they become used to life here?'

Alex smiled up at Samarah.

'I was thinking that just now. I shouldn't stay. There are reasons why I should return to work at home but, yes, I won't leave the children until I know they feel comfortable in their new surroundings.'

Samarah reached out and Alex felt her light touch, like a blessing, on her head.

'You work too hard. I knew that when I met you, though you always pretended it was nothing to be visiting me outside your working hours. You were too tired, too thin, too worn down by work. There is a reason?'

Alex looked at the woman she had grown to admire, and knew she couldn't lie.

'There was—is, in fact—a reason, but it's personal, Samarah. Just something I must do.'

It sounded feeble so she added something she knew Samarah would understand.

'A family thing.'

Samarah studied her for a moment then nodded, as if accepting that to question Alex further would be rude.

'But while you are here,' Samarah continued, 'you must see more of my country than a few rooms in the palace and a destroyed village. A car shall pick you up in the morning. Take the older children with you, for they, too, will enjoy the sights. Hafa will accompany you, and Ghaada will mind the baby.'

'It is I who should be showing you around.'

Alex looked up at the sound of Azzam's voice, and realised that, as ever, he'd rejoined the group in that silent manner he had, so quietly she hadn't heard him come.

'Of course you can't take time to do that.' Clarice must have been right behind him, for the words, cold and dismissive, spun through the air. 'You've already been neglecting your duties, Azzam. Some things can't stop because Bahir is dead. Trade delegations, important politicians visiting from overseas, your own business people—your days will be too full to be taking children and their nanny on a guided tour.'

Alex looked from one to the other. Clarice was probably right, but from what she, Alex, knew of Azzam, he wasn't a man to take orders from anyone.

She knew she'd guessed right when he came to sit beside her.

'Their nanny, as you call her, is my wife,' he said, the coldness in his voice cracking in the air like ice crystals. 'And after what she has done for my country and my people—*my* people, Clarice—I should be spending my life trying to repay her.'

This was entirely too creepy to be true, Alex decided, processing the words but guessing they were being said for a reason beyond the charming compliment embedded in them. The problem was that it was hard for her to work out what was going on when the bits of her that were touching Azzam, so close she couldn't avoid contact, were feeling drawn towards him, as if wanting to cuddle into him, for heaven's sake!

Why was he talking this way? As if he owed her—worse, as if he cared...

Clarice had thrown one look of fury in Alex's direction then stalked away, and suddenly Alex understood. It was a little play for Clarice's benefit.

To make her jealous?

Though why would she be jealous of any woman in her brother-in-law's life? What was Azzam to her apart from her husband's brother?

And worst of all, did Azzam think so little of her, Alex, that he would use her as a weapon against this woman?

The thought killed the treacherous warmth as suspicion wormed its way into her heart.

'She has different ways of showing grief so we must forgive her,' Samarah was saying, and Alex knew she was trying to ease a situation that had grown suddenly tense, for all the women were now looking from the departing Clarice to Azzam, as if asking themselves the same questions Alex had pondered.

'Grief is no excuse for rudeness, Mama,' Azzam said, though he softened the words by adding, 'although I think you would excuse the devil himself, you are so soft-hearted.'

Silence fell on them, not an uncomfortable silence now but one in which Alex's awareness of Azzam had time to grow again, so, in spite of the reservations she was now feeling about this man, her nerves twitched and twittered at each other and sent wayward messages to her brain.

'Unfortunately she is right.' Azzam broke the quiet. 'I do have duties that will prevent me showing you my country, but tonight I'm free. No one has expectations of me tonight. Will you trust the children to Ghaada and Hafa and have dinner with me?'

What could she say? Samarah and the other women were all urging her to agree, and the wild chatter that followed their English words made her think they were suggesting places he should take her.

'Let Azzam plan his own adventure—he's a grown man,' Samarah said calmly. 'But you, child—' she touched Alex on the head again '—wear the silvery gown you will find in your dressing room. I was right in thinking the pale colours would look much better on you than the dark ones you chose for practicality rather than beauty.'

'*You* chose those clothes for me?' Alex asked her. 'Thank you, but there are far too many, and they are way too fancy.'

'Hush,' Samarah said. 'After what you have done for our people, we should be giving you a palace, not just a few articles of clothing. As for the gown, you can wear a cloak over it if you feel it too bare to wear in public, but somehow I think Azzam has a private tour in mind.'

Azzam stirred beside her, while Alex puzzled over the words. She turned to him, but his face revealed nothing, the strong lines giving no hint of what might lie ahead.

Until he smiled and said, very quietly so only she could hear, 'If the silver gown makes you look more beautiful than the outfit you are wearing, it might be best you wear the cloak over it and we go to *very* public places.'

Was it really a compliment? Did he mean it? Alex looked

around, thinking Clarice might have returned to within earshot, but Bahir's widow was nowhere in sight.

Which didn't stop Alex feeling distinctly uncomfortable. How long had it been since anyone had paid her a compliment? Well, sometimes someone at work might remark on a job well done, but a compliment on her looks? And coming from a man who was surrounded by beautiful women?

Suspicion returned, but excitement had sneaked in as well. She hugged Zahid and set him on his feet, watching as he went into the garden to explore with Tasnim, his wounded arm held securely in a sling.

Tonight, she, Alex, would forget all the confusing questions her brain kept throwing at her, and behave as if she'd rubbed her lamp and wished for just one magical night. She'd wear the silver gown, and the high-heeled silver sandals she'd spotted in the wardrobe.

She'd dance with the prince and have the wondrous memory of it all to take home, tucked into her heart. And when work and the life she'd chosen got too much for her, she could take it out and marvel at it, remembering...

'You are rubbing your lamp and wishing again,' Azzam said softly. 'I can tell from your smile.'

Now she smiled directly at him.

'Actually, I'd shifted from the magic lamp to one of our European fairy tales. I was thinking I'd be like Cinderella going to the ball. Do you know the story?'

He grinned at her.

'Can you imagine a father in my culture allowing his boys to be brought up on fairy stories? Oh, my mother told Bahir and I the stories of our land, but fairy stories from another land? I have heard of this Cinderella but I don't know the story. Perhaps later you will tell me.'

Alex needed only an instant to realise that it wasn't a

story she would wish to tell this man—particularly not the bit about Cinderella getting to marry the prince.

'Or we can talk of real life perhaps,' she said, and heard a faint whispering sigh as if a dream had just floated out of reach.

CHAPTER EIGHT

HAFA helped her dress, as excited as if it was she, not Alex, going out to dinner with the prince. She brushed Alex's fine hair until it shone, then plaited two strands of it, one from each side of her parting, linking them behind her head with a silver ribbon.

'Not only will they keep your hair from trailing in your dinner,' she joked when she pushed Alex in front of the mirror to admire her work, 'but they make you look like a princess.'

'Which I'm not,' Alex told her, but Hafa shook her head.

'Of course you are. It is all over the palace that His Highness introduced you as his wife.'

Alex smiled at Hafa's innocent acceptance of what had played out in the colonnade.

'Our *marriage* was to protect both my and his reputation. It wasn't real.'

She didn't add that he'd brought it up—made it public—for some reason of his own, neither did she add her suspicions of this reason. She couldn't work out why, but she was certain it had something to do with his sister-in-law, because if looks could kill, Alex would be dead and buried by now.

She was still thinking about this, while Hafa fussed

over the dress, when a young girl came to tell her Azzam was waiting. The girl led Alex out the back way—the way she'd gone to find the helicopter, and to her surprise it was a helicopter awaiting her. Not the big one, which was probably based at the hospital now, still involved in missions to the ruined village, but a small one, like a monster dragon fly, painted in what she now recognised as the royal colours of black, white and silver.

Apprehension shafted through Alex's body—this was too much, she couldn't do it, she couldn't go flying off into the night in a glamorous silver dress with this man she barely knew. This *wasn't* a fairy story and this kind of thing didn't happen to ordinary, everyday Alexandra Conroy.

Something very like panic built in her head, swirling there, while something that definitely wasn't apprehension slithered along her nerves, and the feelings she'd been beginning to suspect she had for this man made her body tingle with awareness.

'Not a carriage made from a pumpkin, my lady, but the best I could do,' Azzam said, although he'd had to force the words out through a very dry throat, so beautiful did Alex look.

The silvery eyes flashed suspicion. This was not a woman you could win with sweet words or easy compliments.

'I thought you didn't know about Cinderella,' she said, obviously not as impressed by him in his best gown with the silver braid down the front as he'd been by her in the silver gown.

He offered a smile that he hoped looked genuine, although from the inside it felt strained and tight. He, who was normally relaxed with women, was suddenly tense and uneasy in ways he didn't understand.

'I looked her up on the internet,' he said. 'As you seem to know of our Aladdin, I thought I should know of her.'

At least that had her smiling! He took her hand to lead her to the aircraft, helping her into the passenger seat, touching her with hands that felt hot and clumsy.

'We are not going far and this little beauty is not very noisy so you won't need the communication helmet.'

Even more dry mouthed now, he tucked the silver dress around her legs so it wouldn't get caught in the door, and felt the warmth of her flesh beneath the fine material. He should stop right now. This was madness. He could invent an urgent phone call, pretend a text message had come into his cellphone as he walked around the helicopter to take his seat...

Except he'd deliberately not brought his cellphone with him, wanting to give this woman one special night to remember of Al Janeen before she disappeared out of his life.

Or was he hoping for something more?

Hoping she might fall in love with his country and maybe not disappear?

Fall in love with *him*?

He was aware this was the height of stupidity because she hadn't given the slightest indication that she was interested in him, so he had to believe that the attraction, if that's what it was, growing inside his body was totally one-sided.

Although last night attraction definitely had been there—the way she'd responded to the kiss...

That was *physical* attraction, probably heightened by the danger they'd shared...

As for his country, she'd seen the inside of the palace— or a small part of it—and a ruined village, so how could she fall in love with it?

And hadn't he decided, back when he'd still had some working synapses in his brain, that what he needed in the way of a real wife was someone from his own country and background and culture?

'You haven't seen the city so I will fly you over it, but I thought for dinner we would go somewhere special. You have seen flamingos?'

'Flamingos?' she echoed in such delight he had to smile, and the tension that had captured his body began to ease. 'Big birds, long legs, pink?'

'That's them,' he told her.

'You have flamingos here? In a desert country? The leopards haven't eaten them?'

Now he laughed at her disbelief and the little joke, and his laughter dispelled the last of his tension.

'The leopards live in the mountains, the flamingos by the lagoons that are not far inland from the sea. Their habitat, too, is protected.'

He lifted off, and headed for the lights of the city, flying low above it so she could see the mix of old and new that made the capital of Al Janeen unique.

Alex peered down, fascinated by the square and rectangular buildings beneath her, the lights on the roofs showing people preparing to sleep beneath the stars, then, beyond the older area, clustered like jewels in a crown, a clutter of high-rise buildings, brilliantly lit, the new part of the city.

She turned to see this glittery grouping from another angle, then realised they were flying over nothingness again, although now she looked ahead she could see what looked like a huge, shining mirror.

'It is called Shahlah because the birds, when they are there in numbers, turn it pink, and *shahlah* means a blush.'

'A blushing lagoon? None of our fairy stories can compare with that,' Alex told him, as he set the little aircraft down far enough away from the lagoon to not disturb the birds she could now see clustered on its shore.

Were they sightseeing here?

Or had this magic land more surprises to offer her? A fancy restaurant hidden behind the dunes? She'd slipped the fine-spun cloak that went with the gown into the handbag that matched her silver sandals, just in case she needed it, but now she peered around her, she wondered if she should have brought her sneakers instead. Just how practical would silver sandals be, for walking in the sand?

Well, she could always slip them off...

Azzam opened the door and, looking at him as he stood just slightly beneath her, she felt her heart turn over. He was a good-looking man at the best of times, but out here, with the darkening dunes behind him, he *looked* like a prince—the prince of all he surveyed! Was that phrase from a fairy story as well?

He held her hand to help her from the little aircraft, easing her down, not onto the sand she had expected but— she should have guessed—onto a carpet. This one wasn't red but it was patterned and long, like a beautiful path leading her into the night. It was only as they drew near that she saw a darkened area ahead, then lights came on, revealing a long, low tent, as dark as the night itself but lit by filigree lamps, their fractured light, patterns of gold and emerald and crimson, beckoning the visitors closer.

Outside the tent, beneath one raised side of it, more carpets had been spread, with huge soft pillows like the ones in the colonnade plumped down on them.

'Madame!' Azzam said, leading her to the pillows, offering her the choice of where to sit with a sweep of his white-clad arm.

Alex sank down into the largest part of the pile, and realised they were stacked in such a way she could sit, or recline just a little. She chose to sit, bemused by the surroundings—an Ali Baba tent, flamingos turning a lake blush-pink—but not wanting to miss anything.

Which was just as well, for now soft light lit up the lagoon so she could see the pink shapes of the sleeping flamingos clearly now.

'This is a night light for viewing them in the evening, but you must come in daylight to see them picking their way through the shallow water to fully appreciate their beauty and see the mud mounds they build to lay their eggs on.'

Now Azzam had mentioned them, Alex could see the strange-looking mounds clustered together at one end of the lagoon, but although she wanted to learn more about the habits of these beautiful birds, Azzam was explaining something else—explaining the delicacies a silent servant had set down before them on a huge silver platter.

'What you might call appetisers,' he said, 'so don't eat too much or you won't want your dinner.'

Alex felt herself relaxing, although she'd been extremely nervous about this outing with Azzam, about being alone with the man who was occupying so much of her thoughts *and* disturbing her body.

'Try a date—not an ordinary date like you might buy in your supermarket but a date from the family grove. Most of our traditional food traces back to our Bedouin ancestry, when our people roamed the deserts so food had to be easily transportable.'

He was sorting through a bowl of shiny, red-brown dates as he spoke and finally selected one.

'The seed has been removed, so you can bite into it.'

He held it to her lips, and their eyes met, messages that could never be put into words passing between them—provocative messages that sent heat coursing through Alex's body.

She bit into the date, her lips just grazing the fingers that held it, so, before he took the remainder of it to his own lips, his little finger flicked her lip, making the heat spiral downwards.

You're sharing a piece of fruit, for heaven's sake, her head was yelling at her, but her body was way beyond the control of her head, whatever common sense it might be preaching at her.

A small ball of cheese came next, milky and tart, a perfect contrast to the date.

'*Labneh*,' Azzam explained. 'A cheese made from fermented goat's milk.'

He was telling her the tastes of his country, yet the words came into Alex's ears not as words of love but definitely words of seduction.

Or was she imagining it?

She had just decided she must be when he wiped the water dripping from the *labneh* off her chin then once again brushed her lips, this time with his thumb.

Her body was zinging now, so alert she felt he must be able to hear it, the way you could hear the wind through electricity wires in a storm.

And *was* she in a storm!

She should draw back, choose food for herself—the little meatball kind of things looked tasty, but now Azzam's eyes were meeting hers again and she was pinned within this sensual bubble he had woven around them, powerless to resist.

Could she feel it? Was she as aware of him as he was of her? Azzam knew he should stop feeding her, for it was also feeding his need, his hunger for this woman. Nothing could come of it, for all she was his wife. She was a visitor, heading home to her own life as soon as the children were settled.

Heading home considerably richer, he'd make sure of that, for she'd served his country well, and even *misyar* marriages demanded a dowry, although he hadn't mentioned that to her.

Because thoughts of money made him doubt her?

Not anymore!

Whatever suspicions he'd harboured about her when he'd heard of her arrival in his country had been dismissed when he'd seen her in action. He'd come to know she was giving and unselfish, not grasping and avaricious. His doubts had been destroyed by her behaviour...

He offered her the plate of *sfiha*, tiny pies, being careful not to touch her in any way now, for the conjunction of his thoughts—of wanting her and payment—had shamed him so much the fires inside him had...not died, but certainly ebbed.

He began to explain the food, pointing out how each piece was made.

'The dates, grains and legumes, along with dried fruit and nuts, were carried by the tribes, who also had their animals for milk and meat. Because the Bedu acted as guards for the caravans from India and China, they could barter for spices, although saffron was a local spice, and salt a local commodity.'

Had she stiffened when he'd touched her lips?

Alex felt the shift in the atmosphere between them, and felt a sense of loss out of all proportion to the situation, but she hid it behind questions and became fascinated by the answers as he talked of the history of his people.

They ate mysterious meat dishes, drank juices of fruits

she didn't know, and finished with a type of sweet, made from yoghurt and honey, so delicious she didn't deny herself a second helping. Then the shadowy serving people were gone, vanishing as mysteriously as they had appeared, leaving another silver platter behind them, this one laden with the finest fruit. She and Azzam were alone on the carpet with moonlight touching the dunes and turning the lagoon to a shimmering silver, weaving a spell of enchantment about them.

Azzam broke the silence.

'Do you know how beautiful you are? As silver as the lagoon, as beautiful as the moon.'

He half reclined on the cushions beside her, and held a bunch of grapes above her, close to her lips.

'There is an illustration in one of our fairytales of a man feeding a woman grapes in this manner.'

Alex, bemused by the compliment he'd paid her, and still caught in the moonlight's spell, bit a grape off the bottom of the bunch and felt it explode with juice and sweetness in her mouth.

'Looking at the picture,' he said, holding the bunch above his own lips and taking one, pausing while he swallowed it, 'one imagines they are lovers.'

It's the spell, the situation, the magic of it all, Alex told herself, but her body rebelled and, aware in some instinctive way that the first move would have to come from her, she took another grape in her lips, then leant over the man beside her, transferring it to his mouth.

'Ahh...'

The soft sigh seemed to go on forever, floating above them like steam from a boiling cauldron, then Azzam's arms drew her against his body, and his lips, still tasting of grape, brushed against hers.

'I wondered if you felt it,' he whispered between kisses

so light they were like the touch of the moonlight. 'For me, the attraction was so strong I thought surely you must, but you hide your feelings well, Alexandra Conroy.'

She knew no words for this situation, so she answered with a kiss, a proper kiss, capturing the lips that had been teasing hers, pressing hers against them, hard and demanding, greedy now for more, although she wasn't entirely certain what more was.

More was a response like nothing she'd ever felt or imagined, for Azzam took control of the kisses, deepening the contact by sliding his tongue along her lips, delving into her mouth, darting flickers at first, then thrusting in mimicry of what she knew was sex, although she was discovering that knowing something, even viewing it on screen, was very different to the actual thing.

His hands slid along her arms, touching her so lightly the nerve-endings shivered beneath her skin, then his hands moved to her back and explored the contours—her shoulders, sliding to her waist, finishing up on her buttocks, cupping them and pressing her against him so she felt the hardness of his erection.

Should she tell him?

Would it matter?

But how to explain the weird vows she and David had taken, as high-school kids on a youth camp, deciding marriage lay in their future so they would wait…?

David hadn't waited…

She hadn't known it at the time, hadn't even considered he might not be faithful to her, not that it worried her because once he had decamped she'd been so busy there'd been little time to think of him or his betrayal.

Now, here in the present, in the moonlight, one of Azzam's hands still held her close, while the other was moving higher, lifting her hair so he could press kisses on her neck, shifting the strap of the dress so he could kiss the skin on her shoulder.

So far, apart from that first kiss, she'd been the receiver of sensation, but now she wanted to join him in exploration. But could one remove a headdress from a prince to feel his hair? Could one slide a hand beneath the sleeve of his gown to feel his skin, and the muscles beneath it?

Sensing hesitation in the woman in his arms, Azzam drew back, turned her so she lay against the coloured cushions. With unsteady fingers, he spread the silver hair around her head.

'We are at a point, Alexandra Conroy, beyond which there will be no turning back. You must know I want nothing more than to make love to you, here in this beautiful place, in this peaceful setting. You are my wife but that does not bind you to me, neither does it mean you must consent. I would never take a woman against her wishes, but your body tells me you want this as much as I do. Am I right?'

She frowned at him, and Azzam wondered what she was thinking. Had he put it badly? Should he have asked first if she would stay here in Al Janeen and be a real wife? For he felt that things could work well between them for all his misgivings about marrying a foreigner. But telling her that might put extra pressure on her, and this woman had already done so much for his country.

Still frowning, she reached out and touched his head scarf.

'Will you take this off?' she asked, and the smile she gave him told him her answer.

'One piece of clothing each,' he challenged, and though he thought a look of shock had crossed her face, he dismissed the idea. She was a grown woman, no doubt experienced with men.

'Why not?'

She had answered his challenge but now sat up, slipping the ribbon from her hair.

He removed his headdress, then his gown, casting it down on the carpet near their feet.

'Your turn,' he said, as desire burned so fiercely inside him it was a wonder he could speak at all.

She shifted, shuffled, lifted the hem of the beautiful silver dress, then slid out lacy white undies, throwing them on top of his gown.

'That might be cheating,' he whispered, his voice husky with the hunger he felt for her. 'But I will let you get away with it and do shoe for shoe.'

He took off his sandals, setting them aside, then slid off one of hers, his hands drifting up her leg, feeling the swell of her calf, the hardness of knee bones, the soft back of her thigh.

She was shivering, her skin covered with goose-bumps, and that excited him even more, so with the removal of the second sandal he ventured further, sliding his hand high beneath the dress to touch her between her legs, feeling the soft, silken hair there, imagining it, burning to see it—

But she had stiffened, and he knew he'd gone too far, too fast. Slow down, he told himself, standing up in his *wuzar*, the white cloth his people wore as underwear, moving to be close to her again, to kiss her and touch her and feed the fires he knew burned as brightly inside her as they did within him.

She returned his kisses with a fierce need that raged through his blood, and her hands pressed against his naked back, fingers digging into his muscles, fingernails scratching against his skin, so desperate was her touch.

'The dress,' he whispered, when he knew she was riding the excitement once again.

'You do it,' she murmured back, softly acquiescent now, tremulous beneath his questing hands.

He wondered if his hands should be shaking this way as he eased the shoulder straps away, found a zip, then slowly pulled the dress down along her body so bit by bit her pearly skin, luminous in the moonlight, was revealed, and the shape of her body, of small, pert breasts, a tiny waist and swelling hips, was laid out before his gaze.

'You are beautiful.'

He breathed the words then followed them with kisses, not hard and hot but worshipful, kissing the hollow of her neck, her chest, her stomach, leaving the breasts for last then running his tongue across first one and then the other.

She moved now, abruptly at first, as if the caress had startled her, but then she lay back and reached out to pull him closer, kissing his chest as he'd kissed hers, while his hands now found a peaking nipple, and his fingers played with it, her little whimpers of delight exciting him beyond endurance.

Lost in wonder at the delight of Azzam's touch, at the magic of his kisses, at the response of her body to his exploring fingers, Alex drank it in with the thirst of someone who'd been lost too long in the desert. Her body was responding in ways she'd never imagined it could, and a tension beyond anything she'd ever felt was building up inside her.

Now his mouth had taken over the teasing of her breasts, sending fiery pulses down to the place between her legs where his hand worked a subtle new magic. He was touching her so lightly, so gently, yet the heat that had been building inside her had seemed to plateau, and she hung, suspended, in some other world.

Now his fingers probed, but gently, and she knew she

must feel hot and wet for all sensation in her body was now concentrated in that one small area. His thumb moved, touched a part of her she would never have considered sensitive, yet her body jolted beneath him, like someone who'd been hit with an electric charge.

Now he calmed and soothed her again in some way—with kisses on her lips—while she wanted to scream at him to keep going, to show her exactly what she'd been missing out on all these years.

'Soon,' he whispered, as if he sensed her impatience. 'Lovemaking is too special to hurry.'

And once again he took her to that other place, but this time, as she hung there, her body taut with wanting, though what she wasn't sure, his fingers continued touching her, moving into her, his thumb again brushing her clitoris, then one more touch and the world went black, stars exploded in this inky darkness, and her body dissolved into a puddle of sensation too unbelievable for there to be words to describe it.

'Ah,' he said, nothing more, but his hand remained cupped around her and, as more tremors rent her apart, he held her safe.

But this wasn't all—she knew that—and now she'd experienced one part of this sex business she wanted all of it. Boldly she felt for him, found the iron-hard penis that had taunted her earlier, and ran exploratory fingers of her own over it. Of course she'd felt David's excitement, back when they'd been courting and sex had been a fumble in the back seat of his car, but touching David had never made her hot and anxious, never made her move restlessly against him, her body begging to be taken.

Azzam shifted until he was lying above her, his body supported on his strong arms, his undergarment gone.

He was so magnificent in the moonlight she could barely breathe for the wonder of it.

'Guide me in,' he ordered, and she hurried to obey, gasping at first as her body opened to accommodate him, gasping again as a fierce thrust caused a jolt of pain, then she found the rhythm of his movements and moved with him, aware of something primal, something elemental, in this mating dance beneath the stars and moon.

But thoughts became entangled and disappeared altogether as she realised that once again she'd reached that strange plateau, but this time she knew the wonder of the experience that lay beyond it, and she moved beneath him, searching for the connection that would repeat it, moving faster, with him, rising higher, wanting the nearly unbearable tension to break again, to shatter her so she could be new again.

It came, and with it a shout of exultation from Azzam, then his movements slowed and he collapsed on top of her, his body hard and hot, slick with sweat, his lips by her ear, murmuring words she didn't understand.

She held him tightly, aware this might be the only time they could lie this way, and knew she loved him—probably would always love him. She looked up at the moon, silently telling it of her love, and knew, too, that the magic of this memory would light her life just as the moon had added magic to their lovemaking.

Azzam rolled away from her, remaining close, raising his upper body on his elbow, his head on his hand, looking down at her, his free hand running across her skin.

'You are a ghost, an apparition, a thing of wonder and delight. That is what I said to you in my language.'

Now he touched her face.

'You are happy? No regrets?'

Still lost in a place beyond words, she smiled and

shook her head, then, as if remembering something, he frowned.

'Alex?'

Her name was more tentative on his lips than she had ever heard it, then, still frowning he ran his hand down her body, sliding it between her legs, touching the wetness lingering there.

Now he frowned, as if remembering something, studying her, the frown deepening.

'You were a virgin?'

It was more an accusation than a question and it cut into her hazy, drifting thoughts, bringing her back to earth with such a jolt she sat up and stared at him.

'Is that a sin?' she demanded, so annoyed at being shaken out of her little bubble of happiness she could have slapped him.

'Not a sin, no,' he said quietly, touching her on the shoulder. 'But you should have said— I could have hurt you— I wouldn't—'

'If you say you wouldn't have had sex with me if you'd known, I *might* just hit you,' she warned. 'And if you mention it again—as if I had some kind of rare sexually transmitted disease—I will walk home from this place if it takes me all night.'

Angry and feeling somehow humiliated, as if her virginity had been an affront to him, she reached out and grabbed the first thing that came to hand, which happened to be his gown. Clutching it in front of her, she moved away from him.

'Alex!'

Azzam said her name but had no words with which to follow it. Somehow, on top of what had happened, he'd made it worse—offended her in some way he didn't understand.

'Well?' she demanded, his gown wrapped around her body, tucked in above her breasts so she wore it like a sarong while she searched among the tumbled cushions, presumably for her gown and underwear.

'I don't know what to say,' he admitted. 'I don't know what to tell you. I want to say I'm sorry, but I'm not, for what we shared was, to me, truly amazing—something very special and something I will always remember.'

'Then that makes two of us,' she snapped, finding her gown. Discarding his robe, she pulled the silver sheath over her head. But she wasn't done. Grabbing the small silver bag she'd brought with her, she pulled out a cloak. In the haze of what was happening, Azzam still registered the fact that it must have been silk for it to have folded so small. Now she'd donned it over the silver dress and stood, a slender, muted figure all in black, the milky white skin no longer tantalising him, although the shining hair still shamed the moon with its beauty.

'You are still you beneath the gown and cloak,' he reminded her, but she didn't speak and he knew he'd broken the bond between them—a bond he'd been beginning to believe might form a solid foundation for something special.

CHAPTER NINE

THEY flew back to the palace in silence, Azzam wondering if he'd ever understand women. From the helipad behind the palace he could walk her as far as the door to the women's house where she was staying, or to his own quarters—equidistant.

He wanted to do the latter, not because he had any intention of making love to her again this evening but so they could talk and maybe sort this out. But how to ask? The woman was a puzzle to him, an enigma! She must be, what, late twenties? And undoubtedly there were plenty of women of her age who were still virgins, but a woman as beautiful and desirable as she was?

He shook his head, further thought beyond him.

'I don't like to part like this,' he said, when they were on the ground, the engine off and the blades slowing. 'Would you come with me to somewhere we can talk—only talk? I realise you are upset, and with me, but whatever I said it was inadvertent. The experience we shared was very special to me, more special than I can put into words.'

The black-garbed figure shrugged her shoulders.

'I don't think there's anything to talk about,' she finally said. 'After all, I'll be gone before long. As soon as the children are settled I'll be leaving.'

The cool, offhand statement thudded into Azzam's

belly like a punch from an assailant and desperation grew within him.

'We could talk about that—about your plans,' he said. 'Must you go so soon? Might you not stay a while, see my country, learn a little of its ways—maybe stay—'

He'd been about to say 'forever' but had pulled back the word at the last moment, thinking it might frighten her. Women needed to be wooed, not hit with marriage proposals out of the blue. And though they were technically married, he was beginning to realise that what he wanted with this woman was a real marriage...

What had he been about to say? Maybe stay—what? Alex found herself pondering this to stop herself thinking of other things. Like the pathetic way she'd reacted to the virgin thing out there in the desert! Like the way her body was behaving as if the coldness between them didn't exist. Beyond all reason, it was yearning for his touch, and the excitement of his lovemaking...

'I don't think talking will help,' she finally replied, knowing the more she was in this man's presence the less likely she'd be to get over this yearning business. Discovering she was in love with him had been one thing, but discovering what his body could do to hers, that was entirely different. She could hide her love, but was she strong enough to control these new urges of her body, and if she gave in to them, wouldn't he guess the other part?

'Perhaps tomorrow,' he said, his voice sounding strange—hoarse? Strained?

'Perhaps,' she agreed, lying through her teeth, knowing she would do everything in her power to avoid him and, if it was impossible, to see him only in the company of others.

He climbed out of the helicopter and walked around

to help her out. She held the cloak around her as if it was armour that might somehow protect her, but he put his hands on her waist and lifted her easily from her seat, and the heat of his hands burned through the layers of cloth so she felt as if he'd branded her, the outline of his fingers burned into her skin.

He walked with her to the rear door she now knew led to her quarters, and spoke quietly to a man who sat nearby. The man slid off into the shadows, and Azzam stood with her, this time resting his hands on her shoulders and peering into her face.

'You won't change your mind? Won't sit with me a while and talk?'

'No, thank you!'

She knew she sounded tetchy but she was feeling that way too, for the man's hands on her had reawakened the barely diminished fires of earlier and her body clamoured to lean into his, to feel his contours—to know him…

'Then there is only one thing left to say,' he said, with the smile she'd seen so rarely, but which had the power to light up her heart.

'And that's goodnight,' he murmured, and before she could retreat he bent his head and kissed her lips, the softness of his skin accentuating the hard demand behind that simple kiss. Her heart rate soared and imps danced in her head, distracting her from the common sense she knew she needed—desperately.

Now her body was leaning into his, the kiss was deepening, and the longing to be with him, naked, feeling all of him, was all but overwhelming her. Then one small thread of common sense came through for her. If this was how she felt after making love one time, how much worse would it be after two—or four—or fifteen…?

She broke away. What was the point? She didn't want an affair with this man. She didn't want it to be *more* difficult to leave this country. Already it would be bad enough, leaving Samarah and the children, whom she was coming to love.

He released her, and it was only in her foolish heart she felt reluctance in the release.

'We *will* talk,' he said, opening the door for her, waiting until a young woman appeared then speaking to her, no doubt asking her to see Alex to her room.

'Goodnight,' she said, though with sadness. But what else was there to say?

'Goodnight,' he echoed, then he walked away.

Alex followed the young woman to her room, then shooed her away, assuring her she could undress herself. She stripped off the cloak, then the silver dress, casting it into a heap on the floor, wanting to bundle it up and drop it into a rubbish bin then wanting to see it cleaned so she might take it home as a reminder of a magical, if thoroughly disturbing night.

Seeing herself in the mirror made her grimace, faint red marks that would turn to bruises on her limbs and body. But remembering how they'd got there, remembering the pleasure the man had generated in her body, she couldn't regret anything that had happened. The only regret she had for was the way it had ended. But how else could it have ended? There could be no affair—she was going home— and that was quite apart from the fact that for some reason he hadn't liked her being a virgin.

Well, bother him!

She went to bed, wondering if sleep would come, her body more alert, more wired than it had ever been.

Sleep came.

* * *

She woke to sunshine making patterns on the silk coverlet again, and she stretched, lazily, a little sore, but with no regrets.

Sitting up in bed, she realised she had company. Tasnim was sitting by the door, the child as silent as she usually was. Alex opened her arms and the girl ran into them, hugging her tightly, then she slipped off the bed and went away, returning with Zahid and the baby, Masun.

'All my family,' Alex joked, as she hugged them all, then waggled the baby in the air so he crowed with laughter. If only they *could* be her family—*her* laughing, happy children.

Impossible!

A selfish dream...

But one that bit in deep, probably because her own family was all but gone, leaving behind such pain and hardship...

Ghaada was by the door now, and she translated as Tasnim and Zahid rattled on, telling Alex the car was waiting, they were going in a car, please could she come.

Now!

Alex laughed. Typical family! The children had been waiting, not to see her but to go for a ride in a car, obviously something new for them. Ghaada took them out of the room so Alex could dress, reminding the children Alex also had to have her breakfast.

'I will keep the baby here,' she said to Alex, 'for the car would be too tiring for him and you do not need the distraction.'

'But I thought you could accompany us and tell me what I am seeing,' Alex said, and Ghaada shook her head.

'As well as a driver, His Highness has arranged a—is it tour guide you say? He has planned the tour for you and told this young woman where she is to take you. Hafa will bring your breakfast, and the car is waiting when you are ready.'

Soon after Ghaada and the children departed, Hafa entered, carrying a tray with a coffee pot, a cup, sugar and sweet pastries on it.

'I select an outfit for you?' she asked, as Alex sat down to breakfast, surprised at how hungry she was feeling.

'I think for sightseeing my own jeans and shirt,' Alex told her, determined to get her mind off the children and dreams of a new family, and into 'going home' mode.

Hafa seemed about to argue, but in the end she disappeared into the dressing room, returning with the clothes Alex had been wearing when she'd left Australia what seemed like a lifetime ago.

Their tour guide spoke perfect English, acquired, she explained, because she'd grown up in England where her father had run the European end of one of the royal family's businesses. They went first to the markets in the old part of town, where Alex was dazzled by the multitude of aromas—herbs, spices, strange fruit and the ever-present frankincense. But a riot of colour also assaulted her senses, for the vivid yellow of open bags of turmeric powder and the deeper gold of saffron, the bright sheens of bolts of colourful silk, draped across stalls piled high with goods.

The children oohed and aahed as any children would, seeing such an array of goods spread out on either side of narrow alleys. They reached the area where metal objects—pots and pans, urns, vases and lamps—were sold, and Alex stopped to look more carefully. Surely she was entitled to take home one small memento, and if she could discover a small, shapely lamp like the one Tasnim had found, it would be the ideal souvenir.

And she could dream of wishes...

The children poked around among the treasures and it was Zahid who found a tiny lamp, holding it up to show Tasnim, no doubt commenting on how like hers it was. He held it out to Alex, who turned to the guide.

'Can you ask how much—?'

She stopped, an unbelievable awareness striking her. She had no money! Not even Australian money, for her wallet was back at the palace, the last thing she'd thought she'd need.

'It is very cheap,' their guide told her, mentioning a sum in Al Janeen money that meant nothing to Alex.

'No, it doesn't matter,' Alex told her, and she hustled the children on to the next stall, and the next, through the markets and back to the car, her mind in a whirl as she came to terms with just how isolated she was and how totally dependent on Azzam's goodwill to get back home.

Although Samarah would surely help if Azzam's promise to arrange her flight home didn't eventuate—

No way! The thought of borrowing from her kind friend was too much. Bad enough she'd had to ask Azzam for wages.

They drove through the city, visited a museum that had reminders of the past, beautifully bejewelled camel saddles, magnificent gowns and exotic headdresses. Pictures of a distant past were arrayed along the walls, showing nomad camps, and herds of goats summering in the mountains—maybe not far from the children's village. Also on the walls, photographic portraits of memorable faces, ordinary people going about their lives but with the strong, proud profiles of their race, the same profile Alex so admired in Azzam.

Eventually, when the children tired, Alex suggested they return home.

'One more stop,' their tour guide said, and now the big black limo left the city streets, heading out on a bitumen road across the desert. They drove for maybe an hour, then crested a dune and there beneath them spread the shining lagoon, pink around the edges with the daintily stepping flamingos.

'The blushing lake,' the guide said, as the children gazed in wonder at the birds. Alex was less interested in them, orienting herself by the nest mounds but seeing no sign of the tent in which she'd spent such a memorable evening. Wasn't there a saying about desert people folding their tents and disappearing into the night?

Yet her memories couldn't be folded away so easily, and a physical ache started up inside her as she longed to be back at the beginning of the magical night and maybe handling it all differently.

Better—oh, certainly better—for didn't everyone make things better in their dreams?

Both children fell asleep as they drove back to the palace, and Ghaada appeared when the vehicle pulled up, so she carried Zahid while Alex, after thanking their guide, carried Tasnim, feeling the girl's slight body against her breast, feeling the love that had crept into her heart where these children were concerned.

It was a different love from the other love in there—the one that had slammed in without warning over what was a matter of days.

Could love happen like that?

So quickly?

Maybe it wasn't love. Maybe it was nothing more than a strong physical attraction.

But as Alex left the sleeping Tasnim on her bed and returned to her own quarters, she knew that was wrong. Yes, she was physically attracted to the man—even more so after last night—but what she felt was more than that. It was a mix of admiration and respect and something that she couldn't explain—some inner connection to the man—as if they were linked in the way speakers on phones in distant places were linked—brought together by some unseen, and to most people mysterious, power.

Hafa was waiting for her, with a message that Samarah would see her and the children in the colonnade at the usual time.

Alex thanked her and sent her away, assuring the kind young woman she could bath and dress herself, wanting to be alone for a while with her straying thoughts. But being alone didn't help make sense of the chaos in her head, neither did it soothe the agitation of her body, although maybe Azzam wouldn't be in the group at the colonnade this evening.

She lay on her bed, studying the marble fretwork of the window, marvelling as always at the talent of the master craftsman who must have carved it, thinking about shifting patterns to distract her mind and body. The knock on the door was louder than Ghaada's or Hafa's usual light tap, but without stirring much Alex called, 'Come in.'

To her surprise it was Clarice who swept into her room, cast a knowing eye around it, and sniffed in a way that suggested the sumptuous suite was only a small step up from servant's quarters.

'I thought as we're both strangers in this land—although I've been here long enough to be accepted and adored by the locals—we should get to know each other.'

Alex sat up on the edge of the bed, but before she could offer Clarice a chair, the woman had sat down by the window, where the play of light made patterns on her skin, illuminating her golden beauty.

'I'm going home any day now,' Alex told her, then realised it might have sounded rude, so she quickly added, 'not that I wouldn't want to be friends with you, but as I say…'

She left the sentence hanging.

'Really?' Clarice said, and it seemed to Alex that there was relief in the word, although it was a mystery why Alex's departure should please Clarice.

'Once the children are settled here,' Alex expanded, 'I'll be free to go. It just seemed wrong to take them from their village and dump them somewhere strange without a little bit of time for them to adjust.'

Clarice looked perplexed, or as perplexed as someone who had very little in the way of facial expressions could look. Her eyebrows had moved as if to come together in a frown, but no lines marred her smooth forehead.

'But why would you care?' she asked. 'You didn't know the children and they barely know you and they must be so delighted to get out of their squalid little village and come to live in a palace, they wouldn't care who looked after them.'

The local people adored someone who spoke of 'squalid little villages'?

Alex pushed the thought away and concentrated on the main issue.

'These children have lost their mother. No matter where they came from or how magnificent their current circumstances might be, they are grieving and need time to adjust to the worst loss a child can suffer. They need to feel secure in their surroundings, and to know they can trust the adults around them. They need to feel wanted and loved and to know that their little family won't be split up.'

Clarice stretched and ran a hand through her glorious mane of hair.

'Sounds like a load of psychological claptrap to me,' she said. 'Kids are kids, they adapt.'

Swallowing the growl that rose in her throat, Alex rose from the bed.

'I really need to shower. Was there something else you wanted?'

Clarice seemed put out.

'I only came to chat,' she said. 'With Bahir gone, there's no one in this place I can talk to. I should just get out of here—go home to the States, I've houses there—but there's this mourning thing they do and I don't want to upset everyone in case I want to come back some day.'

Alex sat down again. The words sounded false, somehow, but the woman *was* recently bereaved.

'I am sorry for your loss.' It was a trite statement, but Alex meant it.

Clarice waved it away.

'I gather you made a *misyar* marriage with Azzam while you were out there at the earthquake place,' she said, and Alex wondered if that was what her visitor had come to discuss.

'Apparently it was the only thing to do,' she answered, hoping she sounded calmer than she felt because whatever had happened between Azzam and herself was not only private but also precious in a way she didn't fully understand.

'Oh, yes,' her visitor agreed, rather too readily. 'He couldn't have had his reputation tarnished by sharing a tent with a foreigner. Of course, no marriage in these parts, even a *misyar* marriage, is legal until it's consummated.'

Alex's breathing stopped, and her heart stood still, then picked up and raced, while small, shallow breaths saved her from passing out completely.

Had Clarice seen her reaction?

Alex sincerely hoped not, but the statement had raised so many questions in Alex's head that she needed to get rid of the woman so she could at least *try* to sort through them.

Realising some kind of reply was needed, she shrugged her shoulders.

'I wouldn't know about any of that,' she said, hoping she sounded a lot more casual than she felt. 'Now, I really must shower and dress. Samarah wants to see the children.'

Now Clarice stood up.

'Oh, well, whatever Samarah wants Samarah must have,' she said, not even attempting to hide the bitchiness in the words. And on that note she swept out of the room.

Alex lay back on the bed.

Azzam would have known this thing about marriage and consummation.

She'd sensed the previous afternoon in the colonnade that he was using her against Clarice in some way.

Introducing her as his wife.

When, apparently, she wasn't his wife.

Was that why he'd taken her to that magical place last night?

Was that why he'd seduced her?

Be honest, she told herself, it had hardly been a seduction—she'd wanted it as much as he had.

Maybe more?

She sighed and rolled over on her stomach, pressing her hot face into the pillows, aware of how little she knew of male-female relationships, aware of how lost she was...

She'd go home. The children would adapt. They were already at ease with Ghaada, for Alex had seen them laughing and playing with her in the courtyard gardens, and Samarah would give them love. They would be all right.

She heaved herself off the bed, showered hurriedly, then stood in front of the wardrobe. Much as she'd have loved to put on her jeans and a clean shirt, she didn't want to hurt Samarah's feelings by not wearing one of her gifts.

Sorting through them, she found a pale pink tunic and trousers, less fancy than the other sets, although once she was dressed she realised the pink material took on a life of its own, deepening in colour in the folds, paling almost to white where it crossed her breasts and hips.

It was beautiful and a tiny little bit of her was glad because *she* looked beautiful in it—or as beautiful as someone as nondescript as she was ever could look. She hooked her hair up using two of the jewelled combs from the bathroom, wrapped a scarf around her head and once again put pale pink lipstick on her lips.

The children came bounding in just as she finished and she knew from their excited chatter that they were complimenting her. Ghaada translated their exuberant comments so Alex was blushing as she made her way with them, Ghaada carrying Masun today, along the colonnade to where Samarah held her daily court.

In Alex's mind, as she approached the gathering, she had it sorted that she didn't want Azzam to be there, but when she saw him, seated beside his mother, her heart gave a treacherous little leap, and warmth flooded recently excited parts of her body. Breathing deeply so she appeared calm and focussed, she greeted Samarah, nodded hello to Azzam as if he hadn't ignited her body in ways she still couldn't believe possible the night before, then urged the children forward to greet both adults.

Zahid greeted Azzam like an old friend and showed him a treasure he had found—a small white stone from the lagoon—while Tasnim drew close to Samarah, who lifted the child onto her lap and gave her a hug.

'I am blessed to have these children in my life,' Samarah

said. 'Last night I read to them before they went to sleep. I had forgotten what a simple joy that was.'

Hearing Samarah's sincerity in the simple words, Alex could only smile, certain that the children had found a secure home here at the palace and a very special guardian in Samarah.

'I, too, have something special,' Azzam said, and, thinking he was speaking to Zahid, Alex barely glanced his way, but he was handing a little lamp to Zahid, speaking to him in his own language, although when the little boy came and shyly presented the lamp to her, Alex could only stare—first at it, and then at Azzam.

'The guide told me you admired one,' he said, as she turned it around in her hands, looking at it from all angles, aware that it was very different from the market lamp, yet not understanding how.

'It's beautiful,' she said, 'but it looks expensive. I can't accept expensive gifts from you.'

Samarah waved away her protest.

'You are his wife so he can give you anything—far better things than an old lamp—although I suspect objects, possessions aren't as important to you as people, isn't that so?'

'Not important at all,' Alex assured her, remembering how it had been the need for possessions—a fine house for his wife, good art works, the best furniture—that had started Rob's gambling.

Azzam had watched her approach, drinking in the sight of her. She'd tied a pale pink scarf across her head, the material so fine he could see, beneath it, the combs she'd used to hold her hair back from her face.

She'd looked so serenely beautiful his mouth had gone dry and he'd wondered if he'd be able to speak to her at all, let alone say the things he wanted to say.

Now he watched her turning the lamp in her hands, answering his mother, rejecting any wish to have possessions. Something in her past has made her this way—not only about possessions, but had made her remote, untrusting, Azzam decided.

If he managed to speak, how could he bridge the gap between them—a gap he very definitely wanted to bridge?

He accepted that they barely knew each other, but he believed the bond between them, forged in the chaos of the disaster, was rare and special, something that should be nurtured so it could grow and flourish into a deeply loving marriage.

But he'd upset her, and she'd drawn away, and he had no idea how to bring her close again. He watched her, still studying the little lamp—a trinket, nothing more—and wondered what she'd think if he told her he'd, foolishly he knew, already wished on it—wished for her to stay here in Al Janeen, to stay as his wife and consort.

Ask her, his mother had said when he'd sought her advice, but how to ask? When?

She held the lamp, showing it to the children, then smiled at him, a smile that seemed to rip his heart apart, so much did it hurt him.

'Thank you. It will be a wonderful reminder of Al Janeen for me to take home with me.'

'Must you go?'

Really smooth move, brother, the ghost of Bahir teased, but desperation had prompted the words.

Now she smiled again, a sad smile this time that tore a bit more of his heart.

'You know I must. Originally I came to tend Samarah on the flight—I've already stayed longer than I should.'

'There is family back at home? You miss them? Is that why you are so determined to leave us?'

He was saying this all wrong, but he badly needed to know she had pressing reasons to go—apart, of course, from putting a vast distance between herself and him.

'Family obligations,' she replied, not meeting his eyes but with enough emotion in her face for him to know it hurt her to say it. Because she didn't want to leave?

Or maybe it was the obligation that hurt her?

How could that be?

He wanted to know more.

Put bluntly, he wanted to know everything about her, but for him to learn about her, and she about him, she had to stay.

Could he order it? Wasn't he the ruler—couldn't he command it?

Command this woman?

Of course he couldn't. Not her or any other woman, realistically…

'But now you have obligations here, too,' he said, speaking quietly, although his mother's women friends had withdrawn, taking the children into the garden so only he, Alex and his mother remained on the carpets. 'There are the children, and as my…'

He hesitated before saying the word 'wife', knowing it wasn't right for he'd told her there'd be no strings attached to their *misyar* marriage but desperate to get her to change her mind about leaving. Fortunately, before the word came out, Clarice had appeared, coming to stand beside him, taking his arm, urging him a little apart.

'This conversation isn't finished,' he said to Alex, then he followed Clarice a little way along the colonnade.

'Your mother is finding happiness in the children,' she began, and Azzam wondered where the conversation was leading for Clarice rarely gave a thought to other people's happiness.

'She is,' he replied. 'I think it takes her mind off her loss.'

Clarice smiled at him—more a smirk than a smile for it sent coolness through his blood.

'Then perhaps soon I will give her more pleasure—the greatest pleasure of all. I'll give her a child with real meaning for her.'

He heard the words but they made little sense, but as he turned to look at her he saw she was patting her stomach and looking unbearably pleased with herself.

'You're pregnant?'

He spoke quietly, not wanting to raise false hope in his mother, should she hear the quiet conversation.

'It would seem so,' Clarice said, but now the smile he'd once let light his world seemed smug and even devious.

'That would be good news indeed,' he said, wondering why he was feeling so doubtful.

'The child, if it's a boy, will be the true heir, of course.'

She was looking at him now, as if the words might hold some hidden meaning.

Did she think it would hurt him? That he might resent his brother's child? How could he, he who'd loved Bahir better than himself?

Of course Bahir's son would be the heir. Perhaps, even, should the child be a girl, his country would have grown enough to accept *her* as the ruler. Such a time, he was sure, wasn't that far away.

But Clarice was still talking to him, standing a little behind him and speaking quietly so no one else would hear the conversation.

'That's the real reason I thought we should marry, you and I. That way the succession is protected. Bahir's child grows up as yours, and becomes the prince in due time.'

The conversation that had begun, he felt, at the worst possible time, had now taken such a truly outlandish turn that it took him a moment to get his head around it.

'We do not have to be married for the child to grow up to be the ruler,' he told her. 'Bahir's child would be the heir, my place that of a regent until he was of age.'

'And if I were to marry someone else? Take my child back to my homeland of America so he grows up there? How would that suit your ideas of national identity?'

Cold fear gripped him as he realised what the woman was doing. She was bartering with the life of her unborn child, for how could a child raised in another country understand the people and the land he was born to rule?

And how could he allow Bahir's child to be raised by another man—particularly the kind of man Clarice, now she had more than enough money than she would need to keep her in style for life, might choose?

He took her arm and led her down into the garden courtyard, staying away from the children and in the shade of trees for the sun was still hot. But for all the heat, his body shivered as the dreams he'd spun of a real marriage between himself and Alex vanished into the ether, dreams of love crumbling to dust beneath his feet, lost forever because of the obligation of family.

The obligation he felt towards his beloved brother, his twin, his other half...

CHAPTER TEN

This conversation isn't finished. Wasn't that what he'd said? Yet he'd walked away with Clarice. Alex excused herself to Samarah and went to play with the children in the garden, chasing the two older ones around the beautifully crafted hedges and topiary shaped as balls. Tired at last, she sat on the edge of the fountain and took Masun from Ghaada, dabbling his feet in the water, making him laugh, his innocent chuckles bruising her heart because she would never see him grow up.

'It is time for the children's dinner,' Ghaada said, taking the now sleepy baby from Alex and leading the children back to their rooms.

Alex remained by the fountain. Trailing her fingers in the water, drinking in the peace of the tranquil setting, seeing the fierce red sun dropping below the high walls of the palace. Darkness fell swiftly and she saw the women moving back towards the building that housed them, next to what she now knew was the visitors' building, where she and the children had rooms. Looking around, she realised it was more a series of houses than one large palace, for there were other buildings she didn't know, but all were linked by the colonnade.

One would be Azzam's, of course, and presumably Clarice still lived in what had been Bahir's building, and from what Samarah had said, there were receiving areas where people came to meet their prince, and places where dignitaries were entertained. There were areas also for servants and old family retainers, and for cousins and aunts and the women who were friends. Alex was considering how reassuring it must be, this self-enclosed community, how safe people must feel within it, when she felt, rather than saw, Azzam approach.

'I thought you would be eating with my mother,' he said quietly, sitting beside her but not touching her. Not that touch was needed, for awareness was flaring between them with a galvanic power that singed the skin and burned along the nerves.

On her side, anyway…

'I wanted to see the sun set,' Alex told him, unwilling to admit she'd been lost in thoughts of safeness and community.

'And I need to talk to you, but I find I have no words for what I want to say, or, now, the right to say them,' he said quietly. He took one of her hands in both of his, and held it, warm and—yes, safe!

'I would have asked you to stay,' he said then he gave a short, abrupt laugh. 'Asked? How stupid! I probably would have begged you to stay.'

He turned her hand over and dropped a kiss into the palm, then folded her fingers over it to keep the kiss, the hand again held between his.

'But circumstances have changed and I cannot tell you things I would have said. For that, I am truly sorry. But know that when you go, and it can be tomorrow if you wish, you will take a piece of me with you.'

A feeling akin to panic flashed along Alex's nerves and she stood up, moving slightly away, then turning back towards him because she was puzzled as well, and aching with her love for him.

'Is this to do with my overreaction last night? Is it because of that you cannot talk?'

He stood up, put his hands lightly on her shoulders, and looked down into her face.

'It is not to do with you, but with a—a constraint I suppose you would call it, put on me by family obligations.'

For a moment Alex thought he might kiss her, then he muttered what sounded like an oath of some kind and walked away, heading for a shadowy part of the garden she hadn't yet explored.

Drawn by the pain she'd heard in the words, she followed, finding him beside an ancient, black-trunked, gnarled old tree.

'This tree was here before the palace—here before my ancestors first camped in this place. It symbolises continuation, shows us that life goes on no matter what. It is frankincense—you know it?'

Alex came forward and touched the rough trunk.

'I know the scent of it now,' she said. 'It's everywhere.'

'It made our fortune in the early days—not just this tree but many like it. They grow in only a few places. Here, feel the trunk.'

He took her hand and held it against the rough bark, pressing her fingers into what seemed like a cut in it.

'The frankincense gatherers cut through the rough bark to the living tree beneath and it bleeds. Can you feel the small lump there? We call it a tear, as if the tree cries with pain yet its pain gives us life in the same way as a mother's pain gives life to her child.'

He took his hand away and Alex looked up at the night sky through the fine silvery leaves of the ancient tree, wondering exactly what Azzam had been telling her, knowing it was important to him.

Now, as she watched, he pulled a small pen-knife from his pocket and again ran his hands across the bark of the tree, feeling for a cut perhaps, because when he turned back to her he had two small, clear, tear-shaped lumps of frankincense which he pressed into her hands.

'You take my tears with you when you go,' he said quietly, 'and also my heart.'

Alex closed her fingers tightly around the little buds, and was trying to make sense of his words when he bent and kissed her lightly on the lips, before disappearing as quietly as he had come.

Alex stayed beneath the tree, the tears of frankincense biting into her palm, until the sky was dark enough to see the stars. She tried to find the constellations Azzam had pointed out to her, but their brightness was blurred by the tears that had filled her eyes.

Eventually she made her way back to her room, where Hafa scolded her for sitting outside when the cool night air was descending. Waving away the young woman's concern and fending off offers of dinner—food was the last thing her churning stomach would accept—she went into the dressing room and found the jeans and shirt she'd put on one morning that seemed an aeon ago.

'You can go home tomorrow if you wish.' Wasn't that what Azzam had said?

She didn't wish to but she had to go sometime and the way she was feeling, the sooner she made the break, not only from him but from the children and Samarah, the easier it would be.

She *would* go tomorrow...

She put out the jeans and shirt, telling herself she'd leave in her own clothes, set her socks and sneakers beside them, aware how pathetic they looked on the chair in the sumptuous dressing room. She was contemplating a shower when a knock on the bedroom door sent her back in that direction.

Clarice!

'Hi!' she said, breezing in as if they were best of friends. 'Azzam said you're leaving soon so I thought I'd say good-bye and offer a suggestion. I was going to fly home to the States to see my folks tomorrow, but things have changed so the plane is free. I know the pilot well. Shall I let him know you'll go tomorrow? The plane's all fuelled up and the staff on standby so it's a shame not to use it.'

Had Azzam sent her?

Was this what he'd wanted to say but couldn't?

Pain filled Alex's body but there was no way she was going to show it.

'If that suits Azzam and the rest of the family, tomorrow would suit me too,' she said, enunciating each word carefully in case a careless syllable might open the floodgates of her pain.

'I'll arrange it all and send someone to let you know when the car will pick you up,' Clarice told her, smiling brightly as if she'd just accomplished some difficult mission.

Hafa returned as Clarice departed, bringing a tray with juice and fruit on it.

'You must eat something,' she told Alex, and to please her Alex took a piece of melon, but she knew she'd never get it down past the wedge of sadness in her throat.

'I am leaving tomorrow,' she told Hafa, who cried out and waved her hands, chattering half in her native language and half in English, obviously not happy about it.

'I would like to see Samarah before I go. Would it be best now or in the morning, early?'

Hafa frowned then shook her head, finally going across to the phone and phoning someone, talking volubly with much hand-waving.

'Samarah's woman said to come now. They have finished dinner and are having fruit and sweets. You will join them?'

How could she not? Alex thought. Samarah had become a friend.

'I don't think I like goodbyes,' she said to Hafa as the young woman led her to Samarah's rooms. 'I'm not used to them.'

'But you will return,' Hafa said. 'You will want to see the children, and maybe the village when it is rebuilt.'

And risk seeing Azzam?

Risk renewed pain when just maybe some of the wounds she could feel now in her heart were healing over?

'I don't think so,' she said, but so quietly perhaps Hafa didn't hear her.

'There are visitors,' Hafa explained as they entered the big room. 'They came late but will take sweetmeats with us, as will you.'

Hafa led her to what Alex now realised was a privileged position by Samarah's side. Alex sank down onto a cushion, and smiled at the older woman, who was looking so much better since she'd returned home. Except her dark eyes were concerned and worry creased her forehead.

She touched Alex's hand.

'I am sorry you are leaving,' she said quietly. 'Sorry in too many ways to tell you. My son, I think, is making a mistake, but a mother cannot do more than guide her children, she cannot bend them to her will.'

'I am sorry to hear that,' Alex said, giving Samarah's fingers a little squeeze, wondering what Azzam had done to make his mother looked so worried. 'But he is a good son, you know that,' she added, hoping to reassure the woman.

'Yes, perhaps too good,' Samarah said, then to Alex's surprise she leaned forward and pressed a kiss on Alex's cheek. 'We will meet again, my dear,' she said. 'The genie in the lamp has promised me this.'

And reaching into the folds of her tunic, she pulled out the little lamp and handed it to Alex.

'You left it in the colonnade when you played with the children, but I kept it safe for you, as I will keep the children safe. You may be sure of that.'

Tears were brimming in Alex's eyes again, and the lump in her throat now made speech impossible. She gave Samarah's hand one last squeeze, then stood up and moved towards the door, Hafa behind her, chattering about the children, but Alex's head was too full of sadness to hear the words.

After six weeks back at work it seemed to Alex as if she'd never been away. One day slid into the next. She worked night shifts at the hospital, day shifts at the clinic, slowly but steadily reducing Rob's debt.

She hadn't heard from the money-lender so she'd assumed Azzam had been as good as his word and transferred a week's wages into her account to cover the payment that would have been taken out while she was away. One day she'd have to check the figures, so she'd know how much she had in reserve for an emergency, but right now doing anything apart from going to work, doing her job and coming home was beyond her.

She picked up the little lamp and rattled the tears of frankincense she kept inside it, the only tangible reminders of that magical time. She touched the lamp gently, wanting to rub it, to find a genie, to make a wish...

But what wish?

Not money, that was for sure. She'd pay off Rob's debts in time. No, what she'd wish for was impossible, for how could Azzam suddenly appear in her tiny bed-sit?

Yet her hands still held the lamp, feeling its warmth, wondering if wishes might come—

The sharp knock on the door made her drop the precious object, but she caught it before it hit the floor and she put it down safely on the small table before going to see who was there. Working the hours she did, she rarely socialised, and never had visitors, not ashamed of her tiny home but aware that even two people made it feel crowded.

Azzam barged through the door then stared around him in amazement, before turning to stare at her in what looked very like disbelief.

'Why are you living like this?' he demanded, anger she didn't understand written clearly on his usually inscrutable features.

Not that she was understanding much of anything. What was he doing there? How had he found her? What did he want?

Of course she hadn't rubbed the lamp!

'It's my home,' she managed, eventually, but apparently that didn't satisfy him, for he took a turn, three strides, around the small space and faced her again.

'Your home? What are you? Some kind of stoic? Are you doing penance for some unnameable sin? You have a million dollars in the bank and you live like this? Ah, it's that you won't touch my money! That's it, isn't it? Do you feel I did you such wrong you won't accept it from me? Well, let me tell you, *misyar* marriage or not, you were entitled to a dowry! It is *your* money, Alex, not a gift but an official dowry such as is required by law.'

Alex had slumped onto the end of her divan when

he'd mentioned the money in the bank, and her mind had stopped working about then. However, he was looming over her, still angry, but looking down now as if he expected some kind of answer.

There was only one thing she *could* say.

'*What* million dollars?'

Maybe two things.

'*What* bank?'

All that did was make him angrier, for this time he whirled faster in his pacing around the room while she battled the silly delight dancing in her heart at the sight of him.

'You don't know?' he growled as he came past her again. 'Do you never check your account?'

'My bank account?' Alex queried, but faintly, as it was hard to get her brain working on this subject when it was busy trying to stop her heart misbehaving. 'My pay goes into it and my expenses come out of it by automatic transfer. I usually know, maybe not to the cent, about how much I have in there. A couple of hundred dollars for emergencies—I always try to keep that.'

Azzam shook his head. He'd come to ask Alex to marry him—to be his wife forever—but first he'd had to practically force the woman at the clinic where she worked to give him Alex's address, and now he'd walked into a room smaller than his dressing room, to find it was her home. Now she was telling him she tried to keep a couple of hundred dollars in the bank for emergencies. This was poverty…

'You're a doctor, you earn good money, yet you try to keep a couple of hundred dollars in the bank for emergencies. Where does your money go, Alex? What is this obligation you spoke of that forces you to live like this?'

Wrong question and big mistake! Fire flashed in her

pale eyes and she stood up, tall and proud in front of him, confronting him just as she had in the rose garden so long ago.

'That is none of your business,' she said, her small, determined chin tilted towards him, eminently kissable lips right there.

Which was when his anger died away!

'Oh, but it is,' he whispered, and he leaned forward and brushed the lightest of kisses on those irresistible lips. Then, as she'd neither slapped his face, nor moved away, he put his arms around her and tucked her slight body up against his, holding the precious woman he'd so nearly lost close to his heart.

'You see, I love you,' he said, because there didn't seem any other way to say it. 'Love you so much that to walk in here and see you living like this, I was shocked and hurt and angry. And if you want the truth, because I was so uncertain coming here, so afraid I wouldn't find you, or worse, find that you didn't love me, anger took over.'

She squirmed against him and he realised he was holding her far too tightly. He eased his grasp and she looked up at him again.

'Say that last bit again,' she suggested, frowning at him now.

'Which last bit?'

'The bit about being afraid you wouldn't find me, or worse—the bit after "or worse".'

He tried to think what he'd said but the words had come out in such a rush they'd disappeared beyond recall.

'I can't remember.' He was probably frowning right back at her, but over not remembering, nothing to do with her, with Alex, with the woman he loved.

'You said you were afraid I might not love you,' she

reminded him, speaking sternly and adding, 'what makes you think you no longer need to be afraid of that?'

He had to smile.

'Because you're still in my arms? Because I know that when I kiss you properly in a couple of seconds, you're going to kiss me back? Because the love I feel for you is so strong it cannot possibly be one-sided? We are one, Alex, you and I, destined, some would say, to be together.'

Enough of words, his hunger was for her lips.

He bent and kissed her, *properly* this time.

Alex had told herself she wouldn't respond. But only seconds earlier she'd told herself she'd escape from his hold and that hadn't worked either. Now she tried, really tried, to hold the emotions welling up inside her in check, but as his lips moved against hers, questing and exploring, her good intentions vanished and she kissed him back.

Her lips took on a life of their own, demanding and voracious, as all the pent-up love and disappointment, the heartbreak of parting and the joy of seeing him again melded into an inferno of need, transmitting itself to him through something too volcanic and elemental to be called a kiss.

Yet that was all it was. She realised that as they broke apart, silent, breathing deeply, staring at each other. Alex's legs gave way and she sank back down onto the divan, looking up at the man who'd reappeared, like a genie, in her life.

She shook her head but the image didn't go away so she knew he was real. Actually, the taste of him on her tongue and the slight soreness of her lips told her he was real. He crossed the room, two strides, and took her only chair from beside the table, bringing it across to sit in front of her.

'If I sit on that thing you obviously use as a bed, we

won't talk and we need to talk, Alex, both of us. I will start for I have wronged you in too many ways to count.'

He reached out and took her hand, holding it, as he had once before, in both of his.

Touched her palm.

'Did you keep my kiss?'

She held out her other hand, fingers curled as if holding something.

'It's safe in here,' she said, and the smile he gave her, so full of love, flooded her body with happiness.

'That is good,' he said, serious again, 'for with that kiss I gave you my heart.'

She could only stare at him, words beyond her. Did he mean it? Had he loved her back then but not asked her to stay? What—?

He held up one hand as if he sensed her questions.

'That night, in the colonnade, I came with the intention of asking you to marry me, to stay on in Al Janeen as my wife—a real wife, not just a *misyar* one. In some ways I was confused and uncertain about that because the time had been so short, yet I knew, deep inside me, I had found a very special love, a love that would not only last forever but would grow and flourish into something beyond imagining.'

Alex shook her head. Just so had she begun to feel, although she'd had no idea Azzam had shared those feelings. Should she tell him? Was it her turn to talk? This was so unbelievable, sitting here in her tiny bed-sit with a prince telling her of his love. How had Cinderella managed it?

He touched her lips, telling her he wasn't finished, and she guessed she wasn't going to enjoy whatever was coming next.

'Before I could speak to you, Clarice came to me, she told me she was carrying Bahir's child, and unless I married her, she would return to America and bring him or her up there. Later, when my mind was less confused, I realised she wanted nothing more than to stay on in Al Janeen, but as the queen she'd always believed she was, not just as Bahir's widow. If you understand families, you will understand I could not let her take Bahir's child to America, to grow up not knowing his or her heritage and people; to grow up perhaps with a stepfather with different values and beliefs, who saw no need to instil the right principles in the child.'

Alex imagined the scenario only too clearly. Hadn't Clarice told her the plane was booked to fly her, Clarice, home to the U.S., taking Bahir's unborn child with her?

'She blackmailed you?'

Azzam shook his head.

'It's an ugly word, Alex, one I doubt you even understand, but in effect that's what it was. She…required, I suppose is the word, that I marry her, even wanted it to be immediately, but I could not marry my brother's widow before the mourning period was over—the very idea was beyond consideration. But I knew I had to save the child—my brother's child—and so I agreed.'

'And now?' Alex prompted. 'What's happened now?'

'She isn't pregnant, never was,' Azzam said bitterly. 'She lied when she first told me, even showed proof with a test stick one of her women friends gave her. Later, when she was still insisting on an immediate marriage, I began to wonder and arranged for her to see an obstetrician and that's when it all came out. But in deceiving me that way, she made me hurt you. That is what angers me most, that she made me cause you pain.'

'Oh, Azzam,' Alex said softly, and she slid off the couch to kneel beside him so she could put her arms around his waist and rest her head against him, knowing words alone wouldn't heal the hurt he was feeling. 'You did what you had to do. Believe me, I know about family.'

He didn't answer for a moment then he tilted her chin so he could look into her face.

'Tell me,' he commanded, and she found herself obeying, telling him of Rob, of his job in the bank, of his need for 'stuff', as she'd always thought of it, and the embezzlement, then his stupidity in thinking he could borrow more to pay it back, her mother's shame and drawn-out death from cancer, and her—Alex's—determination to protect her brother's wife and child from the money-lender and to clear the family name.

'I'm getting there,' she said, 'and I didn't thank you for paying me those wages. I know you must have put the money into my account because the money-lender's bully hasn't been to see me.'

'Wages? You thought all I'd paid you were some piddling wages?'

He seemed angry again.

'Why would you have paid me more? Why would I have expected there to be more?'

Azzam found himself groaning again. How stupid had he been to have even thought of judging this woman by his experience with Clarice?

He stood up, lifted the woman he loved with ease then sat down on the divan with her in his lap.

'Later, you will tell me how we can repay these debts, and maybe make life easier for your sister-in-law and niece, but now I need to apologise to you because right from the beginning I let the past and my experience with Clarice when she first came to Al Janeen influence my judgement of you. Yet that first time I saw you in the rose garden I felt something for you, and afterwards, when I watched the way you helped the children at the earthquake village and held the orphans in your arms, I understood you had that rarest of gifts, a love that reached out to all humanity.'

He kissed her neck, lifting her hair and pressing his lips to the pale skin.

'That's when I fell in love, although maybe I fell a little bit in love in the rose garden when you turned on me with such fierce anger. This is a woman with iron in her soul, I thought, and was intrigued.'

'Iron in my soul?' Alex echoed, but she'd turned her head and was kissing his ear as she spoke, teeth nipping at it. 'I'm not at all sure that's a compliment.'

He moved so their lips met.

'Believe me, it is. My country needs women with iron in their souls as leaders of the community, and I—' he kissed her more firmly '—I need a woman with iron in her soul as my consort, and in my bed as well, and as mother of my children, and grandmother of my grandchildren—'

She broke away.

'The children? I didn't think! I was so surprised to see you my mind went blank. The children are all right? Did anyone find out anything about their father? Is the new oasis dug? Is the village being rebuilt?'

Azzam smiled at her.

'The children are well and happy. The baby is starting to walk around furniture, Zahid's arm is out of the cast, and Tasnim asks me every day when you are coming back. She tells me she is learning English words from Ghaada so she can talk to you. As to the rest, you must come and see for yourself. We cannot marry yet, you and I, because of the mourning period, but you will return with me and we will be together as *misyar* man and wife, then in time we will have a more formal marriage, maybe out beside the lagoon, just you and me, Samarah and Hafa as witnesses, and the children, for they, too, are special to us both.'

Had she rubbed the lamp unintentionally? Or was this real? Alex returned the kisses Azzam was pressing on her lips, but her mind was not on kisses. It was whirling, doing sums—if the million dollars was really hers, she could pay off the debt then buy a house for her sister-in-law and niece, and have plenty left over to invest for her niece's future, enough to pay for any equipment or treatment she might need. And surely she, Alex, could fly them over for a visit, take them to the blushing lagoon and out to the village, show them the desert...

'I've lost you,' Azzam said, straightening up and looking at her with a slightly wary expression on his face.

'It's okay,' she assured him. 'I was just tying off some loose ends in my head. I'm with you now.'

And she kissed him to show that she was.

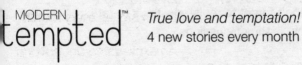